DR. SKULL

BOOKS IN THE ARGOSY LIBRARY:

DR. SKULL

LEWIS CLAY

ABBEY OF THE DAMNED: THE COMPLETE
CASES OF MIKE AND TRIXIE, VOLUME 3

T.T. FLYNN

THE DEATH MESSENGER: THE COMPLETE
CASES OF JIGGER MASTERS, VOLUME 4

ANTHONY M. RUD

BOX 991: THE COMPLETE CABALISTIC
CASES OF SEMI DUAL, VOLUME 5

J.U. GIESY & JUNIUS B. SMITH

BLIND TRAILS AT TONTO: THE COMPLETE
TALES OF SHERIFF HENRY, VOLUME 8

W.C TUTTLE

IN THE MURDERER'S BRAIN: THE COMPLETE
CASES OF THE SCIENTIFIC CLUB, VOLUME 3

RAY CUMMINGS

THE LEGION OF THE LIVING DEAD: THE
COMPLETE CASES OF MR. STRANG, VOLUME 2

CARROLL JOHN DALY

THE MENTAL MARVEL

FRED MACISAAC

THE ADVENTURE OF THE VOODOO
MOON: THE COMPLETE CASES OF
THE LADY FROM HELL, VOLUME 2

EUGENE THOMAS

MURDER ON THE FILM: THE COMPLETE
CASES OF CANDID JONES, VOLUME 1

RICHARD B. SALE

DR. SKULL

LEWIS CLAY

INTRODUCTION BY
WILL MURRAY

COVER BY
RUDOLPH BELARSKI

POPULAR PUBLICATIONS · 2025

TABLE OF CONTENTS

PAULA LANSDOWNE 3

STRANGE THINGS 16

SEIZURE OF HATE 26

THE ULTIMATUM 44

MURDER IN THE AIR 61

THE SECRET 74

MADMAN ON THE LOOSE 85

THE DRUG 97

CONDEMNED TO DEATH 108

POST-MORTEM 122

THE DEFENDANT 134

THE DEFENSE RESTS 148

SPEAK OF THE DEAD 172

SKULL'S AMBASSADOR 183

FIRST BLOOD 197

PLAN OF COMBAT 211

THE DAYS OF THE TERROR 224

STEAM-ROLLER 233

THE RIGHT TRACK 248

FRIEND GONE MAD 265

AT SKULL'S HOUSE 274

CORNERED BUT NOT CAUGHT 297

INSTRUMENT OF MURDER 308

ESCAPE THROUGH FIRE 324

THE GREAT FIRE 337

CITY OF DARKNESS 353

THE FINAL STRUGGLE. 365

THE SUMMING UP 375

INTRODUCTION

LEWIS CLAY'S *DR. SKULL* has the distinction of being
the longest serial ever to appear in the pages of Munsey's
Detective Fiction Weekly. That's going back to its earliest
incarnation as *Flynn's* in 1924.

Dr. Skull ran in the closing months of 1938, beginning
with the September 7 issue, and concluding in the Novem-
ber 19 *DWF*. Ten installments. That's an astounding length
for a Munsey serial. Typically a *Detective Fiction Weekly* or
Argosy serial would run anywhere from two to six installments. It was rare when one went beyond that, and a careful examination of the contents pages of *Detective Fiction
Weekly* shows conclusively that no other serial showcased
in its pages ever ran ten installments.

This suggests that the editors considered *Dr. Skull* an
exceptional novel. Even in the latter years of the Great
Depression, it was difficult for the average reader to keep
up with weekly magazines like *DFW* and *Argosy*. It was
wiser to run shorter serials so that readers wouldn't get
frustrated if they missed or couldn't afford an issue. But
Munsey took that risk with *Dr. Skull*, giving it a strikingly
dramatic Rudolph Belarski cover.

Another remarkable thing about *Dr. Skull* is it author.
The byline Lewis Clay cannot be found in other pulp

magazines before, during, or after the 1930s. One suspects a pen or house name concealing a familiar and prolific writer. But this appears not to be the case.

Assuming he is the same person, the author of *Dr. Skull* resurfaced in 1942 at Columbia Pictures, where he was one of the scripters on the Western serial, *The Valley of Vanishing Men*, which starred the emerging cowboy actor Bill Elliott.

After a hiatus of four years—which might be explained by his having enlisted or been drafted into the armed forces during World War II—Clay began working with producer Sam Katzman, where he specialized in co-authoring Columbia Pictures Saturday matinee serials, colloquially known as "cliffhangers" because each chapter ended with the hero in a dangerous predicament with no clear hope of survival. This gimmick was designed to lure young audiences to return the following week for the resolution— which also ended in another cliffhanger.

Between 1946 and 1951, Clay collaborated on a string of Columbia serials. In keeping with the fantastic theme of *Dr. Skull*, several of these were based on popular comic book or comic strip characters.

Clay, usually in collaboration with George H. Plimpton, Arthur Hoerl, and other writers, wrote chapters for *Jack Armstrong* which was adapted from the radio program, *Jack Armstrong, the All America Boy*. *Brick Bradford* and *Bruce Gentry—Daredevil of the Skies* were based on then-popular newspaper strips. Clay co-scripted three different serials inspired by DC Comics characters, *The Vigilante, Congo Bill,* and the first *Superman* serial in 1948. He was not involved in the 1950 sequel, *Atom Man vs. Superman*.

Typically, an experienced screen writer like George H.

Plimpton would map out a detailed treatment, and then assign a sequence of consecutive chapters to individual writers like Lewis Clay. For example, Clay is known to have scripted the concluding chapters of *Brick Bradford*.

Clay's last serial credit was an adaptation of Jules Verne's *The Mysterious Island*, which Columbia released in 1951. His name never appeared on a feature film, only on multi-chapter cheap serials.

Saturday matinee serials, which consisted of four to five hours of running time but released in 15 to 20-minute installments over successive weeks, began dying off in the 1950s, probably as a result of network television becoming a popular alternative to going to the movies. As was the issue with serializing a long story in a pulp magazine, expecting a moviegoer to commit to catching every episode of a film serial running twelve to fifteen weeks was problematic.

That development appears to have killed Lewis Clay's connection to Columbia Pictures and Sam Katzman Productions. After *Mysterious Island*, his name disappears from the silver screen, only to pop up in 1962 writing a single episode of Warner Bros. *Hawaiian Eye* television show. Two years later a solitary episode of *Bonanza* bore his credit.

After that, Lewis Clay seems to have ceased all screenwriting.

It's an unusual career, to be sure. But it's ironic that the man who wrote the longest serial Munsey ever printed went on to script numerous movie serials of inordinate length. Or perhaps not so ironic. It's widely believed that Hollywood originally got the idea of serializing movies over successive weeks from the identical approach pioneered by newspapers and magazines running long fiction.

Scripting Hollywood serials was a highly specialized and difficult skill. Those who mastered it usually did not also write feature films. So it's not surprising that Lewis Clay did not transition to A or even B Pictures.

Few other contemporary pulp writers broke into that challenging field. Alfred Batson, who sold many stories to *Argosy* and *Short Stories*, contributed to a single serial, the 1941 Republic chapter play, *Jungle Girl*.

The prolific L. Ron Hubbard is said to have contributed to three 1937-38 Columbia serials, *The Spider's Web*, *The Mysterious Pilot*, and *The Great Adventures of Wild Bill Hickok*. But he did not receive screen credit so the precise nature of his contributions are unknown.

As for Lewis Clay, only skeletal information can be learned of his life. Born in Huntsville, Alabama on April 17, 1909, he lost his father, William Lewis Clay, a respected Alabama lawyer, at the age of 2. The author's full birth name was William Lewis Clay, Jr.

In July, 1928, 19-year-old William Clay returned from an ocean voyage to Cherbourg, France, and was living in New York City. According to the 1930 Federal census, he resided in Brookline, Massachusetts, his mother having remarried in 1917. He and his wife, the former Dorothy Handschy, are listed as passengers on the S.S. *Pennsylvania*, which departed New York City on Sept 8, 1934, bound for Los Angeles. The Clays gave their New York address as 383 Madison Avenue.

For an unknown period of time in the 1930s, the childless couple resided in Long Beach. His occupation at that time is unknown, although the Los Angeles city directory for 1938—the year of *Dr. Skull*—lists him as a writer. Clay is know to have attended college, but specifics are absent.

A 1940 draft card states that Clay is employed at Columbia Studio and by RKO Studio. Since this was before his first screen credits, it must be assumed that he was working as a so-called "script doctor," revising other writer's screenplays without receiving screen credit.

The March, 1948 issue of *Mammoth Western* contains a story bylined William Clay—a name that appears in no other pulp magazine. "Cached Calves" is the title. But it's only speculation that this might be the work of William Lewis Clay, who rarely went by his first name as an adult.

The 1950 Federal census lists Clay's occupation as a story analyst in motion pictures, indicating that his screenwriting days were over. By the 1980s, the Clays were living is Tucson, Arizona. Clay lived to the ripe old age of 86, dying in Woodland Hills, California on July 9, 1995.

So what of *Dr. Skull?*

It's a story of Madison Avenue advertising copyeditor Bob Larkin, who becomes embroiled in the challenge of *Dr. Skull,* a sinister criminal mastermind with occult powers who initiates a reign of psychic terror upon Manhattan. At its ten-installment length, it's close to 100,000 words in length. In its way, *Dr. Skull* is the prose equivalent of the Saturday matinee cliffhangers Lewis Clay co-wrote for a decade.

The author displays such an intimate knowledge of New York City and the working life of an advertising agency employee who concocted ads for newspapers and radio that one is compelled suspect that Lewis Clay was in fact writing from direct experience gained during his early career. But that is pure speculation.

Dr. Skull is the kind of fantastic thriller that could easily have run in *Argosy* instead of *Detective Fiction Weekly*, and perhaps it was first submitted to *Argosy*, but Munsey ran it in their popular detective title. William Kostka, assisted by Kendall Foster Crossen, took over as editor for *DFW* in 1937. No doubt the new editor decided to take a chance on an unknown writer with an unusual story. Chandler H. Whipple was concurrently editing *Argosy* at that time.

For all anyone knows, *Dr. Skull* may have been originally written as a treatment for a movie serial that was never produced. In 1938, a great many serials were going before the cameras that were thematically similar to *Dr. Skull*. Sometimes they starred an intrepid investigator, other times a masked vigilante like the Spider, whose first serial, *The Spider's Web*, Columbia released in October, 1938, while *Dr. Skull* was running *DFW.*

It would be amusing if *Dr. Skull* was salvaged from the outline of a serial that was never produced or was abandoned during the script treatment stage. How otherwise to explain its prodigious length?

This absorbing super-serial has never been reprinted in the nearly 90 years since originally appearing in the ragged pages of *Detective Fiction Weekly*. Steeger Books is pleased to bring it back into print, along with Rudolph Belarski's powerful cover and the installment-heading interior illustrations.

Was *Dr. Skull* worth an unprecedented ten installments? Turn the page and judge for yourself....

Will Murray

DR. SKULL

*Of the days of the Terror—and of peaceful,
workaday people caught by a lust for murder*

1

PAULA LANSDOWNE

AT THE TIME it all began, I was a copywriter in the nationally known advertising agency of Rowlandson & Leger,
which had its main offices on Madison Avenue, here in
New York. My place in the organization was certainly
an insignificant one, but since youth is unthinking, and
therefore optimistic, I had no difficulty visualizing a pleasant future for myself: a gradual rise in the company until
I should achieve sufficient success to marry Paula Lansdowne.

Paula was the only child of widowed Professor Alfred
Lansdowne, head of the Department of Applied Psychol-
ogy at the University, an eminent scientist, author, and
authority on mental phenomena. She and I had met during
my senior year, and what started out as a warm friendship
soon developed into love. My own mother and father had
died when I was very young, and Paula was the only person
I'd ever cared about since their death. Twenty-one years
old and equipped with a fine and inquisitive mind, she
was far too much interested in the life which surrounded
her to bury herself in library and clinic in order to become
the psychologist her father visioned. He soon realized the
folly of trying to force her hand in this respect and, in time,

even regarded her proposed marriage to me with complacence. This was a fortunate thing for me, as I would not have missed having his friendship for worlds.

Paula and her father, incidentally, made up all of my social existence. I was never an especially cordial person, making friends slowly and having very few, most of them scattered to the four corners of the earth.

As so frequently happens before events of tremendous importance, no one—least of all myself—recognized the first faint signs of what was to come. People have said that Professor Lansdowne must have known almost from the very first. If he did, he never mentioned the fact, nor did he take any steps to protect himself from a very harrying experience. And, of course, the great mass of New Yorkers went on about their daily tasks, worrying over their petty problems as though nothing could ever happen to upset all their schemes and make a final futility of their pathetic efforts, and themselves, as well.

Even after the first two demonstrations of Skull's sinister

*My reason refused to accept this
situation, yet here it was*

power, only a handful of people realized that something
out of the ordinary was occurring. When more compelling
proof was presented that the world was facing a new and
unknown peril, many supposedly intelligent minds still
scoffed. It was a hoax, they said, a hoax or some strange
insanity that would die out as quickly as it had appeared.

There have been many stories to the contrary, but here
is the truth: the only person who recognized the lower-
ing danger; the only person who ever waged successful
war against it; the one man responsible for whatever final
victory we may have achieved, is Alfred Lansdowne. I
make this statement simply to clear the record, and you
may safely take my word for it, because I am in a position
to know.

It was a warmish evening in early September when
we were confronted with the first sign. The day, as so
frequently happens during the summer slump, had been
a dull one for me. A little work on program ideas for fall
radio shows, the usual routine of newspaper copy for the
tea and baking accounts I handled. By handled, I mean, of

course, that I worked under the cold and fishy eye of John Nash, executive for the accounts concerned. It is perhaps a bad thing to be critical of one's superiors lest such criticism be relegated to the category of sour grapes, but how Nash ever gained anyone's confidence enough to be given one small account—let alone two big ones—is utterly beyond me. Possibly his crisp, authoritative way of speaking, his nervous movements, and his shock of pompadoured gray hair gave him an air of energy and ability that he little deserved. All of which is, naturally, beside the point.

On this particular afternoon, he had been somewhat less critical of my efforts than usual. I could see he was anxious to call it a day and get out to his home in suburban Larchmont where he could play ping-pong. Therefore, I myself was able to duck out a few minutes before five, happy at the extra hour of freedom given me and because that night I had a movie date with Paula Lansdowne.

As was my nightly custom, I bought a copy of the *Express* at the corner of 46th Street and Madison Avenue, turned left on 45th Street and entered the long pedestrian tunnel which connects an office building and a hotel with Grand Central Terminal. This evening, as every evening, it was crowded with hundreds of people wearing that tired, irritable, rather harried look so typical of New Yorkers.

After shuttling over to Times Square, I took a Van Vortlandt Park Express and, hanging onto a strap, glanced at the first page of my paper as the train roared north through the echoing tunnel. The front page was all I ever did look at until the train had unloaded at 72nd Street, it being a physical impossibility to turn pages while jammed in like a sardine. Tonight there was little extraordinary news. The

European situation was threatening; there was agitation for an investigation of the prison system; a chorus girl was suing a noted orchestra leader for breach of promise.

When we pulled out of 72nd, I managed to flip over the first sheet. In the upper left-hand corner of page two, a minor headline caught my eye: HUNDREDS PERILED AS "L" TRAINS CRASH. The accompanying article told how a train on 6th Avenue line had run through a block signal and collided with another one standing at the 50th Street platform. Fortunately, the rear train's speed had been only eight miles an hour, so no damage was done beyond causing a near panic and giving the passengers a pretty thorough shaking up.

There was really nothing about this affair to warrant any special notice. And I wouldn't have given it a second thought if it had not been for the motorman's statement. The man was utterly unable to give any logical reason why he should have run through a clearly visible red light into an equally perceptible train, and all this in broad daylight. Here is what he said—quoting from the account in the paper:

MOTORMAN'S STATEMENT

When I came abreast of No. 2 signal and saw it was yellow, I slowed down to eight miles an hour as required and approached No. 1 signal, which was red. I meant, of course, to stop when I came abreast of it. But when I did, something happened to me. I guess I stopped thinking. But it seemed like something took hold of me and made me go through that signal. What I mean is, I couldn't help it! I couldn't!

The item went on to say that the motorman had been employed by the company for fifteen years and had no black marks against him. A test for drunkenness had shown him to be entirely sober. He was now being held by the police for "observation" and according to the paper was facing discharge.

After reading this, I wondered vaguely if the man had been telling the truth or if he had fallen asleep at his post. Or maybe he'd been thinking about something that was worrying him, poor devil. I made a mental note to call the article to Professor Lansdowne's attention at dinner. It seemed a psychological problem to me, and I never tired of listening to the Professor talk on that subject. At this point in my reverie, the subway rolled into 103rd Street, whereupon I debarked and went to my bachelor apartment to get cleaned up. Gradually, the article slipped out of my mind.

THE LANSDOWNES LIVED in one of those tall apartment buildings on Riverside Drive, just south of 116th Street. The elevator operator greeted me as I entered the car, and let me off on the ninth floor. Professor Lansdowne himself answered the doorbell. Tall and gray-haired at fifty-three, he fairly radiated vigor. You could almost feel it seeping into you when you shook his strong, lean hand. A lot of his life had been spent outdoors, and he had acquired a permanent and becoming tan quite unexpected in a college professor. Much of his time had been passed in India, where he'd taken what he laughingly called "a post-graduate course in mysticism."

"Good evening, Bob," he said cheerily. "How are you? A bit the tired business man, eh?"

He didn't need to be a psychologist to see what I was thinking.

"Paula's getting fixed," he remarked. "She'll be along with drinks after a bit."

We went into the spacious living room and Professor Lansdowne gestured me into the big, leather easy-chair over in what he called his corner of the place. The whole room had a quality which had appealed to me the first time I laid eyes on it. It looked as though it had been arranged primarily for comfort and restfulness, in direct contrast to so many homes I've seen which reflect far more the personality of a hired interior decorator than that of the people who are supposed to inhabit them. A large fireplace, big enough for real logs, commanded the north wall. This was flanked right and left by bookshelves reaching from knee height nearly to the ceiling, well filled with volumes of every kind and description. The books gave the impression of being in frequent use, which was the case. Huge casement windows, becomingly draped, overlooked the broad Hudson on the west. In another corner was a grand piano which Paula frequently played.

In short, no room could have better reflected the friendliness and charm of those who lived in it. It is probably superfluous to say that I found it altogether to my own liking.

Paula herself joined us in a few minutes, beautiful as usual in a shimmery gown that blended perfectly with her auburn hair, her soft, brown eyes and her ivory skin. My heart skipped a couple of beats when I saw her appear, and Paula hesitated ever so slightly in her approach as though she, too, had felt electricity in that quick glance we exchanged. There was, however, no sign of intimacy in her greeting.

"How do you do, Mr. Larkin?" she said distantly, offering her father a cocktail.

"Very well, thank you, Miss Lansdowne," I replied. "You're looking quite lovely this evening. All especially arranged for my benefit, I suppose?"

"You may suppose nothing of the kind. I dress for the gaze of the multitude, not for any lone man. Particularly a man who fails to keep his promises."

"Here, here!" said the Professor. "What's all this? Save your lovers' quarrels until you're alone and let's drink our cocktails to more interesting conversation."

"We shall drink them," said Paula complacently, "to this conversation."

"What do you mean I failed to keep my promise?" I demanded, not having the faintest idea what she was talking about until the words were out of my mouth. Then I remembered an understanding we'd had. I was supposed to look up some data for her and phone it out that after-noon. My expression must have registered my thoughts fairly well because Paula pounced it with renewed vitality.

"You were too busy to telephone, weren't you?" she said with what I hoped was only mock sarcasm. "Ah, yes, I seem to remember the formula. You were called into a confer-ence about that rat-poison account, weren't you? And by the time you got out, it was too late to phone, wasn't it?"

"If you must know," I said, nettled, "yes. Only I have nothing to do with any rat-poison account."

"Well, what's the difference? Rat-poison, Superba Bread—"

"Paula!" said the Professor sharply. "Stop acting like an imbecile and remember that Bob is a guest in our house." Professor Lansdowne wasn't really old enough to be mid-Victorian, but he had tendencies in that direction and Paula shocked him on occasion. Heaven knows he should have gotten used to it. Paula liked few things better than raising the roof about my various shortcomings in such a way that I could never be sure whether she was joking or not, until she'd finally burst out laughing at my discomfiture.

"To please you, Dad, I'll pipe down," she said now. "As for Mr. Larkin, he should take a memory course."

BY THE TIME dinner was announced, the conversation had gotten onto another track, an article that Professor Lansdowne was writing for a popular magazine. It was, he said, an expose of so-called supernatural phenomena, and the point he wished to make was the fact that nothing is really supernatural.

"It is remarkable," he said, "the number of otherwise fairly sane people who spend their good money having their fortunes read, or their future forecast, by some charlatan claiming to have supernatural powers. These psychic quacks gain the confidence of their—clients, I suppose you'd call them—by giving them a string of facts about their past lives, and this simple trick of fact transference, is considered evidence of tremendous supernormal power. Tommyrot! As if anyone could read the future!"

"Maybe they can," put in Paula. "Once when I was a kid, a gypsy told me I was going to travel and the next day you took me to Staten Island to see Aunt Bessie. Maybe there's some natural law there you don't know about."

"I'll be glad to overlook the weak humor," remarked her father. "If you don't let it happen again. Another thing— spiritualism. More quackery. Occasionally you find a pretty good telepathist among the mediums, but more often they're merely contortionists. Yet thousands of people are sufficiently gullible to support these tricksters in grand style. If the public considers this nonsense supernatural, what would it say about a few really good examples of psychic phenomena?

"You know, Bob, I once knew a couple of chaps in Tibet who could do things that would make you doubt your own senses. And they were rank amateurs, too, mere *chelas* at the bottom of the ladder, compared with some of the real magicians."

"Who are they," I asked, "Yogi?"

Professor Lansdowne shook his head. "Yoga is a philos- ophy, and its adherents seldom go in for theatricalism. I'm referring to members of the Ghalat-kan and the other secret orders, societies which have probed into the secrets of the human mind for hundreds of years. They've unearthed knowledge that would make the average person consider them God-like in their power. But they are not, in a true sense, and their unusual abilities are merely the result of following perfectly natural laws.

"We Westerners have been very busy developing a purely mechanistic civilization, and we've been highly successful. There's no doubt about that. But we've neglected sciences that are understood thoroughly by inhabitants of countries we consider quite benighted. Of course, only a compar- atively small number of initiates have this knowledge, and they guard it carefully. Too carefully, perhaps. If their powers were turned to practical purposes, the world might be a much better place to live in. So many things which we are now unable to understand would become quite simple."

"What things in particular?" I asked.

"Insanity, for example. Modern science knows pathetically little about it—either its causes or its cure. We've made strides, yes. Men like Freud and Jung and a few others have done much. But there is still so far to go. Complete cures—by which I do not mean the more or less temporary discharge of a patient from a hospital—are discouragingly rare. Yet, I've seen lunatics—paranoiacs, manic depressives, dementia praecox cases—brought before one old guru I have in mind. He'd look into their eyes for a few seconds, and they'd be cured. Don't ask me why. I've spent more time in India than most psychiatrists, but what I know doesn't amount to a row of pins."

"Some of the boys do tricks, too, don't they, Dad?" asked Paula, knowingly.

"Yes, they do tricks. Disappearing tricks and levitations and many far more remarkable than that. Such as apparently transferring themselves to spots miles away in the twinkling of an eye, or making a flower burst into bloom at the touch of a hand. To the uninitiated, they are magicians at the very least, if not gods. Yet, I repeat, they do nothing more than make use of natural laws white men haven't bothered to discover."

At that moment, a thought occurred to me.

"You say that if this knowledge were properly applied, it could do a great deal of good. If a man were to apply it the wrong way, he could do lots of harm, too, couldn't he?"

"Indeed he could. It is because they fear the consequences of misuse that the secret brotherhoods keep their knowledge so well hidden."

"And let's hope it stays hidden," laughed Paula.

WE FINISHED OUR coffee in the living room, and by then it was time for Paula and me to go down to our movie. We left Professor Lansdowne to put the finishing touches on his article and headed downtown. En route, we put everything out of our minds except those matters of the greatest personal concern to us, to wit: how my bank balance was coming along, where we would live after we got married, when we'd formally announce our engagement with a party, and so on. I suppose that all young people plan their marriages down to the last small detail with the same confidence and enthusiasm that we had that night. Remarkably enough, Skull had already begun to play the game which would place not only our plans, but our very lives, in jeopardy, but neither we, nor anyone else, recognized that fact then.

"Goody!" said Paula savagely when she saw the "stills" outside the theatre. "Gore!"

"Women," I averred loftily, "have lost all of the delicacy that used to entitle them to masculine deference. In the good old days a horror movie would have had you fainting in the aisles. Now you yell for more."

"And men," Paula snapped back, "are getting to be effeminate."

Whereupon we went inside.

After the picture was over and Paula had been diverted from her intention of remaining to see the most trying part of it over again, we went to the top of the Empire State Building to enjoy the cool evening air, the view, and the beautiful isolation of being eighty-six stories above the seething millions that make New York what it is.

We walked over to the north parapet and stood there holding hands, looking down on Fifth Avenue and Times Square and Broadway stretching into the distance. The scattered lamps of Central Park were far beyond us, and to left and right flowed the two great rivers, streams of darkness that divided the lights of Manhattan from the rest of the world.

We stood in silence, looking, and it was then that I had a sudden, intense fear for no accountable reason. There was certainly nothing to cause it, no logic to it. Yet it was there, and would not be thrown off.

It was then that I remembered about the elevated wreck.

So you see, I had never spoken to Professor Lansdowne about it, although my failure in this respect did not now worry me. The persistent, dull premonition of some unseen menace did however, until finally I put it out of my mind with thought of Paula.

We didn't know it that evening, but the Terror had begun.

2

STRANGE THINGS

WORK, THE NEXT day, monopolized my attention to the exclusion of all else. There had been client trouble, a standard advertising agency headache. It was not until late afternoon that things simmered down enough for me to take a much-needed breathing spell, and at that time Harry Saunders came into the cubbyhole that passed with me for an office. He had a newspaper in his hand.

Dropping into my long visitor's chair and helping himself to one of my cigarettes, he demanded:

"Got a match?" I provided a lighter and he settled back in a cloud of smoke.

"Were you here two or three years ago when Smythe, Anderson, Pogue & Walker were thinking about putting on a string of shows to promote stock and bond investments?"

"No," I replied. "That was before my time."

The fellow we had to fool with was Walker, the junior partner. If you think this guy you were worried with today is tough, you should have known Walker. Talk about client trouble! I handled the auditions, and we put on three the same day, two at Columbia and one over at NBC. Walker was one of those eggs who want a five grand show for five hundred—time included. Worst tightwad you ever saw. They say he's one of the few brokers who came through the depression with more than he went in with."

"Huh," I grunted. "So what?"

"So there's justice, after all. Walker just got taken for ten thousand dollars. It's a funny kind of a situation, too. Look." He shoved the paper into my hand and indicated an item on the front page.

PROMINENT WALL STREET BROKER STORM CENTER OF STRANGE AFFAIR

Mysterious circumstances attended today a $10,000 cash donation made by Edward J. Walker, prominent Wall Street financier, to a supposed representative of United Charities. Late yesterday afternoon, Mr. Walker gave this unusual story to detectives from the Chambers Street Station.

"About eleven o'clock this morning, I was informed by my secretary that a Miss Agnes Russell, of United Charities, was waiting to see me. Since it is my custom to make regular donations to charitable institutions, I asked my secretary to have the lady shown in. After informing me of her connection with United Charities, the woman requested that I contribute $10,000 to her organization, and that I give her that sum in cash. I realized, of course, that this was an unusual procedure, but, wishing to be as helpful as possible, I directed my secretary to take that amount from our vault. I then gave the money to the woman, who thanked me and left.

"Shortly after she had gone, I began wondering if everything about the transaction was according to Hoyle, as it were. Accordingly, I had my secretary telephone United Charities and inquire if the money had reached them safely.

To my great astonishment, they told us that they had not seen the money, and that, furthermore, they had no representative by the name of Agnes Russell. Quite naturally, I feel that this is a case for police investigation.

"I realize how gullible I must seem, but the fact is, I really believed the woman was what she claimed to be. I have always prided myself on my ability to read character, and this woman appeared perfectly honest to me. I shall have to revise my method of appraisal."

The description of the woman furnished by Mr. Walker is as follows: About five feet, four inches tall; weight about 120 pounds; about thirty-seven or thirty-eight years old; blue eyes and blonde hair, probably bleached. Mr. Walker was unable to recall how she was dressed. Police have announced that a search is now in progress, but by noon today no trace had been discovered.

Frank amazement has been expressed by officials at Mr. Walker's well-meant, but careless, actions in turning over such a large sum of money to a stranger.

As I finished reading the article my eyes strayed over the page and encountered something else that piqued my interest:

CRASH MOTORMAN RELEASED
AFTER EXAMINATION

Frank Wiggins, motorman of the 6th Avenue "L" train which yesterday afternoon crashed into the rear of another train standing at the 50th Street station, was released today from the psychopathic ward of Bellevue Hospital where he had been undergoing examination. Although it had been believed the accident might have been due to temporary insanity, psychiatrists were unable to find anything wrong with Wiggins' mind, or to suggest any reason for his alleged lapse. The examination came through Wiggins' inability to explain why he had run through a block signal. Transit Company officials said there would be no legal action brought against Wiggins, though they admitted he has been discharged from the position he held for fifteen years.

Believe it or not, even with these articles in such close juxtaposition, I did not at the moment see any connection between the two affairs they described.

"Well," demanded Harry Saunders, "what do you think of it?"

"I think Walker must be cracked. He certainly doesn't sound like either a tightwad or a shrewd broker to me."

"Sure doesn't. Now, I'll tell you something else. I got a coupla pals on the papers, and they tell me that there's more in this than meets the eye."

I raised an inquisitive eyebrow.

"When a guy gives that much cash money—cash, mind you—to a dame, you can bet your bottom dollar there's something screwy somewhere. Now, these fellows I know tell me that this woman had something on Walker, and—"

"Nuts!" I retorted. "If he was giving out hush money, he wouldn't have called in the police on the case, and he certainly wouldn't have tried to pin it on United Charities."

"That may have been some kind of a blind," said Harry, illogically. "Mark my words, there's something behind this. These guys never miss, and I got the tip straight from them. You mark my words."

"Okay," I laughed. "I'll mark them—in red ink. But now I've got to go back to work, so kindly scram, will you?"

HARRY DEPARTED AND I thought no more about Edward J. Walker until I telephoned Paula Lansdowne after dinner that evening. Then:

"Hello, darling," she said.

"Hello, darling yourself," I replied. "How did you know who it was?"

"What makes you think I did?"

"That's an old one. What's new?"

"Quite a bit, when you look at it one way," she said. "Dad's becoming famous. People are beginning to seek him out, and I, as his daughter, am not utterly devoid of recognition. Not if a cute, curly-headed reporter counts, anyhow."

"Curly-headed reporter, eh? I'll be right over. But first, what's it all about?"

"About somebody named Edward J. Walker," Paula answered. "Ever hear of him?"

"Why, yes," I said. "The man who gave the woman the ten thousand dollars."

"That's it. I see you read the newspapers."

"Well," I prompted, "what about him?"

"It'd take too long to explain over the phone, but if by any chance you decide to drop around—"

"Remarkably enough, I was just about to do that very thing."

Fifteen minutes later, Paula met me at the door of the Lansdowne apartment. "Okay," said I, kissing her, "spill it."

"It's like this," she began. "This afternoon the phone rang, and it was a man Dad has known for quite a while.

He wanted to know if Dad would have a look at this Mr. Walker and find out if he were sane. It was on account of that ten thousand dollar business. It seems that Walker had been worrying about his sanity and wanted to consult a psychiatrist, only wanted to be sure that no one would ever find out about it. So he asked a friend who was also a friend of Dad's to recommend one."

"And—"

"And so this afternoon Walker came to see Dad."

"Well," I said, "go on. Was he or was he not sane?"

"Dad said he was more or less sane, whatever he means by that. Perhaps you'd like to talk to him about it, you seem so interested. Is Walker a friend of yours?"

"No, but I've heard some things about him. Besides, it's an interesting case."

We interrupted the Professor, who was doing a bit of research in his study, a little den that Paula had fixed up for him. As usual, it was a mass of confusion, with papers and books scattered all over the place. The scientist seemed rather glad of the excuse to stop work, and after we had exchanged a few pleasantries, I questioned him about the Walker affair. Looking at me rather sharply, Professor Lansdowne removed the horn-rimmed spectacles he had been wearing and leaned back in his chair.

"Are you acquainted with Mr. Walker?" he wanted to know.

I explained that my interest was casual.

"A queer thing, that," Professor Lansdowne went on. "I suppose you read the newspaper account. It didn't give even a hint of the real circumstances, which are quite unusual, quite unusual."

I would like to state categorically that up to, and including, this stage of the game, my interest in the Walker affair
was every bit as casual as I had said it was. I certainly
attached no special significance to it. My curiosity was
merely that of a person whose life is sufficiently unevent-
ful to make him grasp at such small excitement as comes
his way.

"How do you mean, sir?" I asked.

"In strict confidence, here's what I mean: Walker told me
that he definitely did not give the money to this woman of
his own free will. He said it would never occur to him to
do such a foolish thing, and that he cannot account for his
actions, except to say that he had a very strong impulse to
do exactly as his visitor asked. He told me that this impulse
was remarkably strong, and quite irresistible. Not until the
woman had gone did he fully appreciate the foolishness of
what he had done."

"Why, that's funny," I said. "That's the same thing that
the elevated motorman said."

"What elevated motorman?" queried the Professor.

"Why, the one who ran into the train." And I hurriedly
recounted the episode to him. When I had finished, he
looked very thoughtful, and it was several minutes before
he said anything.

"Most remarkable," he finally murmured. "I wonder—
but, of course, not. It would be impossible."

"What's that, sir?"

Professor Lansdowne waved his hand through the air
in a gesture of dismissal. "Merely an absurd thought," he
said. "But there does seem a great similarity."

"If you mean between the motorman and Walker, I

certainly agree with you. By the way, Paula says you found nothing wrong with the man?"

"He's rather a confirmed neurasthenic," said the scientist, "and he's very badly frightened, or was. He was quite convinced that he was going mad. Actually, there are no psychopathic symptoms whatever. So his actions can't be explained that way."

"They couldn't find anything wrong with the motorman, either," I put in.

"Very interesting. Walker's case—to be frank with you—I've permitted myself a bit of fancy, and wondered if he were possibly under a hypnotic influence. The woman—"

"Might have hypnotized him into giving her the ten grand?" I finished for him. "That's a thought."

"One, however, that will never be proved until the woman is located. In any event, it's a very feeble theory." He paused a moment, then added: "That motorman business, now, coming on top of this. Very queer."

"Could it be the start of an epidemic of insanity?"

"An epidemic of insanity? A very original idea, Bob, but I'm afraid it's no go. I really can hit upon no explanation."

"Then let's call off the discussion," cut in Paula. "I can't imagine why you're both so absorbed about it, anyway. I'd like to go places, myself."

"What do you think I'm made of, money?" I demanded. "We went to the movies last night and now you want to go out again. What's the big idea? And another thing. What about this reporter that has been paying you all the attention. Where does he fit in?"

"Oh, Curly." Paula smiled reminiscently. "He's a sweet boy, trying to make his way in the world. He came out here to see Dad and Dad wouldn't see him. What could I do? He might have lost his job on the paper. I gave him what help I could."

"He came out about the Walker business?"

"Uh-huh," replied Paula. "He heard somewhere that Walker had come to see Dad. Seriously, I didn't really give the show away. But we did have a nice chat."

"Don't let her tease you, Bob," advised the Professor.

"Don't worry, I won't," said I. "Come on, you, let's get going if you want to go. But it'll have to be Dutch!"

"Okay, piker!"

FOR THE NEXT several days, the Walker case was kept alive by the newspapers, but no further trace of the woman was discovered and the affair ceased to be news. Walker never did admit the real circumstances but, undaunted, the *Express* published several items in which it was strongly hinted that there was something very strange about it all. An explanation was not offered by the writer, who, it presently appeared, was the reporter who had talked with Paula, one "Curly" Smith.

Near three o'clock of a morning about a week later, two bums made their way into a police station. They'd stumbled, literally, over the body of a woman lying in a gutter on West Street. When the police reached the scene, "they had no difficulty identifying it as that of Agnes Russell, so-called mystery woman of the Walker case. There was a bullet hole in her right temple, and not far away a small caliber automatic was found. The only fingerprints on the weapon belonged to Agnes Russell. From the position of the body, it was deducted that she had killed herself. There was no money on the dead woman, except less than a dollar in silver, nor was there anything to indicate where she had lived.

The corpse was taken to the city morgue where it lay unclaimed.

A coroner's jury found that Agnes Russell had died by her own hand and the Walker mystery remained unsolved.

3

SEIZURE OF HATE

IT WAS A rainy evening, and enough fog had drifted up from the Bay to remind me of San Francisco, where I'd spent several weeks the previous summer. There was the same wet saltiness in the air, a half-mysterious atmosphere that thrilled and depressed me at one and the same time. It was, in short, the sort of night that writers of mystery stories select for their most gruesome murders. In this weird gloom, not common in New York, anything might happen. Thus it was with a feeling of suppressed excitement that I walked up from the Drive to my apartment.

Whether this was a genuine premonition, or merely the result of my foggy environment, I will leave to those more conversant with mental phenomena than I—to Professor Lansdowne, for instance. Once inside my tiny flat and the lights switched on, the strange feeling relaxed entirely and I sat down before my portable typewriter to write several letters before retiring.

I had hardly put a sheet of paper in the machine when the telephone rang. New York telephones all ring exactly alike—a series of moderately long, evenly spaced signals— yet this call sounded urgent. I picked up the receiver and said, "Hello!"

"Oh, Bob!"

It was Paula, and there was fear and anxiety in her voice.

"Darling!" I exclaimed. "What on earth is the matter?"

"It's Dad," she sobbed. "They've taken Dad and I don't know what they're going to do with him!"

"They've taken the Professor? Who's taken him where? What do you mean?"

"The police. They took him to jail. They came here and took him. They arrested him for murder!"

"Murder!" I exclaimed, utterly dumbfounded. Then I came back to my senses a little. "Now, look here, Paula. You get hold of yourself. There's been some terrible mistake, but it's all going to be straightened out. You're at home?"

"Yes. They wouldn't let me go along. Oh, what are we going to do?"

"You're going to take a stiff drink of whiskey and calm down enough to give me a lucid account of what happened. I'm coming right over." I tried to put as much confidence in my voice as possible.

"All right," said Paula, a trifle more collectedly. "Please hurry."

"Don't worry. I will."

It is normally a fifteen minute walk from my place to the Lansdownes', but that night it only took me half that time, running most of the way. As I loped along, I tried to think. But with the meager knowledge at my disposal, only that Professor Lansdowne had been arrested for killing someone, there wasn't much progress to be made. One thing was definite: that man wouldn't hurt a fly, let alone kill a human being—unless it was a case of kill or be killed.

The elevator boy had the look about him of having been

scared out of his wits. My panting, excited appearance must have been still another shock for him that evening. He began to talk as soon as he'd closed the door and started the car upward.

"I dunno what's coming inta this place," he said, shaking his head. "The cops come bustin' in here, askin' me this and askin' me that and I dunno half what they're talkin' about. Then they bring the Professor down with handcuffs on. I guess he musta done something pretty bad to get handcuffs on his hands. I guess he musta—"

"Shut up!" I commanded angrily. "Get this crate moving faster, you infernal idiot!"

Paula burst into tears all over again when she saw me. She was as pale as a ghost and trembling from head to foot. As would any man under the circumstances, I took her in my arms and tried to reassure her. A little later she quieted down and told me what had occurred.

"**DAD WENT OUT** after dinner tonight. He said he was going over to have a chat with Dr. Amos Carter—you've heard us speak of him—which he does every other week or so. I listened to the radio and read a while until about ten o'clock, when Dad came back. He spoke to me, but went right to his room without staying up to talk as he usually does. This seemed a bit queer, but I supposed he was tired so I didn't bother to find out if anything were wrong. Oh, if I only had!"

She began to cry at the thought.

"There, there!" I said clumsily. "Hang onto yourself. Then what?"

"Well," Paula sniffed, "I didn't hear anything more from him and I kept on reading. Then they came and got him."

"You mean the police came?"

"Yes."

"Tell me what they did," I suggested. "What did they say?"

Paula dabbed at her nose with a handkerchief.

"There was a banging on the door and when I answered it there were two big, burly men outside. They showed badges and said they were from police headquarters and wanted to see Professor Alfred Lansdowne. I couldn't begin to figure it out, but of course I let them in. I had just turned around to get Dad when I saw him standing there in the hallway. He—he looked terrible and said, 'It's all right, gentlemen. I'm ready to go along with you.'"

"Yes," I prompted, "and then what?"

"The biggest of the two put his hand on Dad's shoulder and said, 'I hereby arrest you for the murder of Amos Carter,' or something like that."

"Amos Carter? Why, he's been your father's friend for years!"

"Of course. I felt like I'd been hit by a brick building, but Dad only stood there, not saying anything. The detective told him to get his coat and hat and come along, and so Dad asked me to bring them to him. When I came back with his things, he kissed me and said not to worry, that everything would be all right. He said he would get in touch with Norman Howard, our lawyer, and that he would take care of things."

Paula had herself pretty well under control, but when she finished her story, she sighed deeply.

"I don't know what it's all about. I know Dad didn't kill anyone."

"Of course he didn't," I agreed. "Tell me, did the Professor say when you could expect to hear from him, or ask you to get in touch with him later, or with anybody else?"

"No," answered the girl. "It was just as I told you. He said nothing."

"That's funny. Did he seem shocked or surprised?"

"No, I don't think he did. He acted as though he knew what was going to happen."

"Did the detectives say where they were taking him?" I asked.

"No, and I guess I was too dazed to ask them. It all happened so suddenly."

"Now, look, Paula," I said. "Before I ask you a couple of questions I have in mind, I want you to get this straight: I fully believe the Professor is innocent. Knowing him as I do, I couldn't believe anything else. Understood?"

"Of course. You don't need to say that."

"I'm not trying to be any star detective.

I think we ought to go over a few points, and in case they should ask you any questions later you'll have the answers fixed in your mind. Okay?"

"Okay," Paula replied.

"ALL RIGHT, THEN. To begin with, do you know whether your father has ever had any arguments with Dr. Carter?"

"I can't remember any. I don't know what they could have been about, certainly. They wrangle a lot about their respective theories, but that's all it ever amounts to."

"Swell. So far, so good. Now another: did the Professor seem excited or agitated during dinner, or before he went to see Dr. Carter?"

"Not in the least," said Paula, promptly.

"How long have your Dad and Carter known each other?"

"I suppose it must be twenty-five or thirty years. Since they were in clinical work together."

"And they've been close friends all this time, haven't they?"

"Well," said Paula, "I wouldn't have called them close friends exactly, but they've been very friendly. They have a lot of the same interests you know. Dr. Carter is a neurologist. I mean he *was* a neurologist."

"Uh-huh," I grunted thoughtfully. The whole thing was getting more fantastic by the minute. Feeling that Paula was depending on me absolutely, I racked my brains trying to think of some angle that should be covered. As an avid reader of detective stories, I knew that in such cases there was always an unsuspected angle. Of course, the Professor didn't kill Carter, I told myself. But then, if he didn't, why hadn't he seemed surprised when the police came? Why had he said merely that he was willing to go with them?

"Could your Dad be shielding anyone else?" I asked.

"Why, no, Why would *anyone* want to kill poor old Dr. Carter? Why should Dad have to shield anyone?"

"Well, then," I pursued, "let's have a fling at it from another angle. Did anybody else in your family, either your mother's or your father's people, know Dr. Carter?" It seemed to me that sometimes men killed because of an old grudge. Perhaps Carter had been in love with Mrs. Lansdowne before she married the Professor. This was clearly a wild grabbing at straws, but it's only in detective stories that people manage to think clearly at such times.

"I can't think of anyone who'd even have known him

except Father and, of course, Mother. She used to have him over to dinner quite often before she died."

"There was no particularly close friendship between your mother and Dr. Carter?"

"Of course not," said Paula indignantly. "What on earth are you trying to get at?"

"Now, listen, Paula," I said, getting red around the ears. "I'm only asking questions."

"Yes, and while you're hanging around here asking silly questions, what are they doing with Dad? Why can't we go to him?" Paula was holding back the tears with difficulty, it was apparent. It was also apparent that we should do exactly as she said. Remembering a friend on the police force, I called him up. Tom Higgins had been a red-headed, freckle-faced young giant when I was in grammar school back in Baltimore, and he was quite a hero to me. Six or seven years my senior, he was always sort of a big brother. Just recently he'd been made a Deputy Inspector, the youngest in New York, and it was likely that he could help us if anyone could. With some difficulty, I finally tracked him down.

"Hello, you old blankety-blank-blank!" Higgins greeted me cheerfully. "This is a helluva time of night for you to be gettin' a ticket. Want it fixed?"

"No, Tom," I said. "It's quite a bit more serious than that and I need your help."

"Well, I'll do what I can as long as it doesn't interfere with my duty—and even then we'll see what can be done!"

"It won't interfere with your duty," I informed him. "Just tell me one thing. Where would a couple of plainclothes-men take a man they'd arrested for murder?"

"Murder?" Higgins whistled. "You have got mixed up in something. Who's the lucky corpse?"

"Cut the kidding, Tom. I said this was serious."

"Awright, Bob. If it's an important case—big names—they'd take him down to the D.A.'s office. Otherwise to the Homicide Bureau. That's where they put the heat on if the guy hasn't already confessed. Afterwards, they'll hold him in the Tombs for trial or sentence as the case may be."

"Thanks," I said. "Now, one more thing. I want you to use your influence so I can get to see the man they're holding—tonight."

"Maybe you better tell me the whole story," said Tom.

I didn't care to tell the unpleasant facts over the telephone, so it was arranged for me to go to Higgins' midtown apartment. Paula insisted on going along, naturally enough. After listening to the facts, Tom sent us down to the Criminal Courts Building, promising to do what he could to get us a few minutes with the Professor that night.

"Only remember," he said, "I ain't no blankety-blank police commissioner, so don't expect too much!" Then, suddenly conscious of the strong language he had used, he apologized profusely to Paula. I hoped with all my heart he could do something for us. My stomach had felt like a weight had been dropped into it ever since it became clear that the Professor was either locked up in the Tombs or else being given a third degree by a group of tough detectives. I tried to hide my real feelings from Paula and made a strong effort to treat the affair as lightly as possible. The girl herself tried to smile, but for the greater part of the long ride downtown in the taxi, she clung to my arm fiercely.

AT DETECTIVE HEADQUARTERS we were kept waiting

nearly an hour while necessary red tape was being cut. The anteroom where we sat seemed to reek of all the people who'd ever been there. It was as though an aura of hate and fear and hardboiled justice hung in the air.

Slowly, the hands of the clock slipped from midnight to quarter past, to twelve-thirty, to fifty. Finally, a uniformed officer beckoned us and led the way down a long, musty corridor into a small, bare room. There we waited another ten or fifteen minutes before the door opened and Professor Lansdowne, his face haggard and worn, was brought in by a guard. Paula rushed into his arms, but she didn't cry, as I had expected her to.

"Paula, darling!" said the Professor at last. "And Bob! It was fine of you to come here tonight. Of course, you would naturally come. But it's fine of you anyway. What must you think of me to have done a thing like this!"

"We know you didn't do anything, Dad!" cried Paula. "You didn't, did you?" The guard was standing directly behind the scientist, and I didn't think anything should be said in his presence.

"Wait a minute, Paula," I restrained her, "until we can talk—privately."

"Howard will be back in a minute," said the Professor, referring to his lawyer. "I believe he can arrange for us to talk quietly a short time."

Professor Lansdowne obviously had himself under control, and this made everything just that much more puzzling—his attitude when he was arrested, and the calm, unflustered way he was accepting what had happened, as though it were a matter of course. I felt completely in the dark, as did Paula, poor kid.

There was an awkward silence for the next two or three minutes. Then a smallish, middle-aged man, slightly protuberant about the middle, entered the room. He wore pince-nez glasses and his face was ruddy, whether from sun or spirits it was impossible to judge. I knew one thing immediately, that I disliked the gentleman on the spot. Professor Lansdowne introduced him to me as Norman Howard. The lawyer barely nodded in my general direction and spoke to the Professor. His voice was high-pitched and his words were clipped, precise.

"I've done everything I can, Professor Lansdowne," he said, "but I must admit there isn't very much that can be done. Of course, it will be impossible to arrange any bail for you under the, er, unfortunate circumstances. I'm very much afraid you'll have to remain here for the next few weeks. Perhaps later some new light may be shed on the case. But for now—"

He shrugged his shoulders, and a look of panic crossed Paula's face.

"You mean Dad has to stay here, in this terrible place, for weeks?"

"I'm afraid that's just what I do mean, my dear girl," said Howard. "After all—"

"See here, Mr. Howard," I interrupted, "can't you arrange for us to go somewhere and talk things over? There's a good deal which I, for one, want to know, and I don't care to talk in front of this policeman."

Howard darted a look of anger at me.

"Who is this man?" he demanded.

"Mr. Larkin is my very good friend and my daughter's fiancé," replied the Professor in his dignified way. Leave it to him to be dignified at a time like this! "Can't you do as he suggests and arrange for us to talk privately?"

"It isn't usually permitted, but I suppose so," said Howard testily. By now I was quite ready to choke the pompous little rooster, but he removed the temptation by leaving the room. When he returned, a different guard accompanied him and we were taken down yet another corridor to a tight little room without windows. There we were left alone.

"OH, DAD, DAD!" cried Paula, as soon as the guard had gone. "What does it all mean? You didn't—you couldn't—have killed Dr. Carter! Tell me you didn't! Tell me!"

The Professor sat down heavily on one of the hard wooden chairs. For a moment he buried his face in his hands and then once more regained his composure with an apparent effort. With Paula's arms around him, he said:

"I'd give anything in the world to be able to tell you that, my dear."

Paula looked at him searchingly.

"You mean you *did* kill him?"

Her father nodded mutely.

"But why? Why did you do it?"

"I wish I knew, Paula." The Professor's voice was dull, hopeless. "But I don't. I haven't any idea why I killed him. All I know is, I did."

"Now, there!" said Howard, petulantly. "You see? How am I to make any sort of case with the man talking like that?" Once more I restrained an impulse to take a crack at him.

"Professor Lansdowne," I said, "I know that if you killed him you had a mighty good reason. Won't you tell us the whole story from the beginning?"

"Thank you for saying that, my boy. Certainly, I'll be glad to tell you everything that happened, but I'm afraid, just as Norman has said, there isn't much that can be done about it. No jury would be likely to believe my story."

"We'll believe it, Dad, and we'll help, too. You'll see!" It made me feel very proud of Paula, the way she was standing up to this emergency.

"All right, dear," said the Professor. "Here's the story: As you know, I've known Amos Carter for a great many years. In all that time, the only disagreements we've ever had have been about politics and our respective psychiatric and neurological theories. But these things were merely differences of opinion, nothing more. Hardly worth killing each other about.

"I reached Carter's apartment about eight-thirty and he himself met me at the door. The only person in the house with him was Mrs. Edmunds, his cook and maid-of-all-work. Carter was unmarried. We went into his study, just off the living room, and began talking. I described some research I've made recently about the effect of diet on certain kinds of mental aberration. As usual, we got into one of our arguments which lasted for the next two hours, or perhaps longer. I don't remember exactly.

"Suddenly, I began feeling a very powerful antipathy towards Dr. Carter, for no better reason, as far as I could tell, than that he differed with me about this pet theory of mine. He must have caught something of the way I was feeling. He looked at me sharply and then went on with what he was saying. This was a categorical disagreement with the ideas I'd advanced.

"Never in my life have I been given to violent tempers.

But after Carter's last statement I became so terribly angry that I shook from head to foot. Literally, I saw red. There was a heavy metal book-end within reach, and I picked this up and brought it down on Amos' head with all the strength I had."

The Professor's hands were trembling, and at this point he stopped, overcome by emotion. Paula's cool fingers smoothed his wrinkled forehead, and in a moment he was able to continue.

"Instantly, the horror of the thing I'd done became fully apparent to me. I tried frantically to account for my murderous anger, but it was no use. The more I tried to think, the less I was able to. All I remembered was an intense, unreasoning hatred and striking poor, old Carter. As far as any real reason is concerned, none existed. Nor can I add anything now. The only possible explanation is temporary insanity of a most criminal nature."

"And that's our one chance to make a case out of this mess," said Norman Howard. "Not guilty by reason of insanity."

"Dad, listen!" exclaimed Paula. "Don't you know what this is? It's the same thing that hit that man Walker—the man who gave away the ten thousand dollars! Can't you see?"

"Of course," I agreed, elated at finding a key to the puzzle. "And the elevated motorman. It's some sort of epidemic."

The Professor shook his head.

"I've considered that. The cases resemble each other, yes, but I'm unable to advance a sensible explanation, let alone prove it. I have an idea or two, but at the moment, they're worthless. In fact, they're not altogether credible to me."

"Well, if it's a disease they certainly can't hold you responsible for what you've done," said Paula.

"I never heard of an epidemic of insanity, but if it should be that, they'll put me in an asylum, so there really isn't much to choose. However," he made his voice sound more cheerful, for Paula's sake I judged, "Norman says it will be several weeks before I'm brought to trial. Perhaps in that time something will turn up."

"Can I ask a question, Professor?" I'd had a brain wave.

"Go right ahead, Bob."

"Did anyone actually see you strike Dr. Carter?"

"If you're trying to establish—" began Norman Howard, but was interrupted by the Professor.

"Not that I know of, but Mrs. Edmunds must have heard the blow, because she came running into the study and saw me standing there with the book-end still in my hand. Why?"

"I wondered if it couldn't be called an accident, or self-defense," I said, lamely.

"I'm afraid not, Bob," said the scientist. "Besides, I've already confessed to the murder. The trial is Norman's idea—to prove me insane, which shouldn't be hard."

"Sorry folks, but you'll have to go now." It was the guard.

WE RELUCTANTLY BADE the Professor goodby, and watched him as he was taken down the hall. It was a trying moment for both of us, but the lawyer seemed little impressed. He bade us a brisk good-night and hurried out ahead of us.

As Paula and I were going down the stone steps in front

of the building, we were met by a young man whose disar-
ranged collar and tie seemed indicative of hasty dressing.

"Hello, Miss Lansdowne," he said cordially. "I just heard
about your dad and I rushed down here to see if there was
anything I could do."

"That was sweet of you, Curly," said Paula, then, turning to me, "Bob, this is Curly Smith, of the *Express*." I
acknowledged the introduction with a nod.

"Is there anything I can do to help?" Smith asked. "I
was going in to see your father, but maybe you can give
me the dope. I probably couldn't get in to see him at this
hour, anyway."

"Aren't you pretty tired, Paula?" Frankly, I was in no
mood to have the fellow hang around, although he did
seem a decent sort of chap.

"I thought if I could get the story from you or the
Professor, I might be able to write it up in a way that
would help your dad, Miss Lansdowne. Of course, I don't
know whether he needs any help or not, but favorable press
notices sometimes are fairly important, if you know what
I mean." Curly looked very anxious and sincere and Paula,
womanlike, gave in.

"He can ride up in the taxi with us, can't he, Bob?" she
asked. "We won't be losing any sleep that way. Not that I
could sleep."

"Fine," I agreed, without much enthusiasm.

As the cab swung over to Broadway and headed north,
Paula told the reporter all she knew about the case. I would
have preferred her to be silent, but on the other hand, she
was telling only the simple truth and it couldn't possibly
hurt the Professor's chances. Smith listened quite sympa-

thetically, and although I was not overly anxious to admit virtues in a man who was obviously interested in Paula far more than in her father, I had to acknowledge that he was a pleasant-appearing individual. He had blue eyes and sandy hair which sprawled over his head in a tangled mass of curls. Later I noticed that he always walked as though he were making difficult headway against a heavy wind, his head thrust forward and his chin down. There was an air about him that inspired trust, and it isn't surprising that Paula was glad to find in him a potential ally. Though what he could do I didn't know. Winning public sympathy through the newspapers would never prove Professor Lansdowne innocent.

Much to my annoyance, Curly accompanied us all the way to Paula's door. We both tried to persuade her to have someone stay with her, but Paula was determined to remain alone, except for Martha, the Lansdowne cook. Since there was no promise of compromise in her tone, we were forced to give in to her. I left Smith on his way to the subway, and walked slowly down the Drive home.

Try as I might, there was no way of getting at the problem which we had to face. In some remote portion of my mind, I remembered Professor Lansdowne's remarking that the broker, Walker, seemed to have been under a hypnotic influence. I tried to apply hypnosis to the Professor's case, but could not. There had been no one there to do the hypnotizing. The idea of there being an epidemic of insanity satisfied me no more than the other. It didn't seem possible, in spite of Walker and the motorman. Even if there were an epidemic, the situation would not be improved, as the Professor had pointed out. He'd still run the risk of being shut up in a lunatic asylum for the rest of his life, not a pleasant prospect for a man of Professor Lansdowne's attainments.

Another point troubled me, and its name was Norman Howard. I was not at all pleased with him, and it seemed dangerous to trust the Professor's fate to him. I wasn't sure but what Howard believed the scientist a willful murderer.

ALL NIGHT LONG, I tossed between wakefulness and troubled sleep. My dreams were filled with visions of Paula and her father, harried and hunted from one end of the world to the other. Always I tried to help them and could do nothing. The dreams got even worse towards morning and finally I awoke in a cold sweat to get up and sit on the side of the bed, staring out into the gray dawn, wondering what to do.

One resolve I could carry out, and that was my determination to spend as much time as possible with Paula during this trying period. There was enough money in my bank account to take care of my expenses for a few months if necessary. When, later that morning, I told Paula what I'd decided to do, she tried at first to make me change my mind, but in a little while she gave up and seemed much relieved.

It wasn't hard to make arrangements at the office, even on such short notice. My services were by no means indispensable, and Ralph Stone, Rowlandson & Leger's copy chief, was very nice about granting me an indefinite leave of absence. So Paula and I had a late breakfast together at her place, and talked over ways and means. It was rather pathetic conversation, actually, and we knew we were whistling to keep our courage up. There was so little we could do.

Paula was expecting a call from Norman Howard about eleven o'clock, but while we were waiting for it, something else happened. We heard faint cries in the street below, gradually getting nearer. In a few minutes we were able to distinguish the voices as those of newsboys yelling "Extra!" at the top of their lungs. Comparatively little space had been devoted to Professor Lansdowne in the morning papers, so it was extremely unlikely that an extra would be gotten out about him this late. Nonetheless, Paula looked at me, deathly pale.

"Do you suppose anything could have happened to Dad?" she asked.

"Of course not," I replied. "It's something else altogether. Sit tight, and I'll run down and get one."

On the street, I corralled one of the newsboys and bought a paper. Spread across the front page in screaming headlines were the words: MANIAC DEMANDS CONTROL OF CITY; THREATENS REPRISALS UNLESS POWER GRANTED.

With this first ultimatum, terror began smashing at the gates of sanity.

Dr. Skull was beginning to hit his stride.

4

THE ULTIMATUM

I HURRIED UPSTAIRS with the paper, having a queer, prickly sensation running up and down my back. You can say what you like about the absurdity of premonitions, but this crazy demand—the work, on the face of it, of a lunatic—made me feel heavy with dread from the moment I saw those headlines. Paula was too relieved that the extra did not concern her father to pay more than casual attention as I read the whole article aloud.

In brief, it described how a mysterious note had been sent through the mails to the Mayor of New York. Its text was as follows:

Mayor Patrick O'Hara,

City Hall,

New York City, N.Y.

My Dear Mr. Mayor:

Fully understanding how any public official must be the recipient of countless communications sent by so-called cranks, I can appreciate the possibility that this letter may be thrown into the waste-basket by one of your secretaries. Therefore, let me take the liberty of advising whatever secretary reads this to see that this message reaches its destination.

44

It is a message of the utmost importance, not only to you, Mr. Mayor, but to every one of your seven million citizens.

I shall come to the point: I demand that full and complete power of administration of every phase of municipal government be delegated to an agent whom I shall name at the proper time. This agent is to be given absolute authority over all branches of the city government, most especially those of the police and financial departments. Further details of this arrangement will follow in due course.

You and your advisors will obviously conclude that this letter is the work of a madman—a possibility, Mr. Mayor, which is quite beside the point. Whatever your opinion, I can only beg you to treat this communication with the seriousness you will soon discover it merits, a plea which, I fear, is all too palpably made in vain.

At the meeting of the Board of Estimate which you have convened for three P.M. today, I shall be most happy to give you a more personal message. I trust you will forgive my waiving the formality of awaiting an invitation. There is this which you should bear in mind: if my demands are refused, the punishment which I shall visit on you and your city will be memorable, but not to them that receive it.

Dr. Skull

It was a remarkable enough note, certainly, but I was surprised that it had been considered serious enough to warrant the printing of an extra edition. Still, the letter did have a strange tone to it, it was written by a more than averagely well-educated person, I should say, and it was the first example I'd ever known of a threat's being made, not to one or two individuals, but to an entire city. I gathered from the paper that the police were officially pooh-poohing the whole affair, and the Mayor had already issued a tight little statement to the effect that the meeting of the Board of Estimate would take place as scheduled, at three o'clock.

While I was trying to interest Paula in discussing the curious situation, more in order to take her mind off her father's plight than anything else, the house phone buzzed. It was the reporter, Curly Smith, and he wanted to see Paula. A bit petulantly, no doubt, I remarked to Paula that the young man was certainly working hard on the case.

"Oh, it's just that he might be of some help, Bob," she said soothingly. When she herself was worried to death, she could still find the patience to pamper my vanity.

It soon became apparent that Curly Smith would contribute slight help that particular day, anyway. He merely wanted a chance to see Paula, and was clearly disappointed that I was in the apartment. If it hadn't been for the circumstances, I might have taken pleasure in picking a fight with him. As it was, I tried to be agreeable.

"Thought I could give you a lift downtown if you'd like, Miss Lansdowne," he said presently. "I'm going that way. I have to go to a meeting of the Board of Estimate and I could drop you off on the way."

"About the letter the Mayor got this morning?" I asked.

"That's it. Would you care to go, Miss Lansdowne?"

"So early?"

"Well—" Curly looked at me in some confusion. "I thought maybe we might pick up a bite of lunch on the way."

"Thanks a lot, Curly," Paula smiled, "but I'd better not. You see, there are several things I have to do. For one, I've

"Welcome to our wake," said Warren. "It isn't often that the corpse has an opportunity to join in his own festivities"

got to see four or five of Dad's friends. They might be able to help him. Besides, I'm expecting an important phone call."

"I could wait and drive you around. I have until three."

But, to my satisfaction, she shook her head. "Not today, but thanks just the same. I probably won't be able to get downtown until late this afternoon."

For the next half hour we talked about the Professor in a disjointed sort of fashion, and then Paula sweetly invited us both to leave. My own insistence on staying with her she brushed aside. "Really, Bob, I've got people to see I'd rather see alone. You understand, don't you?"

What was there to say? I agreed to meet her at the Tombs at four-thirty o'clock and found myself trudging up the sharp incline of 116th Street with Curly Smith. From an initial awkwardness, our conversation was going along smoothly enough by the time we'd reached Broadway, so smoothly that the reporter suggested a drink. He knew of a quiet place not far from the University and soon we were installed in a comfortable booth with two rye highballs.

"She's a great girl," mused Curly, after his third refill.

"Certainly, she's a great girl. We're engaged, you know," I said deliberately. Curly looked up.

"You know how lucky you are, I suppose?"

"Damned right I do!"

"Humph!" Curly grunted. There was a period of silence which he broke by saying: "Too bad her dad's mixed up in this murder business."

"He'll be all right," I said, with more confidence than I felt.

"I don't know myself. They're having the inquest tomorrow. Not much doubt about the verdict."

"Hang the verdict," I said. "Professor Lansdowne's as innocent as—as anything."

"Just the same, he's in for a tough session. What's the odds? At best, the booby hatch. At worst, well—"

"What do you mean?" I demanded, alarmed. "They couldn't do anything more than send him to the insane asylum."

"Suppose the D.A. doesn't like the insanity plea? Suppose he bears down and tries to get a first degree verdict? You think the Professor can prove temporary insanity?"

"But," I faltered, "he won't be able to find a motive for murder. And anyway, why would he want to send a man like Professor Lansdowne to the electric chair?"

"Why does he want to send anybody to the chair? You

wouldn't. I wouldn't. But he does. That's his job, and from what I hear, he likes it."

"You're a big help," I said, my tone as flat as my spirits. "There's a way out. If not, we'll have to make one, that's all."

"You can count me in on that *we*, fella. I'd do quite a bit to help that gal—even if she is sap enough to marry you," he added with a grin.

"Thanks," I muttered, quite touched.

"Holy Gee!" Smith's eyes were on his wrist watch. "I've got to get out of here. It's after two-thirty."

"Oh, the meeting," I said. "And the menace. Think he'll turn up?"

"How should I know? By the way"—dropping his voice—"you got a couple of dollars on you?"

"Yeah." I paid the check.

"GOING MY WAY?" he asked, as he climbed into a taxi. I nodded. I was a trifle pickled, and in no mood to be alone. As the cab caromed down upper Broadway, its driver stimulated to a glorious contempt for life and limb by a promised tip, the reporter and I theorized about the author of the crazy threat.

"An educated nut," Curly summed it up. "Delusions of grandeur."

"He at least has the courage of his convictions, sticking his head into the noose like he's doing. I'd like to see the guy."

"Come along then," invited Curly. "But I'll give you ten to one the crackpot never shows."

"I'll take the bet," I said, "but I don't see how I'm going to get in. I'm no reporter."

"Don't give it a thought. It's in the bag."

By the time we reached 34th Street, it occurred to both of us that we could have made much better time on the subway, but it was too late now. Thanks to our driver's lofty indifference to a whole string of traffic lights, as well as to the luck which kept the police off our trail, we lurched to a stop in front of the weather-beaten old City Hall at five minutes after three. Curly's press card got him through, and the Leica he thrust into my hand made me look like a photographer, so that I was permitted to follow him into the inner chamber, the sanctum sanctorum where the clan was already gathering.

In addition to the regular eight members of the Board of Estimate, there were a number of other officials in the room. With the exception of the Mayor himself, I didn't know anyone from Adam, but Curly whispered shreds of information to me from time to time. For example:

"See that dignified old coot with the big belly?" he hissed into my ear. "That's Rufus T. Scott, the mug who was mixed up in the Bronx subway scandal half a dozen years ago." And then, "Pipe the guy with the horn-rimmed cheaters and the diamond stickpin. Ed Sauermann. Bosses everything from Williamsburg to Borough Hall and runs three rackets as a sideline."

We were seated at one end of the long room, on the first of two rows of seats reserved for reporters and photographers. It looked as though a sensational trial with a blonde murderess were the main attraction instead of a mentally-warped poison penner who might never put in an appearance. Grouped around the conference table, nearly every official looked as though he expected a bomb to explode any minute, a fear unshared by the press gallery, which looked bored.

Just as Mayor O'Hara was about to call the meeting to order, the door opened and a man stepped briskly across the room and took a chair to the right and slightly behind the Mayor.

"That," whispered Curly, "is J. Homer Warren."

I nodded, having gathered as much myself. Besides the Mayor, Warren was the only person present who would be recognized by even the most politically uninformed of New York's population. There was never a public reception to a visiting celebrity but what J. Homer Warren was the first to grasp the notable's hand as he stepped off the gangplank. Warren was always in the car that carried the King, Queen, transatlantic flyer, or whoever it might be, up Broadway amid fluttering flags and showers of paper, and it was he who usually acted as master of ceremonies at all the important party functions. It was an open secret that Warren had made his sizable fortune by illicit methods—chiefly graft—but the man's ready smile and thoroughly democratic manner to all and sundry made it impossible not to like him. According to some, he was the power behind the throne in the present administration, but everyone knew him as the best greeter since Grover Whalen.

Mayor O'Hara now started proceedings by banging his gavel. The city's chief executive was a big, red-faced Irishman with a thatch of unruly gray hair and a voice which he always seemed to pitch for an imaginary audience several blocks away.

"The meeting is now in session," he boomed. "Miss

Beckstein, will you please read the minutes of the last meeting."

There was a general restlessness among both officials and newspapermen as the sharp-nosed secretary took seven or eight minutes to rattle off the record of the previous council. When she had finished, the Mayor again rose to his feet and, in a voice calculated to startle pigeons in the next square, announced:

"Gentlemen, I think that before we take up any of the routine business originally scheduled for today, we may as well discuss the note sent me by that lunatic who calls himself Dr. Skull."

There was a general murmur of assent.

"To begin with, I'd like the secretary to please pass the letter to Mr. Warren, who will pass it down the line when he gets through with it. I think it might be a good idea for the members of the press to see it after you gentlemen finish looking."

A sheet of white paper accordingly started a slow circuit of the table, continuing thence to the reporters and eventually into my own hands. It was a plain piece of paper, the sort that might have been bought in the five-and-ten-cent store. In fact, I remembered having purchased an identical kind of stationery there myself a few weeks ago. There was, of course, no letterhead, and the message was neatly typewritten, with wide margins. The signature itself was also printed. The envelope which carried the letter was of matching paper, and had been mailed from the Grand Central Annex of the postoffice. All the words were correctly spelled. Indeed, there were no mistakes of any kind.

"I'll let Commissioner Gallagher tell you what he thinks about this letter," said the Mayor, as the missive was returned to the secretary. "Take the floor, Commissioner."

"THANKS, MR. MAYOR," said the Commissioner of Police, a thin, wiry little man with the keen face of a ferret. As he talked, he shifted nervously from one foot to the other.

"In case you gentlemen think we're taking this thing too seriously, I just want you to know that we're taking no more than ordinary precautions. There are two principal differences between this letter and the kind we generally get that contain threats. First, it's been written by a man who otherwise seems to be in his right mind and is educated besides. In the second place—and this is most unusual—the writer says that he's going to talk to you gentlemen at this Board meeting today."

A mouse-like individual at the foot of the table spoke up in a small, timid voice that sounded like he looked.

"Of course, Commissioner, you have guards stationed at the entrance to the room?"

"That I have, Mr. Milhauser. There need be no cause for uneasiness. We intend to bag this bird here and now, if he shows up. We're going to let him walk into our arms, speak his piece, and then get himself hustled right into the psychopathic ward. Outside of a little amusement for you gentlemen, and something for the newspaper boys to write home about, I don't see why this affair should interrupt your regular business in the slightest respect. Thank you."

As Gallagher sat down, several feet away from the conference table itself, there was a hubbub of excited comment until Mayor O'Hara cracked down with the gavel again in no uncertain terms.

"The gentleman from Richmond has the floor!" he roared, in response to frantic motions from the east side of the table.

"I'd like to ask what precautions the Commissioner is taking to see that no man is brought into this room with a weapon in his possession. Why, he could shoot up the place before the police could stop him!"

There was a chorus of agreement. I couldn't help thinking how these men who were supposed to be the wisdom and genius of the city seemed like a gathering of the Friday Afternoon Sewing Circle. It is certain that no group of old women, however chattery, could have outdone this distinguished body of city fathers in jittery gabbling.

"Mr. Ford can rest assured that nobody is going to get in here until he has been thoroughly searched for any pistols and dynamite bombs he may be trying to smuggle in. Also, he will be admitted only under heavy guard."

The Commissioner made this statement in a tone tinged with considerable asperity.

"Well," chirped up one of the boys, the Brooklyn boss, he was, "bring on your maniac and let's get it over with. I want to get out of this damned meeting and get back to work. It costs me five thousand dollars every time I come over here."

Bang! went the gavel.

"The meeting will continue with the business at hand," pronounced His Honor. "The first matter scheduled for discussion this afternoon..." And on he went into an outline of routine affairs. I looked at my watch—3:31. If the good Dr. Skull still intended to put in an appearance at this particular session, I wished he'd get a move on. At the moment, it seemed to me that some wise guy was pulling a fast one and would get a big laugh at the thought of having a flock of city politicians sitting around getting jittery as they waited for him to turn up. My earlier premonition was no longer with me and my thoughts were beginning to wander. Paula would soon be expecting me to join her and I wished I'd stayed with her instead of hooking myself in on this farce.

The council droned on from one item to another as the hands on my watch climbed slowly up to four o'clock. At first, a few of the voices around the big table had been nervous, and more than one pair of eyes kept straying toward the closed doors But as minutes passed and the doors failed to open, the board members forgot their fears and slumped down in their chairs for all the world like bored schoolboys waiting for the closing bell.

In the press section, boredom also was setting in. Chairs which had been comfortable enough to begin with, now developed unsuspected hardness. There began to be a good deal of shifting around and finally some whispering. This became so noticeable that Mayor O'Hara banged his gavel at us.

"Gentlemen of the Press!" he intoned "I ask you to remember that you, yourselves, requested permission to be present at this session of the Board of Estimate. You should have considered then the likely possibility that there would be nothing out of the ordinary here."

"Nuts!" said Curly, with feeling, and I nodded agreement, yawning at the same time. It was now 4:08 and if the person who wrote that letter were going to be there, he'd already have arrived, I thought. In another minute or two, I caught myself dozing, lulled by the monotony of the conversation. Every now and then, the Mayor's voice would make itself heard above the other talk, and I even got used to that, bull-like as it was.

Perhaps that's why I didn't sit on the edge of my seat when the Mayor started the most amazing speech of his entire career. But he had gotten only one word out before I was all ears, my attention caught and held by something tense and electric in the atmosphere, by the same prickly feeling along my spine that I'd noticed when I first saw the newspapers at noon. From Curly I learned what the first word was, and the rest I heard myself.

"GENTLEMEN," SAID MAYOR O'Hara. Curly said it must have been the quietness of his voice, something soft and velvety about his pronunciation that had never been there before, that focused all eyes and ears upon him. It was certain that Mayor O'Hara had never addressed a group in such moderate tones before.

"Gentlemen," the Mayor went on. Everything he said for the next several minutes was spoken in this same restrained voice, as different from O'Hara's usual delivery as day from night. You could have heard a pin drop in the next room.

"I can see that most of my distinguished friends have given up hope of having me as a guest this afternoon. But, you see, I have kept my word. It is one of my strongest characteristics, keeping my word. I am here among you, perhaps not as you might have imagined, but nonetheless present. In case you haven't remembered my name, let me present myself: Dr. Skull. Yes, that is it—Dr. Skull."

I have to hand it to that official greeter. J. Homer Warren was the first to recover from this shock—it was a whole lot more than mere surprise—and, being next to O'Hara, he grabbed the Mayor by the arm and shook him, violently.

"Pat!" he shouted. "Pat! What the devil's the matter with you, man? Have you gone crazy? I say, what's the matter with you!" He shook the arm again. It was then that he and the rest of us noticed the Mayor's eyes. They were staring vacantly into space, and the faint smile on his lips indicated that he was thinking pleasantly of something that had happened a long way away, and a long time ago."

"Pat! Pat!" shouted Warren, again.

"Compose yourself, Mr. Warren." It was the voice. Though it came from O'Hara's mouth, it was not O'Hara's voice. Though O'Hara now looked at Warren, he really seemed to look *through*, rather than *at*, him. My hair showed a tendency to stand on end. My mouth went suddenly dry and I swallowed hard. The voice was going on.

"If you will kindly take your seat again, Mr. Warren, and if you, gentlemen, will keep quite silent until I have finished what I have to tell you, nothing will happen to the Mayor. If, on the other hand, you choose to act hastily, I assure you, you will not see the Mayor himself again. I trust this is entirely clear?"

By now, even Warren had sunk back into his chair, his face deathly white. There was not a person in the room, I believe, who would have been willing to stand before that weird voice.

"Naturally," it now went on, in the same low tones, "the reporters and photographers have sufficient—I believe it is called 'news-sense'—to remain where they are. So.

We understand each other. Now, let us go on, for time is pressing.

"You are all familiar with my letter to the Mayor. You remember that I demanded complete control over the administrative forces of this city. It is not remarkable that you have chosen to regard these demands as those of a lunatic. I foresaw that likelihood and have planned accordingly.

"In the final analysis, only one thing will make you listen to the counsel of wisdom, which is to say, my counsel. Only one thing will make you obey, without question or hesitation, my commands. That thing is Fear. It is my intention to give all of you, and as many others as require it, an intimate acquaintance with this most annoying of human emotions. In time you will learn to know and respect my power.

"It is unfortunate that your puny reasoning will keep you from accepting the inevitable, and from saving yourselves a great deal of trouble. Yet, I know that will be the case, and I shall now prove it."

The body that was, and yet was not, that of Mayor O'Hara swung around until the vacant eyes gazed on J. Homer Warren.

"Mr. Warren," said the voice, "I am not entirely familiar with your function in this organization, but I presume you have a certain amount of authority. Will you see to it that a credit of one million dollars is placed in the name of Dr. Skull in the London & Midlands Bank, by immediate cable? This is, of course, merely as evidence of good faith on the part of yourself and your colleagues, and is just a small beginning. Do you agree to attend to this matter?"

Warren shook himself, as though from sleep, and slowly rose to his feet.

"Pat, Pat!" he moaned. "For God's sake stop this foolishness!"

"You see, gentlemen," said the voice, "Mr. Warren refuses to believe his own ears. I trust you understand what I'm up against. Is there any one of you here who will negotiate with me?"

There was no answer. Every man present sat as though frozen to his chair.

"Too bad," the voice went on. "However, it is exactly as I expected. Since your intelligence isn't up to this emergency, gentlemen, and since, once I leave you, you will doubt your senses even more than you do now, I shall have to make a practical example of one of you. This is to prove that I must be taken very seriously.

"It shall have to be—" There was a slight pause, as the glazed eyes traveled slowly from man to man and finally came to rest on J. Homer Warren. "—Mr. Warren here. Mr. Warren, I regret to inform you that you will die at exactly twelve o'clock sharp tonight. I hope you will note that I'm following the accepted convention as to the time of your sudden demise, Mr. Warren. Midnight."

I shivered and glanced quickly at Curly. He was as white as a sheet.

"And by the way, Mr. Warren," added the voice, "let me remind you that you will only be wasting the time of the police if you have them surround you with a bodyguard of detectives. They will be entirely unable to cope with the situation, I assure you.

"Now, gentlemen, I thank you for your attention. I trust

that Mr. Warren's being made a victim of your ignorance—
and his own—will not be altogether in vain. However, I
must confess I have little confidence in you.

"Good afternoon, gentlemen. Mr. Warren, until
midnight."

5

MURDER IN THE AIR

"THAT'S THE MOST amazing thing I ever heard of!" exclaimed Paula.

She and I were with the Professor in his cell, by virtue of Tom Higgins' influence and intervention. Although there was barely room for three people, we had a greater sense of privacy than it was possible to feel in one of the regular visiting rooms.

I'd been describing the extraordinary occurrence at the Board meeting, from which I'd just come. When I left the City Hall, the building was in an uproar. A physician had been summoned and the Mayor was undergoing first aid, more for fright than for anything else, it was easy to gather. J. Homer Warren was bending over the shaken man and was pleading with him to explain why he'd spoken so strangely. The Mayor, alas, could do no more than wheeze that he couldn't possibly explain. He had felt like a person possessed of an evil spirit; the words had come, unbidden, and they would not be repressed. That was all. Mr. Warren did not appear to be reassured by this statement.

Curly Smith had made a bee-line for a telephone and I'd lost him in the excitement, so I'd decided to come on to the Tombs alone. The Professor had been listening intently to my story, and for the first time since the death of Dr. Carter, the ghost of a smile hung to the corners of his mouth.

"So the Mayor could give no explanation," he mused. "That's very probable, and it seems to fit."

"Fit what, sir?" I asked. But the scientist didn't hear me and I had to repeat the question.

"Eh?" he grunted, as if startled. "Eh? Why, fits the idea I'm beginning to get."

"Father!" said Paula sharply. "What on earth do you mean?"

"Not a thing. Not a thing, my dear," was the hasty reply. "I was merely thinking out loud. That's all. An old habit of mine, you know."

I could see the Professor was mulling a theory around in his head, but I could also see that he was not yet ready to talk about it, so I switched the subject to Norman Howard's preparations for the inevitable trial.

"They're going to hold the coroner's inquest tomorrow at ten," said Paula. "Mr. Howard says that it will be pretty cut-and-dried. He also said that an indictment would be sure to follow their verdict."

"Well," I said, with feeling, "let them get their indictment. They won't be able to do anything to the Professor. We'll find a way out."

Paula squeezed my arm warmly and the scientist smiled at me, and I felt like a hero. This, mind you, in spite of the fact that the chances of my contributing anything worth while to the Professor's case were microscopically slight.

"Oh, by the way, Bob," said that gentleman, "I don't

suppose there's any way for you to stay with Warren until midnight tonight."

"Bob stay with J. Homer Warren?" demanded Paula. "Why should he do that?"

"Just an idea, my dear."

"Why, I don't know, sir," I replied, at length. "I never met the man in my life. It probably wouldn't be easy to crash his party."

"I thought you might be able to arrange it through your friend, Mr. Higgins, or perhaps a friend of mine would be helpful. I refer to Commissioner Gallagher. Once upon a time I did him a small favor, and he told me he'd always be glad to return it."

"In that case, Professor," I said, "it undoubtedly could be worked, I guess. But why—"

"There will be a guard, don't you think? A police guard?"

"I should think so, although the voice said a guard would do no good. I can find out, if you want me to."

"I don't think you need trouble yourself. They'll have to mount some sort of guard. Conventions, you know."

At which point, Paula intervened again "What's the big idea of having Bob hang around while Warren waits for that creature to kill him? Aren't we in enough trouble now without getting Bob killed too?"

"If I may step for a moment into the vernacular," said Professor Lansdowne, "I suggest, Paula, that you keep your shirt on. There can't possibly be any danger for Bob. It's Warren Dr. Skull is after. No one else. Don't you agree, Bob?"

"Sure I do," I assented, eagerly. "Your dad is right, Paula.

There's no danger to me. Anyhow, I'd like to get a crack at the ghost, or whatever it is."

"Well," hesitated the girl, "I don't like it."

"It'll be all right, darling, and if it helps your dad—"

"How can it help him? That's what I'd like to know. How?"

"An idea of mine, Paula," explained her father. "If it works out, it may shed light on a good many things."

"On you and Dr. Carter?"

"Perhaps."

Paula gave in, and I got busy on the telephone. Using the Professor's name, I had no difficulty getting through to Commissioner Gallagher, in spite of the fact that he must have been rather preoccupied that evening, to say the least. The Commissioner told me he was already quite concerned about the Professor and anything he could do that might help him, he would do gladly.

"That guy just about saved my life once," he added, with warmth.

Accordingly, I was directed to appear at Warren's Fifth Avenue penthouse at nine o'clock that evening. A group of plainclothesmen had been designated as guards in addition to uniformed police, and there would be several reporters from the morning papers. Commissioner Gallagher predicted that my presence very likely would not be noticed.

"We don't necessarily expect trouble," he pointed out, "but we aren't taking any chances, either. I don't know whether O'Hara was drunk or whether there was a ventriloquist in the room or what. All I know is, it's pretty damned queer."

I agreed that it was.

"Well," said the Commissioner in conclusion, "you be up there at nine sharp and you'll get in. We won't let the President of the United States in after that time, so be prompt. Ask for Inspector Higgins. I'll let him know." It was good news to me that Tom Higgins would be there. At least, if anything happened, I'd have a friend in the place.

PAULA AND I dined together at a pseudo-Bohemian restaurant called the Atelier. With the inquest hardly twelve hours away, she was hard put to carry on any very bright conversation. Finally, she gave up and reverted to the subject closest her heart.

"What worries me more than anything else is that Dad is locked up in that terrible jail, helpless, and nobody is trying to discover the real thing that made him do what he did. I don't know what it is, but there's some *reason*. My father doesn't kill harmless old men for nothing!"

What could I say?

Not very much. That I agreed with her heartily, that I was going to do everything in my power to clear the Professor, that I was sure he would be cleared, that I'd give my life to keep her from being unhappy. Then I took her home and, after promising to be very careful and to telephone her the minute I left Warren's apartment, I went to keep my appointment.

NEW YORK BY now was definitely conscious of Dr. Skull, though it was regarding what had happened with more amusement than foreboding. Mayor O'Hara had long been noted for his unpredictable conduct, what with his blunderings and his eternal malapropisms, and he was recognized by the press as a rich source of humorous items. For this reason, although the Mayor's behavior at the Board meeting had transcended even his usual remarkable standards, the public viewed matters with a tolerantly suspicious eye. It had been, of course, a gala day for the papers, and vivid descriptions of the afternoon's mêlée were splashed over every front page in town.

So far, let me record, no one thought of connecting it with the Walker and elevated crash incidents.

Until I entered the home of J. Homer Warren, I had never seen a real, honest-to-goodness penthouse except in the movies. Certainly such splendor that the politician's establishment boasted is seldom encountered outside that financially unfettered medium of entertainment. The front door opened onto a reception hall that looked like the diplomat's waiting room in Buckingham Palace. There was a crystal chandelier and, if you please, a fountain, with colored lights playing rainbow effects on the streams of water.

Commissioner Gallagher had evidently kept his word, for I was immediately ushered into the living room by a butler—after two detectives had "frisked" me for concealed weapons. In the spacious parlor were nine or ten men, two of whom I recognized. One was J. Homer Warren himself, sitting in an easy chair with a highball in his hand, and the other was Tom Higgins. The latter got up and walked over to meet me. He was grinning broadly.

"Hello, runt," he welcomed me. "Muscling in on my territory, huh?"

"It's Professor Lansdowne's idea," I explained. "But don't ask me what it is. I wouldn't know."

"Sure hope you pick up something. But don't look for too much."

"I won't. Anything new on what happened this afternoon?"

Tom shook his head, and spoke out of the corner of his mouth: "I bet it was the D.T.'s myself, and everybody else is afraid to commit themselves. They tell me O'Hara hasn't pulled himself together yet."

As for me, I didn't feel inclined to treat the business quite so lightly, but I certainly hadn't the remotest idea what it was all about.

The living room in which we stood continued the luxurious motif set by the reception hall. The walls were lined entirely with cork, arrestingly decorated with drawings of nude Bacchantes being pursued by Satyrs. Lighting was indirect and subdued, while the side of the room overlooking Central Park was no more than one huge window. Outside, there was a terrace, with box shrubbery, beach umbrellas, tables and chairs. Besides Warren, Higgins and myself, four detectives and a trio of reporters made up the company. The last named were taking their ease in deep, soft-cushioned armchairs enjoying highballs.

Tom said he had men stationed all over the place. Besides the four in the living room, there were two on the terrace outside; one guarding the delivery entrance to the apartment; two doing sentry duty at the front door; another downstairs at the street entrance to the building; a seventh stationed on the only staircase that led from the floor below to the penthouse level. Finally, a man on a roving assignment that kept him patrolling the various rooms of the apartment other than the living room. Tom explained that the detectives in the latter were there more to soothe Warren's fears than for any practical purpose.

It struck me right off the bat that Warren was in slight need of soothing, or else was a very convincing actor. Sitting in his chair, blowing clouds of cigar smoke into the air and joking over his drink with the reporters, he was the one man in the room who appeared unconcerned over what might take place. When Tom introduced me to Warren as a personal friend of Commissioner Gallagher's, the official greeter extended his hand cordially.

"Welcome to our wake," he said, with the geniality which had won him friends from every walk of life. "It isn't often that the corpse has an opportunity to join in his own festivities, so you can see I'm making the most of it. Pour yourself a drink."

While I was doing this, one of the reporters—Nathan of the *Star*—asked a question.

"Mr. Warren," he said, "do you think there's any such person as Dr. Skull?"

Warren took a long pull at his drink. "I haven't the slightest idea. If there isn't, we're going to look mighty silly by the time you fellows get through writing up this party."

"Mr. Warren," piped up Sutherland of the *Gazette*, "if there is such a person, how do you figure he made Mayor O'Hara talk as he did? Ventriloquism or hypnotism?"

"It must have been ventriloquism if what I've heard about hypnotism is true. I understand the subject has to have a mind. Of course," he added, amid general laughter, "you won't print that."

"Warren and Pat O'Hara have been friends for years,"

said Higgins, sotto voce. "Like this." He drew his fingers across his throat.

Sutherland's question about hypnotism started me thinking along that line again. Several of the evening papers had conjectured vaguely about hypnotism's having been used on the Mayor, but the theory wouldn't hold water. A hypnotist must place his subject in a responsive attitude and after that has to go through a good deal of hocus-pocus before the victim passes out. Ventriloquism didn't seem to me any more far-fetched, at that.

ABOUT TEN-THIRTY, COMMISSIONER Gallagher arrived. There was more joking, and another round of drinks was served. I began wondering if perhaps Warren was more frightened than he cared to admit. When he held a light for the Commissioner, his hand shook noticeably.

At eleven o'clock Gallagher got to his feet.

"Higgins," he ordered, "have your men relieved, one at a time, so that they can come here and make a report."

Singly, the detectives came in. From all fronts, the downstairs entrance, the terrace, the stairs, the front door, the delivery entrance, the word was, "All's well." No one had seen or heard anything suspicious. No one had entered the building except regular tenants and, in two or three cases, their guests. When the last outside guard had reported and left. Commissioner Gallagher turned to the detectives in the room.

"All right, men," he cracked out, "it's now five minutes after eleven. This lunatic Skull has threatened to do his dirty work at midnight and that's only fifty-five minutes away. If he's really going to try anything, I believe he will do it at twelve o'clock, just as he said he would. These high-toned criminals like to stick to schedule. So keep your eyes peeled. If anybody tries to enter this room between now and midnight, shoot first and ask questions afterward. Is this thoroughly understood?"

There was a quartette of nods.

As the men awaited the Commissioner's next words, my eyes turned to J. Homer Warren. Definitely, now, he was beginning to exhibit a trace of nerves. Nonetheless, he still had himself pretty well under control, and his nervousness showed only in the slight shakiness of his voice and the trembling of his fingers as he poured himself another highball.

"Higgins!" It was Commissioner Gallagher.

"Yes, sir!"

"See that every entrance to this apartment is securely locked and guarded. Have every window closed and fastened. Lock all the doors that lead into this particular room and place a man in front of each one. Draw the curtains across that front window and put a man there by it. Quick, now!"

Tom threw his 200-pound bulk into high gear and got busy carrying out the orders.

"Look here, Mike," said Warren, trying to be jocular. "You act as though you thought someone were really going to try to kill me tonight. You're not letting your imagination get the better of you, are you?"

"My job is to take no chances, Homer," said the Commissioner, "and I'm just doing my duty."

"Well, you don't have to be so confounded serious about it. After all, how do we know there's any such person as Dr. Skull?"

"If you'll excuse my saying it, how do we know there isn't?"

It was then 11:18. Conversation became more and more forced, until there were longish periods of complete silence. Warren again poured himself a stiff drink and put it down without soda. There were several cigarettes going full blast, as well as the Commissioner's pipe, and since every window was shut tight, the air was getting close. Every detective was at his post, and if anyone got into that room, I thought, he would have to enter in a cloak of complete invisibility.

The electric clock on the mantel chimed once. It was half-past eleven. Only thirty minutes to go. I found myself wondering if Dr. Skull were already in the room. Perhaps one of the men set to guard Warren was the very person determined to kill him. Quickly, my eyes shifted from one to another. At any rate, they all looked okay. There's hardly a flatfoot this side of Suez who hasn't got his profession stamped on his face, and the men on this death watch were no exceptions to the rule. Tom Higgins I knew, and that it could be the Commissioner was out of the question. Which left the three reporters, and if any one of them was Skull, he was a swell dissembler. They were by now the scaredest-looking trio I'd ever seen and undoubtedly wished they'd never so much as looked at a headline. The minutes ticked by.

Eleven forty-five. Fifteen minutes to go. It was getting ghastly.

"Higgins," commanded Commissioner Gallagher suddenly, "close in here with me. You too, Mr. Larkin, if you don't mind."

I did mind, like the very devil, but I couldn't very well

say so. At the Commissioner's direction, Higgins and I stood on either side of Warren, our backs to him, so that we could see anyone trying to approach. Gallagher himself stood in front of the threatened man, looking toward the big window. The three reporters were stationed behind the chair.

"Well, gentlemen," said Warren, and his voice was quavery. "I can't tell you how much I appreciate this wall of protection you are making for me."

I turned my head a moment. He was fiddling with a paper cutter, and his fingers opened and closed nervously on its hilt. Even so, I admired him for doing better than I'd have done under similar circumstances.

"Thirteen more minutes and we can laugh at this, can't we?"

The only reply was a grunt from the Commissioner.

"Well, do you think I'm going to get killed, or don't you?"

"Better be quiet a while, Warren," said Gallagher, without turning his head. "Let's just listen."

"Oh, all right." Warren forced a laugh, and I could hear him at the whiskey again. "But don't forget that in the movies it never makes any difference how many guards a man has, he gets murdered just the same. That's what the voice said, too—that I'd get murdered just—"

"Shut up!" Gallagher ground the words out, and Warren subsided.

THERE WAS NOW complete silence. You could hear the noise of the busses, seventeen floors below. From time to time there would be a faint squeak of leather as someone shifted his weight from one foot to the other. The hands on the clock crawled toward twelve. My eyes had been shooting from window to door to window again so many times they ached.

Suddenly, the clock chimed. It was so unexpected, everyone started, involuntarily. It was striking twelve, and never before did I realize that it took a clock so long to strike that hour. Then, it stopped.

We all looked at each other. It was twelve o'clock, and after. Midnight had come, and gone. Nothing had happened. Sutherland, the *Gazette* man, cleared his throat noisily. It relieved the terrific tension. We relaxed.

Commissioner Gallagher turned around to Warren.

"Well," he said, "I guess—" and stopped.

Warren was seated as he had been, slouched down in the easy chair, looking toward the curtained window. But now his eyes stared blankly. His arms hung down, limp and dangling. The paper cutter was sunk to the hilt in his chest and blood streamed down the front of his starched dress shirt.

J. Homer Warren was dead.

Once again, Dr. Skull had kept his appointment.

6

THE SECRET

"HIGGINS," SAID COMMISSIONER Gallagher, "send for the coroner." Then, to no one in particular: "A fat lot of cops we turned out to be!"

We had all—that is, the newspaper reporters and myself—drawn away from the body of J. Homer Warren automatically. It was not a very pleasant sight, the eyes wide open, staring at something no one else could see; the mouth ajar, the ghastly wound in the chest. Blood still oozed from it, and the wet mess on the shirt slowly widened.

"Now, why would he want to do that?" asked Sutherland, wonderingly.

"Why would who want to do what?" snarled the Commissioner.

"Warren, of course. Why would he want to kill himself?"

"Maybe he got tired reading the lousy tripe you guys print. Or maybe one of you gentlemen bumped him off yourself," said Gallagher, irritated.

"Sure, Commissioner," drawled Nathan with fine contempt. "I did it. Always hated his guts, and I knew there'd never be a safer time to settle him than in a room full of cops."

"Oh, yeah?"

"Oh, yeah!"

The Commissioner shook a bony finger in the man's face. "Make all the cracks you want to, but make up your mind to stay right here until we find out if Warren killed himself, or if someone—someone in this room—killed him."

After that, little more was said until the coroner, a finger-print expert, and a police photographer arrived a quarter of an hour later. The coroner, a quiet, businesslike man, quickly made his examination.

"Warren died less than an hour ago," he said, "maybe only a half hour ago. The blade of the paper cutter appears to have punctured the heart itself and death was practically instantaneous. The blow seems to have been self-inflicted, and must have been done under great stress. It takes a good deal of strength to inflict a wound as deep as that. He probably used both hands on the knife."

"Thanks, Doc," said the Commissioner shortly. "Jake, check the prints."

The fingerprint man went to work with his powder and brush. A few minutes later he raised his head.

"The only prints on the knife belong to the dead man," he reported.

"You must have been on the job mighty quick, Commissioner, to get here so soon after it happened. I thought you left that sort of thing to the hired hands, like Higgins." The coroner smiled pleasantly.

"The Commissioner is very prompt these days," smirked Sutherland.

"Yeah," chimed in Nathan, "the Commissioner was so prompt that he was in the room when it happened."

"In fact," supplemented the third reporter, "he came here especially to see that nothing happened to Warren. Don't you read the papers?"

"Papers?" asked the physician. "I never read newspapers. Do you mean to tell me you suspected this was going to happen, Commissioner?"

Gallagher got pink around the ears.

"You mugs will be plenty sorry about this razzing!" he raged at the newshawks. The coroner had started toward the door, laughing heartily. "Don't forget, my keen-nosed yellow journalists, that you were in the room, too. Don't forget to put that in when you write up this story for your lousy sheets!"

"Can we go home now, teacher?" asked Nathan, in honeyed tones.

"Yes, or are you booking us for murder?" Sutherland wanted to know.

The Commissioner, for a full minute, gave them the benefit of the many years experience he'd had in plain and fancy cussing, and the three left in an aura of sulphur and brimstone.

"I still don't see how it happened," said Tom Higgins, who'd been a silent spectator of the Commissioner's humiliation. "A while ago, he was scared stiff for fear something might happen to him, and then he ups and croaks himself. It don't make sense."

"Neither do you!" snapped his superior, jamming on a battered old felt. "I'm going as far away from this madhouse as possible. One more day like this and I'll give my job back to the city. Call the wagon and have the body taken to the morgue for a post-mortem."

With that, the Commissioner departed, and I decided that there was nothing to keep me any longer either.

"Well, Tom," I said, in a voice that was not as firm as it might have been, "I think I've had enough excitement for one night. Thanks very much for the party. I'm going somewhere and get a stiff drink. I can sure stand one."

Tom bade me goodnight, and as I was leaving the apartment, I could hear him starting on his subordinates of the detective force. He sounded as though he were disappointed at the way they had risen to the emergency.

BY THE TIME I got out on the avenue, my mind went blank. There must have been a certain degree of shock, because for the next half hour, it was impossible for me to think about anything. It took three straight whiskeys at the first bar I could find to bring me back to a semblance of normal. Then I remembered my promise to telephone Paula once the "wake" was over. Well, it was over, and it had turned out to be a wake, all right.

"Hello, darling," she said, as soon as she heard my voice. "Did anything happen?"

"Quite a bit," I replied, "as far as Warren is concerned." And I described briefly what had taken place.

"What do you think it means?" she asked me when I'd finished.

"I haven't the slightest idea," I responded, "and I'm not even going to think about it now. I'm going to bed."

Which was where I made a mistake. There was an interruption and its name was Curly Smith. He nabbed me just as I stepped out of the phone booth.

"They tell me you were up at Warren's place tonight, you lucky stiff. Sit down and tell me about it. Those blankety-blank police wouldn't let me in. Said I could read about it in the morning papers. I saw Nathan and he says they got Warren all right. What do you know about it?"

"I don't know anything except that we were all standing with our backs to Warren. When we turned around, he was dead—killed himself."

"Didn't anybody in the place see him stab himself?"

I explained how the Commissioner and Tom Higgins and the reporters and I had formed a human wall around Warren. "The others wouldn't have been able to see him through us," I added.

"Sure nobody in the room did it?"

"I'm not sure, no. But the coroner was," I answered. "Now let me go home to bed. I'm worn out."

But Curly wouldn't be content until I'd answered a dozen more questions. Finally, "Do you think Warren killed himself because he was in a blue funk, or do you think this guy Skull really got to him?"

"I don't know," I replied shortly, and started away.

"If you get any ideas, let me know," Curly called after me.

My mind was still too dazed to try and evolve theories, but as I walked, the nightmare events of the past few days paraded weirdly through my brain—Professor Lansdowne's killing Dr. Carter, the meeting of the Board of Estimate, and now the suicide of J. Homer Warren. Then there was the curious affair of the Wall Street broker, the death of the "mystery woman," Agnes Russell—even the inexplicable elevated smash. They were all similar, or at least the Wiggins (the elevated motorman), Walker, Lansdowne, and O'Hara cases were. Each one of those men had done peculiar things, not of their own volition. Between them, there must be a connection. Perhaps the deaths of Agnes Russell and Mr. Warren were connected. Perhaps, if they could speak, they, too, would tell of a strange and overpowering impulse which possessed them. What, then, was the connecting link? Was it Dr. Skull? Who was Dr. Skull—if there was any such person—and how did he work? How could he have been responsible for Professor Lansdowne's act, and why?

THE MORNING PAPERS were full of the Warren affair, and much theorizing was done about Dr. Skull—was he or was he not responsible for the noted political figure's death? There was, however, no effort on the part of the press to connect the present happenings with the other peculiar events.

The official attitude toward the last night's suicide was expressed in a statement issued by Commissioner Gallagher, in which it was said that Warren's death was the direct result of fear-induced, temporary insanity. The possibility of there being any other factor—including the unknown "Dr. Skull"—was branded ridiculous. Skull's warning—if indeed the Mayor's speech had been brought about by Skull—was termed a maniacal threat which was never fulfilled.

Down at the Tombs, Professor Lansdowne had already seen the papers and was anxiously awaiting my own version of the evening's events. He questioned me closely about everyone present, even asking me to describe their personal appearance. He was particularly interested in finding out everything that Warren had done prior to his death; if he had showed much fear; if he had cried out as he died.

"I wish you'd let me in on the secret, Professor," I

pleaded. "I feel sure you have a theory. Won't you tell me what it is?"

"Not now, my boy," he answered, "not now. I do have a theory. No, on second thought, it's not really a theory, merely an idea. And it's too much in the experimental stage to talk about. Besides, there are more important things."

"Well," I pursued, "won't you at least tell me if you think this Skull guy might be responsible for more things than the death of Warren? Maybe he had something to do with you."

"But how could he have had anything to do with me?"

"Why," I fumbled, "I don't know exactly. Suggestion, hypnotism maybe."

"And have you any idea why anyone would do such a thing, even if he could?" queried the scientist. This, of course, stumped me. "You see," went on Professor Lansdowne, "we couldn't get very far in a court of law unless we could do more than a lot of vague wool-gathering."

The coroner's inquest on the death of Dr. Amos Carter took place an hour or so after our conversation. That this was a formality pure and simple was indicated by the rapidity with which it was conducted. Testimony was quickly gathered, every shred of which showed beyond question of doubt that Professor Lansdowne had killed the elderly physician. The jury promptly found its verdict accordingly.

Although we knew exactly what was going to happen, this verdict, spoken out in the cramped little courtroom, was a distinct shock. Paula was unnerved and once more on the verge of tears, which, however, she managed to keep from falling. My own voice was husky as I spoke a few would-be encouraging words in her ear. The Professor himself was unaffected. He followed the proceedings with an air of detachment, showing interest only when the Carter housekeeper testified as to his behavior on the fatal night. I wished fervently I knew what was in his mind.

Norman Howard showed even less interest in what went on. My antipathy toward him was not in the least tempered by this apparently callous attitude. Considering his position and his intention to plead not guilty by reason of temporary insanity, I suppose there was nothing he could do at the time, but I still didn't like him.

When the inquest was over, Professor Lansdowne was returned to his cell in the Tombs to await a certain indictment by the grand jury and, later, trial. There was no possibility of his being released on bail, I knew, and as much as I would have welcomed a better defense, it did appear that insanity was the only available one at present. If the Professor could hit upon something before the trial, of course, his prospects would be much improved. Meanwhile, I tried to calm Paula by telling her that, should her father be committed to an asylum, it would be only a short time before we could gain his release on one technicality or another. I had no idea just what "technicality" might do the trick, but it seemed to me that there was usually some loophole in the law. You can see that I'd given up hope of being able to discover any evidence that would completely clear the scientist, in spite of my determination to do so.

NEW YORK, THAT afternoon, was doing a lot of talking about Dr. Skull. No one was really alarmed. How could they take such a thing seriously, in the enlightened twentieth century, and in the safest, greatest, most civilized city in the world? Newspaper and radio reports had provided

descriptions of the original threat sent by Dr. Skull; of
the by now famous Board meeting where Mayor O'Hara
had spoken so amazingly; and of the death of J. Homer
Warren in his apartment the previous night. It was all very
amazing. Nothing like it had ever happened before. Not
even the newspapers, in their editorial columns, dared any
explanation. Their reporters, as in the case of Edward J.
Walker, interviewed dozens of prominent people on their
opinions about Dr. Skull, and there were as many different
interpretations as there were people interviewed. An enter-
prising radio station had an announcer and a microphone
right in Times Square, quizzing sidewalk passers-by as to
what they thought. No one had any explanation, but no
one was alarmed.

Police and city officials were forced to continue their
more or less noncommittal stand. They admitted the existence of a person calling himself or herself Dr. Skull, and
that this unknown was obviously trying to terrorize the
city. But they refused to comment on the Mayor's speech
"until the matter had been given more careful study." As
to the suicide of Warren, they stood firm on their explanation that it was caused by fear.

Unknown to the public, Mayor O'Hara had already
been given a thorough examination by the best physicians
and alienists in a fruitless effort to find a natural cause for
his conduct.

That same afternoon, my friend Tom Higgins was placed
in charge of a special detail whose duty was to investigate
these curious events, and to trap Dr. Skull. As to the last
mission, all that could be done was to notify police to be

on the lookout for a mentally unbalanced person going by that name—description and whereabouts unknown.

Early in the evening, every morning paper received an unexpected communication. Here is what they printed:

AN OPEN LETTER TO POLICE COMMISSIONER GALLAGHER

My Dear Commissioner:

At a recent meeting of the Board of Estimate, I warned the governing heads of New York City that serious consequences would follow their refusal to take my demands seriously. At the time, I could see and understand how you and your associates would doubt my ability to carry out this threat, and I realized that it would be necessary for me to prove my power.

Last night, that proof was provided. One of your leading citizens lies dead. Certainly the death of Mr. Warren should be enough to convince any thinking man that my power is not one to be taken lightly. Before it, your guards were helpless, your precautions a waste of time. Yet there not only has been no effort to negotiate with me along the lines suggested, but there has been an attempt to show that I had nothing to do with Warren's destruction.

This is such an inexcusable blunder that I was forced, through the medium of this open letter which I know the newspapers will print, to call to the attention of the people of New York the stupidity of their leaders, and to inform you, Commissioner, that I hold you responsible for the deception that has been worked.

I can afford to be patient a while longer. You, and the other executives of this city, have three days in which to come to your senses. If, at the end of this period of grace, there has still been no effort to meet my terms, your life, Commissioner, will be forfeit. On this basis, you may calculate the possible time of your death at between seven and eight P.M. Monday.

The citizens of New York are witnesses to my fair dealing.

DR. SKULL

When I'd read this, there was only one thing I could think of, and that was to get to Professor Lansdowne as fast as possible and have a heart to heart talk.

7

MADMAN ON THE LOOSE

I CALLED NORMAN Howard and asked him to make arrangements for me to see the Professor that same night, but, as might have been expected, the lawyer merely stated coldly that such a visit was beyond the bounds of possibility and that I would have to wait until morning. Even Inspector Tom Higgins could do nothing to help, so it was necessary for me to cultivate the gentle characteristic of patience until the next day. Paula and I spent the evening together, but I didn't tell her about the conviction which had without warning obsessed me, fearing to arouse a hope that might not be realized. The first thing next morning, I headed down to the Tombs and was soon in Professor Lansdowne's cell.

"Professor," I began, "I want to talk to you about Dr. Skull."

The scientist raised his eyebrows slightly.

"Indeed," he said, "and what about Dr. Skull?"

"You remember my asking you if you thought he could have anything to do with you and Dr. Carter?"

"Yes."

"Well, although I couldn't give you a motive for his action, I've not been able to get rid of the feeling that he did. Last night, when I read the letter he addressed to Commissioner Gallagher through the papers, this feeling—for some unaccountable reason—became terribly strong. Surely it can't be wrong! And here's something else I've also wondered if you have the same idea. Have you?"

"Suppose you tell me what makes you so sure about Dr. Skull before I answer your question," suggested the scientist.

"All right," I agreed, "but there are plenty of blank spaces in my explanation. Here goes: some time ago, an elevated motorman crashed his train into the back end of another one, although it was a clear day, the signal was plainly set against him, and his brakes worked perfectly. When the man was given a third degree, he had no idea why he hadn't stopped his train. He said something had come over him, or words to that effect. Later on, when he was examined, they couldn't find anything wrong with him, mentally or physically, which would account for his actions, and he wasn't drunk at the time. Check?"

Professor Lansdowne nodded.

"Okay. Next comes our friend, Edward J. Walker. He suddenly goes berserk and gives a perfect stranger ten thousand dollars in cash. Later, he can't explain why. You look him over yourself and can't find anything wrong with him. He had met an irresistible impulse to do what he did, that's all. Nobody knows why, least of all Walker.

"Then what happens? A guy who calls himself Dr. Skull writes a letter to the Mayor threatening disaster unless he's given New York City to play with. At the Board meeting Mayor O'Hara goes off his nut and talks like he never talked before. Why? He doesn't know. The words came to

"The drug makes a person highly susceptible to outside influenses," said the Professor

his mind and he had to say them. No other explanation, and so far as we know, he was neither drunk nor insane at the time.

"What next? J. Homer Warren—who looked like he was in his right mind to me—stabs himself. You can't make me believe he did that only because he was scared stiff. Something *made* him do it.

"And hold on a minute—I've forgotten the 'mystery woman,' Agnes Russell. She was found dead, supposedly a suicide."

"Well?" demanded the Professor. He was regarding me intently.

"Well," I echoed, "consider yourself. One evening you go to call on a friend of yours—a friend of twenty or thirty years standing. You have a discussion, the kind you've been having for years without even as much as a black eye exchanged, when all of a sudden, out of a clear, blue sky—you brain the guy. Why? You don't know. You had a sudden, irresistible impulse, nothing more. You're perfectly sane, too, presumably.

"The parallel is too obvious to mention. The motorman, Walker, O'Hara, and yourself are all possessed by crazy desires you can't control. I'll give you ten to one that both Warren and the Russell woman were, too. Assuming for sake of argument that I'm right about them, that makes six people obsessed. Skull appears in the picture with two of them—O'Hara and Warren. Why not with the others— the motorman, the broker, the mysterious woman, and yourself? Anyhow, that's the way it lines up to me. Of course, I can't prove anything. I can't even offer an expla- nation of why or how it's all happened. I don't know how this Skull creature works, and that's a big stumbling block in the path. I've thought of hypnotism and dismissed it because there was no one around to hypnotize you when you were with Dr. Carter, and I saw no one waving any hands at either the Mayor or Warren. If this were Haiti or some such place, I'd lay it to a voodoo charm. But I stand or fall with my belief that Skull is behind the whole mess."

AFTER WHICH I had to stop for breath. Professor Lans- downe was looking very serious.

"I think," he said quietly, "you're right, and it's up to me to plug up the holes in your theory. Perhaps you'd now like to hear my ideas on the subject in question."

I assured him there was nothing I'd rather hear.

"Then I'll start from the beginning," he said. "I haven't spoken about this for the very obvious reason that you can't expect anyone to swallow what appears to be sheer fantasy unless you're in a position to provide proof. I have not been, and still am not, in that position, but your own deductions make me feel I can confide in you." The scientist pulled a venerable briar out of his pocket and began filling it.

"I knew nothing of your elevated motorman until you told me about him, the evening after I'd seen Walker. So my first contact with the current wave of inexplicable phenomena was the financier, Walker. As you know, the man feared for his sanity. Through a mutual friend, he was sent to me for examination. In the course of this examination, I could discover no mental ailment that would explain his unprecedented gullibility. But I did discover something, and I believe I mentioned it to you at the time.

"There were unmistakable indications that Edward J. Walker had recently been under a hypnotic influence of a most powerful nature. It was no ordinary posthypnotic state that I found him in, but rather a state of severe nervous shock and psychic trauma. As you will understand later, I had reason to recognize these particular symptoms, though I could find absolutely no reason for their appearance here in New York City. When you told me of the motorman, my curiosity was again aroused, but by no means satisfied.

"Now, the circumstances of my killing Amos Carter were, as you pointed out, not without similarity to Mr. Walker's giving away his money. They were, in fact, even more similar than you could know. Besides the overwhelming lust for murder that came without warning, there was also an after-state of mental and nervous exhaustion which was very nearly identical with Walker's. After I'd recovered my balance enough to attempt an analysis, I noted this. Yet, the possibility which I could not fail to visualize seemed so remote that even to myself I attempted to explain my state by assuming it to be the natural consequence of remorse.

"With the peculiar behavior of Mayor O'Hara, and the appearance of the person known as Dr. Skull on the scene, my original fears were strengthened. I was not present to examine the Mayor, but from what you told me, I gathered that his affection was similar to mine, both in its initial and after stages. Although I told myself it was utterly impossible, another link was forged in the chain of my theory.

"The murder—for I believe it was murder—of J. Homer Warren—again indicated that the impossible had occurred."

Professor Lansdowne stopped talking and sucked at his pipe. I found myself sitting on the edge of my chair.

"What do you mean, sir?" I asked.

"I mean, Bob, that I agree with you. All of these queer occurrences have the same cause, and the cause is undoubtedly our friend, Dr. Skull. Had I not been included among his victims, this explanation might have eluded me altogether, but the opportunity to study first hand the methods this lunatic—I think he must be slightly cracked—uses cinched the case, in my own mind. Viewing the matter from a purely selfish standpoint, I'll have a great deal of proving to do before I can help myself, and that isn't going to be easy. From a larger and far more important angle, this entire city—perhaps the world—is facing a very ticklish problem."

I was entirely unable to follow him, but I tried. "You mean," I said, "that Skull is just a hypnotist?"

Professor Lansdowne shook his head, smiling.

"I don't mean that he's—as you say—*just* a hypnotist. That is a gross understatement. Let me go on with my hypothesis.

"As you know, certain mystical societies—I use the term, mystical, purely for convenience—are to be found in comparatively isolated sections of Northern India, along the Tibetan frontier. These societies have conducted researches along lines unknown to western minds, and they have made many strange and wonderful discoveries. As you may also know, I spent quite some time, many years ago, in a kind of lamasery which was located to the northeast of Sprinagar, in the Kara-korams. This was known as the Lamasery of the Golden Throne, so named for the great mountain on whose slopes it was built, and it was maintained by initiates of the Three Brotherhoods. This organization is perhaps the most esoteric of the mystical orders, and its more profound mysteries were never opened to me, nor, so far as I know, to any other white man. Their greatest knowledge, I've been told, is far too dangerous to be given to any ordinary mortal.

"However, the lesser secrets of the Golden Throne are open to certain selected students. By a devious path which I'll not outline now, I was fortunate enough to be chosen as one. I know of only one other white man who enjoyed the same distinction, and I have reason to believe that he went deeper into the mysteries than I did—that, in fact, he learned the secret of a peculiar and superior kind of mind control known only to the Three Brotherhoods. Because there have been unmistakable signs that my own experience with that organization enables me to recognize, I believe this man may now be in New York, using his great knowledge and power for wrong purposes. I think he calls himself—"

"Dr. Skull!" I finished for him.

"Exactly," nodded Professor Lansdowne.

"Then," I said eagerly, "you know who he really is!"

"I THINK I do. You see, after I'd finished college, I spent two years getting practical experience in a mental clinic in Vienna. There I met a very unusual young man. His name was Franz Ehrlich, he was also doing clinical research and though he was about ten years my junior, his background was already better than mine. Never have I encountered, before or since, a mind with such potentialities. His ability was amazing, though he was considered rather eccentric by his associates. A few of them went so far as to believe him insane.

"One of the most remarkable things about him was his power over the minds of others. He was even then a hypnotist of almost supernatural ability, and when I think of this innate power coupled with the occult secrets of the Three Brotherhoods—but I'm digressing. Unfortunately, Ehrlich allowed himself to be embittered by the jibes of his fellow students—jibes which came in large part from their envy. I dare say I was the only man in the clinic that he would talk to, and even that was little enough.

"It was some time after I met him that he disappeared, and I never heard of him again until I went to become a novitiate of the Golden Throne order of the Three Brotherhoods. There I heard of a white man who was also a student, but I never saw him. From descriptions of his appearance, I felt this man must be Ehrlich, but I didn't really know until years later I ran into him on a return trip to Srinagar. He remembered me, but talked very little. He told me of his being a *chela* in one of the Three Brotherhoods, and indicated that his studies were not yet completed. That was the last I ever saw of him. At the time, I decided he was quite mad."

"Then," I cut in, "you think Dr. Skull is this man Ehrlich?"

Professor Lansdowne nodded. "No native member of the Three Brotherhoods would dare to disobey their laws and break his vow of secrecy. He would fear the consequences of such sacrilege. Only a white man would have the necessary contempt, and that characteristic fits Ehrlich perfectly.

"Of course, there is always the possibility that it could be some other white man, but I feel that this is obviated by the fact of Dr. Skull's honoring me with his intentions. Since there is no logical reason for his singling me out, I feel there is only one explanation—Ehrlich, or Skull, wanted to renew an old acquaintance."

"But," I interposed, "what makes you so positive that this type of hypnosis is that of your Three Brotherhoods?"

"The signs are absolutely unmistakable," said the Professor firmly. "Absolutely so. In each case we have to consider, hypnosis was achieved without the necessity of the hypnotist being in the presence of his subject. Moreover, in each case, the hypnotist must have had a clear picture of his subject's surroundings—enough to direct the subject's conversation and actions accordingly. Witness my behavior before Amos Carter, and the Mayor's conversation with Warren at the Board meeting. These things could not have been brought about unless the hypnotist could know what was going on around his subject, unless he could, in short, see through his subject's eyes, hear through his ears, and talk through his mouth. This knowledge is a monopoly of the Three Brotherhoods."

Struck by a sudden thought, I inquired: "Do you understand this hypnotism business yourself, can you do these things?"

"No," said the scientist, "I cannot approach the power of Skull, though, God willing, I may be able to oppose him—in time. My participation in the ancient mysteries was much less than his."

"Well," I said with heat, "it's a cockeyed cinch that nobody else is going to know anything about him. They'll have to let you out of here, immediately. Why, there's no telling what may happen!"

"Hold on, now, Bob!" The Professor raised a restraining hand. "Not so fast! I've told you what I *think*. I do not feel certain enough, even yet, to say that I *know*. You can imagine what people would say if I advanced this theory without something to back it up. In order to clear myself, I would have to convict Ehrlich, or Skull. That's not likely to be simple. We first have to find him, and that's going to be like looking for the proverbial needle in a haystack. Having found him, it is not going to be easy to prove my charge. Skull undoubtedly has made his plans well, and we have a very formidable opponent to fight."

"Wait a minute!" I exclaimed. It was another inspiration. "Skull has threatened to kill Commissioner Gallagher unless his terms are met. You know they're not going to be met and that puts the Commissioner right on the spot."

"Yes?"

"So—there are only two days or so grace. You undertake to save the Commissioner in return for your freedom until you've proved your innocence."

Professor Lansdowne knocked the ashes out of his pipe. "I appreciate your eagerness to help me, Bob," he said, "but your suggestion isn't very practicable for several reasons. Primarily, no police Commissioner, or anyone else, can turn loose a man charged with murder, whatever the inducement. In the second place, I haven't yet formed a plan for checkmating, or even opposing, Skull. I don't even know for a certainty that Skull and Ehrlich are one and the same person, although I have every reason to believe they are. I know a good deal of the sources of his power, but I need more time."

"Anyhow," I said, disappointed, "let me have a talk with the Commissioner. I certainly think he ought to know about your ideas. Do you agree?"

"It wouldn't do any harm," acknowledged the Professor thoughtfully, "although he's likely to consider me crazy. Which will strengthen my defense, if I have to use insanity as a plea." The scientist grinned at me. "Just one thing. Pledge him to keep absolute silence in regard to all that you tell him. I don't care to have this get out yet."

"I understand," said I. "I'll do as you advise."

While the jailer, thanks to strong influence, was lenient about Professor Lansdowne's visitors, it was apparent that I'd overstayed my time considerably, so I now got up to leave.

"Have you told Paula about your theory?" I asked.

"No, because I haven't felt certain enough about it. But I will now. Perhaps it will cheer her up a bit."

As I was about to pass through the iron door of the cell, Professor Lansdowne caught me by the arm.

"You might tell the Commissioner for me," he said in a low voice, "that if he's smart, he'll pretend to capitulate and play for time. If he doesn't, I feel that nothing on earth will be strong enough to protect him from Dr. Skull. A madman on the loose with powers which stagger the imagination is nothing to be taken lightly."

I saw that the Professor was very much in earnest.

"I'll tell him, sir," I said.

8

THE DRUG

THE OFFICE OF the Commissioner of Police was, as might naturally be expected, in a state of wild activity that morning. Telephones jangled at about ten-second intervals, secretaries bustled from one room to another with official-looking documents, and over all hung the atmosphere of a fortress preparing for a siege. I made my appearance shortly before eleven o'clock, but it was ten minutes after one before Commissioner Gallagher found time to receive me.

"I don't mind telling you," he said, "that I'm bothering with you at a time like this only because you're a friend of Professor Lansdowne's. I take it you've read the papers and understand what I mean."

"Yes, I have, Commissioner," I said, "and as a matter of fact, that's exactly why I'm here. The Professor has some information directly pertaining to Dr. Skull which he feels you should have too. Since he couldn't very well come himself, he sent me as messenger."

Commissioner Gallagher pushed a pack of cigarettes across the desk within reach of my fingers.

"Is that so?" he said. "Suppose you continue."

As quickly as possible, I outlined the story Professor

Lansdowne had told me, while the Commissioner listened with unwavering interest. In conclusion, I said:

"The Professor thinks your only safe course of action is to pretend to fall in with Skull's plans long enough to gain a few days' extra time. In those few days, it may be possible for him to hit upon a way of combating Dr. Skull. Professor Lansdowne believes that if you fail to do this, you're as good as a corpse right this minute."

Commissioner Gallagher blew a cloud of smoke at the ceiling.

"I wish it were as simple as that," he said.

"You mean you won't do it?"

"I mean," replied the Commissioner bitterly, "that I *can't* do it. Can you imagine what the public would think upon learning that the head man of their police department were carrying on negotiations pursuant to turning them over to the tender mercies of a madman? Why, there'd either be a panic such as the world has never seen, or else there'd be a lynching mob waiting downstairs for me. Very likely both. And this, mind you, if I had the power to carry on any such negotiations, which I haven't. Neither has any other single man, whatever his capacity. I even doubt if the whole cock-eyed Assembly could do it.

"Besides, how do we know Professor Lansdowne is right? If anyone else had offered such a cock-and-bull explanation of what's been happening, I'd have called for the wagon. As it is, I value the Professor's opinion highly enough to give his theory the benefit of the doubt. Which doesn't mean that anybody else would, so if I tried to offer it as an explanation for fake conversations with Skull, I'd be laughed out of whatever room I was in."

"Professor Lansdowne," I said, "seemed genuinely concerned about your safety, Commissioner. Isn't there anything you can do?"

"Yes," he laughed shortly, "I can pray that the Professor is wrong, that we're dealing with a regular flesh-and-blood assassin, and that a bodyguard will keep him away from me. Beyond that, not very much.

"I don't want Professor Lansdowne to think I don't appreciate his help, because I do. Nothing would give me greater pleasure than following his advice to the letter. In fact"—he grinned broadly—"I'd like nothing better than to hop the first boat for South America. I'm no hero, and I've got a wife and two kids. But so what? My hands are tied."

"Well," said I, rather heavily, "I guess that's that."

"I'm afraid so. We'll have to continue as we've been doing, plugging along ordinary lines, trying to get the finger on this lunatic. Even so, be sure and tell Professor Lansdowne that I'm anxious to have every new idea he gets, and that I'll cooperate with him as much as I can, as long as I'm here to cooperate. Of course, under the circumstances, I can't appear to be conferring with him, so you'll have to continue as liaison man, if you don't mind. And of course, if there's anything I can possibly do to help the Professor, or to make his situation any more comfortable, tell him not to hesitate to let me know."

"I won't, Commissioner," I replied, "and thanks a lot."

"Now," said Gallagher, rising and extending his hand, "get to blazes out of here and let me go to work." As I went through the door, I heard him mutter, "I've got a will to write."

IN THE CORRIDOR immediately outside the Commissioner's office, who should come galloping at me with the momentum of a charging buffalo, but Curly Smith.

"Gangway, mug!" he shouted, breathing with difficulty, "I've got business to do!"

I stepped aside quickly to avoid being trampled under foot and turned my head to see him plunge through a group of men and disappear into the Commissioner's private office. Animated by an overpowering desire to see what all the excitement was about, I followed the reporter as rapidly as possible. Whatever made me think I could get into Gallagher's office again, I don't know. Probably the idea didn't enter my head, and that may have been why no one interfered with my progress. The Commissioner was putting down his telephone. He appeared to be angry.

"See here, Commissioner," Curly began, before the official had time to speak, "what have you got to say about the coroner's finding poison in Warren's stomach?"

Commissioner Gallagher's face had been red when he put down the telephone receiver. Now it became purplish.

"What the devil do you mean, running into my office like this?" he raged. "And who the hell are you, anyway? Get out, get out! Can't you see I'm busy?"

"C'mon, Commissioner," urged Curly. "I'm Smith, from the *Express*. Gimme a break on this, won't you? Everybody knows about it now, anyway. I got my dope from the coroner and now I want your comment. Have a heart, Commissioner!"

With apparent effort, Gallagher got hold of himself.

"Would you mind telling me, please," he said, between clenched teeth, "when you obtained your information?"

"Oh, half an hour ago. Why?"

"Half an hour ago?" echoed the Commissioner. Where-upon he began filling the air with a choice collection of invectives, aimed more or less at the absent coroner who talked to a reporter at least fifteen minutes before report-ing to his own superior. Then his eyes fell on me. "You're in again, too?" he demanded, going on without waiting for a reply: "Now if we just had some tea and a fourth, what fun we could have!"

"Commissioner," began Curly once more, softly, "would you care to give me a comment? We got to print some-thing, you know."

"All right, all right," said Gallagher, wearily. "I surrender, dear. What do you want to know?"

"The coroner says the drug found in Warren's stomach must have been taken only a short time before his death, and that it was a kind of drug that could have affected his brain. Do you think this accounts for Warren stabbing himself?"

"Now, look here," grated the Commissioner, "if you want to print something print this: the police department is making a thorough investigation of the latest develop-ments in the Warren case. As soon as this is completed, a statement will be issued. Meanwhile, there's nothing I have to say. Now, get out—and the next time you come back, knock before you come in!"

"Aw, gee, Commissioner," wheedled the reporter, "don't you even want to say whether you think somebody deliber-ately put that stuff in Warren's drink so he'd kill himself?"

"I told you there'd be a statement when we've completed our investigation, not before. Now, scram, d'you hear? Scram!" the Commissioner yelled the last word, so Curly reluctantly started off, and I with him. Gallagher, however, called me back. When the door had closed on the reporter, he said:

"I guess it's just as well you came back. You heard the latest. I got it over the phone just as that guy busted in. The coroner had an analysis made of the contents of Warren's stomach, and he found this drug—never mind, I'd better write it down." He did so and handed me the slip of paper. The word meant nothing as far as I was concerned. "Tell Professor Lansdowne about it. I don't know whether it will shake his theory or not, but the coroner says this drug might have induced suicide. If this is an indication that Skull uses drugs in his dirty work, it puts a bit of a crimp in the Professor's explanation."

I'll admit to feeling slightly sick at the prospect of seeing the scientist's carefully constructed case threatened, and I must have shown it, for the Commissioner added:

"Of course, we have no proof, one way or the other. In any case, keep this under your hat. I don't know what good it'll do with the coroner blowing his mouth off to every Tom, Dick and Harry he sees, but keep quiet anyhow."

Curly Smith was waiting for me as I emerged from the office, but there was little I could have added to the information he already had, even if I'd wanted to, so he soon gave up.

"So long," he said, when we reached the street. "Remember me to the Professor and Miss Lansdowne. The only reason I haven't been in to see him is because I've been up to my ears in this Skull mess. But as soon as it eases off a bit, I'll be around." He flagged a cab and was whirled away in the sea of traffic. I smiled to myself at the thought of Curly's being too busy with the "Skull mess" to talk to Professor Lansdowne, the one person who could shed any light on it. Then I remembered the drug taken by Warren and sobered right up.

I WENT STRAIGHT to the Tombs, and after a good deal of arguing, got in to see Professor Lansdowne. It was with mixed emotions that I discovered him chatting lightly with Paula and Norman Howard. However, after a few rather labored pleasantries, the latter got up to leave.

"Goodbye, Professor," he said, in his flat, clipped way. "The fact that, through our mutual friends, I've secured such an early date for the trial will greatly shorten these tedious days of waiting. Whatever the outcome may be—and I believe we can make out a fairish case—we will certainly be able to get you into more comfortable surroundings."

"Thank you, Norman," said the Professor, "I appreciate all you're trying to do for me."

"Oh, don't think anything of it," answered Howard. "It's all in the day's work, you know."

The lawyer bowed himself out and his short steps tapped themselves beyond hearing range. Then I opened up and told Professor Lansdowne what I had learned from Commissioner Gallagher.

"Dad!" cried Paula, alarmed. She'd evidently been told about the Professor's hypothesis. "This may mean you're wrong about Dr. Skull. If they prove that Warren killed himself because of a drug that was slipped in his drink—"

"Hold on a minute," I interrupted. "Give your Dad a chance to think it over. It may not mean so much." I hoped fervently I was right. Professor Lansdowne stared vacantly at nothing for a full minute, rolling into a ball the piece of paper the Commissioner had given me.

"As much as I hate to admit it," he said heavily, "this new development may possibly upset my theory. If it is true, that is, that somnocephalaine was administered Warren, and if it is also true that the drug disturbed his mind sufficiently to make him take his own life. Also, if the same drug were given O'Hara and the others who were strangely affected, including myself."

"But, Professor," I said, puzzled, "how could any drug make a person commit suicide? That seems impossible to me."

"Somnocephalaine is a relatively new discovery," the scientist explained. "It has been used successfully to make a person amenable to suggestion, particularly those suffering from various forms of insanity. The drug has a peculiar effect on the brain, numbing to a large extent its natural impulses—those which come from within—and making it highly susceptible to outside influence. Thus, a patient suffering from delusions, say, of persecution, is given a small quantity of somnocephalaine. This is followed by a period during which the psychiatrist suggests the absurdity of the delusion, a suggestion which has a marked effect in restoring the patient's mental equilibrium—as long as the effects of the drug last. This is usually about two hours. There is more than one school of thought on the permanent benefits, if any, of the treatment."

"But," wondered Paula, "what could it do to a man like Warren?"

"This," replied her father. "With the surroundings as foreboding as they were, with all the guards on hand, and the possibility of sudden death within a short time, the drug could have greatly increased Warren's natural pessimism and fear. In fact, these emotions could have been emphasized to the point of profound mental depression which might have made him want to die."

I hauled a pack of cigarettes out of my pocket and passed them around.

"How would you account for the motorman and Walker and the Mayor, though?" I asked. "Could this somnocephalaine explain their actions too?"

"It's within the bounds of possibility, yes. We really know very little about the potentialities of the drug and it may have more effects than we think it has. I can't give any explanation of how it could have been administered to any of the people in question, but if it was, then it could have had a lot to do with their actions. Though, come to think of it, it's pretty hard to account for that speech of the Mayor's except by my hypnosis theory. Still, I can't say for sure that somnocephalaine couldn't have been an influence."

"In your case, though," I pursued, "wouldn't you have been able to tell, with all your experience, that you were under the influence of a drug like that?"

"Not necessarily," was the reply. "My perceptions would have been dulled to a considerable extent. The after-effects of somnocephalaine and the kind of hypnotism practiced by initiates of the Three Brotherhoods are quite similar, I should say, though with much less shock resulting from the drug. It is this last factor that makes me continue to hope for my original theory. Walker, for example, was suffering from shock to an unusual degree."

"Oh, that's good," said Paula. "You can't let anything break up your case like that, Dad!"

The Professor patted her hand. "I'll try not to, dear," he promised. "I certainly can't afford to have it proved that Skull works with drugs and not with a kind of hypnotism superior to any ever seen before. It actually isn't possible that I was under the influence of somnocephalaine when I struck down Amos Carter. It couldn't possibly have been given me because the only food I take is at home and only you or Martha could have administered it.

"Therefore, as far as I'm concerned, it doesn't make any difference how many others may have been under its influence. I was not, and if Dr. Skull doesn't work with hypnotism, then I killed Carter as the direct result of a very real criminal insanity that may return. So you see, my theory must not be disrupted. Frankly, I don't believe it will be. I don't believe that Edward J. Walker had been given any drug, or Mayor O'Hara either. Nor the elevated motorman nor the poor woman who was found dead.

"What I do believe is this:

"Franz Ehrlich, or Skull, developed a hypnotic ability greater even than that of his teachers themselves. Fearing death if he broke his vow of secrecy and used his power in India, he came to America. I can't say for sure, but I believe that that motorman may have been only a sort of proving ground for Skull. Before attempting anything on a grander scale he must have wanted to be sure. In the case of Walker, he may have needed the money. In my case— well, it may have been sentiment, or the desire to try his power on someone he thought might be rather difficult.

"With Mayor O'Hara and Warren, his real campaign

has begun. I am very much afraid that it has *just* begun, and that we may be facing a reign of terror such as the world has never known—unless this maniac can be checked."

Professor Lansdowne stopped talking long enough to light his pipe. Then he added:

"I hope, more than I can say, that the man whom Skull has selected for his next victim—Commissioner Gallagher—may escape the fate which overtook Warren. But, as matters stand, I don't believe he will. In the manner of his death, we will surely find evidence, either to further weaken or greatly strengthen, my theory of hypnosis. There are now less than fifty-three hours to wait."

9

CONDEMNED TO DEATH

PAULA AND I spent that Saturday evening worrying over the latest developments in the Warren case. The fact that there was the barest possibility of Professor Lansdowne's not having been the unwilling tool of Dr. Skull when he struck down Amos Carter was enough to cast a pall over our thoughts.

"Just think, Bob," said Paula that evening, "if Skull uses drugs instead of hypnotism to control his victims, that means Dad killed poor Dr. Carter because he really did go out of his mind. And if he did once, he might again. What if that should be true!"

"But it isn't, Paula," I said, and in my heart believed it. "The Professor is as sane as anybody in the world. If he went out of his head, it was because Dr. Skull had him hypnotized. Your dad wouldn't go crazy that way. He's no homicidal maniac."

"I hope and pray you're right, darling."

"I'm right. As your father says, we must keep our eyes on Gallagher. What happens to him, if anything does, may be the proof of our argument."

If it seems cold-blooded of me to take such an attitude toward the possible death of a fine man like the Commis-

sioner, it should be remembered that the happiness—
perhaps the lives—of those I loved best were at stake. At
that moment, I think I would have been willing to sacrifice all the people in the world, if by doing so I could have
saved the Professor from a lunatic asylum and Paula from
the misery which gripped her.

The next morning as I sat down to breakfast at the
restaurant over on Broadway, I rambled through the
Sunday papers. The front page was full of the threat that
had been made to the police official, and in another column
appeared a statement that a thorough investigation into
the cause of J. Homer Warren's death had been launched.
Also on the first page, a smaller item announced that the
selection of jurors for the Lansdowne trial would begin
almost immediately. The article went on to say that the
State would undoubtedly refuse to permit a plea of not
guilty by reason of insanity, and that the prosecution would
probably be conducted by District Attorney Harkness
himself. The thought that anyone in the world could be
planning ways of putting Professor Lansdowne in the
electric chair caused a chill to run up and down my spine.
It came to me with a rush that the scientist would have to
work fast to build up a satisfactory defense, in the short
time left before the trial.

Professor Lansdowne had asked me to have another
talk with Commissioner Gallagher, and to pass on to the
official several last-minute suggestions. Although it was
Sunday, the Commissioner was hard at work in his office
when I telephoned for an appointment, and set a time a
couple of hours away for our conference. Meanwhile, I
dropped around to see Paula. A few minutes after I arrived,

Curly Smith put in an appearance. After we'd discussed the forthcoming trial and Paula had thanked the reporter for several very sympathetic articles he had written about her father, Curly said:

"You won't be seeing me around for a while. I've been assigned to the Skull case on a full-time basis, and from the looks of it, that means twenty-four hours a day."

Paula and I exchanged a swift look, but said nothing of Professor Lansdowne's concern with the mysterious doctor. Curly went on:

"My paper is all set to offer a big reward for Skull if anything happens to Commissioner Gallagher and I don't mind saying I intend to have a whack at it."

"Better be careful," I warned. "Shrouds don't have pockets, you know."

"And live people don't have shrouds," Curly grinned back at me. A time was to come when I would remember that remark.

I REACHED THE Commissioner's office a few minutes before the time of our appointment, but it was thirty minutes after the hour set before the door of the inner sanctum opened and I was admitted. I was pleasantly surprised to find Tom Higgins already seated in a deep, leather chair and puffing a cigar. We exchanged nods.

"All right, Larkin," said the Commissioner brusquely, "what do you know?"

"I had a talk with Professor Lansdowne," I said, "and he has some suggestions for you."

"Let's have them."

Whereupon I passed on a list of precautions outlined by the scientist: that at the zero hour, Gallagher should surround himself only by trusted men; that he should instruct these men to watch him every second, ready to stop instantly any effort on his own part to injure himself; that lethal weapons should be kept out of his reach. There were several other things, as well.

"Tell the Professor I understand perfectly and am grateful to him for his help," said the Commissioner when I had finished. "In view of what happened to Warren, I'd decided to take somewhat similar precautions myself, and I'm glad to hear that Professor Lansdowne agrees with me. Of course, the finding of that stuff in Warren's stomach may have changed the complexion of things materially, but we certainly don't know that the Professor's explanation has been disproved—not by a long shot. My own disposition should shed light on that question, and I have an idea Professor Lansdowne is quite interested in seeing what happens to me."

"As a matter of fact, Commissioner, he is," I admitted.

"Well," said Gallagher with a rather bitter laugh, "I can't say I blame him, but I'm going to do my damnedest to see that nothing happens. Now, while you're here, I have a few things I want to say to you."

The Commissioner leaned back in his chair and appeared to think a few moments before continuing. Then:

"Should Skull get to me regardless of all we do to stop him, and should the way I die prove Professor Lansdowne correct, his importance in this case will be tremendously increased. In fact, as perhaps the only person in New York City who knows anything about the man we're fighting, he will be the most important factor in the campaign. It's unthinkable that such a person should be in jail where he can't give us the greatest benefit of his knowledge, and if this case cracks his way, he won't be there long.

"Meanwhile, though, you can be the link between Professor Lansdowne and the police. It might even be better that way than for Skull to know the Professor is working with us. He might kill him. Be that as it may, Tom Higgins here is directly in charge of all operations against Skull. If I die, he will be the man for you and the Professor to work with. You two had better make arrangements to keep in close touch with each other. If things break the other way, and the Professor is wrong, you can forget about it."

Commissioner Gallagher rose, to indicate that the interview was closed. "Good luck," he said, "and tell that absent-minded Professor of yours that I expect to cheat him out of his proof by staying alive."

"Of course, sir," I replied, "and the best of luck to you, too."

"Thanks, son. I'll probably need it."

As I left the office in the company of Tom Higgins, I could not still the feeling of apprehension that swept over me, a premonition that I had seen that pleasant and capable man for the last time. The mental picture I had of the way he looked, standing there behind his desk, convinced me that he felt the same way himself. He wore the expression of a man condemned to death.

TOM AND I were silent as we drove uptown together. He undoubtedly felt his grave responsibility, and must also have seen the grim expectation in his chief's eyes. We parted at the corner of 47th and Broadway after making arrangements to keep in touch with each other. I then continued northward to Riverside Drive and the Lansdowne apartment, where I had a dinner engagement with Paula.

That night we went to one of the so-called "concerts" that take place in New York on Sunday evenings, when the regular theaters are closed. In reality a glorified variety program, these affairs provide an entertainment rather higher than the level of the average movie stage show, and are quite popular. We probably wouldn't have gone out at all except for the fact that Professor Lansdowne had been pleading with us to get a little relaxation. I was glad he'd suggested it, because the strain was beginning to tell on Paula. The Professor himself, strangely enough, did not now give any appearance of being under pressure. Rather, he acted like a man who is very much absorbed in an interesting experiment. There was nothing about the scientist's behavior to betray the fact that he, himself, was part of the experiment, and that failure might well mean death.

The concert was fairly good, and for a couple of hours we were able to forget the shadows that hemmed us in. We could even laugh at a well-written skit burlesquing Skull. When the show was over, however, Paula preferred to return home rather than go to a restaurant for a late supper.

It still amazes me that the lights on Broadway that night sparkled just as brightly as ever; that the same crowd of people could saunter up and down the famous street, looking in shop windows and at each other with the same expressions they'd always worn. Nowhere was there anything but the commonplace. There were, of course, occasional snatches of conversation about Dr. Skull. But

these were carried on, for the most part, in tones of amusement or merely mild interest. Only in rare instances was
there the faint tremor of voice betokening alarm.

Paula and I reached the apartment in time for the
midnight news broadcast, to which we listened. I remember that the first item read was one concerning a hurricane
in Cuba, and that not until midway of the fifteen minute
bulletin was any mention made of Dr. Skull. Then:

"The attention of seven million New Yorkers," said the
announcer, "is focused tonight on a mysterious person
known as Dr. Skull, who has threatened to murder Police
Commissioner Michael A. Gallagher unless negotiations are begun which would mean the virtual surrender of New York to him. With the zero hour—seven P.M.
tomorrow—drawing closer, many citizens ask themselves.
'Will Commissioner Gallagher be alive at this time tomorrow night?' The Commissioner himself has refused to be
alarmed by the threat, which he terms that of a madman,
but he has admitted that special police have been assigned
to guard him. So far, all efforts to locate Dr. Skull have been
unavailing, but police officials state an arrest is expected
momentarily. And now for news of the sports world. In
Detroit tonight, the Interstate Basketball League has—"

At which point, Paula clicked off the radio.

All indications pointed to my having a restless night,
but sleep came quickly and I even snored through an eight
o'clock alarm to awaken not until twenty minutes of nine.
Clouds had come up and the day was a dismal one, with
a fine drizzle of rain which looked as though it would go
on for the next week.

Instantly, my thoughts reverted to Commissioner Gallagher. This was the day, and there were ten hours and twenty minutes until the fatal hour, during which the Commissioner was slated to die. The dark sky impressed me as a gloomy omen, and my whole being was weighted with a feeling of dull foreboding. In thinking back to that morning, it is clear that nowhere in my mind was there the slightest doubt that Commissioner Gallagher would really be killed. I may have been concerned as to the exact manner of his passing, insofar as that would reflect on the Professor's theory, but I was absolutely sure he would die. Moreover, my faith in Professor Lansdowne's hypnosis idea was now stronger than ever. Such are the unpredictable ways of the human mind.

But to continue:

AT ELEVEN O'CLOCK, Paula and I taxied downtown and, a few minutes later, we greeted the Professor and Norman Howard at the Tombs. Paula's father looked as though he had slept soundly, and not by so much as a flicker of an eyelash did he show any nervousness. Norman Howard was his usual bantam-y, meticulous self. Clearing his throat in his best courtroom manner, he pulled several sheets of foolscap out of a briefcase and handed them to the Professor.

"Here is a preliminary outline of the argument I expect to make," he said. "It is, of course, based on the premise that you were temporarily insane when you struck Amos Carter." He cleared his throat again.

"I see," said Professor Lansdowne, shuffling the sheets with his fingers. "It certainly takes a lot of material to make such a short argument, doesn't it?"

"Well," replied Howard, head cocked to one side, "this is

an outline of the entire case. In a couple of days, I'll bring you the complete brief, but I wanted you to see this first, in case you have any suggestions to make. You see that I have indicated the line of questioning here. It is intended to establish the fact that you had no motive whatever for wanting Dr. Carter dead, and that for years you have been the victim of repeated attacks of insanity."

"I see," said the Professor again, absently.

"Not being familiar with the history of your earlier years, I have merely suggested incidents, the details of which you can supply yourself. Miss Lansdowne will, naturally, be the principal defense witness. She can testify that you've had—ahem—various flights of fancy, shall we say, during her own lifetime. You, being a psychologist, can hit upon any number of ways in which this unfortunate tendency manifested itself, I presume."

"I dare say," murmured Professor Lansdowne.

"I have been able," Howard continued, "to round up several disinterested witnesses, including former pupils of yours, who seem willing, if not eager, to testify as to your insanity."

The Professor looked up and grinned like a schoolboy. "You should subpoena the Dean. He'd really clinch the case for us!"

"Dad!" reproved Paula. "Please don't joke about such a serious thing as this."

"You think I'm joking?" he shot back. "Why—"

Norman Howard was clearing his throat again.

"Now, Professor," he said, "the examination of veniremen will begin at ten o'clock tomorrow morning. We can expect to have a complete panel in a day or two. There's no reason why the State should waste much time in challenges. Thanks to a number of very influential people, all friends of yours, it is possible that the trial itself will get under way before the end of the week. That means that we'll have to round off our case between now and then, preferably at the earliest possible moment. I ask you to examine this outline carefully, you and your daughter together. We'll go over it tomorrow afternoon, late. Now let me see, is there anything else?"

Howard tapped his teeth with his fountain pen and gazed thoughtfully aloft.

"Oh, yes," he said. "I'd almost forgotten. Dr. Rudolph Kleinschmidt has also offered to testify that you are mentally unbalanced."

"You don't say?" Professor Lansdowne's tone was ironical. "Another friend in need, I see. I'll bet Kleinschmidt has waited twenty years for this chance. Anything else?"

Once more Mr. Howard contemplated the ceiling. "No, I believe that about takes care of everything for the present."

"I suppose, Norman," said Professor Lansdowne, "that you've gone to a good deal of trouble to get your brief and your witnesses all lined up, haven't you?"

"There has been considerable time involved, yes," agreed Howard, "but of course that's part of my work."

The Professor extended the papers to him. "Well," he said, "that's too bad, because I'm afraid you're never going to have a chance to use them. Here."

The lawyer drew back a step. He looked from the Professor to Paula, to me, and back to the Professor. "Why, what do you mean?" he demanded. "I assure you—"

"I mean," answered Professor Lansdowne, "that I have

decided against letting you enter a plea of insanity in order to keep me out of the electric chair."

"But," faltered Howard, "There's no question of first degree murder in any case. I don't—"

"Of course you don't, Norman," said the scientist, kindly. "You just run along back to your office and come in to see me again tomorrow morning, first thing. At that time, I expect to present to you my real case. Or perhaps I won't. In any event, there's nothing further you can do at the present."

Howard looked as though he expected the earth to open up and swallow him.

"Why, why—" he choked, "you're running the risk of going to prison for the rest of your life. Yes, possibly the electric chair, at that! Temporary insanity is the only possible—"

But he was again interrupted.

"Norman, you stop trying to think. Run back to your office and stay there until tomorrow morning, like I told you. Get yourself interested in some other case. Now run along. I mean it."

The lawyer turned to Paula. "Miss Lansdowne. I want you to know that I can accept no further responsibility until you can talk some sense into your father. Apparently," he added maliciously, "it would be only too easy to establish insanity in his case!"

"I think you'd better do as Dad asks, Mr. Howard," suggested Paula. "I'm sure he'll have something quite rational to give you, when the time comes."

"Very well, Miss Lansdowne. But I wash my hands, you understand? I wash my hands! Good day!" With which he picked up his briefcase, grabbed the outline out of the Professor's hand and marched off down the corridor.

"Now see what you've done!" said Paula, bitterly.

"Never mind, dear," her father soothed. "I don't think any great harm's been done. His pride is a bit dented, that's all."

"What do you intend to do, sir?" I asked, not sure of his purpose.

"For the present, some hard thinking. Bob," was the reply. "By tomorrow morning I may have arrived at something."

"You mean that by then, you may know more—about the Commissioner, and Skull?"

"Exactly. And now, I'd appreciate it if you two would kindly clear out of here. As I said, there's hard thinking to be done."

HE WOULD HAVE it no other way, so we left. Although a bit nervous at the Professor's sudden dismissal of the one thing, the only thing, that was certain to get him off, we were both buoyed up by the confidence in his voice.

Shortly after one o'clock, I telephoned Tom Higgins from a public booth. Neither of us had anything new to discuss.

"I'm standing by downtown until after eight tonight," said Tom. "Tell me where I can get you then."

I gave him Paula's number and hung up. As I did so, a pall of deep depression and premonition of disaster fell upon me again. Quarter past one. Five hours and forty-five minutes to go. It was the Warren business all over again, and I didn't like it. Rejoining Paula, I piloted her into the subway, and it seemed like going down into a tomb. The express shot uptown to 72nd, 96th. 103rd, 110th. and finally, 116th Street. The big university buildings loomed up in the misty rain as we came out on the street. Silently, we walked down the hill to the Drive and crossed over to the parapet overlooking the broad Hudson. The river was a wide sheet of dismal gray. On the Jersey shore, the Palisades pushed their bulk into the drizzle. From time to time, a dead leaf would fall to the ground, wet and sodden.

"It's a great day for a murder," I remarked.

Paula nodded, shuddering a little.

We stayed there a few minutes longer and then, pretty well saturated, we went up to the Lansdowne apartment.

Hour after heavy hour dragged by. We tried to talk, but couldn't. Nor were we in any mood for the radio. Try as we would to get our minds off it, our eyes kept going back to the electric clock on the mantel. Outside, the rain continued, the same constant drizzle that had lasted all day. Probably, I thought to myself, it would never stop. The little light that was in the sky faded. By five o'clock it was gone.

Paula turned on a lamp and sat down beside me, her cold hand in both of mine, very nearly as cold. We could think of nothing much to say, so we just sat there, smoking innumerable cigarettes. At six-thirty we mixed a couple of whiskey highballs.

"Did Tom Higgins say what time he would call you?" asked Paula, a few minutes later.

"Eight o'clock. When it's—settled."

"Oh."

Now it was seven.

"It's started," I said.

"Yes."

I wondered how Gallagher felt. I wondered if, like

Warren, he was trying to pass the thing off lightly, trying to hide his natural fear, trying to face death smiling. I knew that no matter how many men he had to guard him, he didn't feel safe. No one could feel safe. I wondered if he were drinking highballs, and if there were any drug in the liquor—the same drug that had been found in Warren's stomach—the same drug that might send the Professor's theory crashing down.

"Seven-thirty," said Paula. "Do you think he's—"

"I wish I knew."

This was different from that night at Warren's. If you have to die, it's nice to do it in style, with reporters, and good whiskey, pleasant conversation and a nonchalant air. Of course, that might be the way Gallagher was waiting, but here in this apartment, just the two of us, it seemed as though he must be as silent, as tense and alone, as we.

Seven-fifty. In ten minutes, it would be over. I swallowed to ease my dry throat.

"If he's held through this long," I said, "he's got a good—"

The sharp, electric ring of the telephone cut me short. In the instant between the first and second ring. Paula and I stared at each other.

I took a deep breath and picked up the receiver.

"Hello...."

"Bob Larkin?" It was Tom Higgins.

"Right. That you, Tom?"

"Yeah." A pause.

"The Commissioner—" I began. "Has anything happened?"

"The Commissioner," said Tom Higgins, "is dead."

10

POST-MORTEM

WE SAT, THE three of us, around a flickering fire in the Lansdowne living room. Outside, the night had grown colder, and the rain that had drizzled down all the long day was now being driven against the window panes by fitful gusts of wind that came down the broad avenue of the Hudson. It was something after eleven o'clock and there were half-finished highballs in front of each of us. Tom Higgins had arrived just a few minutes before.

For some minutes, he had been sitting silently, staring into the flames. Finally he spoke.

"He was a great guy." He took another gulp of his drink.

"I still don't get it," I said.

"Aw, there's nothin' to it, except like the Professor says. It's hypnotism. Couldn't be anything else. And what the devil are you gonna do with a thing like that?"

"But there hasn't been an autopsy yet. When there is one, it may show that the drug found in Warren is also in Gallagher."

"It's gonna be a long time before there's any autopsy," said Higgins. "It's quite a way to the bottom of the East River. Fifty-six feet they tell me, at the point where Gallagher went down. And there's a strong current. They ain't likely to hook that car with the grapples until they've done plenty huntin'."

"They've already started trying?"

"Sure—by searchlight. They got four divers workin' in shifts. I've seen these things happen before. One time a guy took a dive off the back end of a ferry boat goin' to Jersey. That was at 125th Street. Ten days later they found the car, with the guy still inside it, but it was down at 119th."

I crushed out my cigarette and had another pull of whiskey-soda.

"If the Commissioner'd only have stayed in his office—"

Tom cut in almost angrily, as though he thought I was holding him to blame, something that was far from the truth.

"There was no holdin' him, I tell you. Up until just before seven he was jokin' with the fellows. Why, there was so many guys in that place, Houdini couldn't have got in, let alone out. Then about ten after seven the Commissioner says, 'Okay, boys, I've had about enough of this.' Then he starts talkin' about headin' over to Brooklyn. He had it all figured out. Said it would be a sure way to queer whatever plans this Skull guy had. He'd hop into a car with one of the boys to drive and three others to keep their eyes on him. Nothin' could happen that way, he says. If it would make us feel any better, he says, we could even handcuff him. A lot of good that'd 've done!

"To make double sure, the Commissioner says I should follow in another car with a couple of boys and keep an eye on his car all the time. Wouldn't that seem plenty careful—I ask you? And him in a bullet-proof car, to boot!"

"It would have to me," Paula said.

*"That was the last we
seen of them," said Tim,
and lifted his drink*

"Well, it did to me, too," went on Tom, "and what a sap I turned out to be! But the Commissioner was so sure that if he stayed in the office he'd be doin' just what Skull wanted him to do. He figured that if he was drivin' around at the time Skull was supposed to get him, he couldn't be found. If Skull didn't know where he was, he'd be safe, see?"

Tom motioned for me to refill his empty glass.

"It would've taken more men than we had in the office to make him do anything different," he continued, "so around quarter after seven, the Commissioner sneaks down to the back alley and gets into his car—the big sedan, it was— along with Curran, Fraser, Munson, and Goss. Matt Fraser was doin' the drivin'. Then, before he starts out, Grogan and Fred Hazzard and Luke Pearson and me gets in a squad car to tail him. It was rainin' a little and pitch dark. Right then it seemed like a dumb idea to me and I was all set to hop out and say so when the chief's car zooms out of the alley. So there was nothin' to do but for us to follow him and hope for the best.

"We stayed right on his tail, figurin' that he'd be headin' for the Brooklyn Bridge, it bein' closest. But instead, he has Matt Fraser drive down to the Battery first. Then they start back along Park Row and keep on up to the approach to the Manhattan Bridge. They turn onto the bridge and right away Fraser starts givin' the old buggy the gas. They were doin' forty-five in no time, but we didn't have any trouble keepin' up with 'em. Traffic didn't happen to be bad and there was plenty of room.

"Well, you know how for a long time, the bridge is over dry land, with the tenements underneath. All the time it keeps risin', so as to be high enough by the time it hits the river to let ships get under it without any trouble. About a block or so away from the river, Fraser starts pickin' up speed. This seems kinda funny to me and I tell Hazzard to stay with him. In no time, he's doin' sixty, sixty-five, cuttin' in and out between other cars.

"We kept close behind them. Almost too close the way things happen, because all of a sudden the Commissioner's car swerves quick to the right and Hazzard nearly breaks his arm twistin' around to keep from smackin' into it. At the same time, it shoots clear over the car tracks, across the sidewalk, through that iron fence like it was so much kindlin' wood, and dives into the river."

Tom took a deep drink and added, in a voice that shook:

"That was the last we seen of them."

IT WAS THE second time I'd heard the story, but its horrible finish was a shock as it had been when Tom had first told me over the telephone. It wasn't so much that five men had gone to their deaths in a particularly terrible fashion, but that every force of law and order had been working to prevent it, and had failed—miserably. It was final, crushing, overpowering proof that New York and all its people—yes, that we ourselves—were as helpless as babies in the shadow of the cruel, incredible Dr. Skull. How did we know that at any moment he might not decide to strike, there, in that very room! Indeed, at the time that seemed a very logical idea to me, and I freely confess to being badly frightened. After all, were we not closely connected with his grim machinations? Were we not his particular enemies, since we knew something about him and were hoping to find a way of trapping him? Surely, with his vastly superior mentality, he must be aware of it.

Tom Higgins broke the silence.

"He was a good guy, the Commissioner," he said slowly. "They were all good guys, every one of them—Munson, Goss, Fraser, Curran! And where are they now? At the bottom of the East River, that's where—trapped like rats, they were." He rose to his feet. "We've got to get that murderin' lunatic!"

"Yes," I agreed, "but how?"

Characteristically, it was Paula who came forward with the only sensible answer.

"I don't know what you gentlemen think," she said quietly, "but it seems to me that our only chance is to cross our fingers and pray that Dad can think up something, quick."

Looking back on that night, I remember clearly that not one of us considered for a moment that the driver of the death car might have lost control of the machine through ordinary circumstances, such as a mechanical failure of the automobile, or through the failure of his own bodily functions, heart, eyes, or brain. I should not have added "brain" for, as a matter of fact, the brain did fail. It failed in its business of remaining its own master the exact instant when Dr. Skull fastened upon it the icy grip of his own invincible will. We assumed, immediately and spontaneously, that Dr. Skull had made good his threat. Later events were to prove that we had not been wrong.

Police censorship, even of the most rudimentary kind, was utterly impossible for the first several hours after the latest tragedy took place. The shrill cries of newsboys with their extras echoed eerily up and down the rain-drenched streets for the rest of the night, and by morning, nervousness pulsed in the city like an electric current.

Tom Higgins and I sought Professor Lansdowne early. We were both very bedraggled, Tom having been closeted with police officials all night and I having been pacing up and down the Lansdowne living room, determined to stay in the apartment with Paula until daylight. As if Dr. Skull were any less dangerous by day!

With the death of Commissioner Gallagher, an unexpected figure had stepped into the case, that of District Attorney Walter Harkness. At the request of the Mayor and other civic heads, he undertook direction of the campaign against one of the strangest and most fearful enemies New York had ever known. Tom Higgins was to function as director of police facilities in the battle against Skull, but was to work under the District Attorney rather than in an independent capacity, as Commissioner Gallagher had expected. Instead of being disappointed, I felt that Tom was genuinely glad to share his terrible responsibility. Whether Professor Lansdowne's aid would be sought by Harkness—the man scheduled to prosecute him for murder—as it had been by the Commissioner remained to be seen, but for the present, Tom Higgins was most anxious to have the Professor for an ally.

IN HIS JAIL cell, the scientist gleaned every bit of information he could get from Tom before he would offer an opinion. He was particularly anxious to know if either the Commissioner or the man who had driven his car had had anything to eat or drink within an hour of the accident.

"No, sir," said Tom, emphatically. "The Commissioner was makin' very sure that he would get none of the drug that Warren got. He wouldn't even drink a glass of water and he wouldn't let any of us do it, either."

Professor Lansdowne said nothing for a minute or two, and when he spoke, it was with great caution.

"In the light of Commissioner Gallagher's death, and most particularly in view of the way he died, I am convinced that my hypnosis theory is correct. What happens from now on will further strengthen it, I feel sure. For the present, we must move carefully, very carefully. Indeed, I can suggest no action at all for the present."

"Holy gee, Professor," exclaimed Tom Higgins, in evident pain, "can't you give me anything to work on? There's no tellin' what that maniac's gonna pull next. We've gotta beat him to the draw, don't you see?"

But Professor Lansdowne refused to be hurried. "I realize only too well," he said, "the seriousness of the situation that is confronting us. I know that every minute, that every second, counts. Yet, to make a false move might be to lose forever the possibility—and I must warn you it is a pretty slim possibility—of beating Dr. Skull. No, you must go ahead with your ordinary precautions and give me a little longer."

"If you saps would have the brains to get the Professor out of this dive, you'd stand a better chance of catching Skull," I remarked, with no little heat. "It's pretty damned ridiculous, the representative of the high and mighty police department shuttling back and forth between his office and a cell in the Tombs, trying to get help from a man he's trying to convict of murder!"

"That's why I wish the Professor could start something," complained Tom, taking my chastisement with unaccustomed meekness. "Then the D.A.'d have to let him out on bail at the very least."

"On bail!" I snarled back. "That's a hot one! A lot of good that would do with the trial starting the latter part of this week. What your precious district attorney should do is throw the whole case out of court. If he had the sense of an amoeba—"

"Calm down, Bob," interrupted the Professor. "This isn't getting us anywhere. We'll take care of my case when it comes up. Meanwhile, I'm fairly comfortable here. I have plenty of time to think, and there's nothing I could do if I were out."

"You'd have more room to think in," I persisted, doggedly.

"Cut it, Bob," said Tom. "The Professor knows how glad I'd be to see him out of this jug. Maybe he will be soon. Who knows? If he can't think up anything right now, I've plenty work of my own to do. They'll be having the Commissioner's car up any time now and I want be on deck when they do. Of course," he added, for the Professor's benefit, "there'll be an autopsy on everybody in the automobile, but I guess that won't get us anywhere."

Professor Lansdowne shook his head. "Not if you're looking for somnocephalaine, at any rate. I'm sure there won't be a trace of it. I don't know what it was doing in Warren's stomach, but I would now be willing to make a small wager that Skull had nothing to do with it."

"Yeah," agreed Tom, adding, "What do you think will be Skull's next move, if any?"

The scientist stroked his chin reflectively.

"Judging by past performances, his next move is fairly obvious. Dr. Skull will point, not with pride, but with regret, and view with alarm."

"What do you mean by that?"

"I mean," explained Professor Lansdowne, "that Dr. Skull will find a way of communicating with the police, or the public, or both. He will remind us that he has carried out his dire promises. He will make a regretful comment on the lack of intelligence being displayed by the city powers in not granting his demands. He will call the world to witness his fair dealing, and then deliver another ultimatum. This time it will be worse than the last, if such is possible. That, for what it's worth, is my guess."

The Professor never gave a better example of his ability as a seer.

In leaving, I asked him what he had decided about his plea—the new one, that is.

"It isn't formulated as yet," he replied, "so I'm not inclined to discuss it at present. Norman Howard is due here at any moment, and I shall have to give him something to work on because they're picking the jurors this morning, I understand. I expect he's nearly as crazy as he thinks I am, poor chap. It's his first criminal case, you know."

"What?" I said, dumbfounded.

"That's correct," smiled the scientist. "He's really a corporation lawyer. Naturally, he's quite worried."

"*He's* quite worried?" I exploded. "What about you? Trusting your life to a man like that!"

"I expect to help him somewhat."

"I hope so!" I said fervently.

THAT AFTERNOON, DIVERS beat Tom Higgins original estimate by over a week and succeeded in raising the wrecked sedan which held the drowned bodies of Commissioner Gallagher and his four companions. The news was spread across the front page of every evening paper. About four o'clock, I dropped around to a quiet bar on 52nd Street for an early cocktail. I hadn't been there for more than a couple of minutes when Curly Smith eased himself on the stool next to mine.

"Happy days," he greeted me. "Eat, drink and be merry for tomorow we die. *Morituri te salutamus. Sic transit gloria mundi*—and all that sort of thing."

"What's eating you?" I demanded.

"Larkin, I wouldn't mind so much if Skull would just reach out and smack me into perdition and get it over with. It's this death by enforced insomnia that gets me down."

"Insomnia?" I'd had no sleep either, but I decided to say nothing about it.

"Yeah. I was on the back end of a police launch all night, freezing to death in the rain, waiting for those hooks to catch on something."

"Yeah?"

"Yeah." He ordered a sidecar. "They didn't catch until two hours ago. You know, when they brought that auto up and I saw what was in it, it gave me a grudge against whoever did it."

"I wouldn't try to do too much about it."

"But I am. My paper—you remember I told you it would—has offered a five grand reward for the guy that brings in Dr. Skull, dead or alive. Who knows? Maybe it'll do some good. Maybe I'll get it myself. Who can say?"

"Who can say?" I agreed, tossing a half-dollar on the bar. Then, nodding goodby, I left. That reward was a laugh to me, and it must have been a bigger one to Dr. Skull. Five thousand dollars!

At 8:55 P.M. Paula and I were listening to a program of dance music that was coming in over WABC. If it hadn't have been a show produced by my former employers, Rowlandson & Leger, we might not have paid any attention to it. I was interested in seeing what sort of a commercial they were using, so we remained tuned in after the final song had been concluded. I knew the announcer on the program quite well. His voice was as familiar to me as my own, so many times had I heard him read commercials I'd written. Therefore, I can say with certainty that the voice which now spoke was that of Gene Ames, although its quality was queerly altered.

"To the people of New York," it said, "my apologies for intruding upon the privacy of your homes. When you know that it is Dr. Skull who speaks, perhaps you will forgive the liberty. Last night, five more men paid the penalty of folly and disobedience with their lives. Today, though they realize all too well their impotence against the power of my will, your city authorities still refuse to meet my demands—that they publicly indicate their willingness to transfer to me absolute control of New York.

"You who listen, feeling that you will not be touched by my punishment, neglect to force upon your officials a wiser course.

"Now the time grows short. My next blow will fall without warning. Instead of singling out individuals in the vain hope of awakening a citizenry which refuses to be awakened, I shall strike at the people themselves. There is yet one way to stay my hand. Call upon your leaders. Bid them acknowledge my rule—now—at once! There will be no second chance."

The voice, familiar, yet strangely metallic, ceased. A murmuring hubbub of sound came from the speaker. Quickly I shut it off, impelled to do so by a sudden fear that clutched my heart.

11

THE DEFENDANT

GRAY MORNING DAWNED on a city jittery in anticipation of an unknown but terrible fate. A hasty police investigation of the strange broadcast had achieved nothing, other than the expected contention by the announcer that he could not possibly explain his speech—any more than Mayor O'Hara could. The press tried to strike a fine balance between making the most of the sensational news for the benefit of their circulation, and following the advice of the authorities to make no statements that would tend to alarm the public needlessly. As might be expected, the circulation proved the stronger factor, and headlines screamed from every front page.

Police, under the spurs of District Attorney Harkness and Tom Higgins, did their utmost to find Dr. Skull, but it was useless. The description furnished Tom by Professor Lansdowne was years old, perhaps no longer accurate. The scientist could remember little besides the fact that Ehrlich—assuming that he and Skull were the same—was a man of medium size, with prominent eyes and an unusually large head. This was not much to go on, and a cable to the Vienna police, at the Professor's suggestion, added nothing more. The Austrian authorities had no record of the man and could be of no help. Still, the hunt went doggedly on.

Early in the day, there was a special meeting held in the chambers of the Mayor at which it was proposed to find more effective measures for combatting the menace that threatened the peace and security of the world's greatest city. Both the District Attorney and Tom Higgins attended, as did numerous city officials, but the session was a fiasco. Aside from mumbling vague criticisms of the way police were handling the case, none of the participants in the conference could suggest any constructive change in the present procedure. Mayor O'Hara himself was still so shaken by his own experience that he was barely able to discharge the minor formalities of directing the meeting, and his only contribution to the talk was the plea, made in a quavering voice, that "something be done." At the time of adjournment, the buck had been passed, or rather, left, in the hands of Harkness and Higgins. Which was, of course, the best thing that could have happened.

While this classic conversation was taking place at the City Hall, I was with Professor Lansdowne in the Tombs, a few blocks away. There were several morning papers on the iron cot, so I gathered that he had read about Skull's latest move.

"What do you think, sir?" I asked.

"I think that Dr. Skull is going along according to schedule," he replied. "He appears to be gaining confidence in himself at a rapid rate, which is not surprising considering the complete lack of resistance he has so far encountered. I wish I could hope that this confidence will lull him into a false step, but I'm afraid that's a vain hope this early in the game. Later, yes. But how much suffering may be caused meanwhile!"

He shook his head quite calmly but I could see his hands were clenched.

"He can't be very well balanced," I remarked, "or he wouldn't try to get control of New York. Who on earth does he think is qualified to give him any such control? And how long does he think he could keep it? Sooner or later someone would kill him."

"Of course he's not well balanced, Bob. If he were, he would not have the power he has. Unfortunately, he probably wouldn't admit it, and I don't imagine he's giving much thought to the possibility of what may happen to him after he gains his objective. I suspect he feels quite Godlike, and entirely impervious to harm."

I went on to press the scientist about his own plans for combatting Skull, but he would say nothing that satisfied my curiosity.

"This is no time for me to have plans about *combatting* Dr. Skull," he told me. "My first interest is in clearing myself. After that has been done, then perhaps we can take the offensive. To be frank with you, I feel we must if anything is to be done to save this city from what may be a very unpleasant fate. I don't have much confidence in the police."

"They don't have much confidence in themselves," I said drily.

"Well, they're not to blame. As long as Skull has the good sense to work under cover, there isn't anything they can do. After all, where should they begin looking? No," the Professor shook his head, "their chance—and our chance—

is that eventually Skull will make a mistake and show his hand. Until then—" He shrugged expressively.

"Don't you suppose," I asked, "that he must have some sort of headquarters, some place where he makes his plans and directs whatever organization he has?"

"I fail to see what need he has of either headquarters or organization at this stage of the game," replied the Professor promptly. "He must sleep somewhere, but I expect that is as near a headquarters as he has."

"If we could only find where that is—"

"Quite," smiled the Professor. "And there's the rub."

TALK SHIFTED TO the trial, now only two days away. Although I failed to realize it at the time, the sudden setting forward of the trial date was too unusual a circumstance to have been attributed to Professor Lansdowne's personal friends and their influence. A far greater factor was the Professor's growing importance in the Skull affair. However, any interest the higher-ups may have felt in the scientist was not reflected in any other way. The necessity of his proving his innocence in the face of considerable evidence to the contrary was as great as ever, and I was by no means convinced this would be an easy task. When I asked Professor Lansdowne along what lines his defense would be conducted, he would only say:

"I'd rather not talk about it, because I'm not altogether sure, even now. Wait and find out in the courtroom. The mystery will add a bit of zest to what might otherwise be a dull affair." I realized only too well the futility of trying to force the information from him.

"Is Norman Howard still with you?" I wanted to know.

"More or less," chuckled the Professor. "He's now

wondering why he ever troubled to get witnesses to prove my insanity. He's quite sure that my mere appearance would do that, if the jury had half an eye. He's over questioning prospective jurors, and after that he's going to run some errands for me."

"Errands?"

"That's right. He's calling on a few friends of mine. I mean to have an ace or two up my sleeve by the time court convenes."

And having let this shred of information out, he once more shut up like a clam, changing the subject back to Skull and the fact that an autopsy on Commissioner Gallagher had shown no sign of somnocephalaine. "As I predicted," he added with pardonable pride.

For the next forty-eight hours, there was no further demonstration on the part of Dr. Skull. Hour by hour, as nothing happened to bear out the threat he had made over the radio, the city's case of nerves gradually diminished. In this period of quiet, there was ample time for a hundred lurid theories to blossom out, theories which described Skull as everything from a black magician to an avenging ghost. Nor was hypnotism forgotten in the explanations given of his power. On the contrary, it occupied the most prominent position of all, but none of the descriptions recognized the type of hypnotism used, nor its hitherto-unheard-of qualities. Police had issued no explanation, and I was glad to see that so far, they had respected Professor Lansdowne's request not to make public his theory.

ON THE MORNING of the trial, Paula and I taxied downtown and arrived in the courtroom about five minutes before ten, the hour at which the hearing was to start.

Whatever fears Paula had she was brave enough to conceal, and of course I pretended an optimism to encourage her. Actually, we were both very much worried. The Professor had not even told his plans to Paula, and she was as much in the dark as I about what was going to happen.

In accordance with a request of Professor Lansdowne's we sat in the regular seats provided for the public, though in the very first row. We had hardly taken our places when the Professor appeared, accompanied by a policeman and the natty little attorney. Howard carried an imposing batch of papers and surveyed the crowded courtroom with his accustomed supercilious air. They passed very close to us, divided only by a low wooden railing, and as her father went by, Paula reached out and squeezed his hand encouragingly. Though the scientist looked quite cheerful, I could sense that there was considerably more nervousness in his manner than had been the case a day or two before.

The courtroom was filled to capacity, and now the two policemen standing at the rear closed the big doors. At the press table, I saw Curly Smith, evidently taking time off from his pursuit of Dr. Skull and the $5,000 reward to cover the trial. He nodded to me and, catching Paula's eye, smiled reassuringly. There were a half-dozen other reporters present, and a woman artist who was apparently making a sketch of Paula.

At two minutes after the hour, the presiding judge, one Martin F. Somers, entered, and after the usual formalities the trial got under way. The surprise of the morning came when, instead of District Attorney Harkness, as everyone expected, an assistant stepped forward to conduct the case for the State. This individual was named Beale. He was short, chunky and equipped with a ruffled, pugnacious visage.

"May it please the court," he began. "Your honor, ladies and gentlemen of the jury: The people of the State of New York have been confronted with one of the most brutal crimes in the history of jurisprudence; a crime that is the more heinous because of the circumstances under which it was committed, circumstances that included the betrayal of a life-long friendship and the violation of the most sacred rules of common decency. That the murderer is a man of more than ordinary intelligence makes his deed all the more revolting, while, at the same time, it sweeps away any mitigating factors that might be present had his past environment been of a different character.

"During the course of this trial, the State will prove that on the night of September 12th of the present year, the defendant, Alfred Lansdowne, paid a visit to Dr. Amos Carter at his apartment on Claremont Avenue in this city; we will prove that during the course of this visit Alfred Lansdowne and his host, Dr. Carter, entered into a discussion relating to the value of certain researches made by the defendant here; that this discussion soon became an argument, a heated argument during which the defendant berated his friend for disagreeing with him; we will prove that when Amos Carter refused to be coerced into reversing his honest opinion, Alfred Lansdowne flew into a violent rage; that at the height of this rage he picked up a heavy, metal book-end and brought it down upon the unsuspecting head of the man who had befriended him for years, killing him.

"The State will show that this crime was not the result

of this sudden anger alone, but in reality the outcome of a long-standing jealousy on the part of Alfred Lansdowne, jealousy for the scientific recognition accorded certain theories of Dr. Carter's which had never been accorded his own. We will show that, while he pretended friendship, hatred smouldered in the breast of the defendant, a hatred that could be satisfied with nothing less than the death of his rival. We will show that this hatred was consummated in the murder that has taken place, a vicious, coldblooded murder that deserves—and must be given—the supreme punishment provided by law. That punishment is death, in the electric chair."

As Beale concluded his opening address, there was a dead silence in the courtroom, a silence in which could be heard the scratching of pens and pencils as reporters and stenographers took down his closing words. Paula turned a white, strained face to me.

"It's not true, any of it!" she whispered, distractedly. "Isn't somebody going to tell the jury that he's lying?"

"Don't worry," I advised her, with an assurance I did not feel. "It'll be all right."

"I'm not so sure," she said.

There was by now a buzz of conversation in the audience and many necks were craned to afford their owners a view of the man accused of such a terrible act. But that man merely leaned back from the forward position he had held during the assistant district attorney's address, turned around to look at his daughter, and smiled. Paula smiled back, but it was hard going for her.

Beale had conferred in a low voice with the judge, and then with an associate. Judge Somers now intoned:

"The State will proceed with its case."

"Thank you, your honor," said Beale. "Bailiff, please call the first witness, Susannah Edmunds."

THE BAILIFF REPEATED the name several times, and an elderly woman, wearing deep mourning, made her way down the aisle and over to the witness chair. She was sworn in and Beale advanced to begin his questioning. He obtained information as to her place of residence and that she had been housekeeper to the late Dr. Carter.

"Tell the jury, if you will, Mrs. Edmunds," continued Beale, "what occurred at Dr. Carter's apartment on the night of September 12th."

Mrs. Edmunds looked rather fearfully around the room, then, clasping hands tightly together, made the following statement:

"Well, sir, on the evening you was speaking about, I opened the door for Professor Lansdowne. I reckon it was a little past eight-thirty when he got there. Dr. Carter was in the study and I knew he was expecting the Professor, so I showed him right in. I left the two of 'em together and went on out to the kitchen to clean up the supper dishes. I don't guess I'd been mor'n about a half-hour or so when Dr. Carter called for me to bring in some sherry, which I done.

"By that time I was finished with my kitchen work— there never was much dishes dirtied up, on account of there just being the two of us—and then I went back to my room to read the paper. It was about nine-thirty when I heard voices getting louder and louder in the doctor's study. Then all of a sudden like, they stopped, right to once't. The next thing I know, I hear something fall, like it was a body falling. I didn't want to disturb Dr. Carter, specially as he had company, but this was an awful loud bump. Besides I thought somebody might of fell down and got hurt, so I went into the hall and started down to the study. Before I got to the door, I saw Dr. Carter a-lying on the floor like he was dead, and the Professor was standing there, looking kind of dazed with the book-end in his hand.

"I reckon I must of been pretty dazed myself, because I just stood there and didn't do nothing while Professor Lansdowne set the book-end down and walked right out of the apartment. It wasn't until after he'd gone that I got up nerve to go in and look at the doctor. I guess he was dead then all right. I didn't feel like touching him, so I ran out in the front hall and called the elevator boy and somebody else called the police later on."

Mrs. Edmunds paused in her narrative and dabbed a small, white handkerchief against her nose.

"Does that complete your story, Mrs. Edmunds?" asked Beale.

"Yes, sir," replied the woman.

"You are quite sure, are you, Mrs. Edmunds, that the man you saw in the apartment that night is the defendant in this trial"—he pointed to the Professor—"Alfred Lansdowne, the man sitting over there?"

"Oh, yes, sir."

"And you are sure there were no other visitors that evening?"

"No, sir, there weren't no other visitors that night. Just the Professor."

"And you distinctly saw the defendant standing beside the dead body of Amos Carter, with a heavy metal book-end in his hand?"

"I did sir."

Beale took an object from a nearby table and held it for the witness to see. "Is this the book-end you saw him holding?"

"Yes, sir," said the woman.

"I'm submitting the book-end in evidence, marked people's exhibit A. Thank you very much, Mrs. Edmunds. Cross examine."

During the foregoing testimony there had been a great deal of silent agitation on the part of Norman Howard, who repeatedly leaned over to whisper in Professor Lansdowne's ear. The Professor had shaken his head emphatically each time, and now there was another whispered consultation between them. The scientist said something and the lawyer turned a brick red. He rose to his feet.

"No questions," he announced, in a choked voice.

There was immediately considerable mumbling throughout the audience, necessitating several raps from the gavel to restore quiet. Paula looked at me in agitation.

"Why don't they do something?" she asked, pitifully.

"It's all right," I again assured her. "They'll do plenty when the right time comes." At that moment, I was racking my brains trying to figure out what the Professor's game could be, but I got nowhere. Whatever it was, it was too deep for my comprehension.

IN RAPID SUCCESSION, Beale introduced other witnesses: the elevator boy from Carter's building, who testified that he had taken Professor Lansdowne up to the eighth floor, where Carter's apartment was located, about eight-thirty, and that he had brought him down again about nine-forty-five, at which time the Professor had looked very excited. Next there was the doorman, whose testimony was similar; a tenant in an adjoining flat who had heard loud voices, evidently raised in a quarrel, and then the sound of a falling body.

Supporting the State's contention that Professor Lansdowne had long envied Dr. Carter the favorable reception that several of his discoveries had obtained, Beale produced a neurologist friend of the doctor's who swore that Professor Lansdowne had frequently showed great bitterness at any mention of Carter's success. There was also a young Professor of Eugenics from the university who testified that Paula's father had often spoken unfavorably of Dr. Carter and had once expressed the opinion that Carter's ideas had been stolen from someone else. Under questioning, both witnesses stated that they had long expected an open fight to break out between Professor Lansdowne and the doctor.

In conclusion, Beale presented one of the Professor's own pupils, a young man of nineteen or twenty, who stated that Professor Lansdowne had been well known among the students for his sudden, ungovernable rages. At this last statement, the scientist squirmed nervously in his chair and I could see that he was very angry.

During the questioning, Norman Howard had made further and more *serious* efforts—judging by his perturbed and anxious expression—to convince his client of something the latter refused to accept. There were frequent sotto voce colloquies, after each of which Howard would run his finger along the inside of his collar as though it had become uncomfortably tight. At the same time, his face kept getting redder and redder until I thought he was going to break a blood-vessel.

Both turned to scan the courtroom every now and again. Toward the end of the testimony, Professor Lansdowne seemed to see something that gratified him, for a worried look which had been increasing in intensity died away. Not being sufficiently acquainted with the niceties of legal procedure to know whether or not it was permissible for the prosecution to call the daughter of a defendant to testify against her father I was on pins and needles worrying lest Paula be called to the stand by Beale. When he finished his questioning without summoning her, I felt much easier.

The case for the State had been presented in record time, but before Howard could make any effort to start his defense, Judge Somers called a recess until after lunch. Professor Lansdowne was taken out of the courtroom during the intermission, but Paula and I stayed on to ask Curly Smith how he thought things were going. Whether it was solely on Paula's account, I didn't know, but he was very optimistic.

"The prosecution hasn't got a leg to stand on and they know it," he said. "Which is exactly why Harkness is sic-ing little Bealie-boy onto the job—so he, the big shot, won't get mixed up in a washout. They haven't got a Chinaman's chance of proving first degree murder and they know it. That phony motive of theirs smells to high heaven. The most they can hope for is a commission to an insane asylum, once the Professor gets his case going." I noted he thought Professor Lansdowne was going to attempt to prove insanity and let it got at that. Nor did Paula correct his impression. "Another thing," Curly went on, "did you ever hear of the State getting through their entire case in one morning before? Don't you worry a minute, Miss Lansdowne, it's in the bag!"

An hour later, court was reconvened. After taking his place on the bench, Judge Somers rapped for order and Norman Howard stepped before the bar. He cleared his throat ostentatiously and spoke.

"Your honor," he said, "my client has a very unusual request to make, one of which I scarcely approve, I might add."

"What is the nature of this request?" asked the court.

"Professor Lansdowne wishes permission to conduct his own defense, your honor, without my assistance, except in an advisory capacity."

Judge Somers pursed his lips a moment, and then said:

"I can see no reason for denying this request, if it is your client's preference. Let him proceed."

Howard nodded and, looking at the Professor, gestured vaguely toward the bar. Paula's grip on my hand tightened as her father rose to his feet and changed places with Norman Howard. The Professor is a fine looking man, and he never looked to better advantage than in the courtroom that afternoon. Very shortly he demonstrated that he had other good qualities as well, not the least of which was showmanship.

In a simple and straightforward manner, Professor Lansdowne made his opening remarks. As he did so, Paula and I moved forward to the very edges of our chairs and remained there for the next half-hour.

12

THE DEFENSE RESTS

"YOUR HONOR," BEGAN the Professor in a clear, unhurried voice, "and ladies and gentlemen of the jury: before I begin my defense, I must beg your indulgence. I am not well acquainted with the formalities of court procedure. As a matter of fact, this is the first time in my life I've appeared in a courtroom, except once, years ago, when I was a character witness for a Negro servant of mine who was accused of stealing chickens."

There was a murmur of amusement at this remark and a couple of photographers snapped pictures.

"At that time, my word had sufficient value to help set the defendant free. Today, when I myself am the defendant, I shall need something considerably stronger than my mere word. I believe I do have something a great deal stronger, something that will convince you all that I am not guilty of the murder of Amos Carter.

"Right now I should like to make a statement regarding my attorney, Mr. Norman Howard. Mr. Howard has rendered me most valuable service from the very outset of this unfortunate affair, and my present action in taking over my own defense does not in any way reflect—"

"Your honor," shouted Assistant District Attorney Beale,

"I object to all this beating about the bush. We are not interested in the defendant's remarks concerning anything but the matter in hand—"

"I also object," cried Norman Howard, bristling like a bantam rooster, "but my objection is to the bullying attitude of the prosecutor. My client is merely trying to conduct his defense in his own way—"

"I fail to see that your client has begun his defense as yet," snapped back Beale before Howard could finish, "and furthermore—"

Judge Somers banged his gavel several times with considerable spirit.

"You gentlemen should remember where you are," he said, "and adopt more fitting conduct. The defendant will confine his remarks to this case. Continue."

As the excitement subsided, I heard a stirring in back of me and upon turning around, saw Tom Higgins and District Attorney Harkness come quietly down the aisle and take seats in the middle of the room as unobtrusively as possible. Not knowing whether this was a good or bad sign, I said nothing to Paula.

"I'm sorry, your honor," the Professor was saying, as though nothing had happened, "but I merely wished to make it clear that my present action is not in any way a reflection on the ability of my attorney, Mr. Howard. I will now be glad to get down to brass tacks."

HE PAUSED A moment and turned so that he faced the general audience as well as the jury.

"Mr. Beale has presented his side of this case to you in such a way that I could hardly blame you if you thought I should be sent to the electric chair. First, he has shown you that I struck down and killed Dr. Amos Carter on the night of September 12th. Second, he has established the fact that, immediately before the fatal blow was struck, Dr. Carter and I were quarreling. Third, he has made it clear that no one was in the apartment besides myself and Mrs. Edmunds, except, of course, Dr. Carter himself.

"This evidence is certainly damning. The only thing that surprises me is why Mr. Beale went to so much trouble to establish facts which I have already admitted, and which I freely admit now, all over again. I did go to the apartment of Dr. Amos Carter on the night of September 12th; Dr. Carter and I did argue—I will not admit that we quarreled; as a result of this argument, I did strike down Amos Carter, and that his death was the direct result of this blow cannot be denied. I was Dr. Carter's only visitor that evening, the only person who could possibly have killed him. All that I admit.

"But, ladies and gentlemen, Mr. Beale was not content with my admission of these facts, nor with his presentation of them without certain embellishments. The establishment of these facts I have rehearsed for you would be quite sufficient to send me to prison for life, unless I could prove that I was insane when I killed Dr. Carter, in which case the rest of my days would be spent in a lunatic asylum instead of a penitentiary. Mr. Beale however wished to have me sent to the electric chair, and for this reason he had to add the embellishments I've spoken of.

"Of course, he had to show that the murder was premeditated, that for a long time I plotted to kill Amos Carter. Why? Because I was jealous of the recognition that was accorded to Dr. Carter—recognition, Mr. Beale has indicated, that I never received. He also had one witness testify that I have said unkind things about Dr. Carter, while another witness swore that I've always had a murderous temper.

"Now, ladies and gentlemen, the original facts presented by the prosecutor are true enough; but the embellishments are lies, and I believe I can convince you that they are. For the moment, let us concern ourselves with proving that I am innocent of premeditated murder. Later on we will prove other things, but for the present, this will do nicely. First, let us take the motive that Mr. Beale has unearthed.

"According to him, I have long envied the recognition given Dr. Carter, recognition which I myself have never received. Let me read you an excerpt from the Boston *Courier,* dated June 4th, 1936. I quote: 'At its final meeting in the Park-Tremont Hotel this afternoon, the American Society of Psychiatrists and Neurologists elected as its president Professor Alfred Lansdowne by an overwhelming vote of 316 to 84, defeating the only other contestant, Dr. Amos Carter.' End of quotation. May I offer this in evidence, your honor?"

Judge Somers nodded and indicated that Professor Lansdowne should give the clipping to the clerk.

"Another quotation, ladies and gentlemen," continued the scientist, "this time from the New York *Morning Record,* dated December 19th, 1934—about eighteen months before the Boston incident occurred. Quote: 'Dr. Carter's theory on the transference of shock from the conscious to the subconscious mind was actively attacked by his colleagues until Professor Alfred Lansdowne came to his aid. Shortly after the Professor's speech in support of his friend, the College did an about face and showered plaudits on Carter.' Unquote. I might add that this article refers to a session of the New York College of Psychical Research. I will also submit this clipping in evidence.

"Ladies and gentlemen of the jury, does that sound like the act of an envious man?"

Professor Lansdowne walked over to the table where Norman Howard was sitting and picked up two rolled parchments. Then, returning to his previous position before the jury, he said:

"I regret that this display of egotism and conceit is necessary to this emergency. However, here is further proof that Mr. Beale's charge that I envied Dr. Carter his scientific achievements is a lie."

Professor Lansdowne unrolled one piece of parchment. "This, ladies and gentlemen," he said, "is a certificate stating that I have been awarded the Lawrence Prize for Psychical Research. This other," he unrolled the second, "states that one Alfred Lansdowne has been given an award for the most outstanding contribution to psychiatry in the past five years. It is dated this year.

"If you will excuse me, I believe these represent the highest recognition an American psychologist can receive. I regret the necessity of adding that Amos Carter never received any such recognition. I can't imagine where Mr. Beale developed this particular approach."

There was a ripple of laughter at the feint and Beale looked uncomfortable.

"Another thing that puzzles me is what inducement could have been offered Dr. Rutherford to testify that I had indicated to him that I felt bitterly towards Dr. Carter." I remembered that Rutherford was the young neurologist who had testified. "The best evidence I can give to the contrary"—Professor Lansdowne dug in an inside pocket and brought forth a small batch of papers—"is this. I have here perhaps twenty or twenty-five promissory notes of Dr. Carter's, all of them made out to me. They are dated all the way from 1920 to the present time. They total in the neighborhood of four thousand, eight hundred dollars. There has never been a payment made on any of them, and there has never been a suit filed by me. I believe there can be no question about a friendship which stands a strain on the pocketbook."

AS PROFESSOR LANSDOWNE handed the notes to the clerk Beale got to his feet. "I object," he said, "to the statement made by the defendant hinting at the bribing of witnesses by the State."

"And I"—Howard sprang upright—"object to the objection. Why didn't the learned Assistant District Attorney make his objection at the proper time, when the remark was made?"

"Why I—I—" stammered the confused Beale. Judge Somers banged his gavel again.

"Prosecution's objection sustained. Defense's overruled. The defendant should make no statements pertaining to the suborning of witnesses which he is not prepared to prove here and now."

"I withdraw the remark about Dr. Rutherford," said Professor Lansdowne. "I only meant to indicate that he was influenced by other factors than a simple desire for truth."

"I object!" flamed Beale all over again. "Your honor, I ask that you find the defendant in contempt of court. More-

over, I want to object to the manner in which the defense
is being conducted. There has been altogether too much
wandering and—"

"I object to the Assistant District Attorney's uncalled-
for statement!" Norman Howard was flying off now. For
a minute it looked like an old-fashioned free-for-all until
order was once more established. Professor Lansdowne
was reprimanded and warned and the trial proceeded.

"There is just one more embellishment I would like to
mention before getting down to the more serious aspects
of this case," said Professor Lansdowne, "and that is the
statement by one of my own pupils that I am noted for my
fearful temper. I don't have it with me at the moment, but
if necessary I can produce proof that that particular young
man is decidedly prejudiced. This proof would be in the
form of his scholastic record, which would show that he
has failed my course three successive times and that he was
once reported by me for public drunkenness. If the Assistant District Attorney cares to object to this statement as
it stands, I can have proof here within one hour of everything I have just said."

There was no objection.

"I believe any temper I may have shown to this young
man was entirely justified under the circumstances, and I
believe you agree with me."

Paula looked at me questioningly as her father hesitated
before continuing. I squeezed her hand encouragingly
and said: "Don't worry, darling, your dad's doing swell!" I
meant it, too.

"Now, ladies and gentlemen, that we have disposed of
the possibility of my having plotted to kill Amos Carter—

thus removing the premeditation factor in this case—let us consider the deed itself. Considering that I had known Dr. Carter for so many years, and that I had liked him well enough to lend him more money than I could well afford to lend, doesn't it seem surprising that I should have been willing to kill him over a petty, everyday disagreement? Mr. Beale has said that we quarreled that night. If we did, then it was the same kind of a quarrel we had nearly every time we met in the past twenty years. Amos Carter and I had disagreed on a great many of our respective theories, and such disagreement never before led to anything like bloodshed.

"Since this is true—and it can be proved—doesn't it seem strange that, as the result of an argument no stronger than all the others, I should suddenly become angry enough to kill a man for whom I had the deepest admiration and affection?

"Wouldn't this strike you as an indication that something was very much wrong with my mind—insanity, perhaps—a subject the prosecutor has been careful to ignore? Mr. Howard, my attorney, told me he could easily save my neck by pleading me not guilty by reason of insanity, and I have no cause to doubt him. But, my friends, it was *not* insanity. Something equally strong, but not insanity.

"Yet, we have already seen that I had no sane motive for wishing Amos Carter dead. Why, then, did I kill him?"

AS PROFESSOR LANSDOWNE waited a moment after asking this question, you could have heard a pin drop in any part of that courtroom.

"I killed Amos Carter," he went on, "for only one

reason—because I couldn't help myself; because I suddenly felt a tremendous, irresistible, murderous impulse to strike him down, an impulse so strong that my will power was unequal to the task of restraining it. But this was not insanity. I was not insane then; I am not insane now, and no alienist in the world can prove otherwise. My case was not one of insanity, but of a different, a new, a terrifying thing—a thing that had occurred before in New York City, has occurred since, and will occur again—God knows how many times, or at what cost!

"As I sat there with Amos Carter, I became the helpless victim of an alien will, a will so powerful as to make me utterly impotent before it. This will bade me to kill—and I killed. Whatever else it had told me to do, I would have done—just as others in this city have done its bidding, without thought, without resistance, even to the extreme of causing their own deaths."

By now, even Beale himself was listening tensely, his mouth hanging half open.

"If I could not prove this apparently fantastic statement, there would be every reason for you to consider me mad, after all. But I can prove it—I can prove that others have experienced the same enslavement of will that made me kill my friend. To this purpose, I ask the bailiff to call my first witness, Frank Wiggins, to the stand."

As the court official called out the name, a slight figure in unobtrusive gray walked down the aisle and entered the enclosure before the bar. He was led to the witness chair and sworn. Professor Lansdowne stood before him.

"Tell me, Mr. Wiggins," he began, "what was your profession until recently?"

"I was a motorman on the Sixth Avenue 'L.'"

"How long had you held that position?"

"About fifteen years."

"How did you happen to lose it?"

"I was fired for running through a block signal and smashing my train into the one that was ahead of me."

"How did you happen to do such a thing?"

"I don't know, sir. All I know is, something come over me. I was sitting there when the signal changed to red, and all of a sudden I just felt like I had to run through that light."

"So you did?"

"Yes, sir."

"Did you stop to think that you were endangering the lives of hundreds of people?"

"No, sir, not at the time. All I thought of was running through that block."

"Now," said the Professor, "think carefully. Were you ever afflicted by any such impulse before, during the fifteen years you were an elevated railway motorman?"

"No, sir. Not ever."

"Did you ever have spells, during which you were out of your mind, or fits of any kind?"

"Oh, no, sir."

"Were you given a sanity test immediately after the accident by physicians acting under orders of your employers?"

"Yes, sir, I was."

"And what did they find?"

"They didn't find nothing wrong with me."

"Have you ever been able to account for this thing that

happened to you, this sudden impulse to run through a safety signal?"

"No, sir, I haven't."

"Was this affair in the papers at the time it occurred?"

"Yes, sir. In all of 'em."

"Do you happen to have any clipping with you, one that mentions your name?"

"Yes, I have, sir."

"Will you lend it to me for the time being?"

The man reached into his coat pocket and from a battered wallet withdrew a small newspaper clipping which he handed the Professor.

"Your honor," said that gentleman, "I should like to offer this in evidence." Then, turning back to the witness: "Just one thing more, Mr. Wiggins. How do you happen to be here in court today?"

"I was subpoened."

"Thank you very much. That will be all, unless Mr. Beale has some questions to ask you."

Beale had no questions, but again objected to proceedings, this time on the grounds that the testimony of Wiggins was irrelevant, immaterial and without bearing on the case.

"I assure your honor," said the Professor in reply, "that the testimony you have just heard, and all that I will present, has the strongest possible bearing on this case."

"Very well, then. Objection overruled. Proceed."

PROFESSOR LANSDOWNE NEXT called to the stand Edward J. Walker, the stock broker. With a few rapid questions, he quickly established the fact that Walker had given $10,000 in cash to a perfect stranger for no better reason than that he had an overwhelming desire to do so. Next, Walker's private secretary, an angular woman who had been in his service for eight years, testified that in her long experience with Walker, she had never known him to exercise anything but perfect judgment in his financial transactions. A psychiatrist who had examined Walker a short time after the Professor had, testified that Walker showed no signs of insanity.

Although I might have expected it, I was nonetheless shocked to hear the next name called out by the bailiff:

"Patrick O'Hara!"

Instantly, every head in the courtroom swung around to the double doors at the rear of the chamber. The appearance of the man who now entered was familiar to all, but his shuffling gait and shifty eyes were new. As he made his way toward the witness chair with hesitant, uncertain mien, it was all too clear that recent events had taken a terrible toll on Mayor O'Hara. His hand trembled violently as he held it up for the oath, and his "I do" was shaky.

"Mr. Mayor," his inquisitor began, "do you recall the meeting of the Board of Estimate and Apportionment which was held at the City Hall on the afternoon of September 13th, and at which you presided as chairman?"

"I do."

"Do you have any reason to remember that particular meeting?"

"Yes."

"Then please tell us what the reason is, Mr. Mayor."

"It was at that meeting that it—that it happened."

"That what happened, Mr. Mayor?" prompted the Professor.

"That I talked—like I did."

Murmuring rose in the audience until the judge had to rap for silence.

"Will you please describe, briefly, how you talked?"

Mayor O'Hara passed a trembling hand across his mouth. He seemed to be striving for self-control.

"I talked for—for Dr. Skull." Now the words came out quickly, tumbling over each other as though the man were anxious to get the ordeal over with. "Where he said that we would have to give him control of the city, or—something horrible would happen. There were a lot of other things. It was terrible—awful. I haven't slept—"

Beale sprang to his feet. "Your honor!" he shouted. "Please! I protest this line of questioning. This is not an investigation into the activities of that maniac, Skull. We've been very patient, but this is too much. Besides, it's only too apparent that the Mayor is not well enough to testify!"

"If your honor please!" It was Professor Lansdowne. "This testimony of Mayor O'Hara is the most vital part of my defense. If the court will let me proceed, that fact will be most obvious in just a few moments."

Judge Somers looked undecided. He turned to the witness.

"Mr. Mayor," he said, "are you sure that you feel equal to this testimony? I can see that it's a strain on you. Perhaps a recess until tomorrow—"

But O'Hara raised a negative hand. "No, thank you, Judge Somers," he said. "I'm really quite all right. I've been under pressure—under considerable pressure. But I'm perfectly all right. Please let me get it over with now."

The Judge nodded to Professor Lansdowne to go ahead, whereupon the latter continued with his questions.

"Mr. Mayor, how did you happen to make these strange remarks, pertaining, I understand, to come from a certain Dr. Skull who is at present attempting to terrorize this city?"

"Oh, please don't ask me that. I don't know. I've been trying to figure it out ever since."

"Well, then, how did it seem at the time?"

"I don't know. The words came to me and I had to say them. I couldn't have stopped them if I'd wanted to."

Professor Lansdowne stepped close to the Mayor. "Did anything like this ever happen to you before, at any time in your life?"

"Never—never."

"Were you examined by alienists immediately after the meeting in question, that is, within the next twelve to twenty-four hours?"

"Yes, they examined me."

"And did they find any indication of insanity?"

"They told me there was nothing wrong with me that they could see."

"Then, Mr. Mayor, since you did not say these things of your own volition, and since experts concluded that there was no psychic disturbance responsible, have you yourself arrived at any explanation of your conduct?"

"Yes."

The monosyllable was so low it was necessary for me to strain my ears to hear it.

"How do you explain it?"

"It—it was *him!*" the Mayor said in a low, tense voice. "It

was him—Dr. Skull. He made me say what I did. I know
it, and everybody else knows it but they're afraid to say it!
They tell me I was upset. Well, they're going to be upset.
It was Dr. Skull, I tell you—Dr. Skull! That's who it was!"

At these last shrill words, the Mayor half rose in the
witness chair, his face congested with terror, and at the
same time the courtroom became a bedlam of noise that
the pounding gavel was helpless to still. I saw District
Attorney Harkness rush into the enclosure and confer
with his assistant in tones that could not reach my ears
above the general confusion. Now, several policemen threw
themselves into the welter of sound, running up and down
the aisles, ejecting the noisiest, quieting others with less
vigor, and gradually bringing about a semblance of order.

"Thank you, Mr. Mayor, that is all I wish to know." With
the Professor's words there was absolute stillness again.
"Your honor, ladies and gentlemen of the jury, the defense
rests."

THE MAYOR, FOR all his bulk a wilted, pathetic figure,
had to be assisted from the chair. Apparently acting on
orders from his superior, Beale waived cross-examination,
but launched into a shambling, unassured summing up of
the prosecution's case. After rehearsing the evidence which
showed that Professor Lansdowne's hand had administered the death blow to Amos Carter, he next attacked the
Professor's surprise witnesses as an attempt on the part of
the defendant to trade, on fear and superstition to save his
neck. He warned the jurors against permitting themselves
to be engulfed in a tide of popular panic to the extent that
they would attribute supernatural qualities to what was
nothing more than "plain, premeditated, brutal murder."

Beale went on to accuse Professor Lansdowne of trying to play for sympathy by conducting his own defense. There was quite a bit more, and Paula's face, which had taken on a more confident expression, became anxious once more. Beale finished with an appeal to the jurors' Americanism to send Professor Lansdowne to the electric chair, and returned to his table.

The scientist then took the prosecutor's former position before the jury box. While Paula and I said a silent prayer and everyone in the courtroom listened expectantly, he began his final plea.

"Ladies and gentlemen of the jury," he said, "Mr. Beale has once more reminded you that I killed Amos Carter. He has refused to recognize this fact—the fact that the real question in this trial is not, 'Did Alfred Lansdowne kill Amos Carter?' but, 'Is Alfred Lansdowne guilty of the murder of Amos Carter?'

"The answer to that question, my friends, is 'No.' The prosecution has been unable to prove that I hated Amos Carter, but I have proved, by producing uncollected notes totalling thousands of dollars, that I was Amos Carter's friend. The prosecution has been unable to prove that there was a motive behind the death of Amos Carter; I have proved that there could have been no motive. If the prosecution has produced one witness—a witness who is by no means unbiased—to swear that I have a vile and murderous temper, I could produce a hundred who would swear that this witness perjured himself for reasons of personal hatred of me, and that I have always been noted for my extreme mildness of disposition. But I can see by your faces that such a waste of time would be unnecessary.

"The prosecutor in the case has warned you not to be swayed by the four witnesses I produced, witnesses who gave evidence of a new danger which is threatening all of us. You have been warned not to give way to superstition, to remember, in effect, that this is the 20th Century. Well, ladies and gentlemen, I warn you not to close your eyes to facts; do not be blind to a menace that is as real as death itself—however fantastic it may seem.

"Until now, every effort has been made to belittle the activities of a man who possesses strange powers, powers that may wreak havoc on countless thousands of innocent people unless he is stopped. The time for such dissembling is past. Today, we must face facts. We must face them and conquer them, or be conquered by them.

"You all read the papers. You have all followed everything that this creature who calls himself Dr. Skull has done. You know the threats he has made. You should know that, so far, he has made all of them good. I do not here attempt to explain the peculiar power this man has, but it is only too obvious that it is a power to control the minds of others in a way that has never before been thought of; a power to make them do *his* bidding, whatever that bidding may be.

"I have called four witnesses, three of whom have had personal contact with this power. If it were possible, I would call two more. If they could be here, they, too, would testify that a tremendous force gripped their wills and forced them to do things they would never have done without the rout of their own self-control—a force so tremendous that it compelled them to take their own lives. Yes, these absent witnesses would swear that men can do strange, unbelievable, criminal acts, and yet be sane—yet be innocent of any crime.

"The absent witnesses I have in mind are J. Homer Warren, and Matt Fraser—the man who drove the car in which he, three of his comrades, and Police Commissioner Michael Gallagher plunged to their deaths."

Professor Lansdowne paused and let the silence emphasize his last words.

"Ladies and gentlemen," he said, after a moment, "believe me when I say that the man who calls himself Dr. Skull is responsible for all this. The strange speech of Mayor O'Hara, the deaths of Warren and Commissioner Gallagher and his men were the main attractions of a show created by Skull to put fear in the hearts of the people. This show, however, was not put on without rehearsal. Before he staged his important scenes, Skull first tried his terrible tricks on Wiggins, the elevated motorman; on Walker, the broker; and on me, Alfred Lansdowne. When he had tested his supernormal mentality, when he had proved his power on smaller fry, then—and not until then—he stepped into the limelight. The Mayor's speech, the death of J. Homer Warren, and the death of Commissioner Gallagher and his companions were direct results.

"You do not hold Mayor O'Hara responsible for his inexplicable behavior. You do not hold Warren responsible for his own death. You do not blame the driver of the Commissioner's car for the tragedy which occurred. By the same rule, ladies and gentlemen, you must not, you cannot find me guilty of a crime which, so help me God, I did not commit—the murder of a friend whom I held in the greatest affection and esteem.

"I place my fate in your keeping, confident that you will not bring down punishment on an innocent man. Rather, I believe in my heart you will set me free so that we may all unite in a death struggle with the creature really responsible for all this evil, the creature who even now has placed us all under the shadow of his threat—Dr. Skull. I have nothing else to say."

With these final words, the courage of Professor Lansdowne and his strength as well must have run nearly dry, for, as he walked slowly to the chair which Norman Howard held out for him, he wavered in his step. His plea had been received by jury and audience alike in utter stillness.

THE SILENCE WAS broken when the foreman of the jury stood up. In his hand was a small sheet of paper. "Your honor," he said, "we won't need to deliberate. We've heard enough and have already reached our verdict. We find the defendant—"

The pounding gavel broke into his speech.

"The foreman of the jury will kindly make no statement at the present time," ordered Judge Somers, clearly angry. "Never, in my sixteen years on the bench, have I witnessed such astounding behavior. It is the duty of a jury to wait until both sides have made their final plea, and the prosecution has not yet made its rebuttal."

"But your honor," insisted the foreman anxiously, "right after we listened to the Mayor, we reached an agreement. The Professor isn't to blame, it's Skull. We don't want to waste any more time—"

"Silence!" thundered the judge. "Silence! If there is any further interruption of these proceedings I shall discharge the jury, declare a mistrial, and find the first person who speaks in contempt of court!"

There were now disturbances in the audience again, an indignant muttering that started as the Judge began to speak and rose higher when he finished.

"Let him go!" shouted a man.

"Why don't you try Skull?" jeered another.

As half a dozen policemen flung themselves into the by now thoroughly inflamed crowd and tried vainly to subdue the rising chaos, a chorus of catcalls, hisses and boos burst out. Judge Somers continued to pound the gavel, but it couldn't even be heard. His face was fairly purple with rage and I feared that he might be on the verge of apoplexy. Adding to the tumult, several photographers were setting off flash-bulbs for their pictures.

Unexpectedly, it was District Attorney Harkness who was finally able to command attention. He stood before the bench, his arms raised above his head, shouting to make himself heard. The crowd understood that he had something to say and, suddenly docile, they listened.

"Your honor," said Harkness, "the State feels, in view of recent evidence, that it is its duty to ask for a dismissal of the charges against Professor Lansdowne."

"What!" demanded Judge Somers. "You mean to—"

Anything else he may have uttered was lost in the instantaneous wave of cheering that broke out. Paula and I were over the railing with our arms around the Professor almost as soon as the District Attorney had finished speaking, and we found ourselves the center of a friendly but nonetheless crushing mob of people, all of whom wanted to shake hands with the Professor. For at least five minutes, that courtroom was a madhouse. Then police reserves arrived on the scene and quickly cleared it entirely of spectators, leaving only the principals in the case, the reporters, Paula and myself.

Harkness had been conferring with the Judge, and now stepped down from the bench. This time, when Judge Somers struck the gavel it was very loud.

"The prosecution having withdrawn its charge," he announced, "the case of the People of the State of New York versus Alfred Lansdowne is hereby dismissed. May I add that this is the most astounding day I have ever spent in a so-called court of law!"

"Most extraordinary, most extraordinary, to say the very least," mused Norman Howard, neatly gathering together his numerous papers. He now seemed so inoffensive that I wondered what I ever could have disliked about him.

The District Attorney approached Professor Lansdowne, Tom Higgins at his side. Introducing himself, he said:

"Professor, no one knows more than yourself the unusual circumstances of this case. If we hadn't all been working altogether in the dark, you might have been spared a great deal of suffering."

Professor Lansdowne merely smiled.

"I'm too thankful for what has just happened to speak very clearly, but any discomfort I may have experienced will be more than worth while if all this brings you any closer to getting the real murderer."

Harkness made an appropriate reply and moved away. Paula and I tried to extricate the scientist from a determined group of reporters, but with slight success. The newshawks, Curly Smith among them, followed us up the aisle, along the outer corridor, down in the elevator and into the street. There we shook them by ducking inside a convenient taxi. All the long way home, only two remarks were made, and both came from the Professor.

"I wonder what happened to Norman," he said, after we'd been riding a while. The little lawyer had gotten himself lost in the shuffle and there'd been no chance to exchange felicitations with him.

The second remark was made as we turned the corner at 72nd Street and sped north along the Drive. Professor Lansdowne took a deep breath of the cool, damp air.

"That's good," he sighed, "good. Now that it's over, I can admit it just between the three of us. I was badly scared when I first went into that courtroom this morning."

Neither of us had any response to make, but Paula clung to him more tightly than before.

WHEN WE ENTERED the apartment, Martha, the Lansdowne maid, heaped moist congratulations upon her employer. Finally collecting herself, she started off to mix some cocktails, then stopped and went over to a small table by the front door.

"Oh, Miss Paula," she said, "I nearly forgot. This came for you a few minutes ago. I was so excited I nearly forgot to tell you about it." She held out a small box, wrapped in cellophane and tied with a white silk ribbon.

"Why, it looks like flowers!" exclaimed Paula. "Bob, what do you know about this?"

I knew nothing and said so, tartly enough, I expect. It didn't soothe me to think that another man was sending Paula flowers.

Smiling and eager, she untied the ribbon and tore off the wrappings. As she opened the box itself, her expression changed from one of pleasurable anticipation to curiosity.

"It's a rose," she said softly, "but what a beautiful rose!"

She took it from the box and even I, who care little for flowers, was impressed. It was large, fully opened, and a peculiar deep crimson against the delicate green of fern the florist had used for background. Even before I raised my eyes from the flower, I felt that Paula had become very tense. When I looked at her, she was deathly pale. Her right hand still held the rose and her left the box in which it had come, but the latter now fell to the floor from nerveless fingers.

"Paula!" I cried sharply. "Are you ill?" She shook her head.

"In the box," she whispered. "The note."

Professor Lansdowne swooped down on the box before I could get to it. When he stood upright a small piece of notepaper was in his hand. Automatically, I noticed that the stationery was the color of ivory and that there was the letter *S* in gold at the top of the page. The message was written in a clear, delicate longhand, the kind which in days past was called Spencerian.

"My Dear Miss Lansdowne," it read, "please accept this rose, the most perfect I could find, that it may see a beauty greater than its own and blush the deeper at a rival so triumphant. It comes from one whose admiration for you is equalled only by his impatience to prove himself worthy of so exquisite a woman by demonstrating his own superiority to ordinary men. You will not wait long for the first proof.

"Meanwhile, will you not think kindly of my suit and

extend to your distinguished father my congratulations for the cleverness with which he carried the day in court? He is a man deserving of more worthy opponents."

That was the message. The signature—Dr. Skull.

13

SPEAK OF THE DEAD

"WELL," SAID PAULA, weakly, "it looks like I'm elected to a very dubious position, to say the least."

"It does bring things rather close to home again, doesn't it?" remarked the Professor, conversationally.

"What are we going to do about it?" was what I wanted to know. If the others were not, I was very much frightened for Paula and in no mood to treat the matter lightly.

"I'm afraid there isn't much we can do," answered Professor Lansdowne. "I'm not sure but what we may consider ourselves fortunate, for the time being, that is. Perhaps this will give us immunity from the calamities Dr. Skull is visiting on people with less attractive daughters."

Paula shuddered and I began getting angry at the Professor for taking what appeared to be a casual attitude about the girl's danger. I exclaimed, "Let's not stand around making clever conversation! We've got to do something to protect Paula."

Professor Lansdowne regarded me quizzically.

"Protect Paula? For the present, my dear young man, she's in less need of protection than anyone I know."

"How can you say that?" My temper was getting the best of me. "How do you know that blithering moron won't try to kidnap her? Why wouldn't he? He knows damned well none of us or the police either—the police least of all—can do anything to stop him. Think what that means!"

"I assure you, Bob, I'm thinking about what everything means, very seriously. But at the same time, I feel absolutely certain that no harm will come to Paula through Skull, not now. Read that note over again. Before he intends to claim Paula, he means to prove that he's worthy of her. In other words, he's going to murder a few more people, can't you see? And after he does that I'm sure Paula will get another message. Besides, I can think of nothing we can do to protect her, except perhaps to spirit her out of the country."

"Let's do that, then," I said heartily. But the Professor shook his head.

"Seriously, I doubt if even that would be effective. It's quite possible that Skull is having Paula watched. If we make any sudden move, it may force him to take quick action that might prove far more dangerous than for us to bide our time and wait."

"Wait?" I demanded. "For what?"

"For a chance to fight back, Bob," said Professor Lansdowne soberly. "At the moment our hands are quite tied."

"Oh, Dad, I don't like this!" Paula's face was white and I could see she was having trouble keeping calm. Small wonder! Never in my life had I, for one, felt so utterly helpless and hopeless. As time went on this feeling was, alas, to become more and more common.

As we stood there, the doorbell rang. All three of us started.

"Do you think—" I began unsteadily.

"At the front door?" asked Professor Lansdowne, in turn. "Hardly. Wait a moment and I'll go see."

When he swung open the portal, we saw District Attorney Harkness and Tom Higgins standing outside.

"Good evening, Professor," said the former. "I realize this visit must be a surprise, but I'd like very much to have a talk with you. May we come in?"

"Certainly, certainly!" replied the scientist, cordially. IN A VERY short time, we were all grouped around the fireplace—the day was unseasonably chilly—with cocktails in our hands.

"Professor Lansdowne," commenced the District Attorney, "before the death of Commissioner Gallagher, you gave him the benefit of your advice in this Skull affair. The manner of his death seems to have borne out certain explanations which you advanced before the accident. Higgins here has passed the information along to me, feeling that to do so under the circumstances would not be a breach of your confidence."

"Of course," nodded the Professor.

"In addition to this," went on Harkness, "certain statements you made at the trial today, together with the facts you brought out, have convinced me that we are very much in need of all the help you can give us. I've come here to ask for your cooperation. With the trial out of the way, there should be no further obstacles. What do you say?"

"I'll be glad to give whatever help it is possible for me to give," replied Professor Lansdowne, slowly. "Right now though, I'm afraid it would be negligible."

District Attorney Harkness sipped thoughtfully at his Martini. "We're all worth practically nothing just now," he

*When I saw the box my throat contracted
with fear. "Let me have it," I said.*

said, "but we've got to find some way of licking this thing. Our very first problem is a tough one, too. As you know, Skull has threatened to bring about a serious disaster unless the city authorities show signs of meeting his ridiculous demands. Naturally, that's out of the question, so we must prepare to take whatever consequences the maniac has in mind. Unless, of course, we can find a way of forestalling them. Which brings up the first question I want to ask you. Have you any idea in what way Skull will bring about this—calamity?"

"I have an idea, yes. No more than that."

"And that is?"

"I think he'll arrange an accident that will kill a comparatively large number of people. Dynamite a building perhaps, or rather, make someone else dynamite it."

The District Attorney gazed reflectively into the fire. Paula, Tom Higgins and I looked on in silence.

"As bad as that, eh?" mused the official. Then, "You

believe that Skull operates through the use of occult knowledge gained in the East, do you not, Professor?"

"I don't merely believe it. That much I know."

"Isn't there some way by which this power—hypnotism, isn't it?—can be checkmated?"

"At the present, I'm unable to suggest a positive way, and I can do nothing in any case until Skull has been located."

"We've been trying to find him through the description you furnished Higgins," said Harkness, "but we've drawn nothing but blanks."

"That's hardly surprising," remarked the scientist, "for at least two reasons. First, Skull is necessarily a clever man. Second, the description is both incomplete and out of date. As yet there's no tangible proof that my identification of him is correct, although I firmly believe it is."

District Attorney Harkness lit a cigarette and settled back in his chair. "Until we have proof to the contrary we'll assume you're right. We've certainly had no other suggestions worth bothering with. Now, getting back to our problem. Can you think of any precaution we can take to prevent trouble?"

"I know of none, except for you to temporize with Skull. We must try to maneuver him into the open, you know. If public opinion stands in the way of open negotiation—and I can very well understand it would—can't you manage secretly?"

The D.A. shook his hand. "Not a chance. I don't have the absolute authority necessary and by the time I brought in O'Hara and the rest of the boys, it would be on every front page in town."

For the next fifteen or twenty minutes, Harkness and

the Professor discussed every aspect of the case. A dozen plans were brought up by the District Attorney ranging all the way from sending out a general alarm and arresting everyone answering the 20-year-old description of Franz Ehrlich to calling in Department of Justice operatives and the National Guard. All of them were dismissed by the scientist as futile.

"We can do nothing at present but wait for Skull to make a false move," he pointed out. "Arrest all suspicious looking characters, certainly. But Skull won't be among them, I feel sure. I tremble to think how many lives our complete lack of power may cost, but I can find no way to prevent it. We must wait… wait…"

Then Professor Lansdowne did something which surprised me. He produced the note sent by Dr. Skull to Paula. Harkness gave a low whistle.

"We'll put a stop to this, at any rate," he said. "Higgins, get on the phone and have Mulvaney send two men up here to guard Miss Lansdowne. Have him arrange for a relief every six hours, night and day. Snap into it, now!"

Tom was already looking around for the telephone when the Professor held up a restraining hand.

"If you please, Mr. Harkness," he said, "don't send for any policemen. Their presence might serve as an inducement for Skull to attempt something sensational, and, believe me, neither two nor two hundred of your men would save my daughter if he intends her any harm."

"Professor Lansdowne is right," I cut in. "You know what good it did to surround Warren and Gallagher with bodyguards."

"What do you want me to do then?" The D.A. looked questioningly at Professor Lansdowne.

"As far as Paula is concerned, nothing. And please don't mention this note to anyone. I merely wanted you to know about it, so that if we need your help later, you'll understand the situation."

As the dialogue between the two men continued, the clock struck six.

AT TWELVE MINUTES past six, a ten-car express train left the subway station at Times Square. Packed to the doors with hundreds of homebound office workers and shoppers, it picked up speed and roared off toward the next stop, 72nd Street and Broadway. As it was an express, it flashed past stations at 50th, 59th, and 66th Streets on the inside track without occasioning any notice from passengers or the guards stationed at the doors. The usual speed of trains along this run is about 35 miles per hour. Two of the guards later estimated that they were travelling in excess of 45 miles an hour when they passed 66th Street, but both thought, at the time, that the motorman was merely trying to catch up with his schedule.

There is a long, easy curve as the tracks enter the 72nd Street station, and trains invariably slow down upon hitting it. But this one did not. Passengers who were hanging onto straps were thrown against those seated on the left side of the train, violently enough for many to have their first fears that something was wrong. A moment later, all but a few *knew* something was wrong. The express, without slackening pace, swept past the station. Several people waiting on the edge of the platform to board the cars were very nearly sucked against the side of the train by the powerful wind its speed created.

On the train itself, passengers who wished to get off at 72nd Street raised their voices in angry protest at the motorman's failure to stop. Guards, realizing that something serious must have happened, began working their way toward the front car. This was a process that took several minutes, since the aisles were effectively blocked by standees and the nearest guard was the whole length of a car from the motorman. Meanwhile the speed had increased steadily.

The cars now began rocking violently from side to side and the wheels shrieked against the curve of the rails. The anger of the passengers quickly gave way to alarm, and alarm to panic. The train was running wild. There were frantic cries of "Help!" and "Stop the train!" It was fearful.

The guard stationed in the forward car had reached the motorman's booth. Since there is no exact account of what occurred then—it has been determined that the express had probably reached the 86th Street station at that time—we can only surmise what took place. The guard must have opened the door to the motorman's compartment, for his body was found—and identified with considerable difficulty—next to the battered remains of the motorman. It is logical to suppose that he demanded to know what was wrong. One passenger, before he died, said he believed there was a struggle between motorman and guard, but was not positive. Only the guard from the very first car ever reached the motorman, and only one other guard reached the forward car. A woman and two men who survived the wreck told police that two and possibly three red signals

had been ignored—warnings that the track ahead was not
clear. The last one, they remembered, was located about a
hundred feet from the platform at the 96th Street station.

As the wild express careened into the station, it had
a speed of somewhat more than 50 miles per hour. The
controls were advanced as far as possible, and there could
have been no attempt to apply the brakes. The brass lever
used to set them was detached from the connecting rod and
was later found still clutched in the hand of the motorman,
who may have used it to beat off the guard.

Another train was standing at the platform. Its doors
had been closed and in another second or two it would
have started, but that wouldn't have made much difference. As it was, the speeding express ploughed into it with
a deafening crash and the scrape and grind of crumpling
steel. The sound of that terrible collision could be heard on
the surface all the way from 86th to 103rd Streets along
Broadway. The comparative silence which followed was
instantly split with the screams of maimed and dying, the
hissing of compressed air, and the horrified cries of people
on the platform.

The cars on both trains were of steel, and how much
greater the loss of life would have been if the cars were
wooden can be fairly well imagined by recalling accidents
involving such death traps. As it was, the destruction was
horrible. The two cars which had borne the first force of
the smash were nothing but twisted masses of steel and
crushed human flesh. The bodies of the guard and the
motorman previously mentioned were identified only
by their clothing when, an hour later, firemen and rescue

squads succeeded in cutting their way through the wreck-
age.

The collision took place at 6:18.

IT WAS 6:15 when the telephone in the Lansdowne apartment rang. The maid answered it, and came in the living
room and announced that a gentleman wished to speak to
Mr. Harkness.

"Excuse me, please," said the District Attorney, rising.
"I left word at my office that I could be reached here if
anything important came up."

It is an impolite thing to eavesdrop on another person's
telephone conversation, yet it is remarkable how frequently
a silence falls over a group of people when one of its
members is talking over the phone. In our case, perhaps it
was because the ringing of a bell or a knock on the door
might mean so much that we all fell perfectly silent as
Harkness, in an adjoining room, said, "Hello!"

"Yes," he went on, "this is the District Attorney...
Who?... Who?" An explosive sound followed the last
word, then there was a sharp call. "Higgins!"

Instantly, Tom was on his feet and at the D.A.'s side.
Paula, the Professor and I looked at each other in surprise.
The next words we heard were low, and sounded like,
"Quick trace this call!" That must have been correct
because Tom came running back into the room.

"Where's another outside line?" he demanded.

"In the next apartment or downstairs at the desk," said
Paula quickly. Without further explanation, Tom dashed
out the door.

"I can't understand you," came Harkness' voice from the

library. "Would you mind repeating that please? Would you— Hello! Hello!"

There was a brief but comprehensive bit of swearing, then a jiggling of the phone.

"Operator, this is the police. Trace that last call, quick, will you?… Confound it, I know the other party hung up. What the hell do you think… What?… All right, all right. Get busy and call me back. The number? What number? Don't you know anything?… Cathedral 8-6433…. Right. Please hurry!"

The receiver clicked into place. When Harkness did not appear, Professor Lansdowne and I exchanged glances. Without a word, we both rose and went to the library door. Inside, seated at the telephone, was the District Attorney. He was nervously biting his nails.

"Is anything wrong, Mr. Harkness?" asked the Professor, quietly.

Harkness started at the sound, and looked up. His face was ashen and he had to clear his throat before he could speak. When he did, his voice was little more than a whisper.

"I think so," he replied. "I've just been talking to Dr. Skull."

14

SKULL'S AMBASSADOR

QUICK INTERCESSION ON the part of the police toned down the press' report of the subway disaster to some extent, but the facts themselves—49 dead, over 100 severe injuries, a similar number of lesser ones—spoke eloquently. Nor could any degree of censorship keep from the mass of people one spine-chilling certainty—the wreck was caused by Dr. Skull. The man who had already brought about so much death had struck with infinitely greater strength, and the police, all the forces of law and order were powerless to stop him. What he would do next, he alone knew, but there could be no question that it would be terrible.

The morning after the accident, I again discussed with Professor Lansdowne the advisability of leaving town until Skull was brought to justice, but the scientist was convinced that such a move would only hasten the danger to Paula. Moreover, he felt it his duty to remain in New York since only he really understood the force with which New York had to contend. The latter attitude was typical of him, and I cannot recall a moment during the whole dreadful period when he lost heart or appeared frightened. Paula, naturally, trusted her father's judgment implicitly, and was determined to do exactly as he advised. As for myself, there could have been no place for me, except by Paula's side.

Early in the afternoon, every evening paper received a typewritten statement purporting to have come from Dr. Skull, in which the madman pointed out that again he had made good his threat; that again the police had been proven impotent; that until the officials of New York recognized his supreme authority, there would be a continuation of his reign of terror. Under threat of another death stroke within forty-eight hours, the police were directed to indicate their willingness to treat with an intermediary of Skull's. They were instructed to publish their acquiescence in the newspapers within the time limit prescribed, and to name a place where the conference could be held.

Each of these typewritten statements was turned over to the authorities for examination. Quickly, police ascertained that the machine used to write them was of recent manufacture and of a certain popular make; they made notes of all blurred or curiously outlined letters; they recognized the stationery as being of the same cheap variety as that of the letter sent to Mayor O'Hara; they saw that each message had been mailed from a box in Grand Central Terminal some time before midnight of the night before. Having gone this far, the police were thoroughly stymied.

IN VIEW OF the situation, a special meeting of municipal officials was called for eight P.M. at the City Hall. Mayor O'Hara, District Attorney Harkness, Tom Higgins, and a considerable number of other members of the administration were to be present.

At six o'clock, District Attorney Harkness, this time unaccompanied by Tom Higgins who was busy with his investigation into the subway wreck, appeared at the Lansdowne apartment. Ever since Paula had received the note from Skull I had been living there as a member of the family, so I was present when the prosecutor arrived. Wasting scant time on social amenities, Harkness plunged into the current trouble.

"There's no need to tell you, Professor," he began, "that Skull hypnotized the motorman into making that subway train run wild last night. We've done our best to keep the newspapers and the public calm, but it's getting harder and harder. If the present state of affairs is prolonged much longer, the entire population of this city will be in a blue funk, and God knows what will happen then. I'm already being driven crazy by about ten thousand different people, all begging me to catch Skull before he kills everyone in town. And every other official is under the same kind of pressure. I don't believe I'm exaggerating when I say that, unless something is done immediately, we'll either have a revolution or a wave of such sheer panic that New York will be seriously shaken by it. Mayor O'Hara has been practically forced into calling a meeting tonight to discuss the measures to be taken. They say he's getting up out of a sickbed to attend, and why, I can't say. There's nothing much we can discuss. They'll all be looking to me—and what can I tell them? Professor, you've simply got to help!"

Professor Lansdowne smiled faintly.

"No one realizes more than I do how important it is for me to find a way of helping you, and I'm trying to. But first, tell me what Skull said over the phone last night, if you still think it was Skull."

"There's no question about it," replied Harkness, getting

up to pace back and forth before the fire. "The voice itself had a quality I've never heard in any other person, a quality impossible to describe, but which, once heard, is unforgettable. Then, this fact: the accident occurred at eighteen minutes after six. Yet at fifteen minutes after six—three minutes before the crash—this man phoned here and told me that within five minutes an accident would take place on the subway. No one but Skull or one of his confederates could have known this."

"Was Tom able to trace the call?" I asked. Harkness shook his head.

"No. Tracing calls went out when automatic telephones came in. There was a possibility that the call could be traced if I could hold Skull on the line long enough for Tom to get in touch with the main switchboard, but he hung up. Then we were sunk."

"He doubtless phoned from a public place, in any event," remarked the Professor.

"Probably," agreed the District Attorney. "I left here last night without giving any details of the call thinking I might be able to do something to stop the accident, although there certainly was nothing I could have done. Higgins and I heard sirens before we'd reached 110th Street, actually. We followed an ambulance to 96th Street, where the wreck took place. I won't try to describe what that station looked like. It was terrible—terrible. It must have been a duplication of Skull's hypnotizing the elevated motorman, the one who testified at your trial, only this time he really meant business."

"What do you intend doing about this latest demand?"

asked Professor Lansdowne. His tone was mild, but his keen eyes betrayed his deep interest in Harkness' answer.

"That's what I came to see you about," answered the D.A. "We haven't been able to do a thing about locating Skull through the notes he sent the papers today. The clues lead nowhere. We've arrested a thousand or more so-called suspects since this mess started, but not one of them has any possible connection with Skull. After all, what can we do? We don't really know what the man looks like, with only an out of date description to go by. So far, he's been smart enough not to show his hand in a way that would give us a tip-off on his whereabouts. He leaves no finger-prints, no cigarette stubs, no buttons torn off of his clothes. He's one criminal who apparently can work under cover indefinitely. He could pass me on the street ten times an hour and I'd never know it."

"And his latest demand?" Professor Lansdowne repeated his question which was met by another from Harkness.

"What do you advise?"

"My advice is what it was before. Play for time. Pretend to begin negotiations. Try and draw him out. It's your only chance to learn anything about him. The notes sent the papers mentioned an intermediary, didn't they?"

"That's right."

"Agree to meet him, then. But take my suggestion and don't play any tricks on the go-between unless you want Skull to take very strenuous measures in retaliation."

"I have to agree with you, Professor," admitted Harkness, "but it will probably be up to the Mayor to decide such a serious move. I'm not sure he'd approve of anything that looked like surrender. Besides, the people might not stand for it."

Professor Lansdowne knocked the ashes from the pipe he'd been smoking.

"That's where I differ with you," he said. "O'Hara is in no condition to take a strong stand, and mark my words, he won't. As for the people, unless you make an effort to stop this slaughter, whatever the cost in temporary alarm—I don't believe there will be a panic—civic pride, or cash, you'll be contending with something infinitely more serious than a mere shortage of votes at the next election. Strategic surrender is the only way."

District Attorney Harkness gnawed hesitantly at his lip, but eventually agreed to use his influence in favor of doing whatever would bring about the greatest amount of delay. To this end, it was decided that since Skull had allowed 48 hours for the city to take action on his ultimatum, the notice of capitulation would not appear in the press until the last possible moment. Meanwhile, perhaps a new clue might be found, or a new angle developed.

"I wonder," I said, as Harkness was about to leave, "if Dr. Skull knows you are coming here to see Professor Lansdowne. I don't think it's safe, either for the Professor or Paula, if he does."

Harkness turned a quick look on the scientist.

"I've thought of that, particularly since learning of the note sent your daughter. On the other hand, I can suggest no better place for us to meet. My office would be even more obvious. What do you think, Professor?"

"I don't see that it makes much difference where we meet," was the reply. "Skull must be quite aware that I know who he is. He may have been present during the trial, and he certainly read the newspaper account of it. I believe he was at the trial itself, and that that is where he first saw Paula. I don't imagine he's very much worried about our conferences, Mr. Harkness. There is certainly no reason why he should be, so far."

"That's true enough," said the District Attorney grumpily. Then, with a tight-lipped smile, he bade us good-night and departed for his meeting downtown. A short time later, with a significant glance in our direction, Professor Lansdowne announced that he was going to do a little work. So Paula and I found ourselves alone for the first time in several days.

I DON'T REMEMBER what we talked about. I was too worried about the whole situation—what Skull might do; whether the Professor could protect Paula from him; what on earth I could do to stand between her and trouble—to carry on a very brilliant conversation. As a matter of fact, we spent the next hour doing nothing but sitting close together, holding hands, and speaking in monosyllables which conveyed more than they said.

I remained at the Lansdowne apartment again that night, and the next morning, Paula and I went for a walk along the river. It was a clear, crisp day with a touch of fall in the air; too bracing to make much pessimism possible. The worries that had been so overpowering to me the night before now melted away like mist in the sunlight, and once more the world seemed a good place to live in. Skull was relegated in my mind to the position of a dangerous, but definitely conquerable, maniac. That cheery morning, it seemed impossible that he could continue to terrorize New York City very much longer.

When we returned to the apartment shortly before lunch time, Tom Higgins telephoned me to report that a special emergency council had been formed, with District Attorney Harkness and himself in first and second command, to prosecute the campaign against Dr. Skull. It was a signal honor that a person as young as Tom had been awarded such high rank, and he was greatly pleased. While Harkness and Higgins had been in charge of the Skull investigation ever since the death of Commissioner Gallagher, the present arrangement greatly broadened and amplified their powers, cutting red tape that could, under certain conditions, retard their progress.

Harkness' suggestion that a temporary capitulation to Skull be simulated had, according to Tom, been met by a whirlwind of criticism at first. A more violent critic had even accused the District Attorney of personal cowardice as well as incompetence, and a physical battle was threatened. In the end, though, Harkness had won out. Mayor O'Hara had played the weak hand Professor Lansdowne had predicted he would play, and before the session adjourned, the D.A. had been given carte blanche in the form of the emergency powers already mentioned.

Accordingly, in a prominent box on the front page of the following morning's papers, appeared this communication:

> Dr. Skull:
>
> While reserving decision as to the terms of a truce until conferring with your representative, the Emergency Council of the City of New York hereby expresses its willingness to

meet with said representative at 3 P.M. today in Room 2100 of the Municipal Building. This is published in accordance with your wishes and no further communication from you is required before the appearance of your representative at the appointed time and place.

(Signed) Walter A. Harkness,

District Attorney,

Chairman Emergency Council

"How terrible," said Paula, "that the government of a city of seven million people should have to temporize with a madman! It's horrible—unbelievable!"

"But, unfortunately, true," replied the Professor. "I'm only thankful Harkness was able to manage this. It may help."

"I'm going to that meeting," I said, eager for a bit of action for a change. "Tom Higgins ought to be able to get me in."

Paula looked at me anxiously. "Oh, Bob! Do you think you'd better?"

I was about to reply when the doorbell rang. The bell was in the kitchen and we were able to hear it quite plainly, sitting around the dining room table as we were. We exchanged glances. This fearful looking at each other had become a standard reaction to any noise that was not entirely expected.

Martha went to the door and in a few moments entered the dining room with a small box. When I saw it my throat contracted with fear and my stomach felt as though someone had poured a gallon of icy water into it. The box was a twin of the one sent by Dr. Skull a few nights previously.

"For you, Miss Paula," said Martha. She put it down on the table beside the girl's plate.

"Thank you, Martha," said Professor Lansdowne casually. "Will you please get me another cup of coffee?"

Paula was staring at the box, as though it contained a bomb ready to explode.

"Here," I said huskily, "let me have it." Before she could reply I was unfastening the white ribbon tied in a neat bow on top. As I opened the lid and pulled aside the wrapping of tissue paper, my fears were fully realized. There was the rose, a deep crimson as before. Beneath it was the same ivory-colored, gold bordered stationery engraved with the letter *S,* also in gold. In a voice which trembled, I read aloud the message. The delicate, Spencerian hand was easy to follow.

> Beautiful Lady:
>
> Is it too much for me to hope that you have been impressed by my power, so recently displayed in the death which was visited upon the poor unfortunates who rode the subway train? You see how invincible I am, how the greatest city in the world must bow to my will as it is doing today. Yet, all that I am I would gladly lay at your feet, and before such a great love, you cannot be unmoved. It is this belief that sustains me in my impatience, soon to be relieved, to have you at my side forever."

As before, the note was signed simply, "Dr. Skull."

"Are we going to let this go, too?" I demanded, turning on Professor Lansdowne.

The scientist looked at me, and without the slightest

emotion suggested: "You might go downstairs and see who brought this. Or perhaps Martha knows."

I cursed myself for not having thought of this before. "Martha!" I shouted through the door. "Come here, quick!"

The maid entered, drying her hands on her apron. "What is it, Mr. Larkin? I was fixing some more coffee. You folks drunk—"

"Never mind that," I said, impatiently. "Who gave you this box for Miss Paula?" Martha regarded me wonderingly and turned to the Professor, as if for protection.

"Go ahead, Martha," he said reassuringly, "tell us."

"Why, it was the elevator boy, sir, that give it to me."

BELATEDLY, I RUSHED out in to the corridor and rang the elevator buzzer. After an agonizing wait, though it must not have been over a minute or so in actual time, the elevator arrived and the door slid open.

"Did you just bring a box here for Miss Paula Lansdowne?" I demanded of the startled operator, ignoring the fact that there were several passengers in the car.

"Why, yes, sir, I did," he replied. "Miss Paula Lansdowne, Nine-B. That's it."

"Who gave you the box?"

"The doorman gave it to me, sir."

"Take me down," I ordered, "and hurry."

"Yes, sir," said the operator, sliding shut the inner grille. "Is something wrong?"

"Maybe," I replied grimly.

On the ground floor, I pushed out ahead of a huffy dowager and addressed the doorman.

"Joe, who gave you that box for Miss Lansdowne?"

"Oh, good morning, Mr. Larkin. That was gave me by a boy."

"What kind of a boy?"

"What kind of a boy, sir? Why, what kind are there? Just a plain everyday boy, sir."

Holding down an explosion with difficulty, "Listen," I ground out, "try and think what he looked like. Was he a Western Union boy? Where did he go? How long ago was he here?"

"Beg pardon, Mr. Larkin. It wasn't a messenger boy of no kind. Just a boy in plain clothes, about twelve years old. He brought me the box five or ten minutes ago and told me it was for Miss Lansdowne. He left right after he gave it to me."

"Did you notice which way he went?" I asked.

The doorman removed his cap and scratched the back of his head.

"Well, sir," he said, "I just saw him out of the corner of my eye, on account of I was turning around to give the box to Sammy. But I think he went up in the direction of 116th, sir."

"Thanks!" I said briefly, and hurried out on the Drive. There was no boy in sight in either direction, so I ran up to the corner of 116th and looked toward Broadway. Still no boy. Nor was my luck any better at the corner of 116th and Claremont, nor yet 116th and Broadway itself. There wasn't the slightest chance of trailing that kid now. Yet, as I retraced my steps to the apartment building, I did not give up all hope of ever finding him. It was logical to suppose that the boy lived in the neighborhood, and that he had been handed the box by someone in Skull's service, if not

Skull himself. Therefore, he might be around the Lans-downe building again, and if so, the doorman would be able to recognize him. It was a slim hope, but the only one that offered itself.

As I re-entered the lobby, I gave Joe my last five-dollar bill and told him to be on the lookout for the boy who had brought the note.

"I sure will, Mr. Larkin," he promised enthusiastically. "And I won't let him get away until I've located you."

"Fine," I replied, "and there'll be another five for you then."

"Thank you, sir. Is there been any crime done?"

"I hope not. But keep quiet about this, understand?"

Joe said he did, and I hastened back upstairs. Professor Lansdowne and Paula were still sitting at the breakfast table, their heads bent low over the note. Both looked up when I entered. When I'd reported on my activity down-stairs, the scientist nodded at me approvingly.

"Good work, Bob," he said. "Maybe the boy will lead us somewhere. I have a feeling that Dr. Skull's interest in Paula is the first serious mistake he's made."

"It will be if I ever get my hands on him," I muttered, glumly.

The three of us carefully reread the message, but there was nothing in its contents to help us in the slightest. Under the circumstances, it seemed to me that Paula should now have some one with her constantly, and I said so. Professor Lansdowne agreed with me.

"I know an excellent trained nurse who can stay with Paula and keep her out of mischief," he said. "Then we can consider the advisability of a detective guard, too. I'm not quite sure whether that would be a good idea or not, but we must certainly have the nurse."

"Right," I agreed, heartily.

"Nuts," said Paula. "Why so much excitement? After the last note, you both decided that all the guards in creation wouldn't do any good. Why should they help now?"

Soberly, the Professor put his hands on the girl's shoulders.

"My dear," he said, "I am still quite sure that Skull intends you no harm. But I believe now what I didn't believe before—that he may try to hypnotize you into going to him within the next few days. Guards could not protect you if Skull chose to make you kill yourself, but they can keep you from wandering into his arms."

Paula wrinkled her nose.

"Rats. Suppose he hypnotizes the guards too? Then what?"

"We can only hope that mass hypnotism is not one of his strong suits," replied her father, a serious expression on his face. "If it should be—well, we won't think about that. In fact, I refuse to accept even the possibility."

As Professor Lansdowne was talking, my nerves were assailed by the jangling of the telephone. Without waiting for permission, I stepped in to the library and answered it. It was Tom Higgins.

"Hello, Adonis," he greeted me, "Harkness wants the Professor to be at the meetin' this afternoon. You know the one I mean. We're expectin' company."

"Skull's ambassador?" I asked.

"That's it. You might tag along yourself. Get down before three, though."

"Okay," I replied, wondering what would happen next.

15

FIRST BLOOD

PROFESSOR LANSDOWNE IS one of those remarkable people with friends in any number of strange and unexpected places, so it really wouldn't surprise me if, on a safari through Darkest Africa, he'd suddenly be hailed as a long lost brother by a naked Hottentot chief. Miss Ella Ross MacLaughlin was every bit as startling as the Hottentot would be, but knowing the Professor, I withstood the shock fairly well. When he'd said he knew a nurse who could be depended upon to protect Paula, he was guilty of considerable understatement. Ella MacLaughlin looked to me as though she could subdue a herd of rogue elephants without half trying. She was of definitely Scotch ancestry, not too remote for her to have a perceptible burr on her speech, and she was large, big-boned, and big-muscled. Her Amazonian physique was topped off by a red, cheerful face and a twisted mop of carroty hair. She fairly exuded self-confidence.

"You don't have to wor-r-ry about Miss Paula," she assured us. "Ah, I'd love to get my two hands on the creature would try and do her harm. He'd soon want to be back home in the nut house, and you can put your last dollar on it, sir-r-r!"

"I'm quite sure he would, Ella," laughed the Professor.

Though I had been very dubious about leaving Paula and going downtown with the scientist, I no longer had any doubts. Professor Lansdowne had known Ella for a good many years, moreover, and he told me that Skull would find her a difficult subject to handle. She'd had considerable psychiatric experience rather off the beaten path, and her will was every bit as powerful as her vigorous body. I even found myself approving Professor Lansdowne's decision not to ask for police protection for Paula, on the grounds that, if Skull could defeat Ella MacLaughlin and get the girl away, he could also defeat any number of policemen. Unfortunately, there was good reason later to doubt the wisdom of this reasoning, but we felt secure at the time.

Paula herself was in high spirits, and took to her brawny protectress immediately. She shooed us on our way.

"Ella's going to show me a couple of wrestling tricks and I wouldn't want anyone to be hurt by flying bodies— probably mine."

"If it's anyone's, it'll certainly be yours," I said with conviction, glancing at the six-foot length of the Scotswoman, who threw back her head and roared delightedly.

Professor Lansdowne and I took a taxi on the Drive and sped along to our appointment. The tall palisades of steel and stone that bordered the river thrust up into the crisp, fall air like a great barrier, and again the feeling came to me that this was all a dream. New York had been here for so long; it was so big, so ruthless. Surely its great and ponderous stability could not be upset by one puny individual, however remarkable he might be. Yet, it had happened, and any one of the million windows that looked down on us might screen him. This thought—that Skull could be anywhere, any time, and, completely undetected and undetectable, could strike out with his deadly power—was not at all comforting. Telepathy appeared at the moment to be one of the Professor's accomplishments, for he said quietly, "We'll get him yet, Bob."

"We've got to," I muttered, half-choked with sudden returning fear, "before he does anything to Paula."

Professor Lansdowne nodded and turned again to look out the window. Everything was as usual, the same jumbled current of cars and trucks on Broadway, the same throngs of people on the sidewalks. The cry of the newsboys: "All about Dr. Skull!" was the only reminder that Manhattan was facing perhaps the most serious crisis of its history. There were, that day, several outbursts of panic and rioting as a result of the city's apparent surrender to Skull, but we saw no signs of it on our way to the headquarters of the Emergency Council.

Looking backward, I frequently marvel that business could go on as usual, that people could accept the turn of events so casually. To most New Yorkers, Dr. Skull was still remote. Possible, of course, like catching influenza during an epidemic, but not immediately threatening. Everyone read the news about him avidly, but in much the way that they read of things happening to others, things that would never really apply to them.

AT THE APPOINTED time, we were shown into the presence of District Attorney Harkness. He shook hands with the Professor and nodded briefly to me before plunging into the subject of greatest interest to us all.

"We've followed your advice, Professor Lansdowne,"

he began, "and unless he gets cold feet, Skull's ambassador and minister plenipotentiary will be with us in a very few minutes."

The scientist nodded.

"If he does show up," went on Harkness, "he'll presumably have a list of demands to present. No doubt Skull will want the keys to the city and a triumphal procession up Broadway. It is my plan to let the messenger present his ultimatum without interference, but after he gets through I don't mind saying he's going to be in for a hot session. I intend to get a description of Skull out of him to check with yours and bring us up to date, and to find out where Skull is hiding."

I expected the Professor to blow up at Harkness' talk of violence. It seemed a stupid idea to me, one that would only precipitate more trouble. The District Attorney must have expected an objection, too, because when Professor Lansdowne kept silent, he said:

"I suppose you don't think much of that program."

"There are a few holes in it. The messenger may know nothing of Skull, and if we detain him, Skull may try reprisals. He's undoubtedly planned on the meeting's being some sort of a trap."

"You have something else to suggest?"

"Not at present," replied Professor Lansdowne. "I'd first like to see the messenger."

Harkness pulled a watch out of his pocket and consulted it. "You should have that opportunity," he said, "within eight minutes, if he's on time. Let's go into the Council Chamber now, if we have nothing else to discuss."

I had apparently been accepted as an inevitable shadow

of the Professor's, so there was no exception taken when I tagged along. The other members of the Emergency Council were already in their places around a large conference table when we entered the room. There were six besides the District Attorney, but I recognized only Mayor O'Hara and Tom Higgins, who grinned at me. The Mayor was pale and seemed terribly careworn.

Professor Lansdowne and I took chairs slightly in back of Harkness. There was an unnatural silence in the place broken only by the scuffing of feet in the corridor outside where a half-dozen patrolmen stood guard. The time was 2:56 P.M.

Approximately one minute before three, there were sounds of a commotion outside, and an officer entered the Council Chamber and hurried to the side of Tom Higgins. There was a whispered colloquy which I could not catch, and then the policeman rushed back out of the room. This pantomime had been noticed by everyone present, of course. The Mayor cleared his throat nervously and glanced at the clock.

An instant later, all eyes were riveted on the doorway. In it stood two plainclothes detectives, and between them they half-held, half-supported a man. He was young, about 26 or 27 I'd say, and was dressed in a shabby suit with neither topcoat nor hat, though the day was chilly. The most startling thing about him was the fact that his face was scratched and bleeding, his breath came in labored gasps, and it was clear that should the detectives loosen their grip, he would fall to the floor.

"Mr. Mayor," spoke one of the detectives, "this guy claims to be the messenger from Dr. Skull. He staggered in just now, looking like this. Shall we throw him in the cooler or let him stay?"

"Why, I—" faltered O'Hara. He looked appealingly at Harkness.

"Let him stay, Allen," said that official. Then, to the amazed assemblage, "Gentlemen, unless there are objections, I'll question this man."

NO ONE DEMURRED, so a chair was brought up and the mysterious visitor was gently but firmly pushed into it. I now noticed that his clothes had been torn in several places and were covered with dirt. His eyes were glazed and blank, and his lips moved soundlessly.

"What's the matter with him?" I asked the Professor, but he motioned me to silence. He himself was regarding the newcomer intently.

"Who are you?" demanded the District Attorney. "You say you come from Dr. Skull?"

For a moment nothing happened, then the blank eyes turned slowly upon the inquisitor.

"Doctor Skull…" a dull, tired voice repeated the words, giving them no meaning.

"Yes," replied Harkness, "Dr. Skull. You have a message from him?"

"Doctor Skull…" A moan issued from the man's mouth. He twisted his body around, then tried to rise, but could not. "Doctor Skull…" He made an effort to go on. Again he attempted to stand and this time succeeded in reaching his feet, to stand swaying. He shook his head several times, as if to clear it. There was absolute silence in the room and Harkness made no effort to hurry him.

"I come from Dr. Skull." The man's voice took on

more strength as he made this announcement. He stared straight ahead of him. "I come from Dr. Skull to present his terms in keeping with the agreement… with the agreement…" The young man paused. He took a deep breath, swayed dangerously, and his eyes became alive for the first time. Wildly, they swept the room, as if looking for someone. "Where am I?" he suddenly cried out. 'Where am I? What's all this about? I can't seem to—" His voice cut off, and he slumped down into the chair again. Once more, Harkness questioned him, but his eyes had gone blank and the only thing he could say was, "I come from Dr. Skull," which he kept repeating. After five minutes of this, Harkness addressed the Council.

"Gentlemen, it's obvious that this man is in no condition to speak intelligently, or any other way. He appears to be ill. I propose to have him taken where he may be properly cared for until he can be questioned."

"Do you think he is really Skull's intermediary, Mr. Harkness?" asked a member of the Council.

"We'll know more about that later," was the reply. "However, it's quarter past three and he's the only one who's put in an appearance, so I don't believe we need expect any others. Unless there's an objection, I'll have this man taken away. I'll get in touch with the Council as soon as I know anything definite. Meanwhile, I suggest you call in the papers and tell them what's happened. The news that his messenger collapsed through no fault of ours should reach Skull. It might not be pleasant if he thinks he's been doublecrossed."

A couple of burly policemen and Tom Higgins accompanied the dazed stranger out of the Council Chamber and as he followed, the District Attorney beckoned to Professor Lansdowne and me to come along. There was a quiet office a short way down the corridor and into this we went. The battered young man was evidently in a state of collapse, but Harkness no sooner had him placed in a chair than he began firing questions at him.

"What's your name?"

A long pause, then the reply: "Name?"

The question appeared to mean nothing to the man. He stared blankly around the office and muttered unintelligibly. Again the District Attorney questioned him, but with no success.

"Let the boys give him a working over," suggested Tom Higgins. "I gotta hunch he's fakin'."

But Professor Lansdowne intervened. "That would be a mistake, I think," he said. "Let me have a look at that fellow, will you?"

Harkness and Tom were more than willing, so the Professor knelt beside the supposed messenger. In a few moments he rose and turned to the District Attorney.

"This man is in a serious condition," he said. "You'd better get a physician here as quickly as possible. He's been badly injured. In addition to which, he's been hypnotized. That's what makes him so dazed."

The D.A. took a step forward. "Why, damn it all," he exclaimed, "we can't let anything happen to him until we've had a chance to talk to him. Flynn, get a doctor on the jump. And keep it quiet, understand?"

"I get you, boss!" said one of the detectives, and left the room. Within five minutes, a police surgeon was leaning over the stranger. Soon he staightened up and addressed Harkness.

"This man must be removed to the hospital immediately," he said. "He's in bad shape. What was it, an auto accident?"

"Does it look like an auto accident to you?"

"Don't know what else it could have been," answered the physician. "Multiple fractures of the left arm, severe chest bruises, possible internal injuries and maybe a fractured skull. Either an automobile or a steam roller."

Harkness and Tom Higgins exchanged quick glances.

"Will he pull through?" asked the latter.

"Dunno," said the doctor. "He's in a pretty bad way. Friend of yours?"

"No," cut in the District Attorney, "a criminal suspect. We've got to ask him some questions and get the right answers before he dies."

The police surgeon scratched his cheek. "If it's important, you better hang around. He may come around in an hour or so, and if he does you better get your questions in quick, or you may never get them answered."

IT WAS MORE than an hour before the man "came around," however. We'd been pacing the prison ward of Bellevue Hospital for nearly three hours before a white-garbed physician beckoned us.

"He's as conscious now as he's ever going to be," was the information given us, "but that isn't saying much. Maybe you can get something out of him, though, only don't get tough. He'll die soon enough without any extra urging."

Tom Higgins had been called back to headquarters on urgent business, so there were only the District Attorney,

Professor Lansdowne and myself to enter the sickroom. The ashen figure on the bed seemed already to have been touched by the hand of death, but the lips moved silently and the head turned from side to side as though the brain within it were troubled. Tersely, Harkness spoke to the man, desperate to snatch from the grave itself a clue which might lead to Skull. But the staring eyes refused to change expression. Harkness turned to the doctor.

"Can't you do something to bring him around better than this?" he asked. "Confound it, man, it's vital. Do you hear? Vital!"

The physician shook his head and shrugged. "Suppose you try and convince *him*. There's nothing I can do, except write a death certificate in a few minutes. It won't be long now."

"How long do you think it will be?" The question came from an unexpected quarter. I turned to see that Professor Lansdowne was looking closely at the dying man.

"Why, I can't say exactly," answered the doctor. "Maybe a minute maybe an hour."

"Mr. Harkness," said the Professor, "this man can't answer questions because he's still under a hypnotic influence."

"Skull?"

The scientist nodded. "Let me see if I can do anything with him. There's a faint chance—a very faint chance—that I may be able to accomplish something."

"What about it, doc?" asked the attorney. "He's going to die anyway, isn't he?"

"Unquestionably. Go ahead. It doesn't matter now."

At the suggestion of Professor Lansdowne, a hypodermic of adrenalin was prepared and placed within easy reach.

If I had expected to see the impassioned gaze and dramatic gestures of a vaudeville hypnotist, I was doomed to disappointment. Throughout the entire experiment— for that is what it was—Professor Lansdowne's appearance was that of an earnest conversationalist, nothing more spectacular. The intense concentration which the scientist attained was not reflected in his expression, either.

"My friend," said the Professor, very quietly, "do you hear me?"

For a long moment, there was no response, and Professor Lansdowne repeated his question. Then, the head which had rolled uneasily on the pillow lay still. A degree of intelligence drained into the eyes, and this time when the lips moved, they formed audible words.

"Yes, I hear."

"Today you were given an order. Is this true?"

"Yes, it is true."

"Who gave you the order?"

"Dr.—Dr. Skull."

"Did Dr. Skull speak to you himself?"

"Yes."

"Tell me, what does he look like?"

An expression of pain flashed across the dying man's face.

"I have been told to forget, and I have forgotten."

"No, you must not forget. You must remember. Tell me, what does he look like. Think!"

"I—I cannot!" The man gasped out the words. He moved his arms and legs feebly, as though he were trying to escape something, an unseen thing that threatened him even in the shadow of death.

"Easy!" The one word, urgently spoken, came from the physician. As Professor Lansdowne nodded understanding, the surgeon's fingers pressed the hypodermic needle against the stranger's pallid flesh. The tinge of blueness that had crept into his face withdrew. The staring eyes now sought those of the Professor and appeared to plead with him. But the scientist was inexorable.

"Remember," he insisted. "Remember and tell me. What does Dr. Skull look like?"

Finally, we heard the answer.

"He—he's a small man. His head is very large and bald. His—his—"

"His eyes?" pressed the scientist.

"Very strange. Very un—unusual."

"What color are they?"

"Black, and very big."

"His nose?"

"I—I can't remember."

"Very well then. What kind of a mouth has he?"

"Small and curved, like a woman's."

"His hands?"

"He has long fingers."

"How old is he?"

"I can't say. Perhaps thirty, perhaps fifty."

"What kind of clothes does he wear?"

"Ordinary clothes." The tired voice was growing weaker.

"When did you receive your orders?"

"In the morning."

"Where did you receive them?"

"On—on—" the words were gasped out. The man half-raised himself with sudden strength. Agonizedly, he looked at Professor Lansdowne, a look of helpless, dumb pleading. I found myself getting sick.

"Think quickly," urged the scientist, in a final effort. "How can we recognize Dr. Skull? Is there any way he can be told from all other men? Answer me!"

"The voice—the voice! You will know—"

Here the man broke off and fell back against the pillows. There was a great sigh, and he was still.

"Is he dead?" rasped out Harkness. The doctor made a swift examination and nodded.

"Good work," said the District Attorney to Professor Lansdowne, who was mopping his face with a handkerchief. "I made notes of everything he said, and it'll be common knowledge to every cop from Brooklyn to the Bronx inside half an hour. Let's get going."

"Poor devil," murmured the Professor, looking at the dead man. "He was hypnotized by Skull and sent down to the Council with a list of demands engraved right on his mind. Funny, too. It wasn't Skull's usual kind of hypnotism. More the ordinary kind, but a particularly powerful variety. So powerful, in fact, that although this fellow was struck and severely injured by an automobile, he had to drag himself up from the gutter and keep on to his destination. Every step must have been agony." Professor Lansdowne got to his feet. "I'd give a great deal to wrap my fingers around Skull's throat!"

We shot back down town in a police car, and soon telephone and teletype wires were flashing to every precinct the description of the man who held New York in his deadly grip. Though this was far from complete, it checked with the Professor's own memory of Franz Ehrlich. At long last, there was actual proof that his identification of Skull as Ehrlich was altogether right.

We still had no idea where to start looking, and the description might fit loosely a great many men, but there was now something to do besides waiting in utter help-lessness for death to strike. For the first time, someone had pitted his brain against Dr. Skull's—and won!

16

PLAN OF COMBAT

PROFESSOR LANSDOWNE AND I dined downtown with the District Attorney and didn't get back to the apartment until after nine o'clock. When we arrived, Paula met us at the door and reported a quiet day.

"As a matter of fact," she said, "I was bored stiff. What happened downtown?"

"Let Bob tell you," suggested her father. "I'm going to the library for a bit of research. Will you please ask Ella to bring a pot of tea in to me?"

After passing on this order, Paula seated herself beside me on the sofa and listened while I retailed all that had happened at the Council and at the hospital. The evening papers, incidentally, carried the story of how Skull's messenger had collapsed before he was able to deliver any ultimatum, so it appeared that Harkness' wishes had been duly carried out. As I read the account, I hoped that Skull would believe it was the truth. If he should think otherwise, we might have reason to tremble.

While we were thus occupied, Inspector Tom Higgins dropped in to report that Skull's description was thoroughly circulated by now, and that an intensive search was under way for the maniac.

"Also," he stated, "we've got special men detailed to cover the main highways in and out of town in case he should get scared and try to make a break for it. That goes for railroad stations, too, and the big airports, and all ferries and steamships."

"I didn't know there were that many cops," I said, truthfully. "How many have you got on the job?"

"Aw, only about five hundred. That's nothin'."

"Well, as far as I'm concerned, if Skull wants to leave town, I'm for letting him go. But he's probably going to stay right here in New York—if he's here now. He's got nothing to run away from."

"Nuts to you," remarked Tom, and left.

About forty-five minutes afterward, Professor Lansdowne emerged from the library.

"You know," he said ruminatively, "this is a good evening to listen to the radio."

"Huh?" I grunted, startled. Professor Lansdowne was noted for his uncompromising dislike of that medium of entertainment.

"Yes, you mental deficient," he smiled, "the radio. Has it occurred to you that Dr. Skull may want to issue a statement about the fate of his negotiator? Frankly, it only occurred to me a moment ago, but I think it's possible he may have a comment to make—if he hasn't already made it."

"Right you are, sir," I agreed, wondering why I hadn't thought of it an hour ago. "Any particular station?"

"The largest and loudest, I should say."

"We can flip coins between WABC and WEAF, then," I

Tom Higgins came by to report that Skull's
description was thoroughly circulated by now

replied. "They're tied for first place. Or we might take them in alphabetical order, which starts us off on ABC."

For the next half hour, we chatted about the good old days when there was no Dr. Skull to worry about, while the Columbia Broadcasting System hurled a variety program into the ether.

"Why not switch over to NBC for a few minutes?" suggested Paula, finally. "We don't seem to be getting anywhere here."

"Okay." I twirled the dial to WEAF. There was music there, too, a nationally known advertiser's coast-to-coast show. "If Skull says anything on this, he'll sure have a big enough audience," I added.

But the station break came and went without any word from the mysterious individual whose very name spelled such hopeless terror to New York. You'd think that by this time, I'd have learned not to relax on any job where Dr. Skull was a factor, but you'd be wrong. I actually started yawning. Paula also became drowsy, but her father remained alert. He couldn't manage to keep his pipe lit, and was forever getting up to walk across the room to a cigar stand for more matches.

I wondered idly why he didn't bring the tray nearer to his chair, but I can now see that this activity was principally the result of nerves, or perhaps an effort to stave off weariness. It had been a long time since any of us had enjoyed a good night's sleep.

Eleven o'clock came, and still nothing from Skull. The program now on the radio was a sustaining show which was broadcast for New York alone. I was barely paying attention to what was going on, and was sitting next to Paula with my head resting comfortably on her shoulder. I remember a feeling of great satisfaction, being so close to her and knowing that she was safe. At that moment, I couldn't have believed that anything could ever come between us.

Professor Lansdowne must have spoken sharply, for I suddenly snapped out of my lethargy and sat bolt upright. He was inclining his head toward the speaker and was apparently waiting for something. Then I realized that there was nothing on the air, although the station's signal was strong, indicating that there was nothing wrong with their transmitter. My watch, which was dependable, said 11:09—too early for the station break that comes at the end of each program. Yet, there was this dead silence—a condition as abhorrent to radio as a vacuum is to nature.

IT TAKES A long time to describe this in writing. Actually, it probably was not more than fifteen or twenty seconds before the announcer spoke. When he did, it was in a dull, flat parody of his own voice, and the words were those of Dr. Skull.

"People of New York," said the voice. "Today I, Dr. Skull, sent a representative to arrange certain terms with the men who presumably run your city. I did this in good faith. I was willing to effect a compromise when it would have been simpler to have forced a complete fulfillment of my wishes by methods which could not fail. For this display of generosity, my reward was treachery. My representative was betrayed, in an effort to strike at me through him.

"But your officials have failed miserably, as all will fail who try to oppose my will. In spite of this unpardonable duplicity which you, the people of New York, tolerate, I do not wish to cause needless suffering. Instead of inflicting a just punishment on you, I shall visit it instead upon your leaders. They are not worthy to hold the high offices they have been given, and they shall be removed, one by one, until a man comes forward who will heed my commands.

"People of New York, you have seen how I can destroy hundreds of you at one stroke. Profit by what happens to your leaders, that the scourge of my anger need not strike you again."

When the voice stopped its monotonous speaking, Professor Lansdowne clicked off the radio.

"Pray God he won't kill anyone tonight. I haven't yet the strength to fight him," he said, sighing deeply and passing his hand wearily across his eyes. "You two must excuse me. I have so much work to do, and then I must sleep. It's very important. Please disconnect the phone and let no one disturb me. There isn't a thing I could do tonight, if the heavens started to fall."

Thus, leaving Paula and me utterly bewildered, Professor Lansdowne walked slowly out of the room. In the last few seconds after the voice had ceased, weariness enveloped him like a heavy cloak. His face, which had been alert, had fallen into deep lines of worry and fatigue. Then the library door closed behind him and we were left alone.

"Well—" began Paula, in a queer, strained voice, and stopped.

"Exactly," I murmured.

As a direct result of that eerie warning, neither Paula nor I wished to be separated that night. Consequently, we remained where we were, sitting close together on the davenport. Ella MacLaughlin soon appeared with milk and thin toast for Paula but, apparently taking in the situation at a glance, she merely put the food down on a small coffee table and retired without saying a word. Paula and I talked a while, but the silences kept lengthening. I remember vaguely taking the telephone receiver off the hook so the instrument wouldn't ring. Then I remember no more.

It was daylight when I awoke, a queer, gray, rain-streaked daylight. Quickly, I consulted my watch. Nearly 7:30, and every muscle in my body was screaming bloody murder. Paula was still sleeping, as quietly as a child, her head resting on top of the davenport. Remarkably enough, the fire was still blazing cheerily in the hearth and when I next looked at her, Paula's eyes were open.

"Good morning," she said thickly. "What happened?"

"We went to sleep."

"Oh. Did you just build the fire?"

"No, Miss Paula," said the robust Ella MacLaughlin, making a crisp, starchy entrance in her spotless nurse's uniform, "your-r young man didna build the fire. The two of you were sleeping so sound, I built it without making you so much as to stir. I hadna the heart to waken you."

"You're a sweet old darling, Ella," said Paula, "and you've got a romantic heart, too, I'll bet. Haven't you, now?"

Whereupon the massive MacLaughlin blushed, resembling nothing so much as a sunburned cow. "I wouldna go so far-r as to say that, Miss Paula. It's just that I have a bit of a feeling for the young folks, being young once myself." And she bustled off again to go into the kitchen and lord it over Martha in the preparation of breakfast.

"You'll have to excuse me a few minutes, sir," remarked Paula, "while I duck out and recapture my glamour."

"What glamour?" I demanded, laughing.

MY MOUTH FELT like blotting paper, so I headed back to the Professor's quarters to brush my teeth, knowing he would be up by now. He was, and while I industriously scrubbed at my molars, he said:

"Skull intends to kill every prominent official in this city. Perhaps he's already begun. Now, admitting, purely for the sake of argument, that I could save one of them, which one should it be? The Mayor? The Chief of Police? The City Treasurer? The District Attorney?"

I sloshed water around in my mouth, spewed it out, and emerged from the bathroom.

"Do you really think you can save one of them?"

"It's possible, yes."

"But how? And why just one?"

"Dr. Skull," enlarged the scientist, "achieves his unpleasant results through his vastly superior will which completely dominates that of the victim. At least this is a logical supposition backed up by considerable evidence. Right?"

"Right."

"Now, this ability of his to hypnotize by remote control, without the consent of the subject, is not only the result of a superior will, but it requires an understanding of certain fundamental, though generally unknown, laws as well. Should another person wish to challenge Dr. Skull success-fully, he would not only have to have a stronger mind than Skull's, but an equally thorough understanding of the laws involved. If the challenger's will and understanding were superior to that of Dr. Skull, he would be able to dispute Skull's control over a given subject and to impress his own will on the subject instead. Do you follow me?"

"Follow you?" I replied, eagerly. "I'm way ahead of you. You mean you've learned the trick of this thing better than Skull?"

"You're too far ahead of me. I don't mean anything of the kind. But to continue this hypothetical discussion, if the challenger should have merely an equal amount of knowl-edge and will power, he would be able to defeat Skull in whatever he attempted to do with the subject, but would not be able to dominate the subject himself. If the chal-lenger's ability and understanding were somewhat less than Skull's, all he could hope for would be to interfere, and confuse the subject enough to seriously alter the course."

"I see, but where—"

"Here is where I come in, Bob," said the Professor, smil-ing. "I know something of the laws which Skull utilizes—in fact we both got our knowledge from the same source, the Lan Batu, or Three Brotherhoods. My own studies in this field were not nearly so extensive as Skull's—continuing to assume that he and Ehrlich are the same—but with the aid of fresh researches I've been making recently, I believe I know enough to prevent at least one death. I can't defeat Skull, but I may be able to confuse his victim enough to save his life."

Professor Lansdowne stopped talking and stared abstractedly at the wall. I was too absorbed in the possibilities of what he had said to interrupt his thoughts.

"Skull has threatened to kill all of the men who direct the administration of this city," he went on. "I dare say there are no more than six or seven men who are the real brains of this town. Or if they aren't, they should be. There's the Mayor, the head of the police department, the Health Commissioner, and so on. Correct?"

"I suppose so."

"Now, we don't know how Skull will work. We don't know which man he'll kill first, or in what way he'll kill him. But we do know this: the selected victim will either die by his own hand, after being directed to kill himself by Skull, or he will be killed by a person near him who is also under Skull's influence."

"Obviously," I commented.

"Come now," said the Professor. "I'm not as silly as I sound. All we have to do is keep the man from killing himself, protect him from those around him, and he'll be safe. Do you grant me that?"

"Sure I grant you that. But you don't know which man to protect."

"Exactly. Which is why I can protect only one person at a time. All I can do is select one of the men threatened, stick close to him, watch him like the proverbial hawk, and if any unusual symptoms develop, do what I can to bring them under control."

"You mean," I said, beginning to understand, "if you see he's starting to act queerly, you stop it by out-hypnotizing Skull?"

"Not by out-hypnotizing him, as you put it, but by interfering with his control. I can't hope for more than that at present."

"You mean you might be able to do more, later on?" I asked.

Professor Lansdowne shook his head. "I can't say now," he replied. "My present problem is which man to bless with my dubious protection. I believe the answer is District Attorney Harkness. Besides being head of the Emergency Council which is supposed to be directing activities against Skull, Harkness appears to have some common sense, and that's such a rarity. I believe we'll need him most."

I considered it a wise decision. "Do you suppose Skull will strike at the Emergency Council first, or the regular administration?" I wondered.

"I suspect," answered the scientist, "that he'll try to cripple the city government, and that would mean the regular administration first. I dare say he holds the Emergency Council in more contempt than anything else, but there's no telling until he swings into action. I believe New York is in for a rather fearful experience, unless by some miracle, Skull can be beaten."

"Well, if you can't do it, no one else can," I said, with real feeling. "Only don't let anything happen to yourself. Which makes me think of another angle—how are you going to keep Harkness' own associates from bumping him off, in case Skull should go to work on them?"

"By isolating him, if possible. Make him contact no one and handle everything by telephone. Nothing will harm him that way."

"Suppose he won't agree to that?"

"Then, by being as alert as possible with everyone who comes near him. There's a big percentage of risk, but it's the best we can do, Bob."

Even as Professor Lansdowne finished explaining to me the first practical plan for opposing Skull that had yet been offered, I thought of someone more important to me than anyone else—than everyone else put together.

"What," I asked dully, "about Paula?"

Professor Lansdowne laid his hand on my shoulder.

"I'm depending on you for that, Bob," he said.

"But what can I do? Suppose she picks up a paper knife and stabs herself before I can get to her? Suppose she jumps out the window. How can I—"

"Hold on a minute, son. Skull has made no threats against Paula's life. The worst he intends is to take her away with him. We have his own word for that, and he's just insane enough to be thoroughly reliable. If you and Ella MacLaughlin remain here with Paula and see that she makes no effort to leave, she'll be all right. Ella is a very hard subject, even for a hypnotist of Skull's dimensions, I assure you. If she goes under, it will be an audible struggle, and you'll be able to keep her from doing anything fool-ish. The same applies to Ella if you are controlled. More important is this fact—unless I take steps to defeat Skull, there will be no safety for anyone."

"But suppose he hypnotizes all of us at the same time. Then what?" I demanded.

"I don't believe he will ever do that," answered Professor Lansdowne.

We walked together into the living room, and while the scientist settled himself with the morning paper (which contained nothing startling), I stepped into the library and replaced the telephone receiver on the hook.

I HAD HARDLY returned to the living room when the front door bell rang. Without waiting for the servant, I answered it myself. It was a special delivery boy, with a letter for Professor Lansdowne. I signed for it mechanically, and with a feeling of utmost dread, took it to the Professor. The handwriting on the envelope was that of Dr. Skull.

> My DEAR PROFESSOR LANSDOWNE: For a time I have regarded your association with the police in their efforts to trap me with amusement. However, I must now ask you to sever your connection with them, before there is real cause for regret. Although I am grateful to you for having such a charming daughter, my gratitude cannot fail to be tempered by any furtherance of your recent activities. You may appreciate how futile it is to oppose me when you see that you are unable to protect even your own *child*.
>
> DR. SKULL

"Now what?" I asked, scared stiff. But Professor Lansdowne didn't reply.

I had an overwhelming desire to hold Paula close to me, so without further delay I walked down the hallway to her room and banged on the door.

"Paula!" I called. "Come out. The mail man's just been here."

The next moment, I knew instinctively that my joke was ill-timed, for there was no reply. I called again, and when there still was no response, I opened the door of the bedroom and walked in. It was empty.

A peculiar feeling in my stomach, I went back to the living room.

"Paula isn't in her room," I said, with rising excitement. "Have you seen her?"

"No, I haven't." Professor Lansdowne's forehead creased into a worried frown. "Try the kitchen."

I rushed into the dining room and, seeing no one there, I shot through the swinging door into the kitchen. Ella MacLaughlin and Martha, the cook, looked at me in surprise.

"Is anything the matter, Mr. Bob?" asked the cook.

"Where's Miss Paula?" I demanded wildly. "Have either of you seen her?"

"No, sir-r," said Ella. "Isna she in her r-room?"

I waited for nothing else, but went through that apartment like a whirlwind, looking in every nook and cranny and in the hall outside. Paula was nowhere to be found.

"Professor!" I cried, distractedly. "She's gone!"

We stood there looking at each other as though frozen to the spot, and all the while I could hear the telephone jangling its head off in the library. But it made no impression on either of us.

17

THE DAYS OF THE TERROR

HOW LONG WE stood there while the telephone rang crazily, I don't know. I don't even remember why neither the cook nor Ella MacLaughlin answered it. Perhaps they were dazed and frightened, too. It was the Professor who finally came to himself sufficiently to pick up the receiver, and while he listened—he hardly spoke more than three words—I sank onto the davenport and made an effort to pull myself together.

I first tried to think of a logical reason for Paula's disappearance. My numbed mind slowly worked ideas back and forth, weakly analyzing and discarding them as they came. The hero of the very worst adventure story I'd ever read would have shown more intelligence in dealing with the situation than I did. But for whole minutes, I was in a state of shock, unable to do anything but sit and wonder whether or not Paula could have decided to go shopping or to the hairdresser's—before breakfast!

Not until Professor Lansdowne had finished his telephone conversation was I really aware of what was going on around me. The scientist's face was haggard, and before he spoke he took a deep breath, as if to gain strength.

"O'Hara was first on Skull's list," he said heavily.

"He's dead?" I asked, not really caring.

"Entirely so. He jumped or fell from a window in the living room of his apartment on Park Avenue. It was a fourteen-story drop. Nobody missed him until this morning, when his wife noticed his bed hadn't been slept in. He fell into a rear court and his body wasn't discovered until a little while ago."

"Too bad." I buried my face in my hands for a moment, then shook my head violently and succeeded in getting a grip on myself. "I've got to find Paula," I said simply.

Professor Lansdowne looked at me for a long moment, then nodded in his usual slow, thoughtful way.

"Of course you have to find her. There's no use wasting time on the false hope that she hasn't gone to Skull, either. I'll never forgive myself for being so completely off guard, or for not having a battalion of detectives on duty, but that's beside the point. We must find Paula, and the only way to find her now, is to find Skull."

A sudden hope flamed within me. "Maybe," I commenced eagerly, "she hasn't gotten out of the building yet. I'm going to try—"

"Spare yourself the trouble," interrupted the Professor. "She was undoubtedly out of our reach the moment we first missed her. She's entirely under Skull's influence now. She might even harm herself if we interfered. Our one hope is to find Skull, and that's what we must do."

"But how?"

"God knows, but we'll find a way. I must get down to Harkness before anything happens to him. If organized resistance to Skull ever collapses, Paula—and a hundred thousand other people—will be completely at his mercy.

We must find a way to get at Skull, and I must find a way to fight him successfully when we do."

"You're going to notify the police about her?"

"Of course. I'll see that a search is started, but the police must not try to close in on Skull, should they find him. That might be fatal to everyone concerned. After they find him—if they do—then it's up to me. And God grant that I won't be found wanting!"

"What can I do?" I asked, helplessly.

"You can scout around and see if you can pick up any trace of her. You can question the elevator boy and the doorman and follow up anything you find. Only keep in touch, both with the apartment here and with me. I'll have Ella MacLaughlin stay here by the telephone—just in case Paula should come to her senses and try to reach us, which I'm afraid is unlikely. Call me at the District Attorney's office if you need me."

A FEW TERSE instructions to the thoroughly distracted Scotswoman and he was gone. I felt utterly beaten, but I determined to lose the feeling in action, if possible. My initial move was to quiz Ella and the cook as to when they had last seen Paula, but this netted me nothing but expressions of anxiety for the girl's fate. Next, I belatedly interrogated the elevator boy and learned that Paula had taken the car down twenty or twenty-five minutes before, that she had appeared all right, and that she had been dressed in brown clothes. So at least I knew that she hadn't changed from the outfit she was wearing when I last saw her.

Joe, the doorman, had little else to add. Miss Paula, he said, had come down in the elevator and had gone right out, turning north on the Drive in the direction of 116th Street.

"Did she speak to you?" I demanded.

"Why, yes, sir," answered the man, "I think so, though I don't rightly remember. She may of said, 'Good morning, Joe,' and then she mayn't of said anything. She usually spoke very nice to me and all the help, sir, and so she—"

"Thanks!" I cut him short and started out the door.

"I'm keeping an eye out for that boy you want to see, sir!" Joe called after me.

My question in regard to Paula's speaking was a forlorn attempt to find out for sure if she had been hypnotized by Skull. I supposed that if she had been, she probably would not have spoken to anyone. But, as you've seen, this line of attack got me nowhere.

I now ransacked my brain for the names of Paula's few intimate friends, on the absurd chance that she might have gone to see one of them, and actually made three fruitless telephone calls. Uselessly, I asked them to notify me or the Professor should they see her. Foolish? Very—like everything else I did on that despondent day. The thing was to find Skull, and I couldn't find him, or know where to start looking. I had to do something, so I carried on a series of senseless enterprises. It was better than sitting in the apartment, waiting, or outside the District Attorney's office, doing the same thing.

My wanderings eventually led me toward Times Square, I suppose because, as the center of New York, it held out the most likely possibility of something's happening. I boarded a subway train and tried to let the roar of its progress swallow up my gnawing fear.

Although far too absorbed in my own problems to pay much attention to my surroundings, it was impossible for me to ignore the atmosphere of fearful expectancy that permeated even the jaded air underground. O'Hara's death was screamed by big, black scareheads on newspapers held by passengers, and a couple of editors, unmindful of, or indifferent to, the police ban on sensationalism, played with the idea that Skull intended utterly to destroy Manhattan. The killing off of all vestiges of leadership, it was gruesomely pointed out, was perhaps the first step toward the annihilation of the entire population.

Times Square itself seemed abnormally tense, though it is difficult to describe in just what way this quality was made manifest. It may have been the shriller cries of newsboys, the quicker pace of pedestrians, a sharper sound to the squawk of auto horns. In the midst of throngs never noted for their politeness, I found myself pushed and shoved with less gentleness than ever.

I'd had no breakfast and in spite of my depressed state of mind, my physical needs proved strong enough to get me into a restaurant for a bite of food. As he put a steaming cup of coffee before me, the waiter remarked:

"I reckon we all better eat while we still got the chance."

I looked at him, dully.

"I says to my old lady this morning, 'You may as well get that new coat you been wanting. Like as not we won't none of us be around when the first installment comes due.'"

"Yeah," I agreed mechanically. My lack of response to his attempt at pleasantry caused the waiter to subside once more into the customary acerbity of his species. Thumping down a plate of toast, he departed, and I was left to eat in a morose silence. When I'd downed the food, I telephoned Professor Lansdowne and Ella MacLaughlin, drawing a blank in both cases as far as any news of Paula was concerned. The Professor reported, however, that every effort was being made by the police to locate the girl, and I got a bitter laugh out of that. If their future success in this direction was to be judged by what had gone before, we'd never see Paula again.

Once more, I lost myself in the crowds that surged up and down Broadway, looking into the faces of all the women who passed in a hope—instinctive and involuntary—that I might find Paula. Gradually, there came upon me a feeling of black hopelessness, the stark realization that, unless a miracle happened, there wasn't one chance in a million of finding her alive and unharmed. I cursed myself for ever letting her get out of my sight; I cursed the Professor for his inability to beat Skull at his own game; and most of all, I cursed Skull himself.

Satisfying a desire that would not be stilled by cold reason, I went in every place along Broadway that Paula had ever liked, that we had ever visited together. I went into stores, hotel lobbies, two or three movies, half a dozen restaurants, looking aimlessly. People must have thought me insane, as probably I was at the time. Finally, with aching legs and a sense of even deeper discouragement, I whistled down a cab and returned to the Lansdowne apartment. Strangely enough, as we approached the building, I began to hope that she had returned home; that she had not, after all, been a victim of Dr. Skull's weird power. But this feeling was quickly extinguished when the doorman informed me that he had not seen her.

ELLA MACLAUGHLIN WAS seated by the telephone, exactly where she had been posted when I left. Apparently, she hadn't stirred. Her face, set in lines hard enough to have been chiseled in granite, did not relax when she saw me.

"There hasna been a single, solitary wor-rd from the poor-r child," she purred dismally, "and should ill come to her, I'll never for-rgive myself. Have you no encour-rage-ment, sir-r? But no, I see you have not."

"No," I confirmed, pretty woodenly, no doubt. "Anything from the Professor?"

He had not called, so there was nothing to do but sit down and try to figure out a course of action more likely to bring results than the one pursued so far. But this was easier to plan than to do. If I'd had all the armies in the world at my command, I'd have been defeated by one thing: Skull's ability to strike unseen, without leaving the most infinites-imal clue as to his whereabouts. Somehow, though, I told myself, there must be a chink in his armor of invisibility.

Throughout the long afternoon, while I waited in vain for word from Professor Lansdowne or—idiotically—from Paula, I struggled desperately to figure out where that chink could be. But the sun fell lower and shadows lengthened into twilight and I got nowhere. As night fell, my spirits struck rock bottom. There was nothing that could save Paula. The police were a set of fools; Professor Lansdowne was pathetically impotent, for all his experi-ence and study; Paula was at the mercy of a madman, and I was like a man paralyzed for all the good I could do.

At six o'clock I tried to get in touch with Professor Lansdowne at the D.A.'s office, but was informed that he had gone out with Harkness on urgent business and would not return for several hours. I did my best to believe that this business might concern Paula, and while I was in this slightly improved mood, Ella got me to eat some dinner. Afterward, though, my nervousness increased and I became quite desperate to get action. I telephoned Tom Higgins, and was lucky enough to find him at his office.

"I've got nothin' for you," he reported, "about Paula, I mean. But there's been plenty poppin' in other directions. Skull got to Lloyd Taylor, less'n an hour ago. I just come from the City Hall, and Harkness and the Professor are still over there."

"Taylor?" I asked. "Who's Taylor?"

"He's a corpse right now, but he *was* Acting Mayor of New York up to a little while ago. I don't want to say any more over the phone. Come on down here, why don't you? It don't do no good for you to sit up there in that place waitin'. You'll drive yourself nuts."

No invitation was ever more welcome and I accepted it gratefully. That apartment was getting very much on my nerves and, besides, it would be good to have Tom Higgins to talk to. Telling Ella MacLaughlin to remain on duty until further notice, I started to leave. But my attention was claimed by the radio, which I'd had running. It was a news commentator.

"Another death late this afternoon marked the bloody trail of the maniac known as Dr. Skull when Lloyd B. Taylor, Acting Mayor of New York City, shot himself at his desk in the City Hall. Taylor, who had taken over the reins of city government this morning upon the death of Mayor O'Hara, was presiding at a special conference when the tragedy occurred. Eye-witnesses said that the Acting Mayor appeared suddenly to go out of his mind. In this condition, he reached into a drawer, brought out a pistol, and before anyone present could interfere, mortally wounded himself. Mr. Taylor recovered consciousness for a brief interval as a hurriedly summoned physician worked over him in an unsuccessful attempt to save his life. Just before he died, the Acting Mayor was heard to murmur, 'I don't know why I did it.' Five minutes later, he was dead, and for the second time within twenty-four hours, New York found itself without a guiding hand.

"Although officials refused to issue a statement at present, experts pointed out that Taylor's death exactly parallels others which have been attributed to the deadly hypnotic power of Dr. Skull. While admitting themselves temporarily baffled by recent events, police insist that there is no cause for general alarm.

"According to an official spokesman, the direction of city affairs will be immediately undertaken by Lawrence Bates, President of the Borough of Manhattan."

This announcement brought home to me the fact that, while I had been absorbed in my own worry and anxiety, Skull was systematically decimating the executive personnel of New York, exactly as he had promised to do. Worse, no one had yet been able to stop him. What grounds, then, were there for hope that Paula might be saved from whatever fate Skull planned for her?

With a feeling of fear and despair in my heart, I went downstairs and out into the windy darkness of Riverside Drive. I looked at the dying branches of trees, moving fitfully against the gray pallor that was the Hudson. A cold wind had come up, and it cut through my topcoat like a knife. Grimly, I bent my body against the chill and tried not to feel in it the dread presence of Dr. Skull.

18

STEAM-ROLLER

TOM HIGGINS I found amid a welter of activity, going through a sheaf of written reports and keeping his ear cocked to a small radio from which issued at intervals the stentorian tones of a police announcer. He nodded curtly to me and indicated that I was to sit down. In a few minutes he pushed aside his papers, lounged back in his swivel chair, and placed his feet comfortably on the desk.

"Sorry to keep you waitin'," he drawled sardonically, "but it keeps me pretty busy bein' the brains of this terrific campaign against Dr. Skull."

"Has anything new happened?"

"Not since Taylor went to his heavenly reward, but of course the police expect to make an arrest any minute now. That's to say we ain't gettin' nowhere and doin' it fast."

"Nothing about Paula?"

"Not yet, but we'll get her. You look kinda peaked."

"I'm damned worried, if that's what you mean," I said with feeling. "How'd you be with the girl you love kidnapped by a lunatic with the power Skull has?"

"Lousy," answered Tom shortly, "particularly with a bunch of clucks like the New York Police Department to have to depend on. But keep your shirt on, son, and remember that here's one copper who'd break his neck to help you. We'll find her. All we need is just one tip about where Skull's hidin' out."

"He may not be within a hundred miles of here, for all you can tell," I said, disconsolately. "If that hypnotism of his can work at a distance of one mile, why can't it work at a distance of a thousand? Maybe he's still in India!"

Tom Higgins lit a cigarette and took a long drag at it. "Ain't you kinda forgettin' the guy that gave Professor Lansdowne the dope on Skull?" he asked. "Judgin' from the little he said and the fact that he musta been hypnotized here in town, there ain't any question about the big shot bein' right on Manhattan Island. Not in my mind, at least."

I grunted in determined skepticism and Tom shifted the talk to the chances of Lawrence Bates, the city's new chief executive, to stay alive.

"It's a helluva thing for a Deputy Inspector of Police to admit," he remarked, "but I wouldn't wanta be in that mug's brogans. And it's okay with me if nobody ever finds out I'm anywheres on the force. I'll be a whole lot safer."

"Where'll it all end?" I asked of the world in general, whereupon Tom shrugged.

"Maybe Skull'll be dyin' of old age one of these days. That'd be the first break we've had yet on this case."

A sudden influx of matters requiring official attention put an end to our conversation for the next two hours, and I retired behind a newspaper in a corner of the office, making a jittery effort to interest myself in the news it contained. This was mostly a great quantity of supposition about Dr. Skull, some of which was voiced in an article written by Curly Smith. It had been quite a while since I'd seen that zealous individual and thus reminded of his existence, I wondered what he thought now of his chances of collecting five thousand dollars for Skull, dead or alive.

Shortly before nine o'clock, Tom's telephone rang. He listened briefly and gulped several times in rapid succession.

"All right, sir," he finally said, "I'll attend to that and come right over." He had no sooner put down the receiver than he picked it up again and barked a succession of orders into the mouthpiece.

"What's up?" I asked quickly. "Anything about Paula?"

Tom looked at me and shook his head.

"Not Paula. Bates. You remember that crack I made about him?"

"Yes."

"Well."

"You mean Skull's killed him already?"

"Who else? He's dead." Tom threw his cigarette on the floor.

"How'd he die?"

"Hung himself in his closet less'n half an hour ago. That was Harkness that 'phoned."

"But, Tom, didn't you do anything to protect him?" I demanded, rather terrified at the universal helplessness.

"What the hell can you do?" He sighed heavily and heaved himself to his feet. "So long. I've gotta go out to his apartment and do the usual." He started for the door.

"Wait a minute!" I yelled after him. "I'm going with you. I'll go crazy if I don't do something."

"Suit yourself," Tom shrugged.

BATES LIVED IN one of those ultra-swank buildings on

Sutton Place and we were piloted upstairs by an ancient elevator "boy" who appeared jolted out of a twenty-year lethargy. The coroner was already at work when we reached the scene of death, and there was little for Tom to do besides supervise the regulation mechanics—searching uselessly for fingerprints, photographing the body, questioning the widow and the servants, and taking down a few notes. To all appearances, it was a plain case of suicide, but we knew better.

The above formalities complied with, Tom and I got back in the former's speedy coupé and drove downtown to Harkness' emergency offices in the Municipal Building. The whole floor was alive with clerks and policemen, and Tom made me wait outside while he entered the inner office and conferred with his chief. For thirty minutes, I paced up and down the corridor like a caged animal before a secretary approached and said that I might now go inside.

Tom and the District Attorney were still talking in low tones, but Professor Lansdowne met me and immediately answered the unspoken question on my lips.

"There's been no trace yet," he said. "Your friend Higgins and also Chief Inspector Greene have been doing everything in their power to find her, but there's been no trace. She's vanished completely."

"But," I clenched my fists, "what are we going to do? We can't let her disappear and do nothing about it! Tear the town apart—turn it upside down. We've got to find her!"

"We can do nothing until Skull makes a mistake and leaves us a clue somewhere. We've got to wait."

"I can't see that he's ever going to make one."

"He'll make one," replied the Professor, grimly.

The scientist went on to explain that District Attorney Harkness had called a secret meeting of the most important city officials to consider the latest turn of events and decide upon a course of action. It was necessary, among other things, to appoint a man, or a body of men, to direct affairs now that Bates had been killed. Even as we were talking, the conferees began to arrive. Harkness had them shown into an adjoining board room which was equipped with a long table and a dozen or so chairs. At Professor Lansdowne's request, I was permitted to be present at the meeting.

OF THE TEN men who, besides my own friends, were present, most were afraid and all were quite nervous. Various types were represented in the group, ranging from a phlegmatic-appearing, thick-necked individual who chewed cigars and spat tobacco shreds on the floor, to a thin, pedagogic little chap who kept fiddling with his eyeglasses. All of them shifted about, fidgeted and acted generally jittery throughout the meeting, which was short and to the point.

Harkness took a position at the head of the table, leaned forward on his outstretched hands and looked directly into the faces of those he addressed.

"You have been asked to come here tonight for a very grave reason, so grave that I considered it unwise to describe it over the telephone. Lawrence Bates has been murdered by Dr. Skull."

His words were received in a stunned silence. Without allowing time for the shocked thoughts of his auditors to be crystallized into speech, Harkness continued:

"We must, accordingly, consider a number of very serious problems, the first of which is that of finding a successor to Mr. Bates. However much I regret the situation, I nonetheless am in no position to guarantee protection to the man who heads the government of this city. Therefore, it seems to me that it is entirely appropriate to call for volunteers for the post, rather than nominations. You'll excuse me, if under the press of the emergency, I appoint myself chairman of this meeting and ask for a volunteer. Do I hear any offers?"

A general hubbub of excited conversation broke out and a battery of questions were directed at the District Attorney concerning the manner of Bates' death. After satisfying the clamor, Harkness again asked for a volunteer, but in vain. His glance traveled around the circle of men and they, in turn, swapped uneasy looks with each other. Finally, a businesslike old chap with crisp gray hair and an equally crisp manner of speaking rose to his feet.

"I would like nothing better," he began, "than to undertake this task. But, besides the fact that I am clearly outranked by others of the distinguished gentlemen present, my business connections would not permit it. However, I'd like to suggest my good friend Harvey Withers, here, whose modesty has no doubt kept him from speaking out. I am sure there is no one more fitted—"

But the nominee had other ideas. "Please now, John," he said, "after all, I've got a wife and three children and if anything happened to me I don't know what would become of them. I'm afraid I must decline the honor."

Nor were there any more courageous—or more foolhardy—individuals around the table.

"I rather expected this attitude," observed District Attorney Harkness, "and I admit I don't blame you. Perhaps the plan I have to suggest will solve the problem. Roughly, it is this: I favor the creation of an Executive Board to handle the routine business of the city during the present crisis. I suggest that it be modeled along the lines of the Emergency Council, which has been directing the campaign against Skull. Such a board must have drastic powers, and in order to obtain them, I recommend that a special session of the Municipal Assembly be called tomorrow morning, at which the necessary legislation may be enacted. The Executive Board must, of course, be prepared to offer the fullest cooperation to the Emergency Council.

"I suggest further that no permanent chairman be appointed, because I feel sure that his position would make him an immediate target for Dr. Skull. I even suggest that the Executive Board itself be kept as secret as possible, and that it work at all times behind closed doors."

Without giving his listeners an opportunity to register objection—though I doubt if they had the initiative to register anything but fear—Harkness quickly followed up this proposition with several other measures designed to meet the unusual conditions. One of these was a rigid press censorship, in order to prevent the spread of panic throughout New York. Through this censorship, the news of Bates' death was to be kept from the public. Harkness also outlined plans for calling in government and state aid should it be needed, and when he finished, there was not a syllable of dissent.

One question was posed, by the thick-necked gentleman with the deceptively phlegmatic air.

"What are you going to do about catching Skull?"

"That's a fair question," replied District Attorney Harkness, "and you're certainly entitled to an answer, but the truth is, we don't know ourselves yet. One thing we do know, and that is this: beginning early in the morning there will be gotten under way the biggest manhunt New York has ever known. Police are going to comb every building in this entire town, if necessary, to run down Dr. Skull. The search will be under the direction of Chief Inspector Greene. Meanwhile, the special campaign will continue as before under Inspector Higgins. Of course, as many of you already know, we're extremely fortunate in having the help of the only man who really knows anything about Skull, Professor Alfred Lansdowne. Anything else?"

There was nothing else, so the conference adjourned. Slowly the various officials filed out, each pausing to shake hands with the District Attorney en route, and all looking as though they were about to go over the top in the face of a withering barrage. When the last man had departed and the door had been closed, Harkness passed a handkerchief across his forehead and sat down wearily.

"Now that that's over, what next?" he asked helplessly.

"Maybe you'd better grab a bit of shut-eye," advised Tom Higgins. "Looks like a busy day comin' up."

"Did the meeting give you any more ideas, Professor?" inquired Harkness, paying no attention to Tom.

"No, but I'm very glad you talked to them as you did, Mr. Harkness," replied the scientist.

"Oh, it was all your idea."

"Perhaps that's why I approve so heartily," smiled Professor Lansdowne. "Now, if you'll permit me to make a suggestion, take Tom's advice and get some sleep."

RELUCTANTLY, HARKNESS AGREED, but insisted on

sleeping right there in the office. As Professor Lansdowne was determined not to leave him, it was necessary to have two cots brought into the room. The Professor pointed out that it would be safe enough for him to sleep while the D.A. did. He was a light sleeper and would awaken if Skull were to try to force Harkness into suicide. As a safety precaution, however, the room was stripped of everything that could be considered a potential lethal weapon, the windows were locked, and the Professor's cot was placed in such a position that he would be disturbed if Harkness tried to jump out one of them. The doors were also to be fastened, with Professor Lansdowne retaining the keys.

"This is all very fine, but what if I should be commanded by Skull to sneak up and choke you. Then what?" Harkness wanted to know.

"Then I would be awakened and would promptly give you a terrific clout in the solar plexus and summon the guard," answered the scientist. "Don't let my gray hairs fool you. I'm still fairly fit."

Which was the truth. The Professor was remarkably strong for his age, and there wasn't a pound of surplus flesh on him.

"There's one other thing," observed the scientist after a moment's thought. "I want you to have a man sent up here, one that has never been seen in connection with you. I want him to have a duplicate key to the door, and to stand sentry outside until morning. He's to come in if he hears anything suspicious."

I wondered at the qualification, but Professor Lansdowne refused to explain, saying only that the whole thing was little more than an experiment and might not work,

after all, should Skull attempt to hypnotize the District
Attorney.

"But there's nothing else we can do," he added.

I wanted to do nothing so little as return uptown to
the vacant apartment—Ella MacLaughlin and Martha
were there, of course, but it was vacant as far as I was
concerned—but Professor Lansdowne insisted on it.

"You can't stay here and it will do you no good to walk
the streets all night," he pointed out. "Tomorrow is another
day, and if I can be hopeful, there's certainly no reason why
you shouldn't be."

There was no choice so I bade them good-night and
departed, but without the Professor's optimism, if indeed
he really had any, which I rather doubted. During the
twenty-minute taxi ride, I reviewed all that had happened
in the Skull affair and tried to visualize progress in combatting the fiend, vainly. I realize that "fiend" has an especially
melodramatic sound to it, yet it was the only word I could
think of that really fitted the creature. Try as I would, I
could see no progress and the outlook for Paula, as well as
for everyone else in New York, seemed very gloomy.

True, Professor Lansdowne had obtained an incomplete
description of Skull that bore out his previous conviction
that the dread doctor and Franz Ehrlich were the same
person. But even that had gotten us nowhere. It was like
looking in a haystack for a needle that might not even
be there, and the Professor talked about optimism! For
myself, I could only hope against hope, pray, and wait. It
was a dark hour.

The clock had struck two when I reached the Lansdowne apartment and Ella MacLaughlin had fallen asleep

at her post by the telephone. She had maintained a vigil right beside the instrument as though it were vital that she be able to lift the receiver the instant the phone rang. I woke her as gently as possible, verified my belief that no word had come from Paula, and went off to catch forty winks. Ella herself refused to go to bed, but agreed to lie down on the davenport.

I slept fitfully between the hours of three and seven, being thoroughly worn out. There were frenzied dreams in which I pursued a grinning lunatic through city streets, a lunatic who carried Paula thrown like a sack of grain over his shoulder. It was the old, familiar nightmare routine in which, the faster you try to run, the slower you go. Or else I was in a strange room where Skull made threatening gestures towards Paula while I remained rooted where I stood, unable to move a finger to help her. It was a pretty awful night and I awoke unrefreshed, with twitching nerves. Three cups of strong, black coffee steadied me a little. But a jangling telephone and the news that came over it soon fixed that. It was Professor Lansdowne.

"Skull has struck again," he told me. "This time it's Robert A. Beatty."

The name was only vaguely familiar.

"Beatty? Who's Beatty?"

"Beatty was the City Comptroller until he locked himself in his bathroom very early this morning and slit his throat with a razor."

"Skull isn't wasting any time, is he?" I muttered. "I suppose there's nothing to be done about it, as usual?"

"The police are beginning a systematic search of the entire city and Harkness thinks they'll find Skull, in time.

All exits from Manhattan Island are being watched closely, too, of course."

"Well, that's just dandy," I said sarcastically, "unless Skull happens to be living in Brooklyn, or Queens, or the Bronx, or on Staten Island—or in San Francisco!"

"I believe Skull is somewhere on Manhattan Island," the Professor remarked quietly, "but I'm afraid there's not enough police in the city to cover all the places he can hide. However, we must hope for the best."

"And expect the worst," I rejoined. "What can I do?"

"Stay where you are. I may need you later in the day and I want to know where to find you. If you should hear anything, call me down here."

"But I don't want to stay in this place. I'll go off my nut. Why can't—"

"Please don't argue, Bob. That's where you're needed, not here."

WAITING WAS THE toughest assignment he could possibly have given me, but I saw his logic and resolved to make the best of it. There was confusion enough at the District Attorney's office without my adding to it, and there was always the remote possibility that Paula might try to get in touch with us. In which case she would surely try the apartment, not the D.A.'s place.

The morning papers printed nothing about either Bates or Beatty thanks to Harkness' suppression of the facts. Instead, the front page was devoted to speculations, rumors, and opinions which might better have been left out for all the credibility they carried. While much horror was expressed editorially at the state of affairs and considerable opprobrium heaped upon the heads of Harkness,

Tom Higgins, and their associates, no practical suggestions were forthcoming as to how things might be improved. After ploughing through several of these inane outbursts, I threw the paper aside with disgust, switched on the radio and started pacing the floor.

This pacing, accompanied by considerable useless scheming and gnawing of fingernails, went on for the next three or four hours. During this period, there was no word from anyone and nervousness built up in me like static electricity, needing only the throwing of a figurative switch to blow me sky high. Ella MacLaughlin came in every now and then, threw me a look of profound anxiety, and silently went out. The radio blared on and on, program after program came and went, but I heard little of it.

I had turned on the set originally in the possibility that Skull might speak over it through his customary proxy of "controlled" announcer. Or there might be a news flash of interest. Until twelve o'clock nothing happened, but then, in the noon news broadcast, came this announcement:

"A short time ago, the City Editor of the New York *Express* received a telephone call purporting to come from Dr. Skull which contained the following message, addressed to the people of New York. Quote: In an effort to avoid needless suffering, I have been striking at your incompetent leaders. Unfortunately, this program has not achieved the required result—the complete surrender of the people of New York to my superior will. You continue to make the fatal mistake of trying to defy and to defeat me. Therefore, I must again resort to more sweeping measures which, I hope, will soon bring you to reason.

At the same time, I will continue to remove from their offices, the unworthy officials you have chosen. This double punishment will continue without mercy or compromise until my commands are rigidly obeyed. Unquote.

"Police have so far been unable to locate the telephone from which the call was made. Both Chief Inspector Greene, in charge of general operations, and Inspector Higgins, directing a special campaign against Skull, declined to comment on this latest development."

My first emotion was not so much horror at what I had heard as surprise that this message had leaked through the supposedly strict censorship. It could do nothing but arouse dangerous panic, and I roundly cursed the City Editor who had made it public. Surrender to Skull was as unthinkable as ever. The way the creature expressed himself, his fantastic idea that cruelty would make him the absolute master of seven million people, were the most conclusive evidence that he was a raving maniac, the more fearful because of his extraordinary power. And this was the man who held Paula prisoner! I couldn't bear to think about it.

I knew that if Skull carried out his present threat and struck at the masses of people, as he had in the subway crash, there would be no holding down panic. The whole town would be in an uproar of stark terror. If it seemed impossible to help Paula now, how much less our chances would be in a city without leaders, overrun by a crazed rabble! At that particular moment, I would have rated even Professor Lansdowne's chances of conquering Skull too low to be measurable, and as I surveyed an immediate future that loomed black and foreboding, the last vestiges of my sanity vanished into thin air.

I dismissed from my mind the Professor's request that I remain in the apartment. I stopped trying to reason things out, to think logically. Only one thing mattered: somewhere Paula Lansdowne was a prisoner of the most heartless, coldblooded murderer the world had ever known, and I was going to find her if I had to tear every building in town apart, brick by brick, with my bare hands.

Determined not to waste another precious second, I grabbed my coat, crushed my hat down on my head, and rushed downstairs to the street.

Riverside Drive was quiet. Everything was as usual.

It was the calm before the hurricane.

19

THE RIGHT TRACK

WHERE I WOULD have gone, or what I would have done, I don't know. Reason had left my mind and there was nothing there but an insensate desire to search all of New York City until I found Skull, and then to strangle him until the eyes popped out of his head. But as my feet pounded along the sidewalk, someone called my name. I was so intent on my purpose that it must have taken a second or two for the sound to register. Then, not unlike a man fighting off the effects of a heavy soporific, I wheeled around to look stupidly into the perspiring face of Joe, the doorman at the Lansdowne apartment building. He had been running after me and couldn't at once find the breath for speech.

"Mr. Larkin, sir," he gasped, sucking in great gulps of air between the words, "that boy you wanted to see—the boy who brought the package for Miss Lansdowne—you know the one I mean?"

"Yes, of course!" I cried, my desperation eagerly grasping at the straw of hope. "What about him? Did you find him?"

"I did that, sir. He lives right around here. In the neighborhood." Joe removed his peaked doorman's-cap and mopped his brow with a large handkerchief.

"Well," I demanded impatiently, "where is he?"

"He's gone home now, sir, but he promised to drop by again on his way back to school, after he's had his lunch."

"You fool!" I raged. "Why did you let him get away? Do you realize what this may mean? Do you know that a person's life—"

Joe did not know that a person's life was concerned, as his expression of pained surprise testified.

"Oh, never mind," I muttered, "let's hope he decides to keep his promise."

"I'm sure he will, sir," Joe said, encouragingly, and went on to point out that the boy would be around very soon as it was already 12:20 and he would be due back at school by 12:45. Accordingly, I returned to the apartment building and waited in the downstairs lobby. It was easier than not to lapse into a mental stupor during the fifteen minutes which followed, and the time passed more quickly than if I had been alert. Fortunately enough, the youngster I awaited kept his word. At approximately twenty minutes of one he sauntered through the broad doorway, an impudent looking rascal if there ever was one. Joe was away on a brief errand and the newcomer threw back his scraggly-thatched head and let out an ululating yell of "Jo-o-o-e!" in the peculiar, ear-splitting manner of his kind.

"Hey, you!" I barked at him, jumping to my feet. "Are you the kid who brought a box here the other day?"

Before answering, the boy swept me from head to foot with a cold, appraising eye.

"What's it to you?" he demanded, in a way that set my blood to boiling. Restraining myself with great difficulty from more lethal measures, I gripped him by the shoulder and shook violently.

"Listen!" I exploded. "Don't try to get fresh with me or I'll wring your skinny little neck, d'you hear?" Be it said by way of explanation that I am ordinarily a peaceable person and not at all addicted to beating children or kicking old ladies' canes out from under them. But after everything I'd been through, and with the profound anxiety I felt for Paula Lansdowne, having an impertinent brat waste precious minutes was more than I could stand. But my pre-adolescent friend was by now thoroughly alarmed.

"Please, mister!" he squealed, piteously. "I'll talk. Honest, I will. What do you want to know?"

BEFORE CONTINUING, I fumbled around in my pocket and brought forth a dollar bill. "Here," I said, pressing it into the boy's hand, "let's be friends. Would you like to help save somebody's life?"

"Sure, mister, you bet I would. Gee!"

"All right, then, listen. I'm the fellow who asked Joe, the doorman, to find you."

"Oh, *you're* the guy!"

"Yes, I'm the guy," I affirmed. "Who gave you that box?"

"You mean the box I brought here to Joe?"

"That's right."

"Why, a fellow in a taxi gave it to me. He told me to bring it here."

"What did he look like?"

"Oh, he was an Arab, I think."

"An Arab?" I repeated, puzzled. "What makes you think he was an Arab?"

"Well," said my friend, "he just was an Arab, that's all. He had on an Arab turban. I guess maybe he might be a sheik when he's home."

*"I was fool enough
to walk right in"*

Then I recalled that Skull had learned his tricks in India. The wearer of the turban was probably one of his servants, perhaps even Skull himself.

"Where were you when this man gave you the box?" I asked.

"About a block from here." The boy pointed to the intersection of the Drive and 115th Street.

"And after he gave it to you he didn't tell you to come back with an answer or anything?"

"No. He gave me fifty cents and told me to bring the box to this building and tell the doorman it was for Miss—Miss—aw, I forget her name."

"Then he drove away?"

"Uh-huh. That's right."

"You didn't hear him give any address to the driver before you left him?"

"Naw. I was half way here by then, I guess," answered the boy.

Whereupon another faint hope fizzled out into the same nothingness that had swallowed all of our efforts to locate Skull.

"Well, thanks," I said morosely. "I don't think there's anything else you can tell me." I turned my back and stood, chin down, trying to ferret out what to do next. When I turned around several moments later, the boy was still standing there, regarding me with frank curiosity.

"Say," he ventured, "is this a police case you're working on? Are you a cop?"

"In a way, I suppose," I replied, and started out the door.

"What's it all about?" pursued my young friend. "Let me in on it, will ya?"

"I'm looking for a person, that's all," I said, still walking.

"The guy in the taxicab?"

"He's one of the people I'm looking for."

"Is he a crook?"

"Yes."

For a few paces there was silence. Then:

"Maybe I could help you find him," remarked the boy.

"How do you mean?" It didn't occur to me for a moment that he could, and the question was perfunctory.

"Well," he continued, "I know where you can find the fellow who drove the cab he was in. Maybe you could get a clue from him."

I stopped dead in my tracks.

"What makes you think you can find him? There are hundreds of cab drivers in New York."

"Yeah, but this one's name is Gus and he hangs out over

on Broadway by the subway station. On the far side of the street. He always talks to me and the rest of the fellows every time we go by. I know a boy he gave a police whistle to."

"Why the devil didn't you say so half an hour ago?" I demanded. "Will you go over there and point him out to me?"

"Well, I don't know," wavered this priceless child. "It's getting late and I have to be at school at quarter to one."

"You can be late this once, and I'll give you another dollar. Besides, it's very important."

"Well, seeing that it's a police case—"

I headed for Broadway at full speed, dragging the kid along after me in such a way that he had to run most of the time to keep his arm from being pulled out of its socket. But when we reached the hack stand, the right driver couldn't be found. However, there were two other cabs parked and from the driver of one of them I learned that Gus, the man I wanted to see, no longer worked from that stand. He had been transferred to Grand Central Terminal.

"If you're lookin' for him, pal," said my informant, "just go down to th' Toiminal and ask for Gus. Everybody always knows him. He's a great big guy with lots of hair. Number of his cab's 433."

TEN MINUTES LATER, I got off the subway at Times Square and rushed through the crowds that always jam that station toward the shuttle that would take me over to Grand Central. As I was about to board the train, I happened to glance at the headlines on a newspaper carried by another passenger. It immediately became necessary for me to take a deep breath.

29 DIE AS 5th AVE. BUS CRASHES:
ACCIDENT OR SKULL?

As the meaning of these words sank into my consciousness, I felt a sudden desire to get out of the subway, to get above ground in the light and air. But, no. For once, there was a job to do. I stayed where I was and took the Grand Central train, wondering if it would reach its destination only a few short blocks away before being destroyed by Skull. Naturally, he was directing his energies against the engineers and drivers of trains and busses. By controlling men in such positions of responsibility, he could inflict more damage than by hypnotizing a person to go berserk in Times Square with a machine gun.

In the Terminal, I tried to buy a newspaper but discovered that every copy had been sold out. This was true of every newsstand in the entire station. Terribly anxious to learn what had happened, I borrowed a copy of the *Express* from a man. The bus was going north on Riverside Drive at about 73rd Street when it suddenly went out of control. It veered across the street, smashed into a southbound taxicab, and continued on over the far sidewalk. The stone wall which borders this walk held under the impact it received, but the lumbering, top-heavy double-decker reeled like a drunken man and capsized. Occupants of the upper deck were thrown violently to the ground, while many of the passengers below were crushed between the seats. To complete the tragedy, the gasoline tank exploded, and when rescuers arrived only a handful of passengers survived, all of whom had been on the upper deck. Unfortunately for the purposes of investigation, the driver was quite dead when found. His body had been thrown partly out of the window and his back was broken.

The article ended on a question: When and where will Skull strike next? My own lips repeated the phrase.

Still shocked by news of this latest disaster, I went to the taxi entrance of the Terminal. Shaking my head at a redcap who started to call me a cab, I approached a man wearing a company cap who appeared to be the dispatcher.

"Can you get me cab number 433, the one a fellow named Gus drives?" I asked.

"No, I can't," was the prompt reply. "You gotta take 'em as they come. It's a rule."

"Then I'll wait until he turns up. No law against that, is there?"

The dispatcher gave me the once-over with a cold and fishy eye.

"That's up to you," he remarked. "Who you say you're waiting for?"

"Driver by the name of Gus. Know him?"

"Naw," snarled the dispatcher. "I ain't got no time to keep up with two hundred different hackmen."

"The number of his cab is 433. Do you know if there's a cab with that number working out of here?"

With an expression of irritated boredom, the starter walked over to a small rack which was fastened to the wall. He checked through a list there and nodded.

"Yeh, it's working outta here. But I ain't got no idee when it'll be along. Maybe hours."

"Thanks anyhow," I said. "I'll stick around."

I waited there in the half-light of the covered driveway for the next thirty minutes while cab after cab zoomed off with its fare in a blue haze of gasoline exhaust. As each one drew up before the exit from the Terminal, I glanced at the number on its side. They had all been in the two and three hundreds, but as my patience was about gone one rolled up and I knew it was my man. The numerals 433 were painted in black figures on the yellow side.

Before I could get to it, a porter had flung open the door and was shepherding an elderly couple into the tonneau. Realizing that it might be now or never, I brushed past him, ahead of his "clients" and climbed into the taxi.

"Can't ya see I already got a fare?" A glowering face, topped by abundant black foliage, glared at me.

"Get going—fast!" I yelled. "There's five dollars in it for you."

It must have been inducement enough, for the scowl was instantly replaced by a broad and sunny smile. A brawny arm reached out and slammed the door in the face of the bewildered couple. There was the whine of gears and we shot out of the drive onto Vanderbilt Avenue.

"Where to?" the driver called, without turning his head.

I'D ALREADY SEEN from the identification card required by law to be posted in every cab that the man's name was Gus something-or-other.

"Central Park," I directed, accordingly. For five minutes, no more was said. When we swung into one of the park drives, I ordered the cabman to pull up to the curb.

"Listen," I began, "you can help me save a person's life, if you will." At the same time, I shoved a bill through the window of the driver's compartment. "Here's your five-spot first."

Gus removed his cap, tucked the money into the lining and regarded me gravely.

"I ain't got the least idea what you're talking about, buddy. Maybe you better explain."

"Right. Several days ago, you picked up a fellow. He was a foreigner, an oriental, and he wore a turban. Remember?"

"Yeh," said Gus, without hesitation, "I remember. But how'd you know?"

"This guy had you go to a place on Riverside Drive. Then he called a kid who was passing by and gave him a package for someone in a building nearby. That's right, isn't it?"

"Yeh, that's right. Are you a cop?"

"Never mind who I am," I replied. "The kid who delivered the package told me the Hindu, or whatever he was, was in your cab. He knows you. Used to talk to you when you parked on Broadway and 116th."

"That's likely. I used to talk to all the kids. I like kids."

"Swell. He likes you, too," I said, unenthusiastically. "Now here's the thing: the package was delivered to a girl. There was a warning note in it, and since then she's been kidnapped. Naturally, the guy you had in this cab had something to do with it, and I'm trying to find out where he is. Understand?"

"Yeh," answered Gus, "only you got me wrong. I ain't never had nothing to do with any kidnapping, buddy. That's clear outta my line."

"Who the hell said you had?" I demanded, losing patience. "All I want to know is, where did you pick that man up and where did you take him after he got rid of the package?"

Gus rubbed his bristly cheek and looked at me uneasily.

"I dunno as I remember."

"You better remember," I said ominously, and for a moment we glowered at each other. Then the cabman's eyes fell.

"I don't want any trouble," he muttered. He began to rub his cheek again, squinting first at me and then out the window at the passing traffic. Finally: "Lemme see, now," he said. It was at least a full minute before he continued while I held my breath.

"Ain't any trouble remembering where I picked him up," he announced, at length. "That was right at the hack stand on Broadway, by the University. What I'm trying to figure is where I let him out. Can't think whether it was 75th or 76th. One or the other, though." He went to rubbing his cheek again.

"East or west?"

"Oh, East 76th. Or East 75th. That's the trouble. I can't recall which. Now maybe if I had a look at one or the other—"

"Get going," I ordered, crisply.

Cutting across the Park, we were on the corner of 75th and 5th Avenue in no time.

"It's clear over by the river," said Gus, heading that way. We drove past the quietly elegant stone houses that succeed one another between Fifth and Park, and then through less plutocratic neighborhoods farther to the east. On the other side of Second Avenue, we skirted a dozen or so brownstone buildings at which the cabman stared. But he kept shaking his head. When we reached First Avenue, he swung around to the left.

"That's took care of, anyhow. It ain't 75th. It's gotta be 76th. I'll see if I can show you the house."

East 76th Street presented a double row of houses and apartments. The houses were brownstone or dingy gray, and looked very much alike. Gus viewed the scene with satisfaction the minute he rounded the corner and announced:

"No doubt about it, buddy. This is it. This street here."

"Which house?" I asked, as we forged slowly ahead. Gus once more became vague. He muttered something indefinite in tone and made two complete trips around the block before voicing a further opinion.

"It musta been one a' those," he pronounced, gesturing to a row of brownstones in the middle of the block. "Yeh, it musta been."

This information, assuming it to be correct, localized my hunt to a comparatively small area, but since there were five three-story houses in the group, any one of which might contain several apartments, the problem was not solved. I had Gus cruise around while I tried to evolve a practical method of approach that would get me to Dr. Skull, if indeed he were here. To begin, there'd have to be a process of elimination. I'd have to start with the end house and comb each one systematically until I found what I was looking for. After considering the matter from all angles, I decided the wiser course would be to return after dark. There might then be a chance that Skull, or his lookouts, wouldn't see me coming. I might get to his apartment without being hypnotized to run into the path of an automobile beforehand. What I would do then would be decided at the time, but I felt that calling in the police would only confuse things.

My plan—if this bare idea can be called a plan—thus formed, I directed Gus to drive to the Lansdowne apartment. It was my intention to phone the Professor from there and let him know what progress I had made.

WE WERE ON Fifth Avenue when I noticed that a lot of cars were passing us at unusual speed and turning left on 110th. Then there were sirens and Gus skidded to a quick stop to give several pieces of fire apparatus the right of way. We had barely started again when two ambulances shrieked by.

"Looks like a fire down near Lenox," observed Gus. "I better go up to 125th and skip the mob. It's farther, but faster in the long run. Okay?"

"No," I answered, struck with a peculiar desire to see what was causing the commotion. "Go across on 110th."

Traffic was getting thicker by the minute. There was a great roaring, a clanging of bells and shrieking of more sirens. Fire engines plunged at us from several directions at once and the cab narrowly missed the curb as Gus swerved sharply to avoid collision, letting loose a stream of curses that would have singed the ears of a brass monkey. On the sidewalks, men, women and children were walking swiftly or running in the direction of Lenox Avenue. Going got harder and harder, and when we had crawled half a block more, we stopped dead. Automobiles were jam-packed a block ahead of us and frantic police were trying to route them north and south, out of the line of whatever the trouble was.

"Here!" I shouted at Gus, and gave him a couple of dollars, "I'm getting out. So long, and thanks for your help."

"This is a helluva place to leave me, mister," he said, by

way of reply. Quickly, I threaded an intricate path through stalled cars to the sidewalk and caught at the arm of a man as he loped by.

"What's the matter?" I asked.

"Big wreck on the 'L'," he gasped, picking up speed. "Eighth Avenue."

Eighth Avenue was only two blocks away, but I couldn't see anything from where I was, so I hurried on.

At the intersection of Eighth and 110th Street, the elevated railway makes a great curve, just before the station platform. At this curve, the steel structure must be close to a hundred feet above the ground, probably one of its highest points in the city. I had ridden over the line many times and had often reflected that that particular spot was an ideal place for a wreck.

As I tried to keep up with the rushing crowd, I glanced upward. Now less than a block away, the elevated structure reared its straddling framework into the air. But it wasn't the tracks which held my interest. It was the train—or what had been a train—which hung, half on, half off the tracks, its front end dangling downward from the dizzy height like a broken chain.

As a result of my experiences during the reign of Dr. Skull, I have come to the conclusion that a person can stand a great deal of shock before being blessed with the numbness that relieves acute suffering. At this juncture, I had not reached any such desirable condition, and I grew sick all over at the sight before me. My knees were weak, my mouth dry, and the interior of my stomach began to quake horribly. Yet, motivated by a force greater than physical weakness, I pressed on until I reached lines which had been hastily strung up by police in an effort to keep the crowds at a safe distance.

The train had been southbound, which placed it on the inside track of the curve. Three of the six cars were still on the track, or approximately so. Another had its rear trucks off the rails but on the structure, while its front wheels hung over the side. Suspended from this car solely by the strength of the coupling, a fifth coach hung in mid-air, and from it depended a sixth.

As I looked, the cars appeared to sway and I expected to see them break loose and crash to the ground. All around them high, jointed ladders were raised and firemen already swarmed on them, fastening ropes and cables to the coaches. In the square-like intersection below, thousands of people craned their necks upward to watch.

There was a good deal of noise going on, the eternal scream of sirens and the roar of still more fire engines which were finding it impossible to get through the mob to the cleared space within the ropes. There was also the noise of the crowd itself, a disembodied murmuring that advanced and receded in waves of sound. There must have been other noise as well, so that the confusion kept me from noticing any cries from the people on the train. I could glimpse splotches of white inside the lower cars, which might have been faces or might not. From one of the windows, the head and shoulders of a woman extended downward, but she did not move. Perhaps a score of people, evidently passengers of the cars still on the track, were cautiously picking their way towards the platform, assisted by police and firemen.

As I say, I heard no outcries. Not until a plume of smoke

suddenly blossomed from underneath the lowest coach and burst quickly into flame. With incredible swiftness, this blaze raced up the length of the car until its whole side was covered with fire. Then I heard no single distinguishable cry, but a long, wavery moan that held all the anguish and pain in the world. My breath wouldn't come, and I turned away and started to fight back through the crowd again, like a crazy man.

I remember only this of the pushing, shoving and squeezing I had to do in order to reach open ground again: the murmuring of the onlookers had taken on a new quality, that of anger, and I heard more than once the words, "Dr. Skull!"

I DON'T KNOW how long I wandered aimlessly through Central Park, struggling to regain much-needed calmness and perspective. The park was practically deserted, and the few people I did pass hurried quickly by. In time, my innards stopped trembling and I was able to think of purpose again. There could be only one, and that was to find Skull—and, through him, Paula—as soon as possible. I should have notified Professor Lansdowne, I should have tried to formulate a definite plan of action, but my reasoning powers were nil. So it was without any kind of preparation or support that I made my way, on foot and by taxi, to the corner nearest Skull's supposed headquarters.

I can truthfully say that I was not afraid, but there's no use in my taking any credit for this fact. A dull resignation possessed me, and nothing mattered except getting to Paula, if only to die with her.

I needn't go into the details of my devious approach to the peril that lay ahead. It is enough to relate that, inquiring for a fictitious person as pretext, I rang every bell in the first four brownstone houses. My only hope was that the man in the turban might come to one of the doors, or that by some other sign I would know I had come to the right place. There was nothing out of the ordinary about the first four houses. It was about seven o'clock and most of their inhabitants seemed to have been at dinner.

The fifth house was like its neighbors, brown and gaunt and narrow. Except, that is, for one thing. It was dark. There was not a light in any of the windows, or in the vestibule where I fumbled for the bell. Perhaps it was this very darkness which should have given it away. It did make me nervous and brought on a return of fear.

After much groping there in the blackness, my fingers came upon a button. Summoning all my flagging courage, I pressed it. From within sounded a distant, harsh jangling. Then it was swallowed up in a silence as black as the dark that swirled around me.

But only for a moment, while I waited, shivering. Then I felt, rather than saw, the big door swing open. Inside was a blackness greater than any I'd yet seen, and from its midst someone spoke.

"Good evening, Mr. Larkin. Please enter. Dr. Skull expects you."

20

FRIEND GONE MAD

THE OFFICE OF the District Attorney was a bedlam
of telephone calls, anxious visitors and feverish activity.
From the early morning of that fateful day, things had
been happening with stunning rapidity. First, there was the
special session of the Municipal Assembly during which
that body delegated sweeping authority to a Special Executive Board, carrying out Harkness' wishes to the letter. The
Board itself consisted of eight members, each of which was
a key man controlling some vital department of New York's
government. Immediately following its creation, this body
pledged itself to the fullest possible cooperation with the
Emergency Council, thus giving Harkness means by which
he could slash red tape and greatly accelerate the placing
of the city on a fighting basis.

This step forward had hardly been taken when Skull's
radio proclamation burst like a bombshell upon New York.
The panic that had been so carefully avoided threatened
to break out in a hundred scattered areas and the prompt
attempt to suppress news of the maniac's warning was a
pathetic failure. Within an hour after it had been heard
over the air, an influential group of citizens waited upon the
District Attorney, so influential that he could not afford to

ignore it. These men demanded that effective steps be taken immediately to capture Dr. Skull and promised to bring about a comprehensive change in the executive personnel of New York if that result were not achieved forthwith.

News had leaked out that Lawrence Bates and Robert A. Beatty had been killed by Skull, though Harkness had been successful in keeping this information out of the press. The delegation, with the utter lack of intelligence usually displayed by such bodies, insisted upon having the rumors either confirmed or denied. In the latter case, it was pointed out that nothing less than actual production of the men in question alive and unharmed, would be accepted as conclusive evidence. Under the circumstances, the District Attorney could do nothing but tell the grim truth, and beg his hearers to keep the secret lest a serious blow to the morale of the people be delivered. But he was talking to the wind, and knew it. Less than an hour after the delegation left, headlines began shrieking and editors pointed out with incontestable logic that further suppression was absurd and impossible.

Fifteen minutes before one o'clock, the Fifth Avenue bus crash occurred. An investigation—empty formality!—had hardly been launched when the disaster on the elevated took place. Skull was keeping his promises with a vengeance, striking both hard and swiftly, and on the heels of the two catastrophes a series of serious disorders broke out in Manhattan. Perhaps five or six thousand people, all told, engaged in riots, parading through the streets and howling for the blood of Dr. Skull. Police reserves had to be called out to restore order, and this was done only with considerable difficulty.

Only one offensive worthy of the name had been started against Skull, and that was the thorough search of Manhattan island mentioned by Harkness at the previous night's meeting. Even this feeble attempt at definite action was doomed to failure before it had been under way six hours. It had obviously been impossible to provide warrants for every building to be searched and District Attorney Harkness had made a radio appeal to the people to cooperate with the police in their efforts to find Skull. Unfortunately, a sizable minority who stood upon their legal rights and forbade entrance to their property was able to bring about the collapse of the entire campaign. The time had not yet come when such dangerous quibbling would be swept away by the tidal wave of driving desperation, but it would come soon.

In the midst of this numbing discouragement, another delegation arrived to plague the harassed District Attorney. This time it consisted of the chiefs of the transportation companies which served New York. Their employees, they reported, were on the verge of walking out, refusing to work until they could be guaranteed protection against Dr. Skull.

Although Professor Lansdowne was in favor of a greatly curtailed train and bus schedule under such protection as could be devised, Harkness saw only an incentive to more panic in any curtailment of regular subway, elevated, street car and bus services. He promptly called into conference leaders of several employee unions and begged them to do their utmost to keep their members at work.

"I realize that they are taking certain risks, but for that matter so is every man, woman and child who rides on their trains. They have an opportunity to render an invaluable service to the people of New York in this crisis, and they simply cannot back down at this stage of the game. As a matter of fact, I don't intend that they shall be permitted to back down, if I have to invoke martial law. A transportation tie-up is too critical a thing for any halfway measures.

"Tell your men they're patriots; tell 'em they're heroes; promise them a thousand dollar bonus; do everything— but keep those trains running!"

The officials promised to do their best, and their best must have been good enough, for there was no strike.

By the time this conference was over, it was nearly six o'clock. Promptly on the hour, during the twenty second station break of one of the most important metropolitan stations, Skull spoke again, in the flat, toneless voice of a controlled announcer: "People of New York—today you have witnessed the results of my anger. There is more and greater punishment to come."

Just the two sentences, no more. No talk of truce or surrender. It was not another ultimatum, but a simple statement designed to cause the greatest possible amount of fear.

HIGH UP IN the Municipal Building, District Attorney Harkness turned a distracted face to Professor Lansdowne. "My God," he said, "isn't there something we can do to stop this creature? Don't you know any way to beat him at his own game?"

The scientist shook his head.

"There's nothing I can do now," he replied. "First we must find him. Then I'll do all I can. Until then—" He shrugged helplessly.

This brief dialogue was no sooner over than news came that Skull had struck a fresh blow. His latest victim was Martin Blake, an extremely well-liked man who had for ten years been Chief of New York's Fire Department. He had been shot down by his best friend who, returning to his senses, had immediately given himself up to the police. Heartbroken and shaken, the man was brought before District Attorney Harkness for questioning. But there was nothing he could say except:

"I don't know what made me do it. He was my best friend. I tell you, I don't know what made me do it—unless it was Skull."

Harkness sent the stricken man home. It would have been criminal to have held him on any kind of charge.

Throughout the long day, Professor Lansdowne himself had been under a severe strain. Desperate to find a way of combatting Skull, he had to admit his utter helplessness while a veritable reign of terror went on unhindered. He had held himself tense every moment of the day, expecting at any second that Skull would exert his deadly power upon the District Attorney, and steeling himself to intervene and attempt to save Harkness from certain death. It had been impossible to isolate the man who was the directing head of New York, and the Professor had also to keep a wary eye on everyone who came near him lest one of them be under Skull's murderous influence. But Skull had not struck.

It was now getting on toward eight o'clock in the evening. The streets outside the building were filled with more than their usual quota of traffic, and a good deal of noise filtered into the room through the closed window in spite of the fact that it was high above the ground. Both the Professor and the District Attorney were trying to relax their taut nerves after the gruelling day they'd had. As neither had had anything to eat since breakfast, Harkness ordered a dinner sent up to stimulate their waning energies. It was while they were waiting for this food, alone in the big office, that Skull's influence was felt.

The District Attorney was leaning back in the swivel chair behind his desk, with Professor Lansdowne opposite and a little to one side of him in a deep leather armchair. The lawyer yawned, stretched, and sighed with relief as his tense muscles relaxed. Leisurely he got up and strolled over to the window, where he stood for a moment, looking out.

"Does it seem stuffy in here to you?" he asked, turning to the Professor.

"Why, I hadn't noticed it."

"Well, I think it is," said the District Attorney. "I'm going to open the window."

With this remark, he quickly threw up the sash. In the split second it took him to do this, Professor Lansdowne realized that something was wrong. Springing to his feet, he got to the window just in time to keep Harkness from leaping twenty-one stories to the street. But the matter was far from settled. Thwarted in his Skull-inspired attempt to commit suicide, the obsessed attorney flung himself upon Professor Lansdowne with all the fury of a madman. If he had succeeded in getting his hands around the scientist's throat, the issue between Skull and humanity might have been decided then and there. But desperation lent strength and agility to Professor Lansdowne and he managed to put the heavy desk between himself and his would-be assailant.

Summoning all his strength of will, the Professor

directed every bit of the mental force he could muster against the lunatic idea planted in Harkness' brain by Dr. Skull. Exactly what took place in that room for the next five minutes, no one but Professor Lansdowne knows, and he will say little. It is enough to record that, while he could not actually conquer, the Professor was able to nullify the effects of Skull's deadly hypnotism so that both he and the District Attorney survived.

WHEN AN ASSISTANT arrived with a tray of steaming food, as had been ordered, he found Harkness leaning back in the arm chair, hands hanging limply down, eyes staring glassily at the ceiling. Professor Lansdowne was unsteady, but on his feet.

"What happened?" asked the man, putting down the tray and striding over to the District Attorney. "Is he dead?"

"No," answered the scientist, "he isn't, but he's had a bad shock. Send for a doctor and telephone Inspector Greene and Inspector Higgins, will you please?"

The trio arrived simultaneously, in a remarkably short time.

"What's it all about?" demanded Tom, eying the unconscious Harkness.

"A few minutes ago Skull attempted to make Mr. Harkness kill himself," replied Professor Lansdowne. "Luckily enough, I was able to prevent that, but I couldn't spare him a stiff shock to his nervous system. I'm afraid he's going to be out of the running for two or three days. We'll have to carry on without him."

"How did it happen?" exclaimed Tom.

As District Attorney Harkness was taken downstairs to be put into a waiting ambulance, Professor Lansdowne described the events of the past twenty minutes. When he had finished, Tom and Inspector Greene were lavish in their praise of the way he had saved Harkness' life. But the scientist dismissed compliments with a curt gesture.

"That's utterly unimportant," he said. "The big fight is yet to come and we must find a way to meet it successfully. Am I right in assuming that Mr. Harkness intended you to take over authority in the event anything happened to him?"

Tom hesitated and looked at Greene. "The Inspector here ranks me," he answered. But this obstruction to a unified command was quickly removed by Greene himself.

"This is no time to worry about a couple of extra stripes, Tom," he said promptly. "You've been on the inside of all this far more than I have. It's up to you to take charge. I'll give you one hundred per cent cooperation, and you can depend on that."

There followed a short consultation between the three men, in which it was agreed that Professor Lansdowne would continue on as a silent partner and that his advice would be rigidly followed. Inspector Greene then had to return to his headquarters and Tom Higgins and the Professor proceeded to attack the food which had been brought. It was nearly cold by now, but neither man had had any time for eating and it tasted good.

As they finished, a detective who had been on guard outside the door pounded vigorously for admittance. Considerably peeved by the force of the knocks, Tom threw open the door and demanded to know the reason for the racket.

"This, Inspector," said the detective. He extended a piece of white paper, folded in a manner familiar to every child who has ever made a "sailer" and sent it darting through the air of a schoolroom.

"What is this, a gag?" demanded Higgins.

The officer scratched his head.

"I dunno, sir. There's a message on it. A guy found it and brought it in. Maybe it's a fake, though."

While Professor Lansdowne looked on, Tom unfolded the paper and glanced at what was written on it. Then, a peculiar expression on his face, he turned to the scientist.

"Grab your hat, Professor," he said, "we're goin' places!"

21

AT SKULL'S HOUSE

THE DOOR CLICKED shut and I was in a velvety darkness that smelled faintly of some exotic perfume, a darkness that flowed around me like deep water. For the space of several moments, there was absolute silence. Then a hand touched my arm and gently guided me.

"This way, Mr. Larkin," said the voice. "Be careful of the stairs, please."

There was a barely perceptible accent. The words were given a more liquid sound than any American could produce and the voice itself was soft, almost feminine, though plainly that of a young man. The light touch remained on my arm as I stumbled against a staircase and then felt my way up each step.

"Is there any reason why we can't have a light?" It was the first time I found myself able to speak.

"I'm very sorry," said my guide, "but we cannot have a light here. It is an order."

Slowly we continued climbing. When we reached the next floor, the touch left my arm and, fearing to step forward lest I run into an obstruction or (the thought was in my mind!) step through a trap door, I stayed where I was and waited. The wait was brief. A door opened and I saw that I was standing at the head of a staircase and looking down a hallway. At the far end, through the open portal, a dim light showed. There was no one with me, but before I had time to wonder a tall, slim figure, clad in western clothes but wearing a tightly bound turban, appeared in the doorway.

"Please come this way," said the apparition, and the voice was that of my guide.

The carpet in the hall was heavy and my feet made no sound. Crossing the threshold, I found myself in a large room, the four walls of which were draped in heavy velvet of a dark wine color. If the carpet in the hall had seemed thick, the exquisite oriental rug on which I now stood made it seem of the poorest weave in comparison. Of an intricate and beautifully executed pattern, the rug must have come from Turkestan or Persia. The room was dominated by a handsome black walnut desk of American manufacture, which was surmounted by a shaded bronze lamp. There was a telephone, and, to the right of the desk, a big terrestrial globe. Comfortable armchairs and a low divan completed the furnishings.

Naturally, all this was registered on my mind in much less time than it takes to describe it, and my attention turned to the young man who had acted as my guide. He was an Indian, and from my shallow acquaintance with that country's ethnography, I gathered that he was from one of the northern provinces. Though comparatively slight in build, he gave an impression of great physical strength. Professor Lansdowne later recognized him as a Kashmiri, so my guess wasn't far off at that.

"You will please wait," he now said gravely, and noise-lessly left the room.

Automatically, my gaze traveled around the walls in an effort to discover the possibilities of escape, if any. There was nothing to give me any encouragement. The only visible way out was the way I had come in, along the hallway, down the stairs in the dark, and out the front door—if there weren't three hundred grinning orientals on guard, ready to carve me up with razor-edged scimitars. My mind, you see, moved along conventional lines, translating every-thing in terms of the approved motion picture rules. In the presence of Dr. Skull's near-omnipotence, grinning orien-tals and scimitars were a superfluity, but this fact was not impressed on me until later.

My thoughts were suddenly interrupted by a movement of the heavy curtains on the opposite side of the room. An instant later, they parted, and a man stood before me, smiling.

ALTHOUGH I HAD listened to descriptions of him from Professor Lansdowne and from the unfortunate fellow who had tried to deliver his message to the Council, I was in no way prepared for what I saw. While he was barely over five feet, four or five inches tall, it was impossible to consider him a small man, any more than it was possible to tear your eyes away from his long enough to register the details of his appearance. These eyes were large, set wide apart, and liquidly brilliant. Looking into them, I saw the distant flickering of strange lights like the shimmering reflection of stars in a midnight pool.

Nor were his eyes the only remarkable thing about him. Their outre qualities were well matched by the high, domed head which swept up and back from his brow in a white curve unbroken by any growth of hair. Seeing the startling height and breadth of this extraordinary cranium, one instinctively visualized the mighty brain it must hold. Truly, this man had been well named Dr. Skull.

For it was he.

The creature who for days and weeks had terrorized the greatest city in the world; he whose very thoughts were the twin scourges of death and destruction; he whose name made tremble the lips which uttered it; he who held the life of Paula Lansdowne in the palm of his hand; the heartless, merciless madman—Dr. Skull—stood before me, and smiled.

Spurred by the blinding realization that here, within reach of my two hands, was the person who threatened the foundations of sanity itself, I started to spring upon him with the intention of strangling him before he would have time to unleash the power of his mind in defense. But my brain never gave the signal to the rest of my body. As quickly as it had come, the desire to kill departed. I stood altogether motionless, devoid even of the power of moving, and all the while this was going on Dr. Skull was looking at me and smiling. It was not the smile of a cat playing with a mouse, or that of a maniac; on the contrary, it was a smile of friendly amusement. That this mild demeanor could be highly deceptive was proven in due course, but for the moment, Dr. Skull looked at me as you or I would look at a puppy trying unsuccessfully to bark.

"If you will just relax, my friend, I'm sure that we shall get along perfectly. If you insist on trying to play the hero, I shall have to use a bit of discipline on you, and I'm sure that would be unpleasant for both of us. Do we understand each other?"

It was a peculiar voice, a voice that blended with the liqueous eyes and the huge, bald head. It was an indescribable voice, musical and metallic at one and the same time. It was also the most assured voice in the world, and it took obedience completely for granted. There was nothing for me to do but nod mutely.

Dr. Skull seated himself behind the desk and motioned me into a nearby chair. Feeling shaky in the knees, I was grateful for the opportunity to sit down. Nothing further was said until the Indian who had shown me in had passed cigarettes to each of us. As I sucked in a lungful of the gray smoke, I felt somewhat better.

"There is nothing like a good cigarette to steady the nerves, don't you agree, Mr. Larkin? Of course, too frequent indulgence brings about a reverse effect, but in moderation they are very soothing."

It was unbelievable that I could be sitting quite calmly in a room with Dr. Skull, listening to him discuss the merits and demerits of nicotine while somewhere in the same house the person who meant everything in the world to me was in danger. But Dr. Skull demonstrated that he meant to spend little time in idle conversation.

"You succeeded in tracing us to this address through the taxi used by my servant, Ali, did you not?" he inquired.

"What difference does it make?" It was only with the greatest difficulty that I could speak calmly. "I'm here. Where have you got her?"

"She is quite safe, Mr. Larkin," the unreal voice replied. "Unfortunately, it will not be possible for you to see her at the moment, but I certainly have no wish to cause you undue anxiety. You can believe me when I say that she is well provided for."

"What are you going to do with her?"

Dr. Skull smiled, the same amicably, contemptuous, tolerant smile.

"I will be frank with you," he said. "I have not as yet decided. I have a special tenderness for beautiful women and Miss Lansdowne appeals to me greatly, but I'm afraid the attraction is not yet mutual. Perhaps later, who can say? Women have been known to change their minds."

I SWORE AT him, categorically, and derived considerable satisfaction from the act. For the time being, I didn't give a merry hoot whether or not he struck me dead the next instant. The only effect of my outburst was a hardening of his features. The smile which he had worn most of the time slowly faded.

"There is no time to exchange pleasantries with you," he said, without a trace of anger in his tone. "It was most careless of Ali to leave a trail so well-marked that you could follow it. At least, however, I have satisfied my curiosity about the man Miss Lansdowne said she loved." My heart skipped a beat at his words. "I do not appreciate her judgment, but that is natural." He paused and the curtains parted to disclose the Kashmiri, who stood respectfully at a distance.

"While it will be impossible for me to entertain you as hospitably as I might under happier circumstances," Dr. Skull went on, "I can at least provide you with the society of a young man whom you may know. You realize, of course, that I can't very well let you go back to Professor

Lansdowne and his police and tell them where I live, do you not?"

"You'd have a hard time getting me out of here even if you wanted to," I replied grimly, "as long as Paula is here. You can't get away with this wholesale murder forever, you know!"

"We'll pretend that you have said nothing, yes? For the time being, you will have to be a prisoner. Now, my friend, in spite of rumors to the contrary, I do not enjoy killing. Please do not make it necessary for me to kill you by attempting to escape. I assure you I shall know if you try and I shall be forced to take drastic action. Need I add that there is not the slightest chance of your succeeding?"

"Have it your way now, Skull," I said, melodramatically. "My time will come later."

"*Doctor* Skull, please, my friend," he corrected gently. "I am sensitive on the point. After so many years of hard labor, I value my few honors." He gestured to his servant to take me away, and as he moved to my side, the Kashmiri produced a wicked-looking automatic which he held in readiness. I wondered why it should be necessary, then my mind was jerked off that line of thought by Skull, who had called me back.

"Before you go there are one or two questions I'd like to ask you," he said conversationally. "What is the general attitude toward me, throughout the city?"

"It couldn't be printed," I replied flatly.

"That is very bad," he murmured. "It will only cause more suffering. Is there no feeling in favor of ceasing this ridiculous opposition to me?"

"None," I said, and there was a note of triumph in the word.

Dr. Skull shook his head. "The poor, blind, crazy fools. If they would only think!" There was more than a trace of wistfulness in the last sentence. Then he nodded to the Kashmiri and I was prodded into movement.

WE REENTERED THE outer darkness of the hallway. Grasping the heavy wooden balustrade to keep myself from stumbling, I felt my way down the stairs ahead of my guard, who followed at a distance too great for me to whirl and grapple with him. To have done so could have resulted in nothing but tragedy for me, but the temptation was great, and I explored the possibilities of such an attack. However, I was forced to the inevitable conclusion that the Kashmiri would undoubtedly riddle me with bullets before I could get my hands on him. Although the darkness was impenetrable to me, I had the uncanny feeling that he could see without difficulty.

At the foot of the stairs, I was ordered to turn sharply to the right. After walking down a hallway which apparently paralleled that on the floor above, I brought up short against a door—so short that I cracked my nose on it and saw a galaxy of stars.

"Can't you tell a guy when there's something in the way?" I inquired with heat. But the Kashmiri merely requested me to stand back while he opened the door. The room within was illuminated by an old-fashioned crystal chandelier and in former times had been the dining room. Now the furniture was swathed in white coverings and presumably was not being used by Dr. Skull. The light was a welcome relief from blackness, but I was allowed no time to appreciate it. The Kashmiri urged me on through a butler's pantry which connected with the kitchen, and then into the kitchen itself. This showed signs of recent use, but I wondered at the complete absence of servants.

While I waited, the Kashmiri took a bunch of keys from his pocket and opened a small door in the wall. Preceding him, I once more plunged into darkness and found myself groping down another stairway. When we reached bottom, an electric bulb hanging from the ceiling was switched on, illuminating a typical basement, complete with coal bin and furnace. Following instructions, I marched along a corridor past two closed doors, evidently entrances to storerooms. At a third door, I was commanded to halt. This one was identical with the others, being of heavy wood, but in addition to the regular lock there were staples through which a sturdy padlock was hooked. Using his left hand to keep me covered with the automatic, the Kashmiri fumbled with the padlock. The door finally swung open, and by the dim light which filtered through I could see that the interior was both floored and walled with cement. It was altogether bare of furnishings and all I could see was a pile of old clothes, or something of the sort, in one of the corners.

"In here, please," directed my captor, and I turned once more to calculate my chances in a hand-to-hand encounter before submitting to the imprisonment. But the man eyed me suspiciously and retreated a step, keeping the gun pointed steadily at my stomach. It was not a situation to inspire in me the greatest amount of daring, and forthwith I decided upon discretion.

As soon as my feet were clear of the threshold, the door

banged shut. There was a rattle of metal as the padlock snapped into place, and a second emphatic click followed which meant that the regular lock had been turned, also. Blind as a bat, I stood perfectly still, waiting to see if my vision would improve before making a move. There was a packet of matches in my pocket, but a sense of caution forbade my using them at the moment.

Now, when Dr. Skull had remarked that there was some-one I knew in the house, I was far too concerned with my immediate fate to show much curiosity about my supposed acquaintance. Besides, the only two people I cared about were Paula and Professor Lansdowne, and since I already knew Paula was there and since I was perfectly sure that the Professor was not, it made slight difference who the good doctor was referring to. But as I stood in the pitch blackness of the basement room I was forcefully reminded of the matter by the feeling that I was not alone. There was no sound, not even that of breathing, and it was impossible to see anything. Still the feeling was there.

The logical thing to do, I told myself, was to call out. If there were anyone in the room, he must be a prisoner too and therefore would be friendly, especially if he were the acquaintance Dr. Skull had mentioned. But my vocal chords simply refused to function and I stood there, like a perfect idiot, cold sweat beginning to break on my fore-head. Minutes passed and the absurdity of my panic grad-ually became apparent. After facing Dr. Skull himself and leaving his presence unharmed it was not very mature of me to be afraid of the dark. A hoarse whisper broke from my throat.

"Hey!"

Silence. I wet my lips, took a deep breath and tried again, a bit louder.

"Hey! Anybody in here with me?"

Still no reply, but I could not shake the conviction that some one or some *thing* was in that room. I brought out my matches, gathering my courage for whatever the light should reveal, and struck one. As the orange flame flickered and then burned brightly, its glare kept me as sightless as the dark had done and by the time I was beginning to get used to it, the flame burned my fingers and had to be blown out. The second match was better. The hard, white walls of the storeroom came into view, then the only thing in the place, the pile of clothes in the corner.

As I looked closer, I saw that it was not a pile of clothes, but a man, lying on the stone floor.

With a third match for torch, I gingerly approached him and looked into his face. It was Curly Smith, the reporter on the *Express*.

HE WAS UNCONSCIOUS, and there was an ugly mass of clotted blood on the back of his head where he must have been struck with a baseball bat or something equally lethal. That match flickered out and I knelt on the floor beside him. His hand was warm to the touch and as I felt for his pulse, I could hear him breathing. It was faint, but quite regular. I struck another match and looked hopelessly around for a water tap so I could bathe his head, but there was none. The only thing visible was what had once been a coal shovel, its handle broken off half way up the stem. Nothing else.

I lifted Curly's head to put my coat under it and he stirred, groaned, tried to move, and opened his eyes. Then the match went out. There were just two more. I could feel the reporter trying to sit up, so I risked one of them. He blinked his eyes rapidly in the wavering light and focussed them on me.

"Larkin!" The word was half a groan. "What happened? Where'd you come from? Where—"

"Take it easy, take it easy!" I cautioned him. The match was gone and we were in the dark again. As gently as I could, I pushed him back on my folded coat. "I don't know what happened, but you certainly got slugged. Rest a minute before you try to remember anything."

"Owoo!" He must have investigated his head, with painful results. "I'm bleeding to death! Somebody better get a doctor!"

"Shut up!" I commanded. "You're liable to get us in worse trouble if you don't pipe down."

Curly subsided temporarily and lay still regaining his strength and trying to recall what had happened to him. I explained that we were in the basement of the house where Skull had his headquarters, and then memory came back to him.

"Yeah," he said. "That blankety-blank Hindu smacked me with his gun. I tried to make a break for it. Guess it didn't work out so well."

"Can you remember how you got here in the first place?"

"That's easy. I followed Paula Lansdowne."

"You followed Paula?" This was more of a surprise than finding him there in the first place. "How did that happen?"

"Well, it was like this." I felt him raise himself to a sitting position. "Quite a while ago my paper gave me the chance to do a little private snooping on this Skull case.

I had a couple of ideas and thought I could beat the cops to the kill *and* to the five thousand dollar reward. Which would be a swell scoop for the sheet and a swell bonus for little Curly, see?"

"Yes, I see."

"You remember the woman who took that broker for the ten grand and whose body they found later on? She was my first clue. I figured that there was a connection between her and Skull, and that by getting a line on her, I could lead myself to Skull. Only it didn't work. Neither did a flock of other things. I've been on the verge of getting canned for weeks. Oh, my poor head!" he suddenly moaned. "I must have a skull fracture!"

"Never mind the puns," I shot back. "Go on with the story, for Pete's sake."

"All right, only give me half a chance. Yesterday morning—or was it last year?—I thought I'd have a talk with Professor Lansdowne, figuring he might possibly have an angle on account of the way he talked at his trial. So I grabbed a subway and went out. Just as I was coming up from the platform at 116th, who should I see but Paula. She was about to go through the turnstile in the opposite direction and I spoke to her. But she didn't seem to hear me. She went on through and started down the stairs to the trains. So I chased after her.

"Down on the platform, I spoke to her again, and this time she looked right at me and turned away. I couldn't figure that out, but her face looked kinda strained and I wondered if she were sick. So I caught hold of her arm and asked her if she was feeling all right. This time, she told me to please leave her alone, so I did. In fact, I started to leave the station. I had no idea what had come over her and couldn't think of anything I'd done to make her feel insulted. She'd always been friendly to me before. I was nearly to the street when I had a flash of inspiration, or something. I remembered how funny her face had looked, especially when she spoke to me. Then I thought hard and remembered that the words had come out funny, too, as though she'd been wound up like a mechanical doll.

"So I had a hunch. Maybe she was hypnotized—by Skull, of course. Right away I turned back and ran after her, praying she hadn't gotten a train yet. One had come in and they were closing the doors, but I got on. I had to hunt through three or four cars before I found her. She was sitting down, looking straight ahead of her and didn't seem to see me when I walked by. I knew if she were really hypnotized it wouldn't do me any good to try to keep her from doing whatever she'd been told to do, so I made up my mind to sit tight and follow her. I thought maybe she might need help. I didn't think for a minute, though, that she'd be going to Skull.

"She got off the train at 72nd Street and hailed a cab. I followed in another and she came straight here. This Hindu who conked me let her in the door. I didn't know what to do then. I couldn't be positive, of course, that she'd been hypnotized and it might be that the Hindu was only a fortune teller for all I knew. So there I was. Just the same, I waited, and she didn't come out."

"So—" I prompted.

"So, I waited and waited. The longer I waited, the funnier it looked. She wouldn't stay so long with any fortune teller and I never heard of anybody in New York with a Hindu butler. It looked very much like something was screwy. Thinking I'd go and find out if she were all right, I went up and rang the bell. No answer. This wasn't right so I kept on ringing. Finally, this same mug comes to the door and asks what do I want. I tell him I want to see Miss Lansdowne, and the fun is on."

"Well, go on," I said impatiently, when he stopped again.

"Okay, I'm going. The Hindu lets me in and no sooner gets the door shut than he shoves a gun into my ribs and takes me upstairs. That's where I see Skull for the first time and really know where I am. Boy! I figured my time was up. It would have been, too, if it hadn't been for Paula. Skull looked me over a couple of times without saying anything and gave the Hindu one of those 'you know how to take care of things like this' look—you know. Then Paula steps in—"

"Was she there?"

"Sure she was there. She was talking to this lug when I was brought in. She—"

"Was she all right? For God's sake man, tell me how she was!" I could have choked him for the casual way he ignored facts that meant everything to me.

"Of course she was all right. Wouldn't I have told you if she wasn't? She wasn't even hypnotized, I'm pretty sure. Anyhow, she begged Skull not to have me bumped off by the oriental stooge."

"She would do that," I murmured. "What then?"

"Well, then Skull said he would do whatever she wanted, if it were reasonable. I didn't hear him give any order, but the Hindu brought me down here, and here I am."

"What about the bump?"

"Oh, that. When he brought my lunch, or maybe it was dinner, I took a sock at him, trying to connect with his chin. But he connected first, with the butt of his gun I suppose. That's all."

"I see."

WE WERE SILENT, while the almost tangible blackness of the place eddied around us.

"What's your story?" Curly asked, at length. Briefly, I outlined my own experiences. "I didn't see Paula," I added ruefully, "and I have no idea where he's keeping her. Do you know?"

Curly replied negatively.

"What do you suppose he's going to do with her, and with us, too, for that matter?" he inquired.

"How the hell should I know?" My voice was bitter. "All I know is this: we've either got to get out of here or get word out."

"Well, if that's the way you feel about it, we better begin gnawing right now. I don't see any other way of doing it."

"You know what," I remarked, an idea coming to me, "I don't think Skull has a soul in this house with him except that stooge with the gun."

Whereupon Curly reduced my budding hope to ashes by pointing out that one man with a gun was quite a bit better than two without. Besides, he added, there was Skull himself to consider. If he had no more help than that afforded by one man, it must be because he didn't need it.

"With that evil eye of his he could hit a gnat at a hundred paces or a hundred miles. Bet he knows what we're talking about now, too," Curly enlarged. "Probably getting a big laugh out of us."

Then I remembered something. "Hold on a minute. If Skull's so confounded omnipotent, why does the Indian use a gun?"

"That's right," said Curly. "Why didn't he just put us in a trance?"

But we didn't know the answer. That wasn't to be revealed until later in the game. For the present, I decided to examine the room and the possibilities, if any, of escaping from it. Curly had a cigarette lighter in his pocket and by the dim light it provided I examined the walls and the windows. The walls, naturally enough, offered nothing, and the first window was securely boarded up. Heavy planks were nailed tightly together so that there wasn't a chance of prying them loose, even if we had anything to pry with, which we didn't.

The second window wasn't such a hopeless one. The lower board, though flush with the sill, was not right up against its neighbor. There was a space of perhaps a quarter of an inch between them. If I could get my fingers in there, I might—

"Did that whack on the head knock all the strength out of you?" I asked Curly.

"Yeah, but it's come back now. Why?"

I pointed to the window, several feet above my head. "One of us has to get up there and pry that lower board loose, that's why. Now which do you want to be, the guy that holds me on his shoulders, or the guy I hold on mine?"

"I'll hold you. With this head, altitude might make me dizzy."

The next few minutes witnessed as neat a trick of acrobatics on Curly's part as you'd ever want to see. Besides

holding me upright on his shoulders, he used his right
hand to prop himself against the wall and his left to hold
aloft the lighter so that I might see to work. But in vain. I
couldn't move the board an inch. After repeated attempts,
we wearily gave up the job. Then, in the deep gloom of the
farther part of the room, my eyes fell on the broken shovel.
With difficulty, I suppressed a cry of joy.

"That'll do the trick!" I said, with new cheer.

"Be quiet with it," cautioned the reporter, "or we'll have
the Hindu in our hair and probably Skull, too."

All over again, we went through our gymnastics. Working carefully to keep the blade of the shovel from grating
noisily against the cement sill, I pried with all my strength.
The next thing I knew something gave way and I fell backward from Curly's shoulders and landed on the hard floor
with the breath knocked out of me. In spite of the pain,
my senses were cocked to see if the sound of my fall would
bring investigation. But the silence was not disturbed.

Curly relit his lighter and I went aloft to inspect our
progress. A disappointment awaited me. Only a small piece
had been broken from the thick wood. More to the point,
when I peered through the chink thus made, I saw something which drowned the little hope left in me—bars. Iron
bars an inch in diameter criss-crossed the window, which
contained no glass. Through the hole I could see the street,
our prison cell being in the forward part of the house.
There was the reflection of a street light on the sidewalk
and as I looked two people walked by. Safety was so near—
and so far! Yelling for help would do no good and might
mean death for us all, Paula included. We were hopelessly
stymied. Despondent, I climbed down.

While Curly lay at full length trying to recoup his energies after the strain he'd been under, I told him what I'd seen.

"So I guess we rot here until Skull decides to put us out of our misery," I said heavily. As far as I was concerned, it was only a matter of time. At that, I wouldn't have cared much. With Paula facing God knew what while I couldn't lift a finger to help her, life wasn't exactly sweet. "Maybe Professor Lansdowne will track Skull down and find us," I said, but my heart wasn't in it.

"SAY!" HISSED CURLY, suddenly. "Could you really see people passing by on the sidewalk?"

"Yeah." I felt as listless as I sounded.

"How far would you say they pass from the window—how many feet?"

"Oh, twenty, twenty-five. Too far to whisper to, anyhow, if that's what you're driving at."

"I'm not," he said shortly. "I'm driving at this: why can't we write a note, tie it to something heavy, and throw it at the next person who passes? He could take it to the police and—"

"Where would that get us? If you throw anything heavy, Skull might hear it hit the pavement—assuming he's no mind reader and wouldn't know about it automatically—and he'd do plenty. Besides, even if anybody would take the note to the police, which they probably wouldn't, what good would the cops do? Just force Skull's hand, that's all, with death in the pot for the three of us."

"But he might not hear it, and you could address the note to Higgins—he's a friend of yours, isn't he?—and tell him to be very careful. It's our only chance. What can we lose?"

I thought a minute before replying. Then, "Okay," I agreed. "What can we lose?"

Curly had about a dozen sheets of paper in his pocket, and a pencil. I hastily scribbled a note to the finder, asking him to take a message to Higgins or Harkness. In the message, I gave the street and number, described our precarious situation and begged for extreme caution. Rolling the paper around Curly's lighter—now empty and otherwise useless—I fastened it on with a rubber band. Then I climbed on the reporter's shoulders as before, waited until I heard someone coming and then, taking careful aim, I let fly. The lighter sailed through the air, landed with a dull "tink" just in front of a man who was passing, and bounced into the street. The man looked first up, then in back of him, and went on. The trick had failed.

Worse, there was nothing else to throw except our billfolds. Keys would have made too much noise in a bunch and wouldn't have been heavy enough individually. Our shoes would have been too big to get through the small aperture I'd made. So, painfully scrawling another message in the dark—I hadn't the slightest idea it would be decipherable—I put it in my wallet and threw it at the next passerby, a woman. I thought if anything would stop a person, a wallet would. But it fell far short of the sidewalk. Curly's did better, but not enough better. Hopelessness again descended on us like a pall. Our only comfort was that Skull and his flunkey had apparently not heard us—small comfort, considering our utter lack of results.

"Well," I sighed, "here we are again."

Under his breath, Curly made an exclamation.

"There are still a couple more chances," he said. "Look—did you ever make paper airplanes in school when you were a kid?"

"Airplanes? No."

"Oh, not airplanes, exactly, but gliders, like. You take a piece of paper and fold it over two-three times, so that it has a sharp point and wings, sort of. Then you throw it into the air and it sails. Get what I mean?"

"You mean make paper sailers and throw *them* at people?"

"Yeah. What do you think?"

"I think you're nuts. You couldn't make one of those things go as far as the sidewalk, and even if it did, nobody would bother with it."

"All right, then, you think of something to do."

I couldn't think of anything, so we made "airplanes" with the paper Curly had left, scribbling a note on each sheet before folding it. When we were through there were about ten "ships" in all, and I felt sure not one of them would ever sail as far as the sidewalk.

For the fourth or fifth time, I climbed on Curly's shoulders and looked through the break in the boarding. I waited for what seemed an interminable time for someone to pass. A man finally did, and I shot the flimsy "sailer" at him. It took the air beautifully, then dipped, turned, went into a tailspin and landed on its nose a couple of feet from the window.

For a long time we waited for people to go by and then sailed the pathetic little darts at them. We changed positions to give Curly relief every two or three minutes, but his luck was no better than mine. Too frequently, the papers would go no farther than a few feet. Once, a "ship" glided clear to the sidewalk and dropped right before a man and a woman, but, aside from stepping on it, they paid it no attention.

Then, when I was at the window, Curly handed up a "ship."

"Make a wish," he said. "It's the last one and there's no more paper."

I made a wish. I crossed my fingers and said a prayer, too. Footsteps sounded on the sidewalk and I got ready. It was a man, and the moment he came into range, I took such aim as was possible and let it go.

Maybe the prayer and the wish and the crossed fingers worked a charm, I don't know. All I know is this: the paper sailed beautifully out toward the sidewalk at an altitude of a little over five feet. Straight as a die it went for the man and I held my breath for fear it would fall short. But it didn't. It kept on going until it struck the man on the side of his face and then dropped to the ground beside him.

I saw him stop and feel his cheek. He glanced up and around, and finally—finally—looked down at the "sailer." He started to move on and a cold chill ran through me. Then he looked back at the ground. He stooped, picked up the paper and began to unfold it. I saw him start reading it, in the light from the street lamp.

"Hey!" cried Curly, in a stage whisper. "Any luck?"

My eyes were still glued to the man. He turned his head to glance behind him, turned and walked quickly and purposefully out of my line of vision. Joyfully, I climbed down.

"I think so—" I started to answer, and that was as far as

I got. A streak of light was on the stone wall. Instantly, my head jerked around to the door of the room.

Standing in it and smiling faintly was the Kashmiri, the automatic held carelessly in his hand.

22

CORNERED BUT NOT CAUGHT

"YOU WILL BOTH come with me, please." A motion of the pistol emphasized the Kashmiri's words. While hopelessness coursed through my veins like ice-water, Curly looked at me questioningly.

"Better do as he says," I advised.

The long, fumbling way up the dark stairs to the luxuriously furnished room on the second floor completed, we were left alone for a few minutes before Dr. Skull joined us. When he did, there was no longer a smile on his face. His strange eyes shot sparks of anger and his femininely full lips were drawn down at the corners.

"You have sent a message to the police." It was a statement, not a question. "You were warned to be discreet. Whatever happens to you now you alone are responsible for."

Curly and I shifted uneasily on our feet, but said nothing. The reporter was showing signs of wanting to attack Skull and I quickly flashed him a warning look. His hands, which he had been clenching and unclenching, relaxed.

"To whom was the message addressed?" The question was directed at me and created a doubt in my mind that I decided to have resolved then and there.

"I won't tell you," I said.

Dr. Skull seated himself at the desk and smiled at me pityingly. "You wish to see if I can make you tell, eh?" he said. "Very well, my friend, you shall see. Now, please be so kind as to give me the information I wish."

His baleful eyes fixed themselves on mine, and it was though an electric charge had been sent through my body. When, a second later, he released me from that soul-shaking gaze, I was weak and trembling. I had no volition left, only the desire to do whatever he willed, anything, so long as I would not have to look into those terrible eyes again.

"The note was addressed to District Attorney Harkness or Professor Lansdowne, either one," I said. "I told where I am and asked for help quickly."

"Thank you, my friend," Dr. Skull nodded his great head several times. "Now please do not make me resort to such foolish trickery again."

"What are you going to do with us?" suddenly demanded Curly. "If you're going to kill us, why don't you get it over with?"

Dr. Skull made no reply, but the curtains in back of him opened and the Kashmiri appeared. Without any audible orders from Skull, he advanced on Curly and nodded meaningly toward the door. Apparently, I was supposed to remain. As he preceded the Indian out, the reporter looked at me, smiled a little and shrugged. When the door had closed behind him, Skull invited me to sit down.

"I presume," he began, in that extraordinary voice of his, "that if Professor Lansdowne gets your distress signal he will be out here post-haste with an army at his heels, no?"

"I can only hope."

The Kashmiri returned with Paula.
"Oh, Bob—you're here!" she said

"Naturally, and we must wait and see. While it was not my intention to renew my acquaintance with the Professor so soon, I shall not avoid a meeting. He has told you we are old friends, has he not?" The doctor's eyes, quietly luminous again, questioned, and I nodded. "Yes," he continued, "we are both graduates of the same school, in a manner of speaking, though it might be said that we took different courses. I always expected that Professor Lansdowne would recognize my—work. A very brilliant man, the Professor, but of course not so brilliant as I." He paused to light a cigarette while I regarded him in silence, waiting for whatever was to come next.

"Mr. Larkin," Dr. Skull went on, blowing a thin plume of smoke into the air, "should our mutual friend arrive with his police, I want our reunion to be as pleasant as possible. To make myself clear, there must be no show of violence on the part of the police. They must not attempt to drive me out of this house with any of their machine guns or tear gas bombs until *after* I have had my visit with Professor Lansdowne. They may surround the house, if that will give them any comfort, but their cordon must not approach any nearer than, let us say, five hundred English yards. Please bear this distance in mind—five hundred yards. Then I must be allowed thirty undisturbed minutes with the Professor. After that, they may do as they please. Have you understood me perfectly?"

"Yes," I replied. "I suppose you'll want me to take them your terms?"

"That is entirely correct, Mr. Larkin—if they should come, of course. I rather believe they will. The gentleman who picked up your ingenious little device went away with quite a determined air about him."

"What makes you think the police will do as you ask?"

"I will leave that up to your own eloquence, although I will do my best to enhance your persuasive ability. Consider: if they should not do as I ask, or if there should be any treachery, on your part or theirs, I can guarantee that Miss Lansdowne's fate will be a most unpleasant one."

"That touch is both old and melodramatic, Doctor," I remarked. "Why don't you just hypnotize the lot of us and let it go at that?"

"If the old tricks were not so good, they would never have lived so long, my friend," said Dr. Skull, ignoring my question. "Please do Miss Lansdowne the service of taking me seriously, whatever you may think of my choice of expedients. But let us continue. Should the young lady's danger prove insufficient to dull the enthusiasm of the police, you may inform them for me that a very personal disaster will strike every man who raises his hand against me. To make this part of your argument more convincing, I will provide some small proof of the statement immediately after you make it."

"And what do I get out of it if I do everything you say?" I demanded. "Will Paula—"

"Perhaps your life, my friend, and the knowledge that the woman you profess to love is unharmed. Is that not enough?" Skull rose to his feet.

"That's enough," I said, rather quickly. "Now what if no one turns up for the show? What will you do then?"

"You need not concern yourself about that." Dr. Skull had not called or, as far as I could see, pressed a button, but the Kashmiri again appeared. I came to believe, and later to know, that he and his servant did not have to communicate with each other by the ordinary spoken word but used a form of mental telepathy instead.

Dr. Skull addressed me:

"I am now going to grant you a great privilege, but I must confess that my motives are not altogether altruistic. You are to see Paula Lansdowne for a short time. I believe that after talking to her you will be even more reluctant than you already are, to let any harm come to her. I'm sure you will forgive me if I withdraw."

HE SMILED, BOWED slightly, and disappeared through the curtains. The Kashmiri followed him out, but returned a moment later with Paula. "Darling!" I cried, and never put so much fear and anguish into a single word.

"Oh, Bob. You're here!"

She rushed into my arms and for a brief moment while time and the rest of the world ceased to exist I held her close. When I finally released her, the Kashmiri had gone and we were alone. There was no doubt in my mind that Skull would hear all that we said, however. Not that it could make any difference.

"How on earth did you find this place?" Paula asked me.

"That isn't important. What is important to me is how you got here?"

"I don't know, Bob. I don't remember a thing about it, except that someone seemed to guide me. I must have slipped out of the apartment very carefully."

"Are you all right?" I asked her.

"I'm all right, dear. What about you?"

I nodded absently and noticed for the first time that she was wearing a filmy negligee.

"Paula—!" I held her tightly, at arm's length.

"No, Bob, no!" she answered, before I could say what was in my mind. "He sent this"—she indicated the garment she wore—"with the message that I should wear it. I started not to and then thought maybe I'd better humor him. He's quite insane I think."

"Where's he been keeping you?"

"In a room in the back somewhere. I'm really quite comfortable and he's given me good food, too. I didn't sleep very well last night, thinking I might have a visitor, but I guess I must be losing my allure. Dr. Skull left me severely alone."

"Please, Paula," I said, "don't joke. I haven't any sense of humor left."

"He told me he wants to marry me, and you know, I believe he would, too. He says he will make me queen of the whole world."

"Paula," the word came through clenched teeth, "I'll get you out of here if it's the last thing I ever do!"

"Silly," she said, touching my hand with cool fingers, "I know. But tell me, where's Dad? Has he been frantic?"

"Of course he's been frantic. He may be here tonight. Curly Smith—I guess you already know—is here and he and I got a note out. Then Skull found out about it and now I've got to be the go-between and persuade the police to keep their distance until Skull has talked to your dad. It's going to be like old home week."

"Bob," said Paula urgently, "don't do it!"

"I've got to. It'll be bad for—for everybody concerned, if I don't."

Paula gave me a long and searching look. "Bob Larkin, if that lunatic is using me to force you—don't be a fool! What do I amount to if thousands of other people are in danger? He *is* making threats about me, isn't he?"

Before I could answer, the Kashmiri entered.

"You cannot talk any more now," he announced. "The lady will please go back to her room." He stood aside, waiting. I kissed Paula lightly on the lips and weighed, for the dozenth time, the chances of attack, only to resign myself to waiting for a better opportunity.

"Goodby for now, darling," Paula murmured in my ear. "Remember what I told you. Anyway, I don't think he would hurt me, no matter what he says."

Then she was gone and I was left by myself. In whatever light the fact may put me, not for one moment did I consider sacrificing Paula, no matter if my failure to do so would cost ten thousand other lives. Nor do I think this was any but a natural attitude for me to take.

Dr. Skull did not return to the room as I had half expected he would. The Kashmiri—I was beginning to consider him an old acquaintance—returned and ushered me back to the basement cell where Curly Smith was already reposing. It was as dark as before and for the next hour there was nothing we could do but conjecture about outside developments. We also could—and did—drive ourselves crazy trying to think of a way out that wouldn't mean greater danger for Paula. I explained my unwilling part in Skull's game and felt better when Curly told me it was the only thing for me to do.

I'll say one thing for the police when they came—for our desperate little note got through—they knew how to be quiet. We had both been listening for the sound of sirens and a great deal of screeching brakes and squealing tires, none of which we ever heard. The first intimation either of us had that a rescue was being attempted came when our friend the Kashmiri turned up with his customary anemic smile and the inevitable automatic.

"Mr. Larkin will please come with me," he said. "The other gentleman will remain here."

Without a word, I got up and walked toward the door.

"Good luck, kid," said Curly. "Watch your step!"

DR. SKULL WAS awaiting me in the disused dining room on the first floor. Wasting no time in preliminaries, he came straight to the point. "Your friends have arrived and are now surrounding the house, as I expected," he said. "Professor Lansdowne is with them and they are slowly closing in with a great deal of stealth. In accordance with our agreement upstairs, you're to stand on the outside, in front of the door. As soon as you see anyone coming, call out and identify yourself, then take my instructions to Lansdowne. I will repeat them: Lansdowne to return here with you; the police to retire to positions at least five hundred yards from this house; no attempt to capture me until I have talked to the Professor for thirty minutes. If these conditions are disobeyed, the girl will suffer, and so will every man who takes part in any attack. You understand?"

"Yes," I replied. "Do you guarantee that after thirty minutes the Professor will be allowed to return to the police lines and that his daughter will be allowed to go with him?"

"I guarantee nothing but death if I am disobeyed. Now, go!" His voice was uncompromising and his eyes shone luminously green, like a cat's, in the dimly lit room. I waited no longer. The Kashmiri opened the door for me and I stepped out on the landing at the top of the brownstone stairs.

At first glance, the street appeared deserted, but as I strained my eyes to look down toward the next intersection, I saw several automobiles. They had stopped in the center of the street and were arranged so as to form an effective blockade. I thought I saw men approaching on the sidewalk. Life in the surrounding buildings was going on in normal fashion and as I stood there waiting for the police to get near enough to hail, a woman's shrill laughter pealed forth. What a time to be drunk, I thought, with all hell getting ready to pop right outside your door!

No ray of light shone from any of the windows above and behind me and I felt that Skull was concealed at one of them, watching.

Though advancing with a minimum of noise, the police

did not sacrifice speed for silence, and came on more rapidly than I had expected. They were well within hearing when I yelled at them wildly:

"Don't shoot! Don't shoot! I'm Bob Larkin." Walking toward the advancing scouts with my hands in the air, I kept repeating this phrase. In a moment, I was gripping the hands of Professor Lansdowne and Tom Higgins. As rapidly as possible, I outlined our situation to them and passed on Skull's demands. All the time, the street was filling up with more and more police. There must have been sixty or seventy of them, many armed with machine guns. At the conclusion of my story, there were angry mutterings of dissent from the men clustering around us.

"We ain't going to let that devil get away. No, sir!" said one copper, grimly.

"If you don't do as he says, you may all be killed," I warned.

"Oh, yeah?" There were more protests which were suddenly cut short by a terrible clattering.

It was one of the policemen, one with a submachine gun in his hands, and he was turning it on his own comrades, spraying them with a rain of death. There were men screaming and sprawling on their faces all over the street. Then there was a flash of light, a lone report, and the submachine was quiet. It dropped to the pavement, and the man who had fired it fell on top of it. Near me stood a tight-lipped sergeant, his revolver still smoking.

"Dr. Skull did that." The words fell, hollowly, from my mouth. "He was showing you he means business. If you don't do as he says, there'll be more."

There was the groaning of men in terrible pain. There

were some who lay on the ground without groaning, and they were dead. From the close-packed survivors came a Babel of voices.

"He's right, Professor," said Tom Higgins. "You better see what you can do. We'll form a circle around the house, five hundred yards away. God knows what good it'll do."

Professor Lansdowne grasped me by the arm.

"I'm ready, Bob," he said. "Let's go."

23

INSTRUMENT OF MURDER

STARTLED BY THE noise of the shooting, people were running out of the houses along the street and Professor Lansdowne and I had to push past groups of men who tried to ask questions. Behind us, I could hear Tom Higgins barking out orders to his police, now silent and awed by the calamity which had overtaken their comrades. We looked neither to right nor left, but pressed on to the dark and ominous house ahead. When we climbed the brownstone stairs, the door was opened and we passed inside. As the closing of the old-fashioned portal cut off the sounds from the street, I thought I could hear the Kashmiri breathing heavily, and wondered if he had been running. But there was no time for conjecture. We were directed up the stairs, which were soon illumined by a sliver of light from the floor above.

As we entered the room where my conversations with Skull had taken place, the doctor was waiting. He stood with one hand resting lightly on the polished surface of the desk, looking past me at Professor Lansdowne. We approached silently and stood, leaving the first move up to him.

"Professor Lansdowne." The unforgettable voice was pitched low.

"Franz Ehrlich." Not a flicker of emotion crossed the scientist's face, except perhaps a faint gleam of satisfaction which lit his eyes momentarily. "I have always known you were Dr. Skull."

"I have always been Dr. Skull." There was a tenseness in his features as he uttered these words. "There is no Franz Ehrlich. You will do me the honor, Professor, to bear that in mind. But now, please be seated, so that we may talk comfortably. It has been a long time since we have met."

Unbidden as always, the Kashmiri slid silently into the room and indicated that I was to follow him out. But Professor Lansdowne intervened.

"Larkin stays," he said, in disarmingly mild tones, "or there will be no conversation between us. And my daughter—she must be present also."

"You are very assured, Professor," remarked Dr. Skull, his voice as smooth and mellow as old brandy. "Please do not underestimate me."

"I don't. But I must see my child."

"As you wish. Only remember that her safety rests with you."

Dr. Skull had hardly finished speaking when the Kashmiri left, to return almost immediately with Paula. As she rushed to her father's arms with a cry of joy, the Indian took up a position across the room, his black automatic in visible readiness as ever. Dr. Skull said nothing while Paula and the Professor embraced and each assured the other that everything was all right.

"What do you intend doing with her?" the scientist demanded.

Dr. Skull waved a delicate hand. "I have not decided. There are more important matters to discuss now and besides, much may depend upon yourself."

"In that case, let's begin the discussion."

"I shall begin," said Dr. Skull, "with a question. Tell me, Professor, what made you think I was Dr. Skull?"

"That's not a long story, though it was a long time before I was quite sure. After your little experiment on the stockbroker, Walker, I had the opportunity of examining him. He imagined himself insane."

Dr. Skull laughed softly. "And was he?"

"Not at all. Rather he showed signs of having been under a most unusual kind of hypnotic influence, a type which I could not fail to recognize. I'll admit I could hardly credit my own senses until other things occurred which proved my original ideas correct."

"Indeed!" Under the watchful eye of the Kashmiri, Dr. Skull passed cigarettes to each of us.

"The other things I refer to were, of course, the strange actions of the Mayor, the deaths of Warren and the others. Connecting you with all that had happened was elementary, particularly in view of your causing me to murder Amos Carter. By the way, why did you do that? It was a needless piece of cruelty."

DR. SKULL MADE an impatient gesture. "Time is short, Professor, and I have a great deal to say. Perhaps you will understand more when I have finished. But first let me begin:

"Years ago—how many I do not exactly remember—you

and I were in Vienna, you taking a post-graduate course in clinical work and I interested in only one thing—to learn more about the human mind than anyone else alive. Because you were older than I and had had far more opportunity for study, I was attracted to you. Again, you were one of my few acquaintances—the only one, perhaps—who did not scoff at my theories. You did not agree, but you did not laugh. You doubtless remember some of my fanciful ideas, many of which have been discarded, others retained and enlarged upon."

Professor Lansdowne nodded. "Yes," he said, "I remember."

"In time, you returned to America to enter upon a professional life," went on Dr. Skull. "My own studies were just starting. I found it quite impossible to satisfy my thirst for knowledge, knowledge that would show me the unknown paths to the soul. Years went by, and I traveled from country to country, always seeking those men who were reputed to be wisest in the ways of the mind and learning a little from each one. Where I got the money, I do not remember, nor is it important. I did, though I was held back repeatedly by the stupidity and unfriendliness of my fellow men who chose to consider me insane and to regard my ideas as the hallucinations of a madman. I learned to keep my own counsel, to pander to the vanity of them I wished to use. I sucked each one dry of all that he knew, and went on to the next.

"It was natural that I should eventually go to India, the very cradle of psychic knowledge and power. By then my own knowledge was sufficient to gain me admittance to the lamasery of Uk-Kur-Dan, the stepping stone to the Three

Brotherhoods as you yourself know. Eventually came full membership in that secret society itself, and initiation into the ancient mysteries."

Dr. Skull's eyes took on a queer glow.

"I began to tread the paths I had sought for so long, to know secrets no other white man had ever dreamed of, not even you, who also know the Three Brotherhoods. Compared with mine, your own studies were very brief. For every week that you spent in study, I spent a month, and finally I possessed the power I had so long wanted— the power to enter the minds of others, to make my will their will. No other white man, and only a bare handful of the Brothers, had this power. The minds of them who had taught me were set in well-worn grooves. They were old and cared nothing for earthly things.

"But I was still in my prime, there were many scores to settle, and I felt within me the desire to use my power for great things. I saw that I could rule the world, if I chose, and I decided to make a beginning toward that end. I came here to America—to New York—for the purpose of setting up my dictatorship."

Dr. Skull paused and tapped his huge, bald head.

"In here is the power to enforce my will, as you have seen. When I first came here, I had not used it, except a very little during the period of learning. The Three Brotherhoods"— he smiled contemptuously—"do not believe that the sacred power should be abused. But there may be more than one opinion as to what constitutes abuse. A great power that will make a man king of the world is meant to be used, not to be hidden away in a rocky lamasery.

"To continue. Before I could achieve my objective, it was

necessary that I have a modest beginning, that first there should be plans and tests. Then, when all was prepared, the first swift stroke that would put fear in the hearts of men. Yes, that is it. They must first fear. Obedience comes later.

"So, there were beginnings. Your stockbroker was one of them. You see, I needed the money. You were another of my, shall we say, early experiments. Because your mind is far above the ordinary level, I was very interested in studying its reaction when I commanded you to kill your friend. I was rather disappointed, Professor. You were every bit as simple as the others."

Dr. Skull's expression was that of patient indulgence when he said this. Professor Lansdowne looked grim.

"MERELY AS A matter of publicity—since it was obvious the world would consider me a lunatic and attempt to ignore me—I used your Mayor O'Hara as an instrument to make my will known. I realized that drastic action would have to follow, and was quite prepared for it. People are exceedingly stupid. They learn only those lessons which are written in blood, and even these they do not always learn. It was this basic stupidity, this unwillingness to accept the inevitable, that caused the deaths which took place. You know yourself that these individual examples failed to stimulate the masses to reason. Naturally, punishment on a larger scale has been my only recourse.

"The puny efforts that have been made to oppose me— even yours, my friend—have had no effect whatever. Future attempts will be no more successful and the sooner this fact is generally accepted, the better it will be for all concerned. If necessary, I am prepared to exterminate every person capable of directing organized opposition to my will.

Divesting the masses of leadership and inflicting severe punishment on the people themselves will eventually bring about the proper degree of submission."

"You'll be beaten in the long run," said Professor Lansdowne. "However many you kill, there will always be more to fight you. What do you hope to gain by this horrible slaughter?"

"Absolute power, Professor," replied Dr. Skull. "The establishment of a dictatorship of the intellect—my intellect!—the dream of every thinker since the world began. My rule will bring its own blessings. Civilization itself will benefit."

"There can be no blessings in a rule based on the wholesale massacre of helpless people."

"You fool!" Skull spat the word out. "What do the lives of people amount to in an undertaking as gigantic as this? What about your wars? Does any good come from them? Do not millions die needlessly? Yet you hold the men who cause them in high honor!

"But wait, my friend. We are wasting valuable minutes. I have not brought you here for a contest in sociological polemics. Give me your close attention."

Dr. Skull advanced several steps until he was within reach of Professor Lansdowne's hands. I wondered if the scientist were going to spring, and held myself ready to tackle the Kashmiri, gun and all. But the Professor sat still, waiting for what Skull would have to say.

"I have told you," the latter went on, "that I recognize the superiority of your mind to those of ordinary men. I can use that mind and you can become part of the force that will change the course of the world. I will open your eyes to knowledge that you can never otherwise aspire to. To a scientist like yourself this should be a greater inducement than an offer of unlimited wealth would be to the average man. I shall rule the world and you may share that rule. You will be honored above all but myself.

"Answer, my friend: will you join me?"

As he spoke the last words, Skull's eyes bored down upon the Professor and I dreaded the answer they might evoke. But Professor Lansdowne merely shook his head.

"No, I will not."

Skull's face was an impassive mask. His voice took on an icy calm.

"Have you not learned how helpless you are? If you care nothing for yourself, are you equally indifferent for your daughter? I promise that unless you change your mind, you will never lay eyes on her after tonight. Does this mean anything to you?"

"Don't pay any attention to him, Dad!" cried Paula. Skull's eyes flicked over her briefly and, without an audible command, the Kashmiri caught her by the arm and propelled her toward the curtained exit. Professor Lansdowne spoke, and I sprang to my feet, simultaneously.

"Let my daughter stay here!" demanded the scientist. I had tensed myself for a leap upon Skull when from his pocket the evil doctor produced a pistol.

"It is not for you to say what shall be done with her, Professor," he remarked, conversationally, "and as for you, Mr. Larkin, I suggest you think carefully before you try to attack me. Please take your seat again."

Helpless in the direct path of the first bullet, I was forced to obey. With a last despairing look at her father, Paula had gone from the room. The Professor was holding himself very tense.

DR. SKULL PUT the pistol down on the desk, within easy reach. He turned to the scientist once more. "My friend," he said, in a voice like velvet, "your decision was not a wise one. You are sure you don't wish to change it?"

"I'm quite sure," replied Professor Lansdowne. "Ehrlich, your situation is far more hopeless than mine. This house is entirely surrounded by policemen and more are coming every minute. You can't hope to break through. You can't kill enough of them before they get you. Come to your senses, man!"

Skull's eyes glowed with the first anger I'd seen him show.

"You think I cannot kill enough?" The corners of his mouth drew down. "You are wrong! I can kill and kill until there isn't one person left in the world to stand against me!"

"I will stand against you."

I had never heard Professor Lansdowne make a statement with more assurance than his quiet voice now carried. But Dr. Skull smiled.

"You aspire very high, Professor," he said. "What gives you such confidence?"

"I know the limit of your power."

I watched Skull closely and it seemed to me that there was a barely perceptible change in his expression. He looked like a man caught off guard, but it was a shadow that passed instantly.

"Are you not attributing too much to the small success you had in defeating my purpose with District Attorney

Harkness?" he asked. "You should not place any importance upon that, my friend."

"Only the importance it deserves," was the reply. Dr. Skull looked at the Professor in silence for a moment, then:

"However bad your present judgment," he said, "you are at least a sincere scientist, and I shall cure your doubt."

The Kashmiri had reentered the room and taken up his previous position against the wall, where his gun could sweep the whole place.

"Professor," continued Dr. Skull, "I shall have to change my residence, and, as you have pointed out, this house is completely surrounded by your police. While I could get through their lines without your assistance, were it absolutely necessary, it would be very helpful if you were to request their withdrawal. Of course, you will not do that of your own free will?"

"Naturally not. Even if I would, the police would pay no attention to me."

"I would be willing to trust to your influence with them. But, unfortunately, you will not help me. That is correct?"

"It is."

"Good!" said Dr. Skull. "Then for my demonstration, we have established ideal conditions. Your will is definitely opposed to mine. In order to gain obedience, I shall have to overcome that opposition. When I do overcome it, you will have to admit defeat. That is true?"

Professor Lansdowne nodded, and I steeled myself for the crisis which I felt was at hand.

"Very well, my friend."

My eyes were drawn to Skull's like steel to a magnet, though he was certainly not looking at me, nor at Professor Lansdowne either. There was nothing here to suggest my own recent experience with Skull. He looked, not at the Professor, but at the wall, yet the tension which now began to permeate the room was so tangible it could be felt. Drawn by the sensation that something was happening to him, my eyes shifted to the scientist.

He had grown pale, his breath was coming fast and as I looked he half rose from the chair as though pulled by invisible cords. Though his body was limp, his face showed more strain than I believed anyone could endure and with agonizing slowness he came to his feet, desperately trying to marshal his own will against the mind that was driving him on. If I could have thought of a prayer I would have said it. I knew that if Skull won, the only barrier to his inhuman plans would be destroyed.

Skull's face had become tightly drawn. His eyes were half-closed and his hands were clasped together. My hair was trying to stand on end and there were a million tiny needles sticking in my body. Professor Lansdowne took one faltering step, then another. Dull terror clutched me as I saw he was turning toward the door. Another step. He looked terribly aged, tired, worn.

Even as he was driven forward once again by Skull's merciless will, I could see the muscles of his jaw stand out as he gritted his teeth together. I knew that Professor Lansdowne was making a still greater effort to resist, that he was now drawing on his last ounce of strength to win the battle that would mean life, instead of death, for thousands. Breathlessly I waited for Skull to force him to take the next step.

But there was no next step.

For seconds that seemed like eternities, Professor Lansdowne was motionless, his mouth a thin, hard line. His breath was labored, and came in a series of dry gasps.

Then, as though pivoted, his body swung around. As if pushing against an invisible current, it bent forward.

I saw that Skull's clasped hands were trembling. His forehead was wet with perspiration. He swayed slightly.

At this precise moment, the waves of energy, electricity—whatever constituted the mysterious and indescribable force emanating from Dr. Skull—began to recede. The barest flush of life strained back into the ashen face of Professor Lansdowne, and, like a man in a dream, he retraced his steps. As he did so, Skull pressed a shaking hand against his great head. His incredible eyes, which had been closed, fluttered open. There was an instant when he and the Professor looked each other full in the face, and then the latter regained his chair and sank wearily into it.

THE KASHMIRI, WHO had been watching all that was taking place with growing agitation, suddenly came to life. His automatic snapped up and pointed directly at Professor Lansdowne. It happened too quickly for me to do anything but yell a warning as the Indian's finger tightened on the trigger. Luckily for the Professor, Skull's voice cracked out a sharp command in a language unknown to me and the trigger was never pulled. It was the first and last time I ever heard him address his servant.

"My friend," said Dr. Skull to the scientist after the danger had been averted, "you have done what no other man in the world will ever do again. I will not concede you victory, because you have gained none—merely a stalemate that will be of very brief duration. We will have one final contest, you and I, and this time there can be no doubt as to the outcome. I regret exceedingly that your refusal to join me makes it necessary for you to die. The manner in which your death is to come will prove my complete mastery, I believe."

Though Professor Lansdowne showed signs of recovery from his ordeal with Skull, he still spoke with difficulty.

"Whatever you do to me you'll never get through that cordon."

"Then it will be all the worse for your daughter, because she will be with me."

These words filled me with a cold horror. Had my attention not been attracted elsewhere, I might have thrown myself at Skull and thus committed suicide under the bullets of the Kashmiri.

But I found myself looking into a pair of eyes, eyes that were returning my gaze from between the heavy curtains that concealed the farther entrance to the room, the one used by Skull. As the velvet drapes were cautiously pulled apart another inch, I saw that the eyes belonged to Curly Smith, and that he was waiting for a chance to leap upon Dr. Skull.

The dread doctor had picked up the gun he'd previously put on the desk and was approaching me when Curly felt his zero hour had come. I will never know whether the reporter realized that the Kashmiri's automatic covered the room or not. I wasn't certain that he intended risking his life in a desperate play to defeat Skull until I saw his body flying through the air, directly at the madman's unsuspecting back.

But as the reporter sprang from his hiding place, the

Kashmiri's gun cracked out once, ominously. There was no second shot and none was needed. The bullet caught Curly in mid-air, dropped him clawing and gasping upon the rich oriental rug. His struggles ceased with merciful quickness and I could see by the position of the spreading red stain on his chest that he must be dead.

The swift suddenness of the reporter's death made me numb from head to foot and I sat motionless while Dr. Skull turned and looked down on the corpse. His face showed no emotion, but he shook his head and murmured:

"It is a pity he was such a fool."

I suppose it was in answer to an unspoken command that the Kashmiri dragged the body over to the wall and let it lie there, slumped on the floor. When this operation was finished, Dr. Skull approached closer, the gun in his hand.

As he was about to speak, I became conscious of considerable noise in the street outside the house. I had heard sirens several times during the past quarter hour, but so intent had I been on all that was happening around me, this sound had made little impression on my conscious mind. But now, there was a hubbub of voices and the unrhythmic tramp of many feet. The thirty minutes is up, I thought, and Tom is bringing in his men.

Dr. Skull also heard.

"Professor Lansdowne," he began, "our time has expired and I can hear your police friends preparing for the attack. I must talk quickly. Our meeting has been far less pleasant than I had anticipated, and I'm sorry to say it must end on an unhappy note. In this room tonight you have shown me that there is one person whose mind I cannot fully control. Your will is very strong and it is a pity you refuse to see things my way. We might have done great things, you and I. Since that is not to be, I cannot let you live.

"This young man"—he indicated me—"who is such a good friend of yours will be the instrument of your death. In one moment, I shall give him this pistol I hold in my hand. I shall tell him to keep it trained upon you until the police break in the door downstairs, which I believe they will do at any moment now. At the first blow on the door, he will shoot you through the heart. I am quite convinced, Professor, that you will be unable to defeat my will and save yourself."

A look which I directed at the scientist was answered by one which seemed to advise caution. There was little enough choice, and all I could do was to vow that I would resist with all my strength Skull's murderous commands. If I could retain my faculties for just one second after he gave me the pistol, I might be able to shoot him. At the same time, the memory of that searing shock given me by his eyes less than an hour ago made me fearful. So much would have to depend upon the Professor's help, and he was very tired. Skull undoubtedly was counting on that. He himself appeared to have completely recovered from the strange contest.

THE KASHMIRI NOW vanished through the velvet curtains. Reversing the gun which had been covering me, Skull carelessly laid it in my hand. It was the moment I had been waiting for. I felt no shock such as I had had before, and reason told me I had not been hypnotized.

So far as I know, my memory in regard to what took place during the next few minutes is reliable. I remember taking the gun and thinking that my chance had come.

Then the next moment I wondered vaguely what chance I was thinking about. That's all.

I turned to Professor Lansdowne. His proud, kindly face was haggard but the eyes which he fixed on me were calm and undisturbed. Just so very, very tired. I knew that as soon as I heard any noise at the front door, I was going to shoot him, and keep shooting until he was dead. There was no anger in me, no feeling of any kind except the iron certainty that at the first sound downstairs, Professor Lansdowne would die.

"Goodby, Professor," I heard Dr. Skull say. "For your daughter's sake pray that there will be no trouble when we go through the police lines. Of course," the strange voice added gently, "it will have to be a short prayer."

Then the curtains closed behind him.

I looked down the barrel of the automatic into the eyes of Professor Lansdowne. The pistol fitted my hand very nicely. Its grip was snug against my palm and I felt a growing desire to press my finger against the smooth trigger. Eagerly, I listened.

Yes, they were coming nearer, much nearer. Soon they would climb the brownstone stairs. They would try the door, find it locked, and have to break it in. There would be the crash of rifle butts against the wood. And then—

Lovingly, my fingers tightened around the gun. Over the sight, Professor Lansdowne's face looked so tired, so tired. But soon he would rest....

24

ESCAPE THROUGH FIRE

FOOTSTEPS DOWNSTAIRS CAME nearer. My whole body tense, I waited for the sound that would tell me the police had started climbing up the brownstone stairs to the door. Then, at the first crash against the wood....

"Bob!"

The word cut into my consciousness like a knife. It irritated me that the Professor was going to talk. It was better when he was quiet. If he were quiet, my aim would be steadier, and any moment now it would be time for me to shoot.

"Bob! Look at me!"

What did he think I was doing? I was looking right at his forehead, just above his nose and between the eyes. With the first noise downstairs, there was going to be a neat little hole there.

"Look at me, Bob! Do you hear me? Look at me!"

But I wasn't going to. He wanted me to look at his eyes, and I wasn't going to do that. I must keep looking right at the spot on his forehead where the little hole would be. If I looked anywhere else, I might miss, and I mustn't do that. It was very important that I didn't miss.

Professor Lansdowne was talking again, pleading with

me. Well, let him talk while he could. It wouldn't be for long. The police were right outside the door now. I must be ready, and I wished he would stop begging me to look at him. But he wouldn't stop. He was talking faster now and it was worrying me. I wouldn't look at him, I wouldn't....

Only something kept pulling at my eyes, kept tugging at them until they dropped down from the little spot on his forehead. There was a hollow thud and the sound of splintering wood downstairs. It was my signal. I must shoot.

I squeezed the trigger, but I couldn't seem to squeeze it hard enough. The strength was going out of my fingers. They felt dead, and unless they came to life, I couldn't shoot.

Shoot? Who was I going to shoot?

The room spun and a wave of faintness engulfed me.

"Good God!"

The words broke from my lips as reason came back to me. Realizing what I had been about to do, I let the pistol fall to the floor. Simultaneously, with a tearing and rending of wood, the front door collapsed and heavy-soled feet pounded on the stairs. My hands were shaking violently and I was bathed in a cold, clammy sweat.

"Get hold of yourself, Bob. Everything is quite all right now." Professor Lansdowne, seemingly drained of blood, forced a smile.

Then Tom Higgins, half a dozen bluecoats with drawn guns at his heels, broke into the room.

"Where is he?" Tom wildly scanned the room until his eyes became fixed on the body of Curly Smith. "What the hell is this?" he demanded, and without waiting for a reply repeated, "Where is Skull?" As if in answer, there was the

staccato crackle of machine gun fire, coming from somewhere to the south of the house.

"Not far from that firing, right now," said the Professor,
"but if you don't get a move on he's going to get away. He's
taken Paula with him. Please hurry!"

"He couldn't get through the police lines. We've got this
whole neighborhood surrounded. That shootin' was probably him gettin' a chestful!"

"Listen, you thick-headed Irish mick," I suddenly thundered at him, finding my voice at last, "have you already
forgotten what he did out there in the street? Hurry up, or
it'll be too late!"

"You're right. I must be gettin' slap-happy or somethin'."
And Tom Higgins began bawling orders right and left.
Leaving two men to stand guard in the house, he and the
rest hurried back downstairs. As I watched them go, I
knew instinctively that he would be too late, that Skull
had gotten through. And Paula Lansdowne was with him.

A minute before I had been on the verge of shooting
the man who was already a second father to me, and would
have done so had not the Professor succeeded in wrench-
ing loose my mind from Skull's control. Before I had been
given a chance to recover from that terrible experience the
knowledge that we had our work to do over again dealt me
another staggering blow. Everything I'd been through—
the anxious hours of waiting, the torture of that dark cell
in the basement, the desperation of those pathetic notes
for help, the arrival of the one man I'd pinned my hopes
on—had been for nothing. Paula had been snatched away
from me again, and this time, was there anything Skull
might not do?

I don't know what I'd have done had not Professor Lansdowne been there to collect the remnants of my sanity and focus them on a new hope. His unwavering courage and his grim refusal to acknowledge defeat were examples I could not fail to follow. Accordingly, I gathered together my scattered wits and tried to figure out what the next step should be.

A few minutes later, Tom Higgins returned to confirm our fears that Skull had succeeded in making his way through the lines.

"One of the boys started spraying the neighborhood with his tommy-gun," he said, "and of course, the others near him rushed over to see what all the shootin' was about—like saps. Skull didn't have to do a thing but walk through a breach a block wide. Oh," he added, "another small item. The cop with the tommy turned it on himself before he ran outa bullets. That makes seven dead and twelve for the hospital. A swell night's work, we did."

At this juncture, Tom knelt down to examine the body of the reporter.

"Dead as a doornail," he commented. "The bullet musta went straight through his heart. Ain't he the fellow that worked for the *Express*?"

Professor Lansdowne nodded and explained the circumstances of the boy's death.

"That's tough," remarked Tom. "Well, that makes eight for the morgue. Mooney, send for a stretcher and get this out of here."

"How is the morale of your men?" asked the Professor. I could see that he was under great strain and was keeping himself going by main force of will and nothing else.

"Not so hot. They're pretty burned up about not rushin' Skull when we first got here. I ain't so sure they're not right, either."

"Nonsense. They wouldn't have stood a chance. You saw what Skull did, as a warning. What do you suppose he could do if he were really trying?"

"Maybe you're right, Professor. Anyhow, they all got their orders to keep their lips buttoned about the shootin'. I dunno what difference it'll make. You can't keep a thing quiet when half of New York has a ringside seat."

WHILE AN EXTENSIVE net was thrown out for Skull in the dim hope that he would get caught in its meshes, Tom Higgins, Professor Lansdowne and I went over the house from top to bottom. Nothing of any significance could be found. Either Dr. Skull traveled very light, or his real headquarters was elsewhere. So far as we could tell, he had no one with him but the Kashmiri, not even a cook, and there were no papers, clothes or other effects to shed any light on the mystery that surrounded him. Judging by visible evidence, Dr. Skull was playing a lone hand and had no organization behind him.

In the basement room where Curly Smith and I had been imprisoned, the regular lock on the door had been broken, showing how Curly had made his escape. The padlock was unfastened, the Kashmiri evidently having been either careless or in a hurry when he had shut in the reporter. A back staircase led from the kitchen to an upstairs hallway, and Curly must have used this route. Whether he had spoken to Paula we could not know, but the hallway led past the bedroom in which she was confined. This chamber, by the way, was exotically furnished and showed signs of having been especially prepared for Paula. None of her clothes, or anything else that had belonged to her, had been left in it.

Our inspection completed, there was nothing else to do but leave. The Professor and I rode in the ambulance which carried the body of Curly Smith to the city morgue for the autopsy that would have to be made. Professor Lansdowne characteristically waved aside my weak offer and himself performed the unpleasant duty of informing Mrs. Smith of her son's death. Though she was widowed, there was a daughter to comfort her, and when we telephoned the news to the *Express,* Curly's paper, they promised to take charge of funeral arrangements. I myself was saddened by the boy's death, the more so since he'd been trying to help us, but my anxiety for Paula left scant room in my mind for anything else.

We preceded to the District Attorney's suite of offices in the Municipal Building, where we were to meet Tom Higgins. En route, Professor Lansdowne brought me up to date on all that had transpired during my sojourn in the house of Dr. Skull. Harkness, he said, would be out of the running for several days and full responsibility for the fight against the mad doctor lay on the shoulders of Tom Higgins and himself.

Ready to jump the instant radio or telephone should bring news of Skull's whereabouts, the Professor, Tom and I arranged to sleep in shifts. The scientist and I took the first turn on cots in the adjoining conference room after I had wolfed some sandwiches and hot coffee, my first food in a long time. Exhaustion proved stronger than worry, and we slept.

The next thing I knew, a rough hand was on my shoulder, shaking me violently.

"C'mon, snap out of it!" Groggily, I looked into the agitated face of Tom Higgins. "All hell's breakin' loose!"

His statement was like a dash of cold water in my face and I sat bolt upright. Professor Lansdowne was already awake.

"What's the matter?" I asked.

"Plenty! Skull was on the radio at midnight threatenin' to blow up New York, and he's already made a whale of a start. Ten minutes after he talked an Interborough "L" took an open switch at about sixty per. Half an hour later there was another wreck, this time in the Queensborough tunnel. Then a Madison Avenue bus ran wild all over the sidewalk. God knows what he'll do next!"

"What have you done about it?" demanded Professor Lansdowne sharply.

"Done?" Tom's face was a picture of desperation. "Done? What the hell *could* I do? I've sent men to the scene of each accident to take charge and handle the injured. Don't ask me how many got killed. Right now the score is fifty-odd and goin' up fast. I knew you needed sleep and I didn't want to disturb you, but it's got me down."

"Did Skull talk over the radio himself?" I inquired, curiously.

"Naw, no more'n he ever does. It was one of the announcers again, like it always is. He don't know from nothin', of course, or so he says."

Pulling on my coat, I followed the Professor and Tom Higgins into the office proper. As we entered, two plain-clothes men were talking over telephones and a stenographer was making rapid pothooks on a pad. One of the men cupped the mouthpiece and turned to Tom.

"They're calling for more ambulances," he said. "What'll I tell 'em?"

"Tell 'em?" raged the Irishman. "Tell 'em to call a hospital. They don't suppose *I* got any ambulances, do they?"

"They've called every hospital in Manhattan and they can't get any."

"Then tell 'em to call Brooklyn and the Bronx. Manhattan ain't the only borough in New York. Try Staten Island, too."

The detective nodded and went back to his phone.

"C'mon, Professor," urged Tom. "You're the brains of this jernt. Tell me what I should do!"

"Very well," nodded the scientist, "I will. First, get in touch with every public transportation company in town. Issue orders that no regular subways, 'L' trains, surface cars or busses are to be run until further notice. That shouldn't be hard to manage. The subway motormen wanted to quit days ago. Next, arrange for special trains, just enough to provide emergency transportation for essential needs. These special trains must have, in addition to the regular motorman, a relief motorman and two guards. The guards must stand where they can see the motorman and the track ahead at all times. Understand?"

"Yeah, but that's gonna stop every bit of business in New York. People can't work unless they can get to their jobs."

"If we don't stop this killing there won't be anybody left alive to work," snapped back the Professor. "You'd better do as I advise."

"Check," said Higgins. "I'll attend to it now."

"Hold on a minute! There's something else, and it's very important."

"Yeah?"

"The guards on these trains must not be armed. No guns, no knives, or any other deadly weapon."

Tom looked at Professor Lansdowne as though he thought the scientist had taken leave of his senses.

"No guns?" he repeated, blankly.

I suddenly saw what the Professor was driving at. "If they haven't got guns they can't go nuts and start shooting up the train, see?" I pointed out irritably.

Professor Lansdowne laid a hand on Tom's arm. "Please trust me," he said. "Tell your guards to watch the motorman closely and at the first sign of trouble to pull him away from the controls."

"And shove in the relief," finished Tom. "Okay, Professor. You're the doctor." An instant later he had grabbed an unoccupied phone and was busy making the desired arrangements.

"I realize this is no time for foolish questions, sir," I said to the Professor, "but I'd like to get something clear."

"Fire away, Bob."

"Suppose Skull hypnotizes both of the motorman *and* the two guards. Then what?"

Professor Lansdowne smiled wanly. "He won't."

"How can you be sure of that? If I were in his place that'd be the first—"

The scientist held up his hand. "He won't, Bob, for one very excellent reason. He *can't.*"

I shook my head. "I guess I'm not very smart tonight. I don't get you."

Professor Lansdowne nodded toward a deserted corner of the office, where we repaired.

"BOB," HE BEGAN, in a tired but earnest voice, "when you were with Dr. Skull did you notice anything strange? Anything that seemed out of place with everything else you know about him?"

I tried to think, but soon gave up, shaking my head again.

"A thing would have to be awfully queer to be out of place with that bird," I said.

"Exactly," agreed the Professor. "But this is what I mean: Skull has this extraordinary hypnotic power, which we know about through sad experience. It is, we have assumed, unlimited in its scope, so that he can control the wills of people at any distance, without having to prepare them in any way or even to see them. With such omnipotence, he should fear no one, should he?"

"I shouldn't think so."

"Nor should I. Yet, Skull's lieutenant carries a pistol. He not only carries it, but mounts guard with it whenever Skull talks to anyone, or at any rate, whenever he talks to more than one person at a time. The only occasion when he left his master unguarded was when Skull himself had a gun. Doesn't that seem strange to you?"

"Of course it does!" I cried. "Now I remember! Curly Smith and I noticed the same thing, only we couldn't figure it out. Do you know the answer?"

"I think so," said Professor Lansdowne, "and here it is: Dr. Skull does have a hitherto unheard-of hypnotic ability; he can impress his will on a subject whether the subject is agreeable or not; so far as I know at present, this power is not limited by the distance Skull may be from his victim.

But"—and the Professor struck his fist on his cupped palm for emphasis—"Skull can control only one person at a time!"

"You mean," I said, "that with two of us in the room with him, he could have mastered only one of us, and while he was doing that the other could have settled with him?"

"Exactly."

"So the Kashmiri was on hand to take care of the ones Skull *couldn't* take care of," I mused, "and all this time Skull could have been captured by the simple process of rushing him with half a dozen men?"

Professor Lansdowne shook his head. "Not 'all this time', no. You forget that until yesterday we hadn't the slightest idea where Skull kept himself. Our ignorance of his exact appearance and his whereabouts were two of his greatest assets. Under such conditions he could strike at key individuals—one at a time—and create a veritable reign of terror without running the slightest risk. Since he's unable to control masses of people directly, he does so indirectly, by controlling men who hold in their hands the lives of others—subway motormen, bus drivers, and the like. In this way he brings about the wholesale murders he wants and which he hopes will give him a dictatorship founded on fear."

I had noticed this method of procedure on the day before, when I saw the headlines telling of the first bus disaster, but it had not hinted to me that Skull's powers were limited. Nor had it, I think, to anyone else.

"How long have you known Skull can control only one person at a time?" I asked the Professor.

"I've suspected it for quite awhile. His methods have all

pointed that way, but there was no proof. I made exhaustive researches, using a very rare collection of ancient Tibetan writings brought to this country only a short while ago. But there was as much to support the possibility that he might have the secret of mass hypnotism as there was to the contrary. I believed he did not have this secret, but I dared not depend on mere belief and give advice based on an unproven premise. I was not positive until I actually saw Skull, but then I knew."

I said quickly:

"If Tom and his men had thrown away their guns so that Skull couldn't have had one man shoot up the rest, they might have captured him? With a concerted charge, I mean?"

"They probably could have," admitted the scientist, "but I was not positive of my ground and was unwilling to advise it. Now it appears that through my failure to do so, I'm entirely to blame for Skull's escape, and for whatever may happen to Paula and God knows how many others!"

"You get that dumb idea right out of your head, sir," I said, heatedly. "You couldn't have gotten that bunch of hoodlums to lay down their guns for anything in the world. They'd have gone ahead with artillery support, probably, and been butchered, every one of them. Even if they'd rushed him bare-handed, he could have shot his way through and escaped. Don't forget those guns he and his stooge had."

"Thanks, Bob." Professor Lansdowne's worn face was grateful. "I'll try and look at it that way."

"Now," I went on, "we finally know how to beat him. All we have to do is get him surrounded, then close in. If none of the men have guns, Skull can inflict only minor damage. Even if he goes homicidal, a man can't do much with his bare knuckles. So that's all there is to it."

"Not quite all. First we have to find him again. God grant it's an easier task than it was before!"

With these words, my freshly built optimism toppled in ruins. The thought of Paula in the grip of that madman was like a giant hand squeezing the breath out of me. The search for Skull had to begin all over again. He was loose, like a wild and indescribably vicious animal, with the whole of Manhattan Island for a hiding place. It might take days, weeks, perhaps months, to ferret him out. In that time would there be anyone left alive? Would Paula be alive?

Professor Lansdowne and I had been so engrossed in our conversation we had not noticed that Tom Higgins had ever left the office. Consequently, we were surprised to see him lunge through the door and blunder up to us, his face like a death mask.

"Fires!" he choked out. "Fires! Skull's setting the town on fire!"

Horrified, we followed his pointing finger. Through the windows, the night sky of lower Manhattan was tinged with a dull, red glow.

25

THE GREAT FIRE

THE FIRES WHICH had broken out almost simultaneously were at first restricted to that section of New York to the south of Canal Street and over toward the East River. With Tom Higgins, Professor Lansdowne and I hurried to the scene—it was then about two o'clock in the morning—and were met by all the horror which fire, and particularly fire by night, can bring. The district was a part of the slums, and the buildings affected were tenements put up years before the era of fireproofing and which burned like so many paper boxes.

There was absolutely no doubt that the fires were of incendiary origin and, though this type of death-dealing was slightly out of his line, we knew they had been started by helpless, unknowing agents of Dr. Skull, as later events were to prove.

The doctor could not have chosen a field more replete with the potentialities of great suffering. It would have been hard to find a section of New York more thickly populated or more vulnerable to the rapid spread of fire. Not only were the tenements highly inflammable, but they were packed so closely together that when one took fire it was a physical impossibility to keep the flames from

*Red Thursday dawned a fire-tinged gray as Tom Higgins, the
Professor and I tried to get a perspective on the situation*

spreading to its neighbors and continuing on in this fashion until an entire block would become a blazing inferno.
Most of these dilapidated structures had no fire escapes
worthy of the name and those that did had too few, so that
this one road to safety frequently became clogged with
frantic people who could move neither forward nor backward, or collapsed under their weight.

Although the odds for a staggering loss of life were
heavily in his favor from the start, Dr. Skull had not trusted
to luck alone. His agents had selected one building in each
of a half-dozen squares where they started simultaneous
blazes. As if this were not enough, even the direction of
the wind had been taken into consideration. Since it was
blowing from the east, the tenements selected for the initial
firing were those located on the eastern side of their blocks.
The wind, spreading the flames to westward, did the rest,

and the thousands of poverty-stricken humans who inhabited the five- and six-story buildings were caught in a roaring trap from which, in most cases, there was no escape.

Fire equipment from every part of greater New York was rushed to the scene as quickly as possible and courageous efforts were made to stop the spread of the conflagration, but these were unavailing. The ancient firetraps burned like tinder and soon it became a fight of sheer desperation to keep the flames from swallowing wholesale stores and warehouses far to the west. To the screams of injured and the hysterical cries of men and women trying to find their husbands, wives, children and other loved ones were added thunderous roars as buildings in the path of the blaze were dynamited.

It is utterly impossible adequately to describe the terror of that wild night, the lurid sky, the black skeletons of tenements showing macabre outlines through the flames, the shrill voices of sirens and then the swallowing up of everything in the earth-shaking blast of an explosion.

For hours while Tom Higgins worked like a crazy man to organize adequate relief facilities and preserve order, the Professor and I did what we could to administer first aid and help evacuate the more critically injured. At dawn, smoke-blackened and weary, the three of us returned to the Municipal Building offices, which were rapidly becoming the nerve center of Manhattan. As the eastern sky turned a gray still tinged with the red aura of fire, Tom Higgins, Inspector Greene, the Professor and I sat around a table and tried to get a perspective on the situation. Steaming black coffee and doughnuts were restoring a measure of sanity that we could well use.

REVIEWING THE SITUATION to date, we confronted the following actualities: Skull was still at large. The giant net that had been hastily spread for his capture the night before had caught nothing. There had been many sensational reports, many false leads, innumerable rumors that Skull had been seen on the West Side near 94th Street; on the East Side near 43rd Street; at the corner of 59th Street and Broadway; that he had been seen in a hundred other places. None of them proved a key to his real whereabouts, although every one of the thousand-odd bits of information that filtered in during the night was meticulously checked. There was, naturally, no trace of Paula, or any message from her. We couldn't know positively if she were yet alive, though Professor Lansdowne refused to countenance the thought that Skull might have killed her. As for myself, I hardly dared think about her at all for fear of going altogether crazy. It was a blessing for both of us that Tom Higgins kept us busy.

Another fact that had to be faced was this: the incredible series of disasters that had occurred during that never-to-be-forgotten night had delivered a terrible blow to the morale of New York City. From a metropolis which had been apprehensive but still perfectly confident of Skull's eventual extinction, it had changed to a nerve-shocked city of dread. Though no one knew where Skull was, the signs of his awful power and his demoniacal lust to rule through fear were all too numerous. The deaths that he had caused during the night would be counted in the hundreds, and the fear he believed would win him obedience was increasing by the minute.

At the beginning of the day that was to go down in

history as Red Thursday, crowds were already jamming the two great railway terminals in a blind panic to get as far away from New York as possible, in the quickest possible time. A quiet exodus of the more plutocratic elements had been going on for some days, but while flight had previously been limited to members of that class, it had now become general. Highways, too, were crowded with automobiles fleeing into the safer hinterland, and since each departing person had to undergo close scrutiny before being permitted to leave, cars were lined up, four abreast, at the principal exits from Manhattan, especially the Holland Tunnel and the George Washington Bridge.

By ten o'clock, it had become apparent just how seriously New York was being affected. Business for the most part was at a standstill with employees unable to get to places of work because of the transportation tie-up. Subways and elevated lines were being used only for such vital services as the transportation of foodstuffs and other essential supplies, the trucking companies which usually performed this job having had their efficiency greatly reduced by the absence of their workers who either could not, or would not, get to work.

Public utilities, except transportation, were still functioning satisfactorily, though many workers were forced to remain at their posts long hours without relief. Early in the morning at a session of the Executive Board, measures were hurriedly adopted to keep electricity, gas, water, and telephone services running efficiently. Two or three of the larger department stores opened with greatly reduced personnel, no doubt a good many smaller businesses operated to some degree that day, and scattered business offices—and a very jittery stock exchange—managed to carry on a portion of their usual activities.

So far—up until ten A.M., that is—panic had been expressing itself mainly in a concerted rush to get away from the theater of Skull's operations. Only in occasional instances had there been any dissatisfaction shown at the administration's hopeless fight against the terror, and police had been able to handle these streetcorner insurrections without difficulty. However, with the spreading of rumors as the day progressed—rumors that were hardly wilder than the truth—further disturbances of a more serious nature began to take place and it became more and more troublesome for Inspector Greene, into whose lap the assignment fell, to maintain order.

Accordingly, Professor Lansdowne advised a move which both Greene and Higgins had kept as a last resort, the summoning of National Guardsmen to patrol the city and the proclamation of martial law. After considerable discussion, Tom finally agreed to contact the Governor in Albany and set in motion the machinery which would make the several thousand Guardsmen already in New York available for duty. Professor Lansdowne suggested that, upon their mobilization, the soldiers be allowed to retain their arms while on patrol, but that the rifles be withdrawn should any encircling maneuver against Skull be performed. The same procedure was recommended for police, and Tom and Inspector Greene agreed to follow the scientist's advice to the letter. Fortunately for everyone concerned, the United States Army Colonel in command of the National Guard units showed an equal willingness to cooperate when the time came.

NEWSPAPERS ON RED Thursday, such as were published at all, contained only sketchy accounts of the night's holocaust on the lower East Side, and their reports of the subway, elevated and bus accidents greatly minimized the death toll, in accordance with police instructions. This attempt to hold down panic was more reflexive than practical, as such measures were useless in the face of the lightning-like spread of news by word of mouth. Somewhat more useful in the maintenance of a slight degree of calm were front page editorials appealing to the population of Manhattan to keep its head and its courage. Remarkably enough, though, the greatest help in the battle against chaos came from the people themselves—the very people we were so afraid would go completely to pieces under pressure—but more about that in due course.

I have neither space nor inclination to go into detail about the innumerable appeals that were made throughout the day to what was left of the city administration; the blustering and outraged merchants who protested singly and in committee; the threats of the rich, the appeals of the middle classes and the curses of the proletariat. Tom Higgins merely moved to a secret office on a different floor and left the storm to beat against the tough skins of specially selected subordinates. It was a highly necessary precaution if anything was to be accomplished.

There were no further warnings from Dr. Skull, but his silence was neither unexpected nor reassuring since his words over the radio the previous night had been:

"People of New York: This is the last time I will speak to you. If you wish to live, force your leaders to acknowledge my authority. Unless this is done immediately, I will destroy New York and every man, woman and child in it."

That was all. Skull had not even mentioned his name.

Needless to say, there were uncountable people who begged in person, by wire and by telephone that such concessions as Skull desired be made without a moment's delay. Many of these appeals were genuinely pathetic, sincere, unselfish efforts to save other lives than the petitioner's, but an equally great number were no more than the cowardly whining of men and women who would sacrifice the lives and liberty of millions to save their own skin. Of whichever kind they may have been, all such pleas necessarily fell on deaf ears, and the fight went on. An altogether one-sided fight it was, with Skull delivering his paralyzing blows from God knew where and with the seventeen thousand police under the command of Tom Higgins and Inspector Greene powerless to strike back. Noon came, and afternoon, and still Skull could not be found.

He was not idle all this time, however, and his threat to destroy New York was being fulfilled with demoralizing swiftness. Thus, in the neighborhood of one P.M. Skull appeared vicariously at a mass meeting held in Madison Square Garden, using as his instrument of destruction nothing more frightening than a woman in the audience. Under the influence of his remarkable mind, she suddenly sprang to her feet and shrieked, so that all could hear:

"Skull! The building will collapse. We'll be killed!"

At least, this is one report of what she said; there were as many variations as there were people questioned. Whatever she said, a blind, raging panic was the instantaneous result. Ten thousand people rushed the exits at once and in the mêlée the weaker were beaten and trampled upon. The loss of life was beyond immediate calculation.

For the first time, Skull had let the mere fear of his name wreak destruction, and it had been more potent than a dozen rifles. Ironically, the meeting had been held, in defiance of an emergency ban on public assemblies, to devise ways and means of combatting the mad doctor.

Due to the epidemic of rioting which broke out in the midtown section following this occurrence, National Guardsmen were ordered to report to previously selected concentration depots where they were equipped with guns and organized into patrols. An offer of Federal aid was not accepted at the time being, but news of its receipt was promptly circulated to stimulate the waning morale.

Dr. Skull's next attack followed within an hour and came about in this fashion: Below the surface of 6th Avenue, between 39th and 40th Streets, a group of workmen were engaged in blasting through the hard rock a tunnel designed to carry part of Manhattan's water supply. Because of its urgency, the work had been carried on in spite of the threatening general situation, and when preparations had been completed for another blast, a worker was sent up to the street level to bring down a supply of dynamite and the requisite number of detonating caps. The man got the explosives from the temporary construction shack where they were kept, but failed to return to the tunnel with them. Instead, he unostentatiously slipped the deadly sticks beneath his overalls, pocketed the detonating caps and began walking away from the excavation. He walked to 34th Street, across to 7th Avenue, and then turned south to the Pennsylvania Station. That terminal, like Grand Central, was filled to overflowing with crowds who were trying to get out of New York before they were overtaken by the terror.

Unfortunately, many of them never lived to take their trains, for, as they stood waiting, a violent explosion shook the vast building from track level to roof. Almost immediately, this first explosion was followed by a second one, and it by a third. Windows were shattered in skyscrapers a block away. When police and ambulance surgeons arrived on the scene, the concourse was a charnel house of death and agony, and amid the scenes of horror stalked the figure of a man in overalls, his arms stretched out before him, his bloody, sightless eyes insensitive to the devastation he had been made to wreak.

This hideous demonstration of Skull's power had an unexpected effect on the people of New York.

Tens of thousands of them put aside fear and became obsessed with but one idea: "Either Skull dies or we do."

THIS NEW MANIA, for mania it was, now spread as quickly as panic had spread before, from person to person, from group to group, from block to block. Where it started, no one will ever know, but soon men were getting on soap boxes, on the tops of automobiles, on street corners, shouting that Skull must die. There was no leadership, no organization, no coordination, only numberless human beings possessed with the grim resolve: Find Skull. They had no idea what to do or where to look, but roamed the streets, in wild, crazy, dangerous mobs, crashing into stores and running through apartment buildings, yelling and screaming for the blood of Dr. Skull.

There were still those who feared, but they either left town or their whimperings were drowned in the mighty roar for Skull's death that was now heard through the streets.

As new recruits kept pouring into the constantly swelling ranks of these disorganized mobs, Tom Higgins and Inspector Greene, influenced by the lamentations of shopkeepers and merchants who feared their goods might be destroyed in the rampage, decided to use all the facilities at their command to disperse the frenzied crowds. It was at this stage of the proceedings that Professor Lansdowne gave the advice that brought about the salvation of New York.

"Gentlemen," he said, "you and I have done everything in our power to effect the capture of Dr. Skull, and we have failed. We know he is hiding somewhere on Manhattan Island because there has been no chance for him to leave it undetected, should he have wished to do so, which I doubt. There are literally millions of places where he might live for weeks before police could ever find him. There are not enough police in New York City to prosecute the kind of a search that could find him, or drive him into the open where we might have a chance of fighting him.

"I see in this providential mass rising against Skull our one chance to close in on him. From what I have heard of the numbers of people already engaged in rioting, as well as the fact that more are taking up the hunt every minute, I think we will find in these mobs an army of sufficient size and ruthlessness to succeed where the police have failed. Seventeen thousand police cannot cover enough territory in a short enough time, but—seventeen thousand police *plus* fifty or a hundred thousand other searchers is something else again. I advise you not to send troops against those people, but instead, to take full advantage of the help they can give."

"Perhaps you're right," said Inspector Greene dubiously, "but a hundred thousand people out for blood can be ten times as dangerous as Skull ever thought of being."

Professor Lansdowne nodded. "True enough," he admitted, "if they're allowed merely to run wild. It's your job to see that they're organized. Get your police in with them, and bring about some degree of discipline, but let them have their own way, within reason. Let them examine every square inch of territory on this island, but make sure they're being led by your men. Do you follow me! In this way, you can avoid dangerous and purposeless rioting, prevent panic, and—if you handle your army carefully—trap Skull to boot. What do you say?"

Tom Higgins brought his clenched fist down on the table with an emphatic thud. "The Professor's absolutely right," he said, "and I'm for gettin' on the job right away. Come on, Greene, let's go to work!"

Within an hour, carefully spotted police agents were beginning to guide the growing mass hysteria into productive channels, and by late afternoon the greatest manhunt in history was under way. How many actually took part in it will never be known, but there were enough to form a determined, implacable horde which stretched its ranks clear across the upper strip of Manhattan Island. Starting from this northernmost point, the gigantic citizen army moved southward with police stationed at strategic points along the line maintaining a fair amount of evenness in the advance. Most of the searchers were young men, but there were plenty of older heads in the ranks, and women, too. As they surged onward, block by block, not a room, cellar or roof was left unsearched.

It was to be expected that Dr. Skull would quickly know of this mass attack and would do what he could to instill terror in the hearts of his enemies. To render him as powerless as possible, Professor Lansdowne had urged that both police and soldiers, as well as the civilians, be permitted no weapons any more lethal than clubs or night sticks, and for the most part his advice was carefully followed. However, two National Guard officers saw fit to disregard his counsel as well as the orders of their own military superiors and permitted several fully equipped machine gun detachments to take places in the advance "to preserve order."

With that keenness of perception which made us feel he must be gifted with clairvoyance, Dr. Skull discovered their presence and their positions in the line. As soon as he did, he struck in characteristic fashion. One of the machine guns suddenly swung around to face in the opposite direction and from its ugly nozzle leaden death was sprayed into the close-packed ranks of the people. Hardly had this gun shot through a cartridge belt than another a block away began spluttering.

But the guns were silenced and removed from the line, and instead of being terrified by what had happened, the people were made all the angrier, all the more unswerving in their resolution to find and destroy Skull. Gaps created by the machine gun bullets were quickly filled and the search went on.

PUBLICITY, OF COURSE, had been given to the fact that

Skull could control only one person at a time, and by radio and through police in the "battle lines," Professor Lansdowne had appealed for the use of as much caution as possible to keep Paula from harm. But at the most, we could only hope and wait, wait, wait for news that Skull had been located.

Whether because his attention was directed to more pressing problems brought about by the mass hunt for him or whether he felt there was no one else worth killing, Dr. Skull did not bring his fatal concentration to bear on any more civic officials on Red Thursday. Professor Lansdowne had expected an attempt on the life of Tom Higgins and remained on the alert to make a quick intervention should one be necessary, but none was. I have always believed that Skull gave up this line of attack for a very elementary reason: that it would do him no good to kill every official in New York as long as Professor Lansdowne stayed alive, and that he knew he could not hope to bring about the Professor's death by suicide since here was one mind too strong for him to control. Professor Lansdowne would never confirm this theory, but I am convinced it is the right one. Why Skull did not hypnotize someone to kill the scientist is a question not so easily answered, but the Professor has always thought that this was due to one of two reasons. First, because it was a matter of fierce pride with the mad doctor to settle his score with Professor Lansdowne in a personal, direct way that would clearly demonstrate his mental superiority; or, second, because in the last few days of his war against civilization Dr. Skull's attention was focussed on his most immediate enemies— the masses of people themselves.

To return to my subject, toward nightfall another huge civilian arm was formed under the leadership of police, this time on the extreme south of Manhattan Island, at the Battery. This new horde swept relentlessly northward to meet the other which moved in the opposite direction. Every exit from the city was hermetically sealed—no one was permitted to leave the island on any excuse whatever— and the rivers were diligently patrolled to make sure that Skull would not slip from between the narrowing jaws of the two pincers.

While Tom Higgins busied himself somewhere else in the city, Professor Lansdowne and I sat in his office, waiting as hopefully as we could for news. A million times during the day I had thought of Paula with a horrible feeling of helplessness and had repeatedly staved off hysteria by finding something useful to do. But now, all the things that could be done had been done, and there was nothing left but this nerve-racking waiting. Seven, seven-thirty, eight o'clock came, and still no word. Through the closed window we could hear the vast murmur, like heavy waves breaking on a shore, that was the voice of the southern horde, and I found myself vaguely wondering if Skull were himself part of it by now, laughing up his sleeve and biding his time for an opportunity to bring about more death and suffering.

Then the private phone on Tom's desk rang, imperatively, and Professor Lansdowne nodded for me to answer it. I did so, and heard Tom Higgins on the other end of the line.

"Bob," he said, "I think we've got a line on Skull. It looks like Paula's still with him. You two better get up to

Grand Central fast. I'll be waitin' for you at the 42nd Street
entrance."

In less time than it takes to tell, I was speeding north in a
borrowed squad car with Professor Lansdowne at my side.

26

CITY OF DARKNESS

I HEADED UPTOWN at a good rate of speed. New York was like a city of the dead, and fifty miles an hour was easy to maintain on the deserted streets. Only occasionally did we see a furtive figure moving along the sidewalk, or an anxious face silhouetted for a moment in a window. Union Square and the whole stretch of 14th Street had no more than a dozen people in sight, all men, and though lights blazed from movie marquees and the gaudy shop windows were bright, they played to an empty house.

Tom Higgins met us as we pulled up in front of Grand Central. A policeman took charge of the coupé and we followed the young Irishman across the marbled concourse, filled to overflowing with would-be emigres waiting hopefully for trains, the schedules of which had been suspended, to start running again. They stared at us apathetically as we passed, their expressions like those of war refugees registering dull, unmitigated despair. At the Lexington Avenue exit, Tom shoved us into another car and drove in silence until we were rolling swiftly past 57th Street. Then he spoke.

"I got word that Skull tipped his hand and put himself in a tight spot. They got him surrounded up on 179th Street near Broadway—Mitch Maurer and his gang. I told 'em to hold their lines tight but not to close in until I got there. Thought you two'd like to be in at the finish."

"Did they actually see Skull?" I demanded.

"Yeah. He was drivin' down Broadway in a car. There was a dame with him—that'd be Paula—and they ducked outa the car and into a row of flats. Mitch says he had the net around him in less 'n five minutes. Mitch says he can't get out. And this time they ain't usin' guns, Professor!"

"That's very wise of them," commented the scientist. "Let's hope Dr. Skull isn't either." Struck by the absence of enthusiasm in his tone, I glanced at him in the semi-darkness but his face conveyed nothing.

Somewhere on the upper part of the West Side, we were stopped by a row of cars parked across the street. A burly officer swaggered up and demanded our business, then snapped to attention as he recognized Tom Higgins.

"The lieutenant's waiting for you, sir," he announced. "Two blocks up, corner of 178th."

When we reached the designated intersection we were met by the swarthy, stockily-built officer in command and he and Tom went into a huddle. After a couple of minutes' conference, the latter turned to the Professor.

"They're ready to close in. Any suggestions?"

"You're sure the men are unarmed?"

"They just got billies, and maybe a few brass knucks."

"That's good," said Professor Lansdowne. "Better give two or three of the men—not the leaders—pistols, in case Skull is armed. Be sure that these guns are kept out of sight so that Skull won't know who is carrying them. Instruct a man to watch each of the officers who are armed and at the first sign that they are being controlled by Skull, tell them to knock them out with a club, or their fists. Don't let there be any shooting unless Skull shoots first. Understand what I mean?"

"Right!" snapped Tom Higgins and the swarthy lieutenant of police nodded.

"These are the only suggestions I have, except one. Please be careful—for the sake of my daughter."

"You bet, Professor," Tom assured him, and the next moment was gone. The scientist turned to me.

"A lot of lost motion," he remarked. "Skull's not going to be caught this time."

"What makes you think so?"

"There are still too many hiding places for him to have been cornered so soon. Of course, it's merely a hunch."

BUT IT WAS a good hunch. As we looked down the dim, vacant street, we could see dark forms warily making their way toward a group of apartment buildings. This sortie was performed so quietly that every element of surprise was preserved and had Skull been in one of the apartments, his chance of escaping would have been slight, regardless of his extraordinary abilities. But he was not, and, after combing each building from top to bottom, Lieutenant Maurer and his men returned, empty-handed and downcast.

"Sorry, Professor," apologized Tom. "He musta got away again, or else it was never him in the first place."

"I rather incline towards the latter view," observed the Professor, drily.

From where we were, a kind of subdued roar was audible, similar to the far-off jumble of voices which we had heard from the Municipal Building downtown. This low, mumbling sound was punctuated every now and then by the high treble notes of individual cries.

"That's our 'Army of the North'," grinned Tom Higgins. "C'mon. Let's go look it over."

In the car again, we sped four or five blocks farther on and soon came face to face with a crowd of perhaps two hundred people, stretching in unbroken ranks several units deep from curb to curb. There were young men and middle-aged men, quite a few girls and young women and even a sprinkling of children. This, then, was a "detachment" of the "Army of the North," as Tom had jokingly called it.

Although there was so much noise and confusion it was not readily apparent at first, the mob was slowly advancing southward. As it moved along, a score of its members swarmed into each building in its path. I assumed correctly that they were searching every apartment, and when I began to realize the thoroughness with which the job was being performed, I felt that here was something not even Skull could defeat. The faces of these people showed no fear, and little anger—only grimness and determination. About the scene there was visible a vague sort of discipline, at least to the extent that no time was being wasted.

The entire block was systematically searched in a matter of minutes and we were soon forced to choose between moving back or being swarmed over by the crowd. We decided to move, so Tom swung the car in a circle and headed west on the first cross street he came to. As we passed each intersection, the streets to the north—all of them—were seen to be boiling with masses of yelling humanity. Here and there were distinctively colored armbands which Tom said indicated a police-instructed leader, and even more numerous were uniformed police themselves and National Guardsmen.

It was difficult for me to grasp the significance of the picture thus presented, though we were seeing it on no more than a very small scale. When I tried to visualize this same deep line of human beings as stretching clear across Manhattan Island, from the Hudson to the Harlem River, I found my imagination unequal to the task. Yet, this apparent impossibility was a fact, and literally every foot of earth, steel, brick and mortar was being minutely examined. At the time, as on more than one occasion during the Great Search, I shuddered to think of the property damage which was necessarily being done, but in reality there was very little of it. Officials did their best to impress everyone with the urgency of care and their strenuous efforts were later proven successful.

About midnight, as the human net was drawn ever tighter, we were still cruising the streets in Tom Higgins' car, well within the narrowing limits of unsearched territory. I was driving with the short wave radio turned on and from time to time there were terse instructions directed to the roving police who were acting as coordinators between the two "armies." Tom, worn out by the enforced wakefulness of recent nights, was snoring loudly between the Professor and myself. For hours now there had been no sign from Dr. Skull, no stunning blow delivered out of nowhere. We were on Lenox Avenue, just north of 116th, and the heavy silence which surrounded us was oppressive.

"It reminds me," I commented, "of once when I was in Florida, just before a hurricane struck."

Whereupon, as though my remark had been the cue,

there was the high-pitched whine of a siren, another, and then another. Fire engines, or ambulances—or both.

"Speak of the devil," said the Professor. Tom snored serenely on.

The trio of sirens were augmented by others until it seemed that every such contraption in the world were concentrated within earshot. The noise was to the eastward, and without further conversation I swung the coupé in that direction and stepped on the gas. By the time we had reached 5th Avenue, I could see the cause of the alarm.

"Fire again," I announced to Professor Lansdowne, and added: "I guess Skull must have found a box of matches." The attempted humor was as forced as it was weak, because the sight that now unfolded itself unbalanced my choice of repartee. Perhaps a dozen squares to the north and east, a weird aurora of dancing flame seared the sky.

The Professor swore, and his vehemence brought Tom Higgins to life.

"What the hell you waitin' for, an invitation?" he shouted at me, taking in the situation at a glance. "Get goin'!"

I got.

DR. SKULL, WE soon discovered, had brought about a repetition of the inferno of the night before, except that this time it was on a grander scale. He had chosen an identical field of operations—row upon row of anachronistic, red-bricked tenements whose wooden interiors were as inflammable as dry tinder and as thickly populated as beehives. Tonight, instead of six blocks, some fourteen blocks were being converted into flaming pyres for their terrified, trapped inhabitants. The suddenness with which the fires had broken out showed that Skull had worked even more efficiently than before, and Professor Lansdowne expressed the opinion that he had used a succession of "controls" to carry out his inhuman plan. Besides which, the direction of the wind had again been taken into consideration, with deadly results. A freshening breeze from the northeast was sending the flames to lick hungrily at more ramshackle buildings to the south and west.

By the time we arrived on the scene, there was nothing we could do that was not already in capable hands. Since we were all three anxious to follow the advance of the two hordes of searchers, Tom turned the small car downtown and put the roar of the flames and the steady thudding of the pumpers behind us.

It had been arranged for us to be notified by short wave immediately there was any trace of Skull, so all night long we roamed the streets of Manhattan, watching the twin hordes gradually work toward one another through the steel and concrete canyons. Slowly, but with never-slackening speed, the giant citizen armies surged ever closer together, drawing tighter and tighter the one net which Skull—we fervently-hoped—could not slip through. Police and soldiers worked untiringly to keep the unwieldy mobs in some degree of coordination, and contact between different sections of each line, and between the two hordes, was constantly maintained by radio patrol squads.

I have never learned how the searchers managed about sleep. I don't know whether they were relieved by others, whether they slept on their feet, on the ground, or whether they slept at all. I only know this: the relentless advance of the human flood gained rather than lost momentum throughout the long night. At the first crack of dawn, scalding hot coffee and doughnuts were served by National Guard field kitchens to as many people as the limited equipment could supply. All through the night, the search had never paused. News of the disastrous fire merely sharpened a mass determination already aimed at Skull's utter destruction, nothing less.

As I beheld in the chill dawn light a New York which had never before, has never since, and I hope will never again, be presented to my eyes, I was afraid. Somewhere in this strangely changed metropolis was Paula, if she was still alive. What was happening to her? What would happen when the mob hemmed Skull in closely? My tortured imagination visioned a thousand and one terrible possibilities, while I struggled to hold down the fear that threatened to drive me mad.

During the day which followed, the two forces moved nearer and nearer together. Momentarily, we expected further evidences of Skull's continued presence, although every possible precaution had been taken to spike his guns. Public assembly, except in the disarmed hordes, had been forbidden to prevent his being able to strike at people made especially vulnerable by grouping together. Transportation in Manhattan was completely at a standstill with the exception of the special elevated and subway trains previously mentioned, so there was no chance for Skull to make his power felt in this direction. There were not even facilities for leaving the island, either by train, automobile, or boat, and the nearest airport was on the inaccessible mainland of New Jersey.

If Red Thursday had seen the serious crippling of business activity, Friday witnessed its complete cessation. When at noon, after two or three hours of stolen sleep, Professor Lansdowne and I drove around the Times Square district, we were unable to find open a single store where we could buy a pack of cigarettes. Even the regular distribution of food had stopped, and no markets were operating. With the exception of the thousands engaged in the Great Search, few people were to be seen on the streets and these few could do nothing but stand idly around, discussing the incredible situation in which they found themselves.

Dr. Skull did not manifest himself in any way during either the morning or the afternoon, and with practically everyone I encountered the impression was gaining ground that he was being cowed into nonaggression by the conviction that his destruction was impending. I must admit that this happy idea took root in my own brain, but the wish was probably father to the thought. Tom Higgins was openly optimistic and was even predicting the surrender of Skull within the next several hours. Not so Professor Lansdowne, who maintained a non-committal silence.

BY NIGHTFALL, THE two hordes were within a couple of miles of each other. The army surging down from the north had reached 80th Street, and the other was sweeping northward along the line of 38th Street. As the two forces came closer together, their progress was slowed somewhat by the large number of people who were leaving their homes in the territory as yet uncovered. These refugees, fearful that they would be trapped between two battle lines should Skull be located, passed through inspection posts to the rear of the armies, and though this movement was hurried as much as possible, it was delaying the advance.

Accordingly, Tom Higgins arranged to have the remaining inhabitants removed by subway and elevated railways. In view of the special guards assigned to each train, Professor Lansdowne believed that this speedier method of evacuation would prove safe enough, which it did. Close inspection of each passenger by police nullified the possibility of Skull's escaping. Where there was any doubt, suspects were refused admittance to trains and were held in improvised concentration depots for further examination.

Another maneuver is worth mentioning. Towards nine P.M. police and National Guard officials supervising the Great Search held the centers and the eastern wings of both hordes at a standstill while the two western flanks executed a pivoting movement which, two and a half hours later, brought them in contact with each other. Thus, the separate masses had become one huge company, deployed in the form of a giant letter U. The top, or open part, faced the East River; the bottom, or closed part, advanced foot-by-foot eastward from the Hudson. In order to keep this semi-oval of humanity from becoming musclebound as its size constantly decreased, the various leaders began reducing the number of its members. The cooperation of the citizenry in this strategy, as in the campaign as a whole, was close to one hundred per cent. The few malcontents who preferred to have matters their own way rather than that of greatest benefit to the majority were summarily dealt with by their fellows.

As soon as they were detached from the tightening ring, citizens were either sent home or organized into vigilante bodies to patrol streets in the rear and help in the very necessary work of preventing looting and other disorders.

On the off chance that Skull might have gotten through the net, sharp lookout was kept in all sections of the city, but nothing at all was reported.

Throughout the day food, in scanty but strength-sustaining measures, was supplied the searchers by National Guard, police, and other organizations, and even by private citizens. Water, of course, was plentiful at all times.

If we had been lulled into a sense of security by Dr. Skull's inactivity, we were due for a rude awakening. Tom Higgins and I were in the Grand Central Station about midnight when without warning every light in the place flickered out. The Terminal was still jammed with people trying to flee the city and among the several hundred who were camped in the big concourse, panic was instantaneous. Screams and curses sounded on all sides. Everyone, including myself, thought the building was going to be blown up.

In the tiny room where Tom Higgins was conferring with police officers, a dozen matches flamed up at once. In the wavery light, every face showed strain and uncertainty.

"Find your men at once," rapped out Tom. "Get every flashlight you can lay your hands on. Go into the concourse and calm that gang down. Hop, now!" The men hopped. A flashlight in his own hand, Tom called to me, "C'mon. We've got to see how far this has gone. If it's general, we're in for trouble."

It was general. Not an electric light shone from any building on the street outside, and there were none in sight. Private automobiles had been banned and the lights of a few police cars constituted the only illumination visible. Back into the Terminal dashed Tom, and when I caught up with him he was yelling orders into three or four telephones at once; they were still working. Quickly, he arranged for squad cars to patrol the streets and do whatever they could to quell alarm. Fortunately, there were comparatively few people left in the midtown district and the job wasn't as impossible as it might appear.

A moment later word came that only the Times Square and Grand Central sections had been affected; for the rest, electric service was as yet unimpaired. A quick check told us that the power failure had been caused by a crazed employee at the transmitting station who had managed to put four dynamos out of commission before he could be stopped. There was no question in our minds that he was obeying the unspoken commands of Dr. Skull. It would take quite a while to repair the damage, we were informed, and meanwhile the hordes of searchers were well within the darkened area, their progress seriously impeded by the light failure. To remedy this, a quantity of flashlights, flares and searchlights were rushed to various points along the lines, together with every other kind of portable illuminating equipment that could be found.

As soon as it appeared that the emergency was being handled as well as could be expected, Tom and I drove northward up Park Avenue to inspect the searching lines. Professor Lansdowne had gone to a nearby hospital to see District Attorney Harkness, who was making a good recovery from the nervous shock of his encounter with Skull. As we rode along, the luxurious apartment houses that flanked the broad avenue were as dark as Eblis and not a soul was in sight. It was just as we were passing 55th Street, peering along the white shafts from the headlights, that it happened.

27

THE FINAL STRUGGLE

THE WHOLE WORLD shook. A fraction of a second later my eardrums seemed to burst. The car veered crazily to one side and screeched to a stop as Tom instinctively jammed on the brakes. Before we could get our breath four more explosions followed in rapid succession, and then, after a brief pause, a fifth. There were blinding white flashes and when at last the shocks were ended the tall apartments around us stood out in bold relief against a background of brilliant orange.

"The storage tanks!" I heard Tom's voice, as if from a distance.

I knew the tanks he referred to, a half dozen or so big affairs located at the edge of the East River up near the Queensborough Bridge and used for the storage of gasoline. They were each about twenty-five feet high and perhaps twenty in diameter.

"Well," Tom grated, "let's go count the bodies!" His voice still appeared to have only a tenth of its normal volume, I was so deaf from the noise of the explosions.

The destruction wrought by this latest catastrophe was greater than any engineered to date, in loss of life, in the number of people injured, and in the amount of prop-

"Keep away," he screamed, "or the girl dies!"

erty damaged. To make matters worse, a sizable breach
had been blown in the line of searchers converging from
the north, a section of which was only a block from the
storage depot when the explosion took place. While fatal
injuries were not so numerous among the searchers as
among the people living immediately to the west and south
(the explosion having for some reason taken its greatest
force in this direction), hundreds of members of the horde
were showered with blazing gasoline and bits of metal
from the wrecked tanks. Under this unendurable rain, the
line wavered and broke. Keenly appreciating the danger
of Dr. Skull's making his escape through the open space
thus created, Tom hastily took command and marshalled
together an emergency brigade which he threw into the
breach. We could only hope that Skull had not already
gotten through.

Once the first shock had subsided, the morale of the
searchers, strengthened by a fresh outburst of fury at what

had been done, was better than ever. With renewed vigor they flung themselves into their task and by three A.M. only the small area of a few square miles was untouched.

It was at this time, when man's courage is said to be at its lowest ebb, that the steel nerves of Dr. Skull were shattered. As the horde came closer and closer to his hiding place and the mad murmur of angry men and women reached his ears, he—the omnipotent, the invincible—knew the meaning of fear.

Exactly where he was first sighted no one now remembers, but in the small hours of the morning the word passed: "Skull has been driven into the open!"

Tom Higgins and I—Professor Lansdowne had come from Harkness' bedside, but was helping burned and injured in the horde—rushed to the spot where the mad doctor had last been reported. But he was no longer there and we were forced to scour a dozen streets and alleys before we found what we were looking for.

We were approaching one of the ramps leading up to the Queensborough Bridge, barely inside the iron ring of searchers, when we sighted two police cars. Both had their front ends smashed in and were partially blocking the street. As Tom pulled up alongside, a fusillade of shots rang out and was lost in a strangling, bubbling cry that came from some human throat. Half a block away in the direction of the bridge, a medium-sized private sedan stood motionless. In the middle of the street, its appearance was inexplicably strange, uncanny, ominous. Groups of police and a handful of civilians were keeping a respectful distance between themselves and the sedan and no one was making an effort to close in.

Even as I took in this scene, a policeman standing near me raised his pistol and fired two shots at the car. The echoes had not died away when the same man, his face suddenly transformed, swung around and aimed the gun directly at me. It's a cinch that I never hit the ground faster in my life. The bullet whistled harmlessly over my head, but with a second report, I heard Tom Higgins groan. There was an incisive crack from another quarter and with it the berserk policeman crumpled to the pavement.

"Are you badly hurt, Tom?" I gasped, picking myself up.

"Naw," he replied ungraciously. Then, raising his voice to a yell: "You guys throw away your guns unless you want to be corpses, d'you hear me? This is Tom Higgins talkin'." There were murmurs of assent and Tom added, for my benefit, "Just grazed my arm. It ain't bad."

"It's Skull all right," I said excitedly. "That cop turning his gun on us proves it. Don't let anybody shoot, on account of Paula. She may be with him."

"Right." The previous order was amplified.

We could now see why the sedan was standing still. The street behind it was blocked, as well as the nearest cross street. A police car was swung across the only other avenue of escape, the ramp leading up to the bridge, but as I looked it turned and zoomed toward the huge span, quickly gathering speed. Instantly, Skull's sedan moved after it. I judged that the doctor had hypnotized the police driver and was planning a getaway across the river, not knowing that a strong cordon of men reinforced by a heavy iron chain blocked the center of the bridge.

IGNORING HIS WOUNDED arm, Tom Higgins shoved me into the coupé. Dousing the headlights and yelling to the nearest group of policemen to find Professor Lansdowne—quick!—he shot the car after Skull. It was a risky thing to do, but God knows that made no difference to me. Paula might be in the sedan ahead, and that was all that mattered. Our best chance lay in the possibility that Skull might not look back and see us following until it was too late for him to do anything about it, and in this the doused lights would help.

As we neared the first tall pillar of the bridge, the gap between the two cars was closing rapidly.

"Here!" Tom thrust a pistol into my hand. "Get the tires before Skull puts the evil eye on you. If you make a move at me, I'll slug you, no foolin'." I knew he meant it, too.

Fortunately, I'm something of a marksman, thanks to a youthful penchant for target practice, and this ability never stood me in better stead than that night on Queensborough Bridge. I leaned out the window, took careful aim, and started pulling the trigger. The red tail light on the fender had given me a pretty good idea of where the wheel was and in spite of the semi-darkness, I scored a hit on my fifth try. The sedan lurched from side to side and slowed down. As it did so, there was a staccato rattle of shots from its rear window and bullets whined around us. One crashed through our windshield and came much too close to my ear for comfort.

"There's two of 'em shootin'," said Tom. "D'you s'pose he's got Paula—"

"It's his servant," I interrupted.

The police cordon which guarded the center of the bridge had been standing with the lights of their cars turned off, but now they came to life and a battery of headlamps flooded the roadway. Simultaneously, the fleeing sedan jerked to a complete halt and Tom slammed on his own brakes barely in time to avoid a crash. Stealing a quick glance in back of us, I saw that more police cars were coming from that direction, and coming fast.

The door of the sedan ahead flew open and a man emerged. Ignorant of the perfect target he made outlined against the glaring lights of the cars on the bridge, he dropped into a kneeling position and fired two shots at us pointblank range—and missed. I let fly with the remaining bullet in Tom's gun and was rewarded by seeing the man throw up his hands and fall.

Two more figures now got out of the sedan and I was unable to check the cry that rose to my lips when I saw that one of them was Paula. The other was Dr. Skull. I could see his face in the eerie light cast by the soaring flames on the waterfront.

"Bob!" Paula cried out the word.

Before I could reply, Skull's arm flashed out. There was the sound of a blow and Paula started to fall, only to be caught by the mad doctor. Skull, his face impassive no longer, glared at me. If fifteen feet had not separated us, I would have rushed him; as it was, I feared for Paula should I attack, and held my ground. The cold familiar voice of the maniac came to me across the intervening space.

"Call off the police or I will kill the girl!"

The words put the chill of ice in my breast. I looked appealingly at Tom and swept the bridge with my eyes. From both directions, police were rushing toward us and I knew that a crazy mob of people was following them.

I realized I couldn't hope to stop them and a cold sweat broke out on my body.

"I'll do what I can!" I said to Skull. "Don't hurt her, for God's sake!"

But, whipped into action by the sight of the oncoming police, Skull ran. He carried the unconscious Paula as though she had no weight and loped to the high granite tower from which the bridge cables were strung.

"Keep away," I heard him scream over his shoulder, "or the girl dies!"

There was a narrow iron ladder on the side of the tower and up this, holding Paula limply in one arm, Skull began to climb.

"Holy Saints!" cried Tom Higgins. "What's he gonna do?"

Impulsively, I ran forward, only to be jerked back by Tom's uninjured right arm.

"Let go, you fool!" I yelled at him. "I've got to help her, can't you see?"

"You're gonna do nothin' until—"

That was as far as Tom got when there was an unexpected interruption.

"Let him go, Tom," said a quiet voice. It was Professor Lansdowne and he'd come in one of the first cars to follow us. I was never so glad to see anyone in my life.

I said fervently, "Skull's got Paula and I've got to go after him!"

"Go to it, Bob," he said. "I'll help you."

I waited for no more. My previous fears that Skull would harm Paula if I tried anything were swallowed in the certainty that he would do worse if I didn't. Throwing all my strength into my legs, I sprinted for the bridge tower and swung onto the highest rung of the ladder I could reach. Looking up, I could see Skull far above me struggling to climb fast in spite of the encumbrance of Paula's hundred-odd pounds of dead weight. Having to use one arm to hold the girl, it was a miracle that he kept his balance as he made his way up the ladder, and I kept praying for Paula's sake that he would not fall. The river was two hundred feet or more below.

SUDDENLY SKULL PAUSED and looked down at me. As he did so, I had a violently terrible attack of giddiness. The world spinning before my eyes, I clung to the narrow ladder with all my might and fought desperately a nearly irresistible desire to jump into the river. For a timeless moment, my life—and Paula's—hung in the balance. Then I commenced to feel, like a physical force, courage flowing back into my veins. There was no longer the temptation to jump and my head was clearing. I glanced down and saw the reassuring figure of Professor Lansdowne standing far beneath me in the midst of a great crowd of people.

But above me, Skull had started to climb again. The human mind is a strange mechanism, and even as I pulled myself after him, I was capable of noticing how quiet and tense everything had become. There was no sound from the crowd below and I could feel the intentness of their gaze as they watched.

There was a faint cry from Paula. Regaining consciousness, she was weakly struggling with Skull.

"No, Paula, no!" I cried to her. "Don't fight him. You'll fall. Be still!"

She heard me and stopped trying to free herself, but Skull had also heard.

"Stay where you are!" His cold voice was like a blow in the face. "Come no nearer!"

Panting with fear and exertion, I raised my eyes. Skull was only a few feet away now and his face, no longer that of a world-conqueror, was indescribably terrible in the lurid light.

"You think"—the words fell from his lips like stones— "that you will beat me—you and your brilliant Professor Lansdowne. But you won't! Do you hear?" His voice was raised to a scream. "I'll kill her! Try and stop that! I'll—"

Paula had sensed in advance the move that Skull now made to push her from him and send her hurtling to her death, and strove frantically to grasp the iron rung over her head. The mad doctor himself was struggling to loosen the hold she'd fastened around his neck, but, having to use one arm to hold onto the ladder, he was making slight progress. Yet it would be only a matter of seconds before his greater strength would win, and I launched myself upward to catch hold of Paula.

Something about Skull's face caught my eye as I climbed a step higher. It contorted as though he were battling an unseen antagonist. A snarl of protest came from his loose mouth, like the growl of a wild beast. He pulled at Paula's hand more desperately and her hold loosened. I inched up another rung before Skull saw me and ground his heel on my fingers. With the piercing pain, a wave of nausea engulfed me and again I nearly fell. A second time his heavy heel came down, crushing the fingers of my other hand, but I gritted my teeth and somehow held on, though I was worthless as far as helping Paula was concerned.

Through a mist of agony, I saw her losing the battle. Inch by inch her hand was slipping and only one of her feet was on the ladder.

Then, for no apparent reason, those awful eyes of Dr. Skull's opened wide. His efforts to dislodge Paula became feebler, then ceased altogether. Sobbing, the girl reached upward and gripped the iron rung over her head. Seeing my chance and numbed by an anger that was sheer insanity to the pain from my bruised and bleeding fingers, I crawled up until Skull's face was within reach of my fist. His eyes fastened themselves upon mine for a moment, but they held no terror for me now.

"No!" he choked out. "You will not—you will—" His face worked convulsively.

A piercing shriek poured from Paula's throat. I felt a terrific jolt that nearly knocked me off the ladder. There was a fearful animal cry, receding with the speed of an express train. Paula was clinging to the ladder with one hand, the other hanging loosely at her side.

Skull was no longer there.

Just as Paula started to sway dizzily, I was at her side, using my free arm to support her.

"It's all right, darling," I said.

"Yes," she answered brokenly, "it's all right. Everything's all right now."

We both looked down through the chill air to the dark waters of the river, the dark waters that held in their depths the body of Dr. Skull.

28

THE SUMMING UP

ABOUT TWO WEEKS after Paula and I had picked our perilous way down the narrow ladder of the Queensborough Bridge tower, a dinner party was in progress at the Lansdowne apartment. New York had once more returned to its accustomed pursuits and it was no longer necessary to live in constant dread of a power that was as evil as it was invincible. No longer were radio programs being interrupted by the demands and threats of the mad doctor, and the previously universal shadow of fear had been routed. New York would never forget the horror of those terrible days, and many of its wounds would never be healed, but it had survived.

Because of the commanding role he played in making this survival possible, Professor Lansdowne's grateful fellow citizens wanted to bestow various public honors upon him, all of which he politely refused. He was interested only in returning to his classes at the University and continuing his beloved scientific researches in untroubled obscurity. Since there was no way of weakening his resolve in this matter the Professor's wish was granted, though reluctantly.

Tom Higgins came in for his share of acclaim as the

result of his capable and tireless work during the emergency, and it was made known that he would soon be appointed to one of the highest positions on the force.

District Attorney Harkness, who had completely recovered from his temporary prostration, was being talked of as a candidate for governor.

As for myself, having done nothing during the Terror but produce countless acres of gooseflesh on my shrinking anatomy, I was naturally in line for no medals. There was some undeserved praise for my small part in getting word of Skull's whereabouts to the police, but fortunately this was soon forgotten. It would have been embarrassing for me to have long accepted plaudits that rightly belonged to the person who really made it possible for the Professor and Tom Higgins to find Skull's headquarters—Curly Smith. In any event, it strikes me that the feat was inconclusive to say the least, since the doctor won that encounter hands down and forced us to do our work all over again.

My present interest was in getting back to my advertising job with Rowlandson & Leger, quickly accumulating a modest nest egg, and marrying Paula. If I add, with pardonable egotism, that she was more interested in marrying me than in the several motion picture offers she received, then I have described the condition of every member of our small band of veterans.

As I was about to say some distance back, we were having dinner at the Lansdowne's, Tom Higgins, District Attorney Harkness and myself. The occasion had two *raisons d'etre*, the formal celebration of Paula's engagement to me, and to commemorate our survival of an ordeal as trying as anyone ever lived through.

DURING THE MAJOR portion of the excellent meal, conversation kept to a light and cheerful plane, but by the time coffee and liqueurs were served it inevitably reverted to the individual we all wished to forget—Dr. Skull.

"I'll never understand the secret of that man's uncanny power," mused Mr. Harkness.

"Comparatively few people will, I suppose," said Professor Lansdowne, "although it was based on laws as natural to the initiated as the force of gravity is to us. A knowledge of these laws, together with an extremely remarkable mind, made Dr. Skull's hypnotic ability possible. What a pity that a brain capable of imposing its will on a subject without that subject's knowledge or consent, should be put to such terrible use! If only he had used it for good, what miracles he might have performed!"

"But he didn't," commented the District Attorney, sipping at his brandy, "and I'm only surprised that he didn't do a great deal more harm than he did. An utter madman with an unlimited power—"

Professor Lansdowne interrupted. "Ah, but that's where you're wrong. His power was by no means unlimited. God help us and the world if it had been! It was limited, in the first place, by the fact that it could be used against only one person at a time, and to make it effective against this one person, Skull's steady concentration was required throughout the entire period of control. Thus, he couldn't start one subject on a task, leave him with the task incomplete, and go on to another. He had, in short, to follow through, and this was a serious limitation. Looking at it in this light, it's remarkable that he could have held New York City at bay as long as he did when he could use only one person at a time as a weapon against millions. He wouldn't have, had he not been able to keep his whereabouts a secret. As soon as this was known, and the limitation of his power understood, he was doomed."

"But," objected Harkness, "if he could control only one person at a time, what about the woman he used to get the money from the broker, Walker? Wasn't she hypnotized just as thoroughly as Walker was?"

"Very probably, but not in the same way. While Skull had the secret of a hypnosis that didn't require the subject's consent and generally used it, he was also acquainted with the more conventional forms of hypnotism which, while necessitating the placing of the subject in a properly receptive and willing state, do not demand the constant concentration of the hypnotist. In the Walker affair, Dr. Skull used both types.

"By one means or another, he must have induced the woman, Agnes Russell, to agree to be hypnotized, although she probably had no idea of what she was going to be made to do. When she had been placed in a hypnotic state, she was instructed to visit Walker, pick up a sum of money by saying she was a charity worker, and return with it to Skull. Once this idea was planted in her mind, Dr. Skull was not compelled to give it any further thought. Unless she were stopped by insurmountable barriers, Agnes Russell would carry out his instructions.

"But Walker was a different case altogether. Skull had no access to him, so it was necessary to use the more complex and infinitely more powerful variety of hypnotism—the kind known only to members of the Three Brotherhoods. He did this, imposing his will on Walker quite without

Walker's knowledge or consent. The money was delivered to the woman and she returned with it to Skull, and that was that."

"And all the time," asked the District Attorney, "Skull had to keep concentrating on Walker?"

"Exactly. Later, when he feared she would reveal his identity to police, Skull controlled Agnes Russell in his usual way and forced her to take her own life. His use of her in the first place was probably due to an unwillingness to have Walker bring the money himself because of the possibility that the movements of so prominent a man might have been traced, and Skull discovered.

"On only one other occasion did the doctor use a regular kind of hypnotism. This was when he sent his messenger— the unfortunate young man who died—to confer with us. I presume this was done so that Skull might keep his mind free in case some emergency developed that would require his full attention. This, of course, was a mistake, since it was from the messenger that we obtained our first description of Skull to check with my own, but Skull couldn't have foreseen this. It very likely would not have been possible had not the man's mind been severely shocked and weakened by the accident he was in. Incidentally, Dr. Skull made two other major mistakes. The first was in selecting me as a victim, an act that supplied the first clue as to his identity. The second was in kidnapping Paula, which, together with the notes he sent, put Bob on his trail."

"When you thought of examining the fellow who came to the Council," inquired Harkness, "did you recognize the type of hypnosis and see your way clear to get information about Skull?"

"Not altogether. But there were signs which made me determined to investigate.

"Getting on with Skull's limitations, though, here's another: it was necessary, except under one special condition, for him to have seen, at one time or another, each person he intended controlling. Unless he had, he would be unable to attain the proper degree of concentration. He had to see each one of his victims with his own eyes, or—and this is the special condition—indirectly, through those of a trained intermediary. The trained intermediary was, I probably needn't add—"

"The stooge," I supplied. "The Kashmiri, or whatever he was."

"You mean," demanded Tom Higgins, "that Skull saw *all* his victims in advance? He sure musta been busy."

"I mean," explained Professor Lansdowne, "that either Skull had seen them, or else the Kashmiri had. As for his being busy, he must have made advance preparations for all of his activities so that the people he wished to control were thoroughly fixed in his mind. It was hardly a serious problem for him to arrange to see Mayor O'Hara, or J. Homer Warren, or any of the others. It's rather more remarkable that he should have taken the care to see not only Commissioner Gallagher, but most of his assistants as well, yet he must have done so. Otherwise he would not have been able to control the man who drove the Commissioner's car the day it plunged into the river."

"What worries me," remarked the District Attorney, "is how Skull knew exactly when to strike and what words to put in the mouths of his victims when they were talking to other people who certainly were not controlled. For example, how could he have Mayor O'Hara carry on a conversation with Warren, as was done at the meeting of the Board of Estimate? Also, how could Skull know exactly when to have Warren stab himself, just at the time when everyone's back was turned? That's what I'd like to know!"

"The explanation of that isn't exactly elementary, but it's simple enough when you understand the mysteries of the Three Brotherhoods. When Skull, using their hypnotic formula and his own remarkable mind, controlled a person, he could also look through that person's eyes, hear through his ears, feel through his fingers. He knew precisely what was happening around the subject, and could direct the subject's every reaction, of whatever kind. This ability was demonstrated on a great number of occasions, not alone with O'Hara and Warren. Without it, Skull's efficiency would have been considerably reduced."

TOM HIGGINS SEEMED to have been mulling something over for the past few moments, and finally he spoke. "What I don't see," he complained, "is what good it would do for Skull's assistant to see a victim if Skull himself had to do the spellbindin'."

"It did a great deal of good," smiled the scientist. "The Kashmiri, by the comparatively academic trick of telepathy, communicated the image to his master, and that was all that was required."

"Would a photograph work just as well?" I asked.

"Apparently not, and we can thank our lucky stars for that much," replied Professor Lansdowne. "We can also be thankful for what appears to be a third limitation on Skull's power—distance. While there is no tangible proof that he couldn't operate just as well at a thousand-mile distance from his subject as a mile away, there's plenty of circumstantial evidence. First, the fact that Skull remained in New York, where he was most likely to be trapped, instead of running the whole show from the next state, or the next continent. Second, the fact that Skull did not put his reign of terror on a national, or even, an international, basis. Assuming that he could have if he so desired, it is hardly compatible with his megalomania that he didn't. For these two reasons alone I think we can safely conclude that he *was* limited by distance. To just what extent, I can't say, but probably his power was ineffective beyond, say, ten or fifteen miles. I can see no logical basis for this limitation, and only point to the facts."

During the pause that followed this explanation, I felt inclined to inquire about a theory that had intrigued me for quite a while.

"Tell me, sir," I asked the Professor. "Aren't your powers of hypnotism every bit as great as Dr. Skull's? After all, you defeated him in that house when he wanted you to get rid of the cops. And when Paula and I were upon that bridge—well, you kept him from making me jump. In fact, you made *him* do the jumping. So why couldn't you start taking over Skull's old territory?"

Professor Lansdowne broke into a laugh. "I think you all have a right to know where I stand, at that," he said, "so you can nip any dictatorial ambitions I may have in the bud. The fact is though, I couldn't possibly take over Dr. Skull's territory, as Bob puts it. I must confess to knowing more than is good for me about the Three Brotherhoods, and I've spent a lot of time sticking my nose into every kind of psychic phenomena I could find. Naturally, I've picked up quite a bit of odd knowledge and even a few tricks of hypnotism. But my studies in India were not nearly so exhaustive as Dr. Skull's, and my abilities are correspondingly much slighter—not to mention the fact that my own brain is hardly as weighty as his. He, for instance, must have known what the attitude of the Three Brotherhoods would have been toward his evil use of their power, and this may have had something to do with his end.

"As for beating down Dr. Skull at his house that evening, I didn't really beat him. I only managed to get a stalemate. Although his brain's weightier, as I've just said, I know perfectly well that he's no more bull-headed than I am. All my life I've been known as a stubborn old mule, and this characteristic helped quite a bit, that's all."

"More likely your will was every bit as strong as Skull's, seems to me," remarked the District Attorney, and I agreed with him, but the Professor only smiled.

"What about the way you kept me from shooting you?" I persisted. "You certainly must have licked Skull on his home grounds there."

"I'm not so sure of that," said the scientist. "I may have held you off a while—as I was lucky enough to hold off our friend Mr. Harkness on another occasion—but I think it's highly possible that your return to sanity was due primarily to Skull's relinquishing control. You remember that he got through Tom's surrounding cordon by 'controlling' one of the policemen. The shooting we heard came very soon after you recovered, and Dr. Skull's attention must have been taken away from you a few moments before that happened. I might add at this juncture that his concentration wouldn't interfere with a purely physical activity like walking, or even a minor mental one like bidding me a sarcastic farewell."

"Uh-huh," I grunted, not sure but what the Professor's modesty, rather than his reason, was talking. "But what about the bridge business?"

"I've an alibi for that, too. One thing absolutely essential, if Skull was to control people effectively, was an undisturbed, undivided mind. I feel sure that he realized his own destruction was near, and that that realization, coupled with the distraction caused by his pursuers, was quite sufficient to keep him from giving you the full attention you deserved. You'll recall that he didn't try to control you when he first jumped out of his car, but only made threats and tried to use Paula as a means to force you, and through you, the police, to terms. I know you owe your life far more to those circumstances than to any help I was able to give."

"And," I kept on, "I suppose you didn't keep me from jumping and finally made Skull jump instead?"

"I tried to keep you from doing anything foolish, but my efforts might have failed had Dr. Skull's mind not been confused. As for making him jump, I don't really see how I could have since I was devoting all my thought to making him climb down the ladder with Paula. I wouldn't have dared try to make him jump. The possibility that he might have pulled Paula down with him was far too great, even if it was only one chance in a thousand. No, Bob, Dr. Skull was under the influence of the Three Brotherhoods, or he slipped and fell without any help from me."

"Dad," said Paula, when we all fell silent, "I'm ashamed of you. You're just a sissy!" But there was pride in her eyes. "A COUPLE OF more things, if you don't mind, Professor."

District Attorney Harkness blew a cloud of mild Havana smoke into the air. "How were those fires and the gasoline tank explosions managed?"

"From what I've learned from Paula and Tom, the Kashmiri acted as a scout while Skull was in hiding those last two days, and through contacts made by him, Skull controlled several men who started the tenement fires. In the same way, he controlled an oil company employee who blew up the tanks by igniting a leak in an important pipe line that connected them together. The Kashmiri admitted as much to Tom before he died, and I learned from Paula that Skull handled everything by proxy while the search for him was on."

"Yeh," said Tom, rather sheepishly. "I meant to tell you about that, only I musta forgot."

"Skull was scared stiff, I honestly believe, those last few days," put in Paula. "He kept dragging me from one dark basement to another and when the mob got close enough for him to hear it, he tried to get across the bridge."

"One more question, Professor, and I'll let you alone," said Harkness, leaning forward. "Was there any time when you could have used your own hypnotic powers to control Skull and force him to surrender?"

Professor Lansdowne smiled faintly. "Do you think I would have passed up such an opportunity if it had ever presented itself?" he asked.

"Of course not," answered the District Attorney hastily. "It was a foolish question. I merely wondered."

"That's natural enough," said the Professor. "And now, if you gentlemen are through with your questions, I should like to ask one of my own, one that has been troubling me for a long, long time. Here it is:

"While I was still languishing in jail and trying desperately to gather evidence that I was not responsible for the death of Amos Carter, J. Homer Warren committed suicide in his apartment with a considerable number of police, I believe, surrounding him. To me, that appeared to be an ill wind that might blow me some good. I thought it might prove that an outside influence could force a man to do things that would ordinarily be unthinkable.

"Then, just as I was developing my argument, it was discovered that Mr. Warren's stomach contained a quantity of the peculiar, mind-affecting drug, somnocephalaine. Now, what I want to know is this: has it ever been discovered who put that drug in his stomach?"

"I could've cleared that up weeks ago, Professor," said Tom Higgins. "Only I guess I was too busy with other things to think about it. Here's how it was:

"On the day that Mayor O'Hara—God rest his soul— went off his bat and told Warren he'd be dead at midnight, Warren was scared stiff. You couldn't hardly blame him. Now, he'd been goin' to a doctor for a long time on account of his punk nerves, and that afternoon after the meetin' he went and asked for somethin' to steady him up.

"The doc had already been givin' him quite a bit of dope, and wasn't keen to give him any more than was really needed, so he just told Warren to go on takin' his regular medicine. But the guy kept on beggin' for somethin' special and the sawbones finally gave in. This doctor—name's Flemming—went in for experiments and things like that and had a lot of equipment around the place, so he always mixed his own prescriptions. Or else his nurse, who was a pharmacist, too, mixed 'em for him. This day, the doc had to go some place in a hurry so he wrote out a prescription and gave it to the nurse to take care of. Before he left he told Warren not to take the powder unless he's about ready to go through the roof.

"So—the nurse goes to make up the stuff—just one dose, mind you, on account of that's all the doc will trust Warren with—and somehow gets her signals mixed. Instead of what she should of used—this is her story—she uses this somno-whatchamacallit. Never discovered the mistake until the next mornin' and then Warren was dead anyhow so it didn't make no difference.

"Well, so Warren takes the powder home. He keeps it in his pocket until that night. Then when he gets so scared he's about to pop a blood vessel, he slips it into his drink. The coroner says there was enough of the drug to have knocked him out cold instead of just affectin' his mind, but it never got a chance, because Skull beat it to the punch. We never thought of pressin' charges against the nurse because it wasn't her carelessness that cooked Warren's goose, but Skull. Anyhow, we nearly scared her to death askin' her questions, so what are the odds?"

"Thank you very much," said Professor Lansdowne. "That satisfies a curiosity of long standing."

We then adjourned to the living room, and on the way I asked Tom if they'd ever found Skull's body.

"Naw," he replied, "and they ain't very likely to. There's a strong current in the East River and that blankety-blank-blank is probably out in the Gulf Stream by now, feedin' the sharks. And will *they* have a bellyache!" he added.

We both laughed heartily at the joke. It was very pleasant, being able to laugh like that at a creature who had inspired so much fear. The peril that had threatened all that we held dear, even life itself, no longer existed, and the very air was cleaner.

We'd brought our replenished brandy glasses into the living room with us and now, as Paula and I sat beside each other on the sofa, Professor Lansdowne proposed a toast.

"To Paula and Bob: May they always be as happy as they are tonight."

Smilingly the toast was drunk.

At that moment, the doorbell rang and I started involuntarily. Then, realizing that that sort of thing had gone forever, I gave an apologetic laugh and relaxed once more. Ella MacLaughlin, who had become a family fixture, appeared and went to answer the bell. I heard her thanking someone, after which she approached Paula, proudly bearing a small box wrapped with tissue paper and ribbon.

"For-r you, Miss Paula," she burred. "Nae doot in honor-r o' the occasion!" Whereupon, in her motherly way, she plumped the package down on the girl's lap and left the room.

"Aha," I said, in mock suspicion. "A rival, eh?"

Paula looked at the box wonderingly. "I haven't the faintest—"

"Open it, my dear, and find out," smiled her father.

While we all stood by, Paula untied the ribbons, removed the tissue and opened the box. Inside, a written message first met our eyes.

"On the happy occasion of your betrothal, will you deign to accept the best wishes of one who admires you greatly and hopes for your future happiness?" Paula read the words in a voice which trembled increasingly with each syllable. And though there was no signature to the note, my body turned to ice and the old, terrible fear gripped my heart. The fear I thought gone—forever.

For the message was written in a fine, Spencerian hand on gold-bordered, ivory-colored stationery engraved with the letter *S*—and in the box reposed a single, crimson rose.